VANITY FAIR

VANITY FAIR

A NOVEL WITHOUT A HERO

by

W. M. THACKERAY

Abridged Edition

PRINTED IN
DEAN & **SON Ltd.**
41/43 Ludgate Hill
GREAT BRITAIN
LONDON EC4
TRADE MARK

MADE AND PRINTED IN GREAT BRITAIN BY PURNELL AND SONS, LTD.
PAULTON (SOMERSET) AND LONDON

603 03020 3

CONTENTS

Chapter   Page

CHAPTER I

CHISWICK MALL

WHILE the present century was in its teens, and on one sunshiny morning in June, there drove up to the great iron gate of Miss Pinkerton's academy for young ladies, on Chiswick Mall, a large family coach, with two fat horses in blazing harness, driven by a fat coachman in a three-cornered hat and wig, at the rate of four miles an hour. A black servant, who reposed on the box beside the fat coachman, uncurled his bandy legs as soon as the equipage drew up opposite Miss Pinkerton's shining brass plate, and as he pulled the bell, at least a score of young heads were seen peering out of the narrow windows of the stately old brick house. Nay, the acute observer might have recognized the little red nose of good-natured Miss Jemima Pinkerton herself, rising over some geranium pots in the window of that lady's own drawing-room.

"It is Mrs. Sedley's coach, sister," said Miss Jemima. "Sambo, the black servant, has just rung the bell; and the coachman has a new red waistcoat."

"Have you completed all the necessary preparations incident to Miss Sedley's departure, Miss Jemima?" asked Miss Pinkerton herself, that majestic lady—the Semiramis of Hammersmith, the friend of Dr. Johnson, the correspondent of Mrs. Shapone herself.

"The girls were up at four this morning, packing her trunks, sister," replied Miss Jemima; "we have made her a bow-pot."

"Say a bouquet, sister Jemima—'tis more genteel."

"Well, a booky as big almost as a haystack. I have put up two bottles of the gillyflower-water for Mrs. Sedley, and the receipt for making it, in Amelia's box."

"And I trust, Miss Jemima, you have made a copy of Miss Sedley's account. This is it, is it? Very good—ninety-three pounds, four shillings. Be kind enough to address it to John Sedley, Esquire, and to seal this billet which I have written to his lady."

Miss Pinkerton's "billet" was to the following effect:

"THE MALL, CHISWICK, *June* 15, 18—.

"MADAM,—After her six years' residence at the Mall, I have the honour and happiness of presenting Miss Amelia Sedley to her parents, as a young lady not unworthy to occupy a fitting position in their polished and refined circle. Those virtues which characterize the young English gentlewoman, those accomplishments which become her birth and station, will not be found wanting in the amiable Miss Sedley, whose *industry* and *obedience* have endeared her to her instructors, and whose delightful sweetness of temper has charmed her *aged* and her *youthful* companions.

"In music, in dancing, in orthography, in every variety of embroidery and needlework, she will be found to have realized her friends' *fondest wishes*. In geography there is still much to be desired; and a careful and undeviating use of the backboard, for four hours daily during the next three years, is recommended as necessary to the acquirements of that dignified *deportment and carriage*, so requisite for every young lady of *fashion*.

"In the principles of religion and morality, Miss Sedley will be found worthy of an establishment which has been honoured by the presence of *The Great Lexicographer*, and the patronage of the admirable Mrs. Chapone. In leaving the Mall, Miss Amelia carries with her the hearts of her companions, and the affectionate regards of her mistress, who has the honour to subscribe herself,

"Madam, your most obliged humble servant,
"BARBARA PINKERTON.

"*P.S.*—Miss Sharp accompanies Miss Sedley. It is particularly requested that Miss Sharp's stay in Russell Square may not exceed ten days. The family of distinction with whom she is engaged desire to avail themselves of her services as soon as possible."

This letter completed, Miss Pinkerton proceeded to write her own name and Miss Sedley's in the fly-leaf of a Johnson's Dictionary—the interesting work which she invariably presented to her scholars on their departure from the Mall. On the cover was inserted a copy of "Lines addressed to a young lady on quitting Miss Pinkerton's school, at the Mall; by the late revered Doctor Samuel Johnson." In fact, the Lexicographer's name was always on the lips of this majestic woman, and a visit he had paid to her was the cause of her reputation and her fortune.

Being commanded by her elder sister to get "the Dictionary" from the cupboard, Miss Jemima had extracted two copies of the book from the receptacle in question. When Miss Pinkerton had finished the inscription in the first, Jemima, with rather a dubious and timid air, handed her the second.

"For whom is this, Miss Jemima?" said Miss Pinkerton, with awful coldness.

"For Becky Sharp," answered Jemima, trembling very much, and blushing over her withered face and neck, as she turned her back on her sister. "For Becky Sharp: she's going too."

"MISS JEMIMA!" exclaimed Miss Pinkerton, in the largest capitals; "are you in your senses? Replace the Dixonary in the closet, and never venture to take such a liberty in future."

"Well, sister, it's only two and ninepence, and poor Becky will be miserable if she don't get one."

"Send Miss Sedley instantly to me," said Miss Pinkerton. And so, venturing not to say another word, poor Jemima trotted off, exceedingly flurried and nervous.

Miss Sedley's papa was a merchant in London, and a man of some wealth; whereas Miss Sharp was an articled pupil, for whom Miss Pinkerton had done, as she thought, quite enough, without conferring upon her at parting the high honour of the Dixonary.

As we are to see a great deal of Amelia, there is no harm in saying, at the outset of our acquaintance, that she was a dear little creature; and a great mercy it is, both in life and in novels, which (and the latter especially) abound in villains of the most sombre sort, that we are to have for a constant companion so guileless and good-natured a person. As she is not a heroine, there is no need to describe her person; indeed I am afraid that her nose was rather short than otherwise, and her cheeks a great deal too round and red for a heroine; but her face blushed with rosy health, and her lips with the freshest of smiles, and she had a pair of eyes which sparkled with the brightest and honestest good-humour, except indeed when they filled with tears, and that was a great deal too often; for the silly thing would cry over a dead canary-bird; or over a mouse, that the cat haply had seized upon; or over the end of a novel, were it ever so stupid; and as for saying an unkind word to her, were any persons hard-hearted enough to do so—why, so much the worse for them.

Well, then. The flowers, and the presents, and the trunks, and bonnet-boxes of Miss Sedley having been arranged by Mr. Sambo in the carriage, together with a very small and weather-beaten old cow's-skin trunk with Miss Sharp's card neatly nailed upon it, which was delivered by Sambo with a grin, and packed by the coachman with a corresponding sneer—the hour for parting came; and the grief of that moment was considerably lessened by the admirable discourse which Miss Pinkerton addressed to her pupil. Not that the parting speech caused Amelia to philosophize, or that it armed her in any way with a calmness, the result of argument; but it was intolerably dull, pompous, and tedious; and having the fear of her schoolmistress greatly before her eyes, Miss Sedley did not venture, in her presence, to give way to any ebullitions of private grief. A seed-cake and a bottle of wine were produced in the drawing-room, as on the solemn occasions of the visits of parents, and these refreshments being partaken of, Miss Sedley was at liberty to depart.

"You'll go in and say good-bye to Miss Pinkerton, Becky!" said Miss Jemima to a young lady of whom nobody took any notice, and who was coming downstairs with her own handbox.

"I suppose I must," said Miss Sharp calmly, and much to the wonder of Miss Jemima; and the latter having knocked at the door, and receiving permission to come in, Miss Sharp advanced in a very unconcerned manner, and said in French, and with a perfect accent, "Mademoiselle, je viens vous faire mes adieux."

Miss Pinkerton did not understand French; she only directed those who did; but biting her lips and throwing up her venerable and Roman-nosed head (on the top of which figures a large and solemn turban), she said, "Miss Sharp, I wish you a good-morning."

Miss Sharp only folded her own hands with a frigid smile and bow, and quite declined to accept the proffered hand; on which Semiramis tossed up her turban more indignantly than ever. In fact, it was a little battle between the young lady and the old one, and the latter was worsted. "Heaven bless you, my child," said she, embracing Amelia, and scowling the while over the girl's shoulder at Miss Sharp. "Come away, Becky," said Miss Jemima, pulling the young woman away in great alarm, and the drawing-room door closed upon them for ever.

Then came the struggle and parting below. Words refuse to tell it. All the servants were there in the hall—all the dear friends—all the young ladies—the dancing-master who had just arrived; and there was such a scuffling, and hugging, and kissing, and crying, with the hysterical *yoops* of Miss Swartz, the parlour-boarder, from her room, as no pen can depict, and as the tender heart would fain pass over. The embracing was over; they parted—that is, Miss Sedley parted from her friends. Miss Sharp had demurely entered the carriage some minutes before. Nobody cried for leaving *her*.

Sambo of the bandy legs slammed the carriage-door on his young weeping mistress. He sprang up behind the carriage. "Stop!" cried Miss Jemima, rushing to the gate with a parcel.

"It's some sandwiches, my dear," said she to Amelia. "You may be hungry, you know; and Becky, Becky Sharp, here's a book for you that my sister—that is, I—Johnson's Dixonary, you know; you mustn't leave us without that. Good-bye. Drive on, coachman. God bless you!"

And the kind creature retreated into the garden, overcome with emotion.

But, lo! and just as the coach drove off, Miss Sharp put her pale face out of the window and actually flung the book back into the garden.

This almost caused Jemima to faint with terror. "Well, I never!"—said she—"what an audacious——" Emotion prevented her from completing either sentence. The carriage rolled away; the great gates were closed; the bell rang for the dancing lesson. The world is before the two young ladies; and so, farewell to Chiswick Mall.

CHAPTER II

IN WHICH MISS SHARP AND MISS SEDLEY PREPARE TO OPEN THE CAMPAIGN

WHEN Miss Sharp had performed the heroical act mentioned in the last chapter, and had seen the Dixonary, flying over the pavement of the little garden, fall at length at the feet of the astonished Miss Jemima, the young lady's countenance, which had before worn an almost livid look of hatred, assumed a smile that perhaps was scarcely more agreeable, and she sank back in the carriage in an easy frame of mind, saying, "So much for the Dixonary; and, thank God, I'm out of Chiswick."

Miss Sedley was almost as flurried at the act of defiance as Miss Jemima had been; for, consider, it was but one minute that she had left school and the impressions of six years are not got over in that space of time.

"How could you do so, Rebecca?" at last she said, after a pause.

"Why, do you think Miss Pinkerton will come out and order me back to the black hole?" said Rebecca, laughing.

"No; but——"

"I hate the whole house," continued Miss Sharp in a fury. "I hope I may never set eyes on it again. I wish it were in the bottom of the Thames, I do; and if Miss Pinkerton were there, I wouldn't pick her out, that I wouldn't. Oh how I should like to see her floating in the water yonder, turban and all, with her train streaming after her, and her nose like the beak of a wherry!"

"Hush!" cried Miss Sedley.

"Why, will the black footman tell tales?" cried Miss Rebecca, laughing. "He may go back and tell Miss Pinkerton that I hate her with all my soul; and I wish he would; and I wish I had a means of proving it, too. For two years I have only had insults and outrage from her. I have been treated worse than any servant in the kitchen. I have never had a friend or a kind word, except from you. I have been made to tend the little girls in the lower schoolroom, and to talk French to the Misses, until I grew sick of my mother-tongue. But that talking French to Miss Pinkerton was capital fun, wasn't it? She doesn't know a word of French, and was too proud to confess it. I believe it was that which made her part with me; and so thank Heaven for French. *Vive la France! Vive l'Empereur! Vive Bonaparte!*"

"O Rebecca, Rebecca, for shame!" cried Miss Sedley; for this was the greatest blasphemy Rebecca had as yet uttered; and in those days, in England, to say, "Long live Bonaparte!" was as much as to say, "Long live Lucifer!" "How can you—how dare you have such wicked, revengeful thoughts?"

"Revenge may be wicked, but it's natural," answered Miss Rebecca. "I'm no angel." And, to say the truth, she certainly was not.

Miss Sharp's father was an artist, and in that quality had given lessons of drawing at Miss Pinkerton's school. He was a clever man, a pleasant companion, a careless student; with a great propensity for running into debt, and a partiality for the tavern. When he was drunk, he used to beat his wife and daughter: and the next morning, with a headache, he would rail at the world for its neglect of his genius, and abuse, with a good deal of cleverness, and sometimes with perfect reason, the fools, his brother painters. As it was with the utmost

difficulty that he could keep himself, and as he owed money for a mile
round Soho, where he lived, he thought to better his circumstances by
marrying a young woman of the French nation, who was by profession
an opera-girl. The humble calling of her female parent Miss Sharp
never alluded to, but used to state subsequently that the Entrechats
were a noble family of Gascony, and took great pride in her descent
from them. And curious it is, that as she advanced in life this young
lady's ancestors increased in rank and splendour.

Rebecca's mother had had some education somewhere, and her
daughter spoke French with purity and a Parisian accent. It was in
those days rather a rare accomplishment, and led to her engagement
with the orthodox Miss Pinkerton. For her mother being dead, her
father, finding himself not likely to recover, after his third attack of
delirium tremens, wrote a manly and pathetic letter to Miss Pinkerton,
recommending the orphan child to her protection; and so descended to
the grave, after two bailiffs had quarrelled over his corpse. Rebecca
was seventeen when she came to Chiswick, and was bound over as an
articled pupil; her duties being to talk French, as we have seen;
and her privileges to live cost free, and, with a few guineas a year,
to gather scraps of knowledge from the professors who attended the
school.

She was small and slight in person, pale, sandy-haired, and with
eyes habitually cast down: when they looked up they were very large,
odd, and attractive—so attractive that the Reverend Mr. Crisp, fresh
from Oxford, and curate to the Vicar of Chiswick, the Reverend Mr.
Flowerdew, fell in love with Miss Sharp; being shot dead by a glance
of her eyes which was fired all the way across Chiswick Church from
the school-pew to the reading-desk. This infatuated young man used
sometimes to take tea with Miss Pinkerton, to whom he had been
presented by his mamma, and actually proposed something like marriage in an intercepted note which the one-eyed apple-woman was
charged to deliver. Mrs. Crisp was summoned from Buxton, and
abruptly carried off her darling boy; but the idea, even, of such an
eagle in the Chiswick dovecot caused a great flutter in the breast of
Miss Pinkerton, who would have sent away Miss Sharp, but that she
was bound to her under a forfeit, and who never could thoroughly
believe the young lady's protestations that she had never exchanged
a single word with Mr. Crisp except under her own eyes, on the two
occasions when she had met him at tea.

By the side of many tall and bouncing young ladies in the establishment, Rebecca Sharp looked like a child. But she had the dismal pre-
cocity of poverty. Many a dun had she talked to, and turned away
from her father's door; many a tradesman had she coaxed and wheedled
into good-humour, and into the granting of one meal more. She sate
commonly with her father, who was very proud of her wit, and heard
the talk of many of his wild companions—often but ill suited for a
girl to hear. But she never had been a girl, she said; she had been a

woman since she was eight years old. Oh why did Miss Pinkerton let such a dangerous bird into her cage?

The fact is, the old lady believed Rebecca to be the meekest creature in the world, so admirably, on the occasions when her father brought her to Chiswick, used Rebecca to perform the part of the *ingénue*.

The catastrophe came, and she was brought to the Mall as to her home. The rigid formality of the place suffocated her: the prayers and the meals, the lessons and the walks, which were arranged with a conventual regularity, oppressed her almost beyond endurance; and she looked back to the freedom and the beggary of the old studio in Soho with so much regret that everybody, herself included, fancied she was consumed with grief for her father. She had a little room in the garret, where the maids heard her walking and sobbing at night; but it was with rage, and not with grief. She had not been much of a dissembler, until now her loneliness taught her to feign. She had never mingled in the society of women: her father, reprobate as he was, was a man of talent; his conversation was a thousand times more agreeable to her than the talk of such of her own sex as she now encountered. The pompous vanity of the old schoolmistress, the foolish good-humour of her sister, the silly chat and scandal of the elder girls, and the frigid correctness of the governesses equally annoyed her; and she had no soft maternal heart, this unlucky girl, otherwise the prattle and talk of the younger children, with whose care she was chiefly entrusted, might have soothed and interested her; but she lived among them two years, and not one was sorry that she went away. The gentle, tenderhearted Amelia Sedley was the only person to whom she could attach herself in the least; and who could help attaching herself to Amelia?

Worthy Miss Pinkerton, although she had a Roman nose and a turban, and was as tall as a grenadier, and had been up to this time an irresistible princess, had no will or strength like that of her little apprentice, and in vain did battle against her, and tried to overawe her. Attempting once to scold her in public, Rebecca hit upon the before-mentioned plan of answering her in French, which quite routed the old woman. In order to maintain authority in her school, it became necessary to remove this rebel, this monster, this serpent, this firebrand; and hearing about this time that Sir Pitt Crawley's family was in want of a governess, she actually recommended Miss Sharp for the situation, firebrand and serpent as she was. And as Miss Sedley, being now in her seventeenth year, was about to leave school, and had a friendship for Miss Sharp (" 'Tis the only point in Amelia's behaviour," said Miss Pinkerton, "which has not been satisfactory"), Miss Sharp was invited by her friend to pass a week with her at home, before she entered upon her duties as governess in a private family.

Thus the world began for these two young ladies. For Amelia it was quite a new, fresh, brilliant world, with all the bloom upon it. It was not quite a new one for Rebecca—(indeed, if the truth must be told with respect to the Crisp affair, the tart-woman hinted to somebody,

who took an affidavit of the fact to somebody else, that there was a
great deal more than was made public regarding Mr. Crisp and Miss
Sharp, and that his letter was *in answer* to another letter). But who
can tell you the real truth of the matter? At all events, if Rebecca was
not beginning the world, she was beginning it over again.

By the time the young ladies reached Kensington turnpike, Amelia
had not forgotten her companions, but had dried her tears, and had
blushed very much and been delighted at a young officer of the Life
Guards, who spied her as he was riding by, and said, "A dem fine gel,
egad!" and before the carriage arrived in Russell Square a great deal
of conversation had taken place about the drawing-room, and whether
or not young ladies wore powder as well as hoops when presented, and
whether she was to have that honour: to the Lord Mayor's ball she
knew she was to go. And when at length home was reached, Miss
Amelia Sedley skipped out on Sambo's arm, as happy and as handsome
a girl as any in the whole big city of London. Both he and coachman agreed on this point, and so did her father and mother, and
so did every one of the servants in the house, as they stood bobbing,
and curtseying, and smiling, in the hall to welcome their young
mistress.

You may be sure that she showed Rebecca over every room of the
house, and everything in every one of her drawers; and her books, and
her piano, and her dresses, and all her necklaces, brooches, laces, and
gimcracks.

When Rebecca saw the two magnificent Cashmere shawls which
Joseph Sedley had brought home to his sister, she said, with perfect
truth, "that it must be delightful to have a brother," and easily got
the pity of the tender-hearted Amelia, for being alone in the world,
an orphan without friends or kindred.

"Not alone," said Amelia; "you know, Rebecca, I shall always be
your friend, and love you as a sister—indeed I will."

"Ah, but to have parents, as you have—kind, rich, affectionate
parents, who give you everything you ask for; and their love, which
is more precious than all! My poor papa could give me nothing, and
I had but two frocks in all the world! And then to have a brother, a
dear brother! Oh, how you must love him!"

Amelia laughed.

"What! *Don't* you love him? You, who say you love everybody?"

"Yes, of course, I do—only——"

"Only what?"

"Only Joseph doesn't seem to care much whether I love him or not.
He gave me two fingers to shake when he arrived after ten years'
absence! He is very kind and good, but he scarcely ever speaks to
me; I think he loves his pipe a great deal better than his . . ." but
here Amelia checked herself, for why should she speak ill of her brother?
"He was very kind to me as a child," she added; "I was but five years
old when he went away."

"Isn't he very rich?" said Rebecca. "They say all Indian nabobs are enormously rich."

"I believe he has a very large income."

"And is your sister-in-law a nice pretty woman?"

"La! Joseph is not married," said Amelia, laughing again.

The meaning of the above series of queries, as translated in the heart of the ingenious Miss Sharp, was simply this: "If Mr. Joseph Sedley is rich and unmarried, why should I not marry him? I have only a fortnight, to be sure, but there is no harm in trying." And she determined within herself to make this laudable attempt.

CHAPTER III

REBECCA IS IN PRESENCE OF THE ENEMY

A VERY stout, puffy man, in buckskins and Hessian boots, with several immense neckcloths, that rose almost to his nose, with a red-striped waistcoat and an apple-green coat with steel buttons almost as large as crown pieces (it was the morning costume of a dandy or blood of those days), was reading the paper by the fire when the two girls entered, and bounced off his arm-chair, and blushed excessively, and hid his entire face almost in his neckcloths at this apparition.

"It's only your sister, Joseph," said Amelia, laughing and shaking the two fingers which he held out. "I've come home *for good*, you know; and this is my friend, Miss Sharp, whom you have heard me mention."

"No, never, upon my word," said the head under the neckcloth, shaking very much,—"that is, yes,—what abominably cold weather, Miss;"—and herewith he fell to poking the fire with all his might, although it was in the middle of June.

"He's very handsome," whispered Rebecca to Amelia, rather loud.

"Do you think so?" said the latter. "I'll tell him."

"Darling! not for worlds," said Miss Sharp, starting back as timid as a fawn.

"Thank you for the beautiful shawls, brother," said Amelia to the fire-poker. "Are they not beautiful, Rebecca?"

"Oh, heavenly!" said Miss Sharp, and her eyes went from the carpet straight to the chandelier.

Joseph still continued a huge clattering at the poker and tongs, puffing and blowing the while, and turning as red as his yellow face would allow him. "I can't make you such handsome presents, Joseph," continued his sister, "but while I was at school, I have embroidered for you a very beautiful pair of braces."

"Good Gad! Amelia," cried the brother, in serious alarm, "what do you mean?" and plunging with all his might at the bell-rope, that article of furniture came away in his hand, and increased the honest fellow's confusion. "For Heaven's sake see if my buggy's at the door! I *can't* wait. I must go. D—— that groom of mine! I must go."

At this minute the father of the family walked in, rattling his seals like a true British merchant. "What's the matter, Emmy?" says he.

"Joseph wants me to see if his—his *buggy* is at the door. What is a buggy, Papa?"

"It is a one-horse palanquin," said the old gentleman, who was a wag in his way.

Joseph at this burst out into a wild fit of laughter; in which, encountering the eye of Miss Sharp, he stopped all of a sudden, as if he had been shot.

"This young lady is your friend? Miss Sharp, I am very happy to see you. Have you and Emmy been quarrelling already with Joseph, that he wants to be off?"

"I promised Bonamy, of our service, sir," said Joseph, "to dine with him."

"O fie! didn't you tell your mother you would dine here?"

"But in this dress it's impossible."

"Look at him, isn't he handsome enough to dine anywhere, Miss Sharp?"

On which, of course, Miss Sharp looked at her friend, and they both set off in a fit of laughter, highly agreeable to the old gentleman.

"Did you ever see a pair of buckskins like those at Miss Pinkerton's?" continued he, following up his advantage.

"Gracious heavens! Father," cried Joseph.

"There now, I have hurt his feelings. Mrs. Sedley, my dear, I have hurt your son's feelings. I have alluded to his buckskins. Ask Miss Sharp if I haven't. Come, Joseph, be friends with Miss Sharp, and let us all go to dinner."

"There's a pillau, Joseph, just as you like it, and Papa has brought home the best turbot in Billingsgate."

"Come, come, sir, walk downstairs with Miss Sharp, and I will follow with these two young women," said the father, and he took an arm of wife and daughter and walked merrily off.

Joseph Sedley was twelve years older than his sister Amelia. He was in the East India Company's Civil Service, and his name appeared, at the period of which we write, in the Bengal division of the East India Register, as collector of Boggley Wollah, an honourable and lucrative post, as everybody knows: in order to know to what higher post Joseph rose in the service, the reader is referred to the same periodical.

Boggley Wollah is situated in a fine, lonely, marshy, jungly district, famous for snipe-shooting, and where not unfrequently you may flush a tiger. Ramgunge, where there is a magistrate, is only forty miles off, and there is a cavalry station about thirty miles further; so Joseph wrote home to his parents, when he took possession of his collectorship. He had lived for about eight years, quite alone, at this charming place, scarcely seeing a Christian face except twice a year, when the detachment arrived to carry off the revenues which he had collected, to Calcutta.

Luckily, at this time he caught a liver complaint, for the cure of which he returned to Europe, and which was the source of great comfort and amusement to him in his native country. He did not live with his family while in London, but had lodgings of his own, like a gay young bachelor. Before he went to India he was too young to partake of the delightful pleasures of a man about town, and plunged into them on his return with considerable assiduity. He drove his horses in the Park; he dined at the fashionable taverns (for the Oriental Club was not as yet invented); he frequented the theatres, as the mode was in those days, or made his appearance at the opera, laboriously attired in tights and a cocked hat.

On returning to India, and ever after, he used to talk of the pleasure of this period of his existence with great enthusiasm, and give you to understand that he and Brummel were the leading bucks of the day. But he was as lonely here as in his jungle at Boggley Wollah. He scarcely knew a single soul in the metropolis; and were it not for his doctor, and the society of his blue-pill, and his liver complaint, he must have died of loneliness. He was lazy, peevish, and a *bon-vivant*; the appearance of a lady frightened him beyond measure; hence it was but seldom that he joined the paternal circle in Russell Square, where there was plenty of gaiety, and where the jokes of his good-natured old father frightened his *amour-propre*.

Downstairs, then, they went, Joseph very red and blushing, Rebecca very modest, and holding her green eyes downwards. She was dressed in white, with bare shoulders as white as snow—the picture of youth, unprotected innocence, and humble virgin simplicity. "I must be very quiet," thought Rebecca, "and very much interested about India."

Now we have heard how Mrs. Sedley had prepared a fine curry for her son, just as he liked it, and in the course of dinner a portion of this dish was offered to Rebecca. "What is it?" said she, turning an appealing look to Mr. Joseph.

"Capital," said he. His mouth was full of it; his face quite red with the delightful exercise of gobbling. "Mother, it's as good as my own curries in India."

"Oh, I must try some, if it is an Indian dish," said Miss Rebecca. "I am sure everything must be good that comes from there."

"Give Miss Sharp some curry, my dear," said Mr. Sedley, laughing. Rebecca had never tasted the dish before.

"Do you find it as good as everything else from India?" said Mr. Sedley.

"Oh, excellent!" said Rebecca, who was suffering tortures with the cayenne pepper.

"You won't like *everything* from India now, Miss Sharp," said the old gentleman; but when the ladies had retired after dinner, the wily old fellow said to his son, "Have a care, Joe; that girl is setting her cap at you."

"Pooh! nonsense!" said Joe, highly flattered.

Being an invalid, Joseph Sedley contented himself with a bottle of claret besides his Madeira at dinner, and he managed a couple of plates full of strawberries and cream, and twenty-four little rout cakes that were lying neglected in a plate near him, and certainly (for novelists have the privilege of knowing everything) he thought a great deal about the girl upstairs. "A nice, gay, merry young creature," thought he to himself. "How she looked at me when I picked up her handkerchief at dinner! She dropped it twice. Who's that singing in the drawing-room? 'Gad! shall I go up and see?"

But his modesty came rushing upon him with uncontrollable force. His father was asleep: his hat was in the hall: there was a hackney-coach stand hard by in Southampton Row. "I'll go and see the *Forty Thieves*," said he, "and Miss Decamp's dance;" and he slipped away gently on the pointed toes of his boots, and disappeared, without waking his worthy parent.

"There goes Joseph," said Amelia, who was looking from the open windows of the drawing-room, while Rebecca was singing at the piano.

"Miss Sharp has frightened him away," said Mrs. Sedley. "Poor Joe, why *will* he be so shy?"

CHAPTER IV

THE GREEN SILK PURSE

Poor Joe's panic lasted for two or three days; during which he did not visit the house, nor during that period did Miss Rebecca ever mention his name. She was all respectful gratitude to Mrs. Sedley: delighted beyond measure at the Bazaars; and in a whirl of wonder at the theatre, whither the good-natured lady took her.

As if bent upon advancing Rebecca's plans in every way—what must Amelia do, but remind her brother, on his reappearance, of a promise made last Easter holidays—"when I was a girl at school," said she, laughing—a promise that he, Joseph, would take her to Vauxhall. "Now," she said, "that Rebecca is with us, will be the very time."

"Oh, delightful!" said Rebecca, going to clap her hands; but she recollected herself, and paused, like a modest creature, as she was.

"To-night is not the night," said Joe.

A goblet of champagne restored Joseph's equanimity, and before the bottle was emptied, of which as an invalid he took two-thirds, he had agreed to take the young ladies to Vauxhall one evening.

"The girls must have a gentleman apiece," said the old gentleman. "Jos will be sure to leave Emmy in the crowd, he will be so taken up with Miss Sharp here. Send to 96, and ask George Osborne if he'll come."

At this, I don't know in the least for what reason, Mrs. Sedley looked at her husband and laughed. Mr. Sedley's eyes twinkled in a manner indescribably roguish, and he looked at Amelia; and Amelia, hanging down her head, blushed as only young ladies of seventeen know how to blush, and as Miss Rebecca Sharp never blushed in her life—at least not since she was eight years old, and when she was caught stealing jam out of a cupboard by her godmother. "Amelia had better write a note," said her father; "and let George Osborne see what a beautiful handwriting we have brought back from Miss Pinkerton's. Do you remember when you wrote to him to come on Twelfth-night, Emmy, and spelt twelfth without the f?"

"That was years ago," said Amelia.

On the evening appointed for the Vauxhall party, George Osborne having come to dinner, and the elders of the house having departed, according to invitation, to dine with Alderman Balls, at Highbury Barn, there came on such a thunderstorm as only happens on Vauxhall nights, and as obliged the young people, perforce, to remain at home. Mr. Osborne did not seem in the least disappointed at this occurrence. He and Joseph Sedley drank a fitting quantity of port-wine, *tête-à-tête*, in the dining-room—during the drinking of which Sedley told a number of his best Indian stories; for he was extremely talkative in man's society; and afterwards Miss Amelia Sedley did the honours of the drawing-room; and these four young persons passed such a comfortable evening together, that they declared they were rather glad of the thunderstorm than otherwise, which had caused them to put off their visit to Vauxhall.

Osborne was Sedley's godson, and had been one of the family any time these three-and-twenty years. At six weeks old, he had received from John Sedley a present of a silver cup; at six months old, a coral with gold whistle and bells; from his youth, upwards, he was "tipped" regularly by the old gentleman at Christmas; and on going back to school, he remembered perfectly well being thrashed by Joseph Sedley, when the latter was a big, swaggering hobbadyhoy, and George an impudent urchin of ten years old. In a word, George was as familiar with the family as such daily acts of kindness and intercourse could make him.

"Let us have some music, Miss Sedley—Amelia," said George, who felt at that moment an extraordinary, almost irresistible impulse to seize the above-mentioned young woman in his arms, and to kiss her in the face of the company; and she looked at him for a moment, and if I should say that they fell in love with each other at that single instant of time, I should perhaps be telling an untruth, for the fact is, that these two young people had been bred up by their parents for this very purpose, and their banns had, as it were, been read in their respective families any time these ten years. They went off to the piano, which was situated, as pianos usually are, in the back drawing-room; and as it was rather dark, Miss Amelia, in the most unaffected way in the world, put her hand into Mr. Osborne's, who, of course, could see the way among the chairs and ottomans a great deal better than she could. But this arrangement left Mr. Joseph Sedley *tête-à-tête* with Rebecca, at the drawing-room table, where the latter was occupied in knitting a green silk purse.

"There is no need to ask family secrets," said Miss Sharp. "Those two have told theirs."

"As soon as he gets his company," said Joseph, "I believe the affair is settled. George Osborne is a capital fellow."

"And your sister the dearest creature in the world," said Rebecca. "Happy the man who wins her!" With this, Miss Sharp gave a great sigh.

When two unmarried persons get together, and talk upon such delicate subjects as the present, a great deal of confidence and intimacy is presently established between them. There is no need of giving a special report of the conversation which now took place between Mr. Sedley and the young lady; for the conversation, as may be judged from the foregoing specimen, was not especially witty or eloquent: it seldom is in private societies, or anywhere except in very high-flown and ingenious novels. As there was music in the next room, the talk was carried on, of course, in a low and becoming tone, though, for the matter of that, the couple in the next apartment would not have been disturbed, had the talking been ever so loud, so occupied were they with their own pursuits.

Almost for the first time in his life, Mr. Sedley found himself talking, without the least timidity or hesitation, to a person of the other sex. Miss Rebecca asked him a great number of questions about India, which gave him an opportunity of narrating many interesting anecdotes about that country and himself. And as he talked on, he grew bold, and actually had the audacity to ask Miss Rebecca for whom she was knitting the green silk purse? He was quite surprised and delighted at his own graceful familiar manner.

"For any one who wants a purse," replied Miss Rebecca, looking at him in the most gentle winning way. Sedley was going to make one of the most eloquent speeches possible, and had begun—"O Miss Sharp, how"—when some song which was performed in the other room came to an end, and caused him to hear his own voice so distinctly that he stopped, blushed, and blew his nose in great agitation.

Having expended her little store of songs, or having stayed long enough in the back drawing-room, it now appeared proper to Miss Amelia to ask her friend to sing. Rebecca sang far better than her friend, and exerted herself to the utmost, and, indeed, to the wonder of Amelia, who had never known her perform so well. She sang a French song, which Joseph did not understand in the least, and which George confessed he did not understand, and then a number of those simple ballads which were the fashion forty years ago, and in which British tars, our King, poor Susan, blue-eyed Mary, and the like, were the principal themes.

Conversation of a sentimental sort, befitting the subject, was carried on between the songs, to which Sambo, after he had brought the tea, the delighted cook, and even Mrs. Blenkinsop, the housekeeper, condescended to listen on the landing-place.

When the parents of the house of Sedley returned from their dinnerparty, they found the young people so busy in talking, that they had not heard the arrival of the carriage; and Mr. Joseph was in the act of saying, "My dear Miss Sharp, one little teaspoonful of jelly to recruit you after your immense—your—your *delightful* exertions."

"Bravo, Jos!" said Mr. Sedley; on hearing the bantering of which well-known voice, Jos instantly relapsed into an alarmed silence, and quickly took his departure.

CHAPTER V

DOBBIN OF OURS

Cuff's fight with Dobbin, and the unexpected issue of that contest, will long be remembered by every man who was educated at Dr. Swishtail's famous school. The latter youth (who used to be called Heigh-ho Dobbin, Gee-ho Dobbin, and by many other names indicative of puerile contempt) was the quietest, the clumsiest, and, as it seemed, the dullest of all Dr. Swishtail's young gentlemen. His parent was a grocer in the City: and it was bruited abroad that he was admitted into Dr. Swishtail's academy upon what are called "mutual principles"—that is to say, the expenses of his board and schooling were defrayed by his father in goods, not money; and he stood there —almost at the bottom of the school—in his scraggy corduroys and jacket, through the seams of which his great big bones were bursting —as the representative of so many pounds of tea, candles, sugar, mottled-soap, plums (of which a very mild proportion was supplied for the puddings of the establishment), and other commodities. A dreadful day it was for young Dobbin when one of the youngsters of the school, having run into the town upon a poaching excursion for hardbrake and polonies, espied the cart of Dobbin and Rudge, Grocers and Oilmen, Thames Street, London, at the Doctor's door, discharging a cargo of the wares in which the firm dealt.

Young Dobbin had no peace after that. The jokes were frightful, and merciless against him. "Hallo, Dobbin," one wag would say, "here's good news in the paper. Sugar is ris', my boy." Another would set a sum—"If a pound of mutton-candles cost sevenpence-halfpenny, how much must Dobbin cost?" and a roar would follow from all the circle of young knaves, usher and all, who rightly considered that the selling of goods by retail is a shameful and infamous practice, meriting the contempt and scorn of all real gentlemen.

"Your father's only a merchant, Osborne," Dobbin said in private to the little boy who had brought down the storm upon him. At which the latter replied haughtily, "My father's a gentleman, and keeps his carriage;" and Mr. William Dobbin retreated to a remote outhouse in the playground where he passed a half-holiday in the bitterest sadness and woe.

Cuff, on the contrary, was the great chief and dandy of the Swishtail Seminary. He smuggled wine in. He fought the town-boys. Ponies used to come for him to ride home on Saturdays. He had his top-boots in his room, in which he used to hunt in the holidays. He had a gold repeater: and took snuff like the Doctor. He had been to the Opera. and knew the merits of the principal actors, preferring Mr. Kean to Mr. Kemble. He could knock you off forty Latin verses in an hour. He could make French poetry. What else didn't he know, or couldn't he do? They said even the Doctor himself was afraid of him.

It happened that Mr. Cuff, on a sunshiny afternoon, was in the neighbourhood of poor William Dobbin, who was lying under a tree in the playground, spelling over a favourite copy of the *Arabian Nights* which he had—apart from the rest of the school, who were pursuing their various sports—quite lonely, and almost happy.

Well, William Dobbin had for once forgotten the world, and was away with Sindbad the Sailor in the Valley of Diamonds, or with Prince Ahmed and the Fairy Peribanou in that delightful cavern where the Prince found her, and whither we should all like to make a tour; when shrill cries, as of a little fellow weeping, woke up his pleasant reverie; and looking up, he saw Cuff before him, belabouring a little boy.

It was the lad who had peached upon him about the grocer's cart; but he bore little malice, not at least towards the young and small. "How dare you, sir, break the bottle?" says Cuff to the little urchin, swinging a yellow cricket-stump over him.

The boy had been instructed to get over the playground wall (at a selected spot where the broken glass had been removed from the top, and niches made convenient in the brick); to run a quarter of a mile; to purchase a pint of rum-shrub on credit; to brave all the Doctor's outlying spies, and to clamber back into the playground again; during the performance of which feat, his foot had slipt, and the bottle was broken, and the shrub had been spilt, and his pantaloons had been damaged, and he appeared before his employer a perfectly guilty and trembling, though harmless, wretch.

"How dare you, sir, break it?" says Cuff; "you blundering little thief. You drink the shrub, and now you pretend to have broken the bottle. Hold out your hand, sir."

Down came the stump with a great heavy thump on the child's hand. A moan followed. Dobbin looked up.

"Hold out your other hand, sir," roars Cuff to his little schoolfellow, whose face was distorted with pain. Dobbin quivered, and gathered himself up in his narrow old clothes.

"Take that, you little devil!" cried Mr. Cuff, and down came the wicket again on the child's hand. Dobbin started up.

I can't tell what his motive was. Torture in a public school is as much licensed as the knout in Russia. It would be ungentlemanlike (in a manner) to resist it. Perhaps Dobbin's foolish soul revolted against that exercise of tyranny; or perhaps he had a hankering feeling of revenge in his mind, and longed to measure himself against that splendid bully and tyrant, who had all the glory, pride, pomp, circumstance, banners flying, drums beating, guards saluting, in the place. Whatever may have been his incentive, however, up he sprang, and screamed out, "Hold off, Cuff; don't bully that child any more, or I'll——"

"Or you'll what?" Cuff asked in amazement at this interruption. "Hold out your hand, you little beast."

"I'll give you the worst thrashing you ever had in your life," Dobbin said, in reply to the first part of Cuff's sentence; and little Osborne, gasping and in tears, looked up with wonder and incredulity at seeing this amazing champion put up suddenly to defend him: while Cuff's astonishment was scarcely less.

"After school," says he, of course; after a pause and a look, as much as to say, "Make your will, and communicate your last wishes to your friends, between this time and that."

"As you please," Dobbin said. "You must be my bottle-holder, Osborne."

"Well, if you like," little Osborne replied; for, you see, his papa kept a carriage, and he was rather ashamed of his champion.

Yes, when the hour of battle came, he was almost ashamed to say, "Go it, Figs:" and not a single other boy in the place uttered that cry for the first two or three rounds of this famous combat; at the commencement of which the scientific Cuff, with a contemptuous smile on his face, and as light and as gay as if he was at a ball, planted his blows upon his adversary, and floored that unlucky champion three times running. At each fall there was a cheer; and everybody was anxious to have the honour of offering the conqueror a knee.

"What a licking I shall get when it's over!" young Osborne thought, picking up his man. "You'd best give in," he said to Dobbin; "it's only a thrashing, Figs, and you know I'm used to it." But Figs, all whose limbs were in a quiver, and whose nostrils were breathing rage, put his little bottle-holder aside, and went in for a fourth time.

As he did not in the least know how to parry the blows that were aimed at himself, and Cuff had begun the attack on the three preceding occasions, without ever allowing his enemy to strike, Figs now determined that he would commence the engagement by a charge on his own part; and accordingly, being a left-handed man, brought that arm into action, and hit out a couple of times with all his might—once at Mr. Cuff's left eye, and once on his beautiful Roman nose.

Cuff went down this time, to the astonishment of the assembly. "Well hit, by Jove!" says little Osborne, with the air of a connoisseur, clapping his man on the back. "Give it him with the left, Figs, my boy."

Figs's left made terrific play during the rest of the combat. Cuff went down every time. At the sixth round, there were almost as many fellows shouting out, "Go it, Figs!" as there were youths exclaiming, "Go it, Cuff!" At the twelfth round, the latter champion was all abroad, as the saying is, and had lost all presence of mind and power of attack or defence. Figs, on the contrary, was as calm as a Quaker. His face being quite pale, his eyes shining open, and a great cut on his under lip bleeding profusely, gave this young fellow a fierce and ghastly air, which perhaps struck terror into many spectators. Nevertheless, his intrepid adversary prepared to close for the thirteenth time.

If I had the pen of a Napier, or a Bell's Life, I should like to describe this combat properly. It was the last charge of the Guard—(that is, it *would* have been, only Waterloo had not yet taken place)—it was Ney's column breasting the hill of La Haye Sainte, bristling with ten thousand bayonets, and crowned with twenty eagles—it was the shout of the beef-eating British, as leaping down the hill they rushed to hug the enemy in the savage arms of battle—in other words, Cuff coming up full of pluck, but quite reeling and groggy, the Fig merchant put in his left as usual on his adversary's nose, and sent him down for the last time.

"I think *that* will do for him," Figs said, as his opponent dropped as neatly on the green as I have seen Jack Spot's ball plump into the pocket at billiards; and the fact is, when time was called, Mr. Reginald Cuff was not able, or did not choose, to stand up again.

And now all the boys set up such a shout for Figs as would have made you think he had been their darling champion through the whole battle; and as absolutely brought Dr. Swishtail out of his study, curious to know the cause of the uproar. He threatened to flog Figs violently, of course; but Cuff, who had come to himself by this time, and was washing his wounds, stood up and said, "It's my fault, sir; not Figs's —not Dobbin's. I was bullying a little boy; and he served me right." By which magnanimous speech he not only saved his conqueror a whipping, but got back all his ascendency over the boys which his defeat had nearly cost him.

In consequence of Dobbin's victory, his character rose prodigiously in the estimation of all his school-fellows, and the name of Figs, which had been a byword of reproach, became as respectable and popular a nick-name as any other in use in the school. "After all, it's not his fault that his father's a grocer," George Osborne said, who, though a little chap, had a very high popularity among the Swishtail youth; and his opinion was received with great applause. It was voted low to sneer at Dobbin about this accident of birth. "Old Figs" grew to be a name of kindness and endearment; and the sneak of an usher jeered at him no longer.

Dobbin was much too modest a young fellow to suppose that this happy change in all his circumstances arose from his own generous and manly disposition: he chose, from some perverseness, to attribute his good fortune to the sole agency and benevolence of little George Osborne, to whom henceforth he vowed such a love and affection as is only felt by children—such an affection, as we read in the charming fairy-book, uncouth Orson had for splendid young Valentine his conqueror. He flung himself down at little Osborne's feet and loved him. Even before they were acquainted, he had admired Osborne in secret. Now he was his valet, his dog, his man Friday. He believed Osborne to be the possessor of every perfection, to be the handsomest, the bravest, the most active, the cleverest, the most generous of created boys.

So that Lieutenant Osborne, when coming to Russell Square on the day finally appointed for the Vauxhall party, said to the ladies, "Mrs. Sedley, Ma'am, I hope you have room; I've asked Dobbin of ours to come and dine here, and go with us to Vauxhall. He's almost as modest as Jos."

That evening, when Amelia came tripping into the drawing-room in a white muslin frock, prepared for conquest at Vauxhall, singing like a lark, and as fresh as a rose—a very tall ungainly gentleman, with large hands and feet, and large ears, set off by a closely-cropped head of black hair, and in the hideous military frogged coat and cocked-hat of those times, advanced to meet her, and made her one of the clumsiest bows that was ever performed by a mortal.

This was no other than Captain William Dobbin, of His Majesty's —— Regiment of Foot, returned from yellow fever in the West Indies, to which the fortune of the service had ordered his regiment, whilst so many of his gallant comrades were reaping glory in the Peninsula.

He had arrived with a knock so very timid and quiet, that it was inaudible to the ladies upstairs: otherwise, you may be sure Miss Amelia would never have been so bold as to come singing into the room. As it was, the sweet fresh little voice went right into the Captain's heart, and nestled there.

His history since he left school, until the very moment when we have the pleasure of meeting him again, although not fully narrated has yet, I think, been indicated sufficiently for an ingenious reader.

CHAPTER VI

VAUXHALL

LET us step into the coach with the Russell Square party, and be off to the Gardens. There is barely room between Jos and Miss Sharp, who are on the front seat; Mr. Osborne sitting bodkin opposite, between Captain Dobbin and Amelia.

Every soul in the coach agreed, that on that night, Jos would propose to make Rebecca Sharp Mrs. Sedley.

The party was landed at the Royal Gardens in due time. As the majestic Jos stepped out of the creaking vehicle the crowd gave a cheer for the fat gentleman, who blushed and looked very big and mighty, as he walked away with Rebecca under his arm. George, of course, took charge of Amelia. She looked as happy as a rose-tree in sunshine.

"I say, Dobbin," says George, "just look to the shawls and things, there's a good fellow." And so while he paired off with Miss Sedley, and Jos squeezed through the gate into the Gardens with Rebecca at his side, honest Dobbin contented himself by giving an arm to the shawls, and by paying at the door for the whole party.

It is to be understood, as a matter of course, that our young people, being in parties of two and two, made the most solemn promises to keep together during the evening, and separated in ten minutes afterwards. Parties at Vauxhall always did separate, but 'twas only to meet again at supper-time, when they could talk of their mutual adventures in the interval.

What were the adventures of Mr. Osborne and Miss Amelia? That is a secret. But be sure of this—they were perfectly happy, and correct in their behaviour; and as they had been in the habit of being together any time these fifteen years, their *tête-à-tête* offered no particular novelty.

But when Miss Rebecca Sharp and her stout companion lost themselves in a solitary walk, in which there were not above five score more of couples similarly straying, they both felt that the situation was extremely tender and critical, and now or never was the moment, Miss Sharp thought, to provoke that declaration which was trembling on the timid lips of Mr. Sedley.

"How I should like to see India!" said Rebecca.

"*Should* you?" said Joseph, with a most killing tenderness; and was no doubt about to follow up this artful interrogatory by a question still more tender (for he puffed and panted a great deal, and Rebecca's hand, which was placed near his heart, could count the feverish pulsations of that organ), when, oh, provoking! the bell rang for the fireworks, and, a great scuffling and running taking place, these interesting lovers were obliged to follow in the stream of people.

Captain Dobbin had some thoughts of joining the party at supper—as, in truth, he found the Vauxhall amusements not particularly lively—but he paraded twice before the box where the now united couples were met, and nobody took any notice of him. Covers were laid for four. The mated pairs were prattling away quite happily, and Dobbin knew he was as clean forgotten as if he had never existed in this world.

The two couples were perfectly happy then in their box, where the most delightful and intimate conversation took place. Jos was in his glory, ordering about the waiters with great majesty. He made the salad; and uncorked the champagne; and carved the chickens; and ate and drank the greater part of the refreshments on the tables. Finally, he insisted upon having a bowl of rack punch; everybody had rack punch at Vauxhall. "Waiter, rack punch!"

The young ladies did not drink it; Osborne did not like it; and the consequence was that Jos, that fat *gourmand*, drank up the whole contents of the bowl: and the consequence of his drinking up the who e contents of the bowl was, a liveliness which at first was astonishing, and then became almost painful; for he talked and laughed so loud as to bring scores of listeners round the box, much to the confusion of the innocent party within it; and, volunteering to sing a song (which he did in that maudlin high key peculiar to gentlemen in an inebriated state), he almost drew away the audience who were gathered round the musicians in the gilt scollop-shell, and received from his hearers a great deal of applause.

"Brayvo, Fat un!" said one; "Angcore, Daniel Lambert!" said another; "What a figure for the tight-rope!" exclaimed another wag, to the inexpressible alarm of the ladies, and the great anger of Mr. Osborne.

"For Heaven's sake, Jos, let us get up and go!" cried that gentleman, and the young women rose.

"Stop, my dearest diddle-diddle-darling," shouted Jos, now as bold as a lion, and clasping Miss Rebecca round the waist. Rebecca started, but she could not get away her hand. The laughter outside redoubled. Jos continued to drink, to make love, and to sing; and, winking and waving his glass gracefully to his audience, challenged all or any to come in and take a share of his punch.

Mr. Osborne was just on the point of knocking down a gentleman in top-boots, who proposed to take advantage of this invitation, and a commotion seemed to be inevitable, when by the greatest good luck a gentleman of the name of Dobbin, who had been walking about the Gardens, stepped up to the box. "Be off, you fools!" said this gentleman—shouldering off a great number of the crowd, who vanished presently before his cocked-hat and fierce appearance—and he entered the box in a most agitated state.

"Good Heavens! Dobbin, where *have* you been?" Osborne said, seizing the white cashmere shawl from his friend's arm, and huddling up Amelia in it. "Make yourself useful, and take charge of Jos here, whilst I take the ladies to the carriage."

Jos was for rising to interfere, but a single push from Osborne's finger sent him puffing back into his seat again, and the lieutenant was enabled to remove the ladies in safety. Jos kissed his hand to them as they retreated, and hiccupped out, "Bless you! bless you!" Then, seizing Captain Dobbin's hand, and weeping in the most pitiful way, he confided to that gentleman the secret of his loves. He adored that girl who had just gone out; he had broken her heart, he knew he had, by his conduct; he would marry her next morning at St. George's, Hanover Square; he'd knock up the Archbishop of Canterbury at Lambeth—he would, by Jove! and have him in readiness; and, acting on this hint, Captain Dobbin shrewdly induced him to leave the Gardens and hasten to Lambeth Palace, and, when once out of the gates, easily conveyed Mr. Jos. Sedley into a hackney-coach, which deposited him safely at his lodgings.

George Osborne conducted the girls home in safety; and when the door was closed upon them, and as he walked across Russell Square, laughed so as to astonish the watchman. Amelia looked very ruefully at her friend, as they went upstairs, and kissed her, and went to bed without any more talking.

"He must propose to-morrow," thought Rebecca. "He called me his soul's darling four times; he squeezed my hand in Amelia's presence. He must propose to-morrow." And so thought Amelia, too. And I daresay she thought of the dress she was to wear as bridesmaid, and of the presents which she should make to her nice little sister-in-law, and of a subsequent ceremony in which she herself might pay a principal part, etc., and etc., and etc.

That next morning, which Rebecca thought was to dawn upon her fortune, found Sedley groaning in agonies which the pen refuses to describe. Soda-water was not invented yet. Small beer—will it be believed?—was the only drink with which unhappy gentlemen soothed the fever of their previous night's potation. With this mild beverage before him, George Osborne found the ex-Collector of Boggley Wollah groaning on the sofa at his lodgings. Dobbin was already in the room good-naturedly tending his patient of the night before. The two officers, looking at the prostrate bacchanalian, and askance at each other, exchanged the most frightful sympathetic grins. Even Sedley's valet, the most solemn and correct of gentlemen, with the muteness and gravity of an undertaker, could hardly keep his countenance in order as he looked at his unfortunate master.

"Mr. Sedley was uncommon wild last night, sir," he whispered in confidence to Osborne, as the latter mounted the stair. "He wanted to fight the 'ackney-coachman, sir. The Capting was obliged to bring him upstairs in his harms like a babby." A momentary smile flickered over Mr. Brush's features as he spoke; instantly, however, they relapsed into their usual unfathomable calm, as he flung open the drawing-room door, and announced "Mr. Hosbin."

"How are you, Sedley?" that young wag began, after surveying his victim. "No bones broke? There's a hackney-coachman downstairs with a black eye, and a tied-up head, vowing he'll have the law on you."

"What do you mean,—law?" Sedley faintly asked.

"For thrashing him last night—didn't he, Dobbin? You hit out, sir. like Molyneaux. The watchman says he never saw a fellow go down so straight. Ask Dobbin."

"You *did* have a round with the coachman," Captain Dobbin said, "and showed plenty of fight, too."

"And that fellow with the white coat at Vauxhall! How Jos drove at him! How the women screamed! By Jove, sir, it did my heart good to see you. I thought you civilians had no pluck; but *I'll* never get in your way when you are in your cups, Jos."

"I believe I'm very terrible, when I'm roused," ejaculated Jos from the sofa, and made a grimace so dreary and ludicrous, that the Captain's politeness could restrain him no longer, and he and Osborne fired off a ringing volley of laughter.

Osborne pursued his advantage pitilessly. He thought Jos a milksop. He had been revolving in his mind the marriage-question pending between Jos and Rebecca, and was not over well pleased that a member of a family into which he, George Osborne, of the —th, was going to marry, should make a *mésalliance* with a little nobody—a little upstart governess. "You hit, you poor old fellow!" said Osborne. "You terrible! Why, man, you couldn't stand—you made everybody laugh in the Gardens, though you were crying yourself. You were maudlin, Jos. Don't you remember singing a song?"

"A what?" Jos asked.

"A sentimental song, and calling Rosa, Rebecca, what's her name, Amelia's little friend—your dearest diddle-diddle-darling?" And this ruthless young fellow, seizing hold of Dobbin's hand, acted over the scene, to the horror of the original performer, and in spite of Dobbin's good-natured entreaties to him to have mercy.

As George walked down Southampton Row, from Holborn, he laughed as he saw, at the Sedley mansion, in two different stories, two heads on the look-out.

The fact is, Miss Amelia, in the drawing-room balcony, was looking very eagerly towards the opposite side of the Square, where Mr. Osborne dwelt, on the watch for the lieutenant himself; and Miss Sharp, from her little bedroom on the second floor, was in observation until Mr. Joseph's great form should heave in sight.

"Sister Anne is on the watch-tower," said he to Amelia, "but there's nobody coming:" and laughing and enjoying the joke hugely, he described in the most ludicrous terms to Miss Sedley the dismal condition of her brother.

"I think it's very cruel of you to laugh, George," she said, looking particularly unhappy; but George only laughed the more at her piteous and discomfited mien, persisting in thinking the joke a most diverting one, and when Miss Sharp came downstairs, bantered her with a great deal of liveliness upon the effect of her charms on the fat civilian.

All that day Jos never came. But Amelia had no fear about this: for the little schemer had actually sent away the page, Mr. Sambo's aide-de-camp, to Mr. Joseph's lodgings, to ask for some book he had promised, and how he was; and the reply through Jos's man, Mr. Brush, was, that his master was ill in bed, and had just had the doctor with him. He must come to-morrow, she thought; but she never had the courage to speak a word on the subject to Rebecca; nor did that young woman herself allude to it in any way during the whole evening after the night at Vauxhall.

B

The next day, however, as the two young ladies sate on the sofa, pretending to work, or to write letters, or to read novels, Sambo came into the room with his usual engaging grin, with a packet under his arm, and a note on a tray. "Note from Mr. Jos, Miss," says Sambo.

How Amelia trembled as she opened it!

So it ran—

"DEAR AMELIA,—I send you the *Orphan of the Forest*. I was too ill to come yesterday. I leave town to-day for Cheltenham. Pray excuse me, if you can, to the amiable Miss Sharp, for my conduct at Vauxhall, and entreat her to pardon and forget every word I may have uttered when excited by that fatal supper. As soon as I have recovered, for my health is very much shaken, I shall go to Scotland for some months, and am

> "Truly yours,
> JOS. SEDLEY."

It was the death-warrant. All was over. Amelia did not dare to look at Rebecca's pale face and burning eyes, but she dropped the letter into her friend's lap; and got up, and went upstairs to her room, and cried her little heart out.

Blenkinsop, the housekeeper, there sought her presently with consolation, on whose shoulder Amelia wept confidentially, and relieved herself a good deal. "Don't take on, Miss. I didn't like to tell you. But none of us in the house have liked her except at fust. I sor her with my own eyes reading your Ma's letters. Pinner says she's always about your trinket-box and drawers, and everybody's drawers, and she's put your white ribbing into her box."

"I gave it her, I gave it her," Amelia said.

But this did not alter Mrs. Blenkinsop's opinion of Miss Sharp. "I don't trust them governesses, Pinner," she remarked to the maid. "They give themselves the hairs and hupstarts of ladies, and their wages is no better than you nor me."

It now became clear to every soul in the house, except poor Amelia, that Rebecca should take her departure, and high and low (always with the one exception) agreed that that event should take place as speedily as possible. Our good child ransacked all her drawers, cupboards, reticules, and gimcrack boxes—passed in review all her gowns, fichus, tags, bobbins, laces, silk stockings, and fallals,—selecting this thing and that and the other, to make a little heap for Rebecca. And going to her Papa, that generous British merchant, who had promised to give her as many guineas as she was years old—she begged the old gentleman to give the money to dear Rebecca, who must want it, while she lacked for nothing.

She even made George Osborne contribute, and nothing loth (or he was as free-handed a young fellow as any in the army), he went to Bond Street, and bought the best hat and spencer that money could buy.

"That's George's present to you, Rebecca, dear," said Amelia, quite proud of the bandbox conveying these gifts. "What a taste he has! There's nobody like him."

"Nobody," Rebecca answered. "How thankful I am to him!" She was thinking in her heart, "It was George Osborne who prevented my marriage." And she loved George Osborne accordingly.

She made her preparations for departure with great equanimity; and accepted all the kind little Amelia's presents, after just the proper degree of hesitation and reluctance. She vowed eternal gratitude to Mrs. Sedley, of course; but did not intrude herself upon that good lady too much, who was embarrassed, and evidently wishing to avoid her. She kissed Mr. Sedley's hand, when he presented her with the purse; and asked permission to consider him for the future as her kind, kind friend and protector. Her behaviour was so affecting that he was going to write her a cheque for twenty pounds more; but he restrained his feelings: the carriage was in waiting to take him to dinner, so he tripped away with a "God bless you, my dear; always come here when you come to town, you know.—Drive to the Mansion House, James."

Finally came the parting with Miss Amelia, over which picture I intend to throw a veil. But after a scene in which one person was in earnest, and the other a perfect performer—after the tenderest caresses, the most pathetic tears, the smelling-bottle, and some of the very best feeling of the heart, had been called into requisition—Rebecca and Amelia parted, the former vowing to love her friend for ever and ever and ever.

CHAPTER VII

CRAWLEY OF QUEEN'S CRAWLEY

AMONG the most respected of the names beginning in C, which the *Court Guide* contained in the year 18—, was that of Crawley, Sir Pitt, Baronet, Great Gaunt Street, and Queen's Crawley, Hants. This honourable name had figured constantly also in the Parliamentary list for many years, in conjunction with that of a number of other worthy gentlemen who sat in turns for the borough.

Sir Pitt Crawley (named after the great Commoner) was the son of Walpole Crawley, first Baronet, of the Tape and Sealing-Wax Office in the reign of George II, when he was impeached for peculation, as were a great number of other honest gentlemen of those days; and Walpole Crawley was, as need scarcely be said, son of John Churchill Crawley, named after the celebrated military commander of the reign of Queen Anne. The family tree (which hangs up at Queen's Crawley) furthermore mentions Charles Stuart, afterwards called Barebones Crawley, son of the Crawley of James the First's time; and finally, Queen Elizabeth's Crawley, who is represented as the foreground of the picture in his forked beard and armour. Out of his waistcoat, as usual, grows a tree, on the main branches of which the above illustrious names are inscribed. Close by the name of Sir Pitt Crawley, Baronet (the subject of the present memoir), are written that of his brother, the Reverend Bute Crawley (the great Commoner was in disgrace when the reverend gentleman was born), rector of Crawley-cum-Snailby, and of various other male and female members of the Crawley family.

Sir Pitt was first married to Grizzel, sixth daughter of Mungo Binkie, Lord Binkie, and cousin, in consequence, of Mr. Dundas. She brought him two sons: Pitt, named not so much after his father as after the heaven-born minister; and Rawdon Crawley, from the Prince of Wales's friend, whom His Majesty George IV forgot so completely. Many years after her ladyship's demise, Sir Pitt led to the altar Rosa, daughter of Mr. G. Dawson, of Mudbury, by whom he had two daughters, for whose benefit Miss Rebecca Sharp was now engaged as governess. It will be seen that the young lady was come into a family of very genteel connections, and was about to move in a much more distinguished circle than that humble one which she had just quitted in Russell Square.

She had received her orders to join her pupils, in a note which was written upon an old envelope, and which contained the following words:

"Sir Pitt Crawley begs Miss Sharp and baggidge may be here on Tuesday, as I leaf for Queen's Crawley to-morrow morning *erly*.
"*Great Gaunt Street.*"

Rebecca had never seen a Baronet, as far as she knew, and as soon as she had taken leave of Amelia, and counted the guineas which good-natured Mr. Sedley had put into a purse for her, and as soon as she had done wiping her eyes with her handkerchief (which operation she concluded the very moment the carriage had turned the corner of the street), she began to depict in her own mind what a Baronet must be.

Having passed through Gaunt Square into Great Gaunt Street, the carriage at length stopped at a tall gloomy house between two other tall gloomy houses, each with a hatchment over the middle drawing-room window; as is the custom of houses in Great Gaunt Street, in which gloomy locality death seems to reign perpetual. The shutters of the first-floor windows of Sir Pitt's mansion were closed; those of the dining-room were partially open, and the blinds neatly covered up in old newspapers.

John, the groom, who had driven the carriage alone, did not care to descend to ring the bell, and so prayed a passing milkboy to perform that office for him. When the bell was rung, a head appeared between the interstices of the dining-room shutters, and the door was opened by a man in drab breeches and gaiters, with a dirty old coat, a foul old neckcloth lashed round his bristly neck, a shining bald head, a leering red face, a pair of twinkling grey eyes, and a mouth perpetually on the grin.

"This Sir Pitt Crawley's?" says John, from the box.

"Ees," says the man at the door, with a nod.

"Hand down these 'ere trunks then," said John.

"Hand'n down yourself," said the porter.

"Don't you see I can't leave my hosses? Come, bear a hand, my fine feller, and Miss will give you some beer," said John, with a horse-laugh; for he was no longer respectful to Miss Sharp, as her connection with the family was broken off, and as she had given nothing to the servants on coming away.

The bald-headed man, taking his hands out of his breeches pockets, advanced on this summons, and throwing Miss Sharp's trunk over his shoulder, carried it into the house.

On entering the dining-room, by the orders of the individual in gaiters, Rebecca found that apartment not more cheerful than such rooms usually are when genteel families are out of town. The faithful chambers seem, as it were, to mourn the absence of their masters. The turkey carpet has rolled itself up, and retired sulkily under the sideboard; the pictures have hidden their faces behind old sheets of brown paper; the ceiling lamp is muffled up in a dismal sack of brown holland; the window-curtains have disappeared under all sorts of shabby envelopes; the marble bust of Sir Walpole Crawley is looking from its black corner at the bare boards and the oiled fire-irons and the empty card-racks over the mantelpiece; the cellaret has lurked away behind the carpet; the chairs are turned up heads and tails along the walls; and in the dark corner opposite the statue is an old-fashioned crabbed knife-box, locked and sitting on a dumb-waiter.

Two kitchen chairs, and a round table, and an attenuated old poker and tongs were, however, gathered round the fireplace, as was a saucepan over a feeble sputtering fire. There was a bit of cheese and bread, and a tin candlestick on the table, and a little black porter in a pint-pot.

"Had your dinner, I suppose? It is not too warm for you? Like a drop of beer?"

"Where is Sir Pitt Crawley?" said Miss Sharp majestically.

"He, he! I'm Sir Pitt Crawley. Reklect you owe me a pint for bringing down your luggage. He, he! Ask Tinker if I aynt. Mrs. Tinker, Miss Sharp; Miss Governess, Mrs. Charwoman. Ho, ho!"

The lady addressed as Mrs. Tinker at this moment made her appearance with a pipe and a paper of tobacco, for which she had been dispatched a minute before Miss Sharp's arrival; and she handed the articles over to Sir Pitt, who had taken his seat by the fire.

"Where's the farden?" says he. "I gave you three-half-pence. Where's the change, old Tinker?"

"There!" replied Mrs. Tinker, flinging down the coin; "it's only baronets as cares about farthings."

"A farthing a day is seven shillings a year," answered the M.P.; "Seven shillings a year is the interest of seven guineas. Take care of your farthings, old Tinker, and your guineas will come quite nat'ral."

"You may be sure it's Sir Pitt Crawley, young woman," said Mrs. Tinker surlily, "because he looks to his farthings. You'll know him better afore long."

"And like me none the worse, Miss Sharp," said the old gentleman, with an air almost of politeness. "I must be just before I'm generous."

"He never gave away a farthing in his life," growled Tinker.

"Never, and never will; it's against my principle. Go and get another chair from the kitchen, Tinker, if you want to sit down and then we'll have a bit of supper."

Presently the baronet plunged a fork into the saucepan on the fire, and withdrew from the pot a piece of tripe and an onion, which he divided into pretty equal portions, and of which he partook with Mrs. Tinker. "You see, Miss Sharp, when I'm not here Tinker's on board wages; when I'm in town she dines with the family. Haw! haw! I'm glad Miss Sharp's not hungry, ain't you, Tink?" And they fell to upon their frugal supper.

After supper Sir Pitt Crawley began to smoke his pipe; and when it became quite dark, he lighted the rushlight in the tin candlestick, and producing from an interminable pocket a huge mass of papers, began reading them, and putting them in order.

"I'm here on law business, my dear, and that's how it happens that I shall have the pleasure of such a pretty travelling companion to-morrow."

"He's always at law business," said Mrs. Tinker, taking up the pot of porter.

"Drink and drink about," said the Baronet. "Yes, my dear, Tinker is quite right: I've lost and won more lawsuits than any man in England. Look here at Crawley, Bart., *v.* Snaffle. I'll throw him over, or my name's not Pitt Crawley. Podder and Another *versus* Crawley, Bart. Overseers of Snaily parish against Crawley, Bart. They can't prove it's common: I'll defy 'em; the land's mine. It no more belongs to the parish than it does to you or Tinker here. I'll beat 'em, if it cost me a thousand guineas. Look over the papers; you may if you like, my dear. Do you write a good hand? I'll make you useful when we're at Queen's Crawley, depend on it, Miss Sharp. Now the dowager's dead, I want some one."

"She was as bad as he," said Tinker. "She took the law of every one of her tradesmen; and turned away forty-eight footmen in four year."

"She was close—very close," said the Baronet simply; "but she was a valyable woman to me, and saved me a steward."—And in this confidential strain, and much to the amusement of the new-comer, the conversation continued for a considerable time. Whatever Sir Pitt Crawley's qualities might be, good or bad, he did not make the least disguise of them. He talked of himself incessantly, sometimes in the coarsest and vulgarest Hampshire accent; sometimes adopting the tone of a man of the world. And so, with injunctions to Miss Sharp to be ready at five in the morning, he bade her good-night. "You'll sleep with Tinker to-night," he said; "it's a big bed, and there's room for two. Lady Crawley died in it. Good-night."

Sir Pitt went off after this benediction, and the solemn Tinker, rush-light in hand, led the way up the great, bleak stone stairs, past the great, dreary drawing-room doors, with the handles muffled up in paper, into the great front bedroom, where Lady Crawley had slept her last. The bed and chamber were so funereal and gloomy, you might have fancied, not only that Lady Crawley died in the room, but that her ghost inhabited it. Rebecca sprang about the apartment, however, with the greatest liveliness, and had peeped into the huge wardrobes, and the closets, and the cupboards, and tried the drawers, which were locked, and examined the dreary pictures and toilette appointments, while the old charwoman was saying her prayers. "I shouldn't like to sleep in this yeer bed without a good conscience, Miss," said the old woman. "There's room for us and a half-dozen of ghosts in it," says Rebecca. "Tell me all about Lady Crawley and Sir Pitt Crawley, and everybody, my *dear* Mrs. Tinker."

But old Tinker was not to be pumped by this little cross-questioner; and signifying to her that bed was a place for sleeping, not conversation, set up in her corner of the bed such a snore as only the nose of innocence can produce. Rebecca lay awake for a long, long time, thinking of the morrow, and of the new world into which she was going, and of her chances of success there. The rushlight flickered in the basin. The mantelpiece cast up a great black shadow, over half a mouldy old sampler, which her defunct ladyship had worked, no doubt, and over two little family pictures of young lads, one in a college gown, and the other in a red jacket like a soldier. When she went to sleep, Rebecca chose that one to dream about.

At four o'clock, on such a roseate summer's morning as even made Great Gaunt Street look cheerful, the faithful Tinker, having wakened her bedfellow, and bid her prepare for departure, unbarred and un-bolted the great hall door (the clanging and clapping whereof startled the sleeping echoes in the street), and taking her way into Oxford Street, summoned a coach from a stand there. It is needless to par-ticularize the number of the vehicle, or to state that the driver was stationed thus early in the neighbourhood of Swallow Street, in hopes that some young buck, reeling homeward from the tavern, might need the aid of his vehicle, and pay him with the generosity of intoxication.

It is likewise needless to say that the driver, if he had any such hopes as those above stated, was grossly disappointed; and that the worthy Baronet whom he drove to the City did not give him one single penny more than his fare. It was in vain that Jehu appealed and stormed; that he flung down Miss Sharp's band-boxes in the gutter at the 'Necks, and swore he would take the law of his fare.

Let us be set down at Queen's Crawley without further divagation, and see how Miss Rebecca Sharp speeds there.

CHAPTER VIII

PRIVATE AND CONFIDENTIAL

Miss Rebecca Sharp to Miss Amelia Sedley, Russell Square, London.
(Free.—Pitt Crawley)

"MY DEAREST, SWEETEST AMELIA,—With what mingled joy and sorrow
do I take up the pen to write to my dearest friend! Oh, what a change
between to-day and yesterday! *Now* I am friendless and alone; yesterday I was at home, in the sweet company of a sister, whom I shall
ever, *ever* cherish!

"I will not tell you in what tears and sadness I passed the fatal night
in which I separated from you. *You* went on Tuesday to joy and
happiness with your mother and *your devoted young soldier* by your side;
and I thought of you all night, dancing at the Perkins's, the prettiest,
I am sure, of all the young ladies at the ball. I was brought by the
groom in the old carriage to Sir Pitt Crawley's town house.

"Sir Pitt is not what we silly girls, when we used to read *Cecilia* at
Chiswick, imagined a baronet must have been. Anything, indeed, less
like Lord Orville cannot be imagined. Fancy an old, stumpy, short,
vulgar, and very dirty man, in old clothes and shabby old gaiters,
who smokes a horrid pipe, and cooks his own horrid supper in a saucepan. He speaks with a country accent, and swore a great deal at the
old charwoman, at the hackney-coachman who drove us to the inn
where the coach went from, and on which I made the journey *outside
for the greater part of the way.*

"Before the house of Queen's Crawley, which is an odious old-
fashioned red brick mansion, with tall chimneys and gables of the
style of Queen Bess, there is a terrace flanked by the family dove and
serpent, and on which the great hall-door opens. And oh, my dear,
the great hall I am sure is as big and as glum as the great hall in the
dear castle of Udolpho. It has a large fireplace, in which we might
put half Miss Pinkerton's school, and the grate is big enough to roast
an ox at the very least. Then there are Mr. Pitt's apartments—Mr.
Crawley, he is called—the eldest son, and Mr. Rawdon Crawley's
rooms—he is an officer like *somebody*, and away with his regiment.
There is no want of room, I assure you. You might lodge all the people
in Russell Square in the house, I think, and have space to spare.

"Half an hour after our arrival the great dinner-bell was rung, and
I came down with my two pupils (they are very thin, insignificant
little chits of ten and eight years old). I came down in your *dear* muslin
gown (about which that odious Mrs. Pinner was so rude, because you
gave it me); for I am to be treated as one of the family, except on
company days, when the young ladies and I are to dine upstairs.

"Well, the great dinner-bell rang, and we all assembled in the little
drawing-room where my Lady Crawley sits. She is the second Lady

Crawley, and mother of the young ladies. She was an ironmonger's daughter, and her marriage was thought a great match. She looks as if she had been handsome once, and her eyes are always weeping for the loss of her beauty. She is pale and meagre and high-shouldered, and has not a word to say for herself, evidently. Her stepson, Mr. Crawley, was likewise in the room. He was in full dress, as pompous as an undertaker. He is pale, thin, ugly, silent; he has thin legs, no chest, hay-coloured whiskers, and straw-coloured hair. He is the very picture of his sainted mother over the mantelpiece—Griselda of the noble house of Binkie.

"When the repast was concluded, a jug of hot water was placed before Sir Pitt, with a case-bottle containing, I believe, rum. Mr. Horrocks served myself and my pupils with three little glasses of wine, and a bumper was poured out for my lady. When we retired, she took from her work-drawer an enormous interminable piece of knitting; the young ladies began to play at cribbage with a dirty pack of cards. We had but one candle lighted, but it was in a magnificent old silver candlestick; and after a very few questions from my lady, I had my choice of amusement between a volume of sermons, and a pamphlet on the corn-laws, which Mr. Crawley had been reading before dinner.

"*Saturday.*—This morning, at five, I heard the shrieking of the little black pig. Rose and Violet introduced me to it yesterday; and to the stables, and to the kennel, and to the gardener, who was picking fruit to send to market, and from whom they begged hard a bunch of hot-house grapes; but he said that Sir Pitt had numbered every 'Man Jack' of them, and it would be as much as his place was worth to give any away. The darling girls caught a colt in a paddock, and asked me if I would ride, and began to ride themselves, when the groom, coming with horrid oaths, drove them away.

"Lady Crawley is always knitting the worsted. Sir Pitt is always tipsy, every night; and, I believe, sits with Horrocks, the butler. Mr. Crawley always reads sermons in the evening, and in the morning is locked up in his study, or else rides to Mudbury, on county business, or to Squashmore, where he preaches, on Wednesdays and Fridays, to the tenants there.

"A hundred thousand grateful loves to your dear papa and mamma. Is your poor brother recovered of his rack punch? O dear! O dear! How men should beware of wicked punch!

"Ever and ever thine own,
"REBECCA."

CHAPTER IX

FAMILY PORTRAITS

SIR PITT CRAWLEY was a philosopher with a taste for what is called low life. His first marriage with the daughter of the noble Binkie had been made under the auspices of his parents; and as he often told Lady Crawley in her lifetime she was such a confounded quarrelsome high-bred jade that when she died he was hanged if he would ever take another of her sort, at her ladyship's demise he kept his promise, and selected for a second wife Miss Rose Dawson, daughter of Mr. John Thomas Dawson, ironmonger, of Mudbury. What a happy woman was Rose to be my Lady Crawley!

Let us set down the items of her happiness. In the first place she gave up Peter Butt, a young man who kept company with her, and in consequence of his disappointment in love, took to smuggling, poaching, and a thousand other bad courses. Then she quarrelled, as in duty bound, with all the friends and intimates of her youth, who, of course, could not be received by my Lady at Queen's Crawley; nor did she find in her new rank and abode any persons who were willing to welcome her. Who ever did? Sir Huddleston Fuddleston had three daughters who all hoped to be Lady Crawley. Sir Giles Wapshot's family were insulted that one of the Wapshot girls had not the preference in the marriage; and the remaining baronets of the county were indignant at their comrade's misalliance. Never mind the commoners, whom we will leave to grumble anonymously.

Sir Pitt did not care, as he said, a brass farden for any one of them. He had his pretty Rose, and what more need a man require than to please himself? So he used to get drunk every night; to beat his pretty Rose sometimes; to leave her in Hampshire when he went to London .or the parliamentary session, without a single friend in the wide world. Even Mrs. Bute Crawley, the Rector's wife, refused to visit her, and she said she never would give the *pas* to a tradesman's daughter.

As the only endowments with which Nature had gifted Lady Crawley were those of pink cheeks and a white skin, and as she had no sort of character, nor talents, nor opinions, nor occupations, nor amusements, nor that vigour of soul and ferocity of temper which often falls to the lot of entirely foolish women, her hold upon Sir Pitt's affections was not very great. Her roses faded out of her cheeks, and the pretty freshness left her figure after the birth of a couple of children, and she became a mere machine in her husband's house, of no more use than the late Lady Crawley's grand piano. Being a light-complexioned woman, she wore light clothes, as most blondes will, and appeared, in preference, in draggled sea-green, or slatternly sky-blue. She worked that worsted day and night, or other pieces like it. She had counterpanes, in the course of a few years, to all the beds in Crawley. She had a small flower-garden, for which she had rather an affection; but beyond this no other like or disliking. When her husband was rude to her, she was apathetic; whenever he struck her, she cried.

The languid dullness of their mamma did not, as it may be supposed, awaken much affection in her little daughters, but they were very happy in the servants' hall and in the stables; and the Scotch gardener having, luckily, a good wife and some good children, they got a little wholesome society and instruction in his lodge, which was the only education bestowed upon them until Miss Sharp came.

Her engagement was owing to the remonstrances of Mr. Pitt Crawley, the only friend or protector Lady Crawley ever had, and the only person, besides her children, for whom she entertained a little feeble attachment. Mr. Pitt took after the noble Binkies, from whom he was descended, and was a very polite and proper gentleman. When he grew to man's estate, and came back from Christchurch, he began to reform the slackened discipline of the hall, in spite of his father, who stood in awe of him. He was a man of such rigid refinement, that he would have starved rather than have dined without a white neckcloth. Once, when just from college, and when Horrocks the butler brought him a letter without placing it previously on a tray, he gave that domestic a look, and administered to him a speech so cutting, that Horrocks ever after trembled before him. The whole household bowed to him: Lady Crawley's curl-papers came off earlier when he was at home: Sir Pitt's muddy gaiters disappeared; and if that incorrigible old man still adhered to other old habits, he never fuddled himself with rum-and-water in his son's presence, and only talked to his servants in a very reserved and polite manner; and those persons remarked that Sir Pitt never swore at Lady Crawley while his son was in the room.

At Eton his son was called Miss Crawley; and there, I am sorry to say, his younger brother Rawdon used to lick him violently. But though his parts were not brilliant, he made up for his lack of talent by meritorious industry, and was never known, during eight years at school, to be subject to that punishment which it is generally thought none but a cherub can escape.

At college his career was, of course, highly creditable. And here he prepared himself for public life, into which he was to be introduced by the patronage of his grandfather, Lord Binkie, by studying the ancient and modern orators with great assiduity; and by speaking unceasingly at the debating societies. But though he had a fine flux of words, and delivered his little voice with great pomposity and pleasure to himself, and never advanced any sentiment or opinion which was not perfectly trite and stale, and supported by a Latin quotation; yet he failed somehow, in spite of a mediocrity which ought to have ensured any man a success. He did not even get the prize poem, which all his friends said he was sure of.

After leaving college he became Private Secretary to Lord Binkie, and was then appointed Attaché to the Legation at Pumpernickel, which post he filled with perfect honour, and brought home dispatches, consisting of Strasburg pie, to the Foreign Minister of the day. After remaining ten years Attaché (several years after the lamented Lord Binkie's demise), and finding the advancement slow, he at length gave up the diplomatic service in some disgust, and began to turn country gentleman.

Miss Sharp's accounts of his employment at Queen's Crawley were not caricatures. He subjected the servants there to the devotional exercises before mentioned, in which (and so much the better) he brought his father to join. He patronized an Independent meeting-house in Crawley parish, much to the indignation of his uncle the Rector, and to the consequent delight of Sir Pitt, who was induced to go himself once or twice, which occasioned some violent sermons at Crawley parish church, directed point-blank at the Baronet's old Gothic pew there. Honest Sir Pitt, however, did not feel the force of these discourses, as he always took his nap during sermon-time.

Mr. Crawley was very earnest, for the good of the nation and of the Christian world, that the old gentleman should yield him up his place in Parliament; but this the elder constantly refused to do. Both were, of course, too prudent to give up the fifteen hundred a year which was brought in by the second seat (at this period filled by Mr. Quadroon, with carte-blanche on the Slave question); indeed the family estate was much embarrassed, and the income drawn from the borough was of great use to the house of Queen's Crawley.

It had never recovered the heavy fine imposed upon Walpole Crawley, first baronet, for peculation in the Tape and Sealing-Wax Office. Sir Walpole was a jolly fellow, eager to seize and to spend money ("alieni appetens, sui profuseus," as Mr. Crawley would remark with a sigh), and in his day beloved by all the county for the constant drunkenness and hospitality which was maintained at Queen's Crawley.

If mere parsimony could have made a man rich, Sir Pitt Crawley might have become very wealthy; if he had been an attorney in a country town, with no capital but his brains, it is very possible that he would have turned them to good account, and might have achieved for himself a very considerable influence and competency. But he was unluckily endowed with a good name and a large though encumbered estate, both of which went rather to injure than to advance him. He had a taste for law, which cost him many thousands yearly; and being a great deal too clever to be robbed, as he said, by any single agent, allowed his affairs to be mismanaged by a dozen, whom he all equally mistrusted. He was such a sharp landlord, that he could hardly find any but bankrupt tenants; and such a close farmer, as to grudge almost the seed to the ground, whereupon revengeful Nature grudged him the crops which she granted to more liberal husbandmen.

One great cause why Mr. Crawley had such a hold over the affections of his father, resulted from money arrangements. The Baronet owed his son a sum of money out of the jointure of his mother, which he did not find it convenient to pay; indeed he had an almost invincible repugnance to paying anybody, and could only be brought by force to discharge his debts. Miss Sharp calculated (for she became, as we shall hear speedily, inducted into most of the secrets of the family) that the mere payment of his creditors cost the honourable Baronet several hundreds yearly: but this was a delight he could not forego; he had a savage pleasure in making the poor wretches wait, and in shifting from court to court and from term to term the period of satisfaction. What's the good of being in Parliament, he said, if you must pay your debts? Hence, indeed, his position as a senator was not a little useful to him.

Sir Pitt had an unmarried half-sister who inherited her mother's large fortune; and though the Baronet proposed to borrow this money of her on mortgage. Miss Crawley declined the offer, and preferred the security of the funds. She had signified, however, her intention of leaving her inheritance between Sir Pitt's second son and the family at the Rectory, and had once or twice paid the debts of Rawdon Crawley in his career at college and in the army. Miss Crawley was, in consequence, an object of great respect when she came to Queen's Crawley, for she had a balance at her banker's which would have made her beloved anywhere.

CHAPTER X

MISS SHARP BEGINS TO MAKE FRIENDS

AND now, being received as a member of the amiable family whose portraits we have sketched in the foregoing pages, it became naturally Rebecca's duty to make herself, as she said, agreeable to her benefactors, and to gain their confidence to the utmost of her power.

So she wisely determined to render her position with the Queen's Crawley family comfortable and secure, and to this end resolved to make friends of every one around her who could at all interfere with her comfort.

As my Lady Crawley was not one of these personages, and a woman, moreover, so indolent and void of character as not to be of the least consequence in her own house, Rebecca soon found that it was not at all necessary to cultivate her good-will—indeed, impossible to gain it. She used to talk to her pupils about their "poor mamma;" and, though she treated that lady with every demonstration of cool respect, it was to the rest of the family that she wisely directed the chief part of her attentions.

With the young people, whose applause she thoroughly gained, her method was pretty simple. She did not pester their young brains with too much learning, but, on the contrary, let them have their own way in regard to educating themselves; for what instruction is more effectual than self-instruction? The elder was rather fond of books, and as there was in the old library at Queen's Crawley a considerable provision of works of light literature of the last century, both in the French and English languages (they had been purchased by the Secretary of the Tape and Sealing-Wax Office at the period of his disgrace), and as nobody ever troubled the bookshelves but herself, Rebecca was enabled agreeably, and, as it were, in playing, to impart a great deal of instruction to Miss Rose Crawley.

Miss Violet's tastes were, on the contrary, more rude and boisterous than those of her sister. She knew the sequestered spots where the hens laid their eggs. She could climb a tree to rob the nests of the feathered songsters of their speckled spoils. And her pleasure was to ride the young colts, and to scour the plains like Camilla. She was the favourite of her father and of the stablemen. She was the darling, and withal the terror, of the cook; for she discovered the haunts of the jam-pots, and would attack them when they were within her reach. She and her sister were engaged in constant battles. Any of which pecca-dilloes, if Miss Sharp discovered, she did not tell them to Lady Craw-ley, who would have told them to the father, or worse, to Mr. Crawley; but promised not to tell if Miss Violet would be a good girl and love her governess.

With Mr. Crawley Miss Sharp was respectful and obedient. She used to consult him on passages of French which she could not under-stand, though her mother was a Frenchwoman, and which he would construe to her satisfaction; and, besides giving her his aid in profane literature, he was kind enough to select for her books of a more serious tendency, and address to her much of his conversation. She admired, beyond measure, his speech at the Quashimaboo Aid Society; took an interest in his pamphlet on Malt; was often affected, even to tears, by his discourses of an evening, and would say, "Oh, thank you, sir," with a sigh, and a look up to heaven, that made him occasionally con-descend to shake hands with her. "Blood is everything, after all," would that aristocratic religionist say. "How Miss Sharp is awakened by my words, when not one of the people here is touched. I am too fine for them—too delicate. I must familiarize my style—but she understands it. Her mother was a Montmorency."

Indeed it was from this famous family, as it appears, that Miss Sharp, by the mother's side, was descended. Of course she did not say that her mother had been on the stage; it would have shocked Mr. Crawley's religious scruples.

He took Rebecca to task once or twice about the propriety of playing at backgammon with Sir Pitt, saying that it was a godless amusement, and that she would be much better engaged in reading *Thrump's Legacy*, or *The Blind Washerwoman of Moorfields*, or any work of a more serious nature; but Miss Sharp said her dear mother used often to play the same game with the old Count de Trictrac and the venerable Abbé du Cornet, and so found an excuse for this and other worldly amusements.

Before she had been a year at Queen's Crawley she had quite won the Baronet's confidence; and the conversation at the dinner-table, which before used to be held between him and Mr. Horrocks the butler, was now almost exclusively between Sir Pitt and Miss Sharp. She was almost mistress of the house when Mr. Crawley was absent, but conducted herself in her new and exalted situation with such circum-spection and modesty as not to offend the authorities of the kitchen and stable, among whom her behaviour was always exceedingly modest and affable. She was quite a different person from the haughty, shy, dissatisfied little girl whom we have known previously; and this change of temper proved great prudence, a sincere desire of amendment, or at any rate great moral courage on her part. Whether it was the heart which dictated this new system of complaisance and humility adopted by our Rebecca, is to be proved by her after-history. A system of hypocrisy, which lasts through whole years, is one seldom satisfactorily practised by a person of one-and-twenty; however, our readers will recollect that, though young in years, our heroine was old in life and experience, and we have written to no purpose if they have not discovered that she was a very clever woman.

The elder and younger son of the house of Crawley were, like the gentleman and lady in the weather-box, never at home together—they hated each other cordially; indeed, Rawdon Crawley, the dragoon, had a great contempt for the establishment altogether, and seldom came thither except when his aunt paid her annual visit.

The great good quality of this old lady has been mentioned. She possessed seventy thousand pounds, and had almost adopted Rawdon. She disliked her elder nephew exceedingly, and despised him as a milksop. In return he did not hesitate to state that her soul was irretrievably lost; and was of opinion that his brother's chance in the next world was not a whit better.

Old Miss Crawley was certainly one of the reprobate. She had a snug little house in Park Lane, and, as she ate and drank a great deal too much during the season in London, she went to Harrogate or Cheltenham for the summer. She was the most hospitable and jovial of old vestals, and had been a beauty in her day, she said. (All old women were beauties once, we very well know.)

This worthy old lady took a fancy to Rawdon Crawley when a boy, sent him to Cambridge (in opposition to his brother at Oxford), and, when the young man was requested by the authorities of the first-named University to quit after a residence of two years, she bought him his commission in the Life Guards Green.

A perfect and celebrated "blood" or dandy about town, was this young officer. Boxing, rat-hunting, the fives court, and four-in-hand driving were then the fashion of our British aristocracy; and he was an adept in all these noble sciences. And though he belonged to the household troops, who, as it was their duty to rally round the Prince Regent, had not shown their valour in foreign service yet, Rawdon Crawley had already (à propos of play, of which he was immoderately fond) fought three bloody duels, in which he gave ample proofs of his contempt for death.

Silly, romantic Miss Crawley, far from being horrified at the courage of her favourite, always used to pay his debts after his duels; and would not listen to a word that was whispered against his morality. "He will sow his wild oats," she would say, "and is worth far more than that puling hypocrite of a brother of his."

CHAPTER XI

ARCADIAN SIMPLICITY

BESIDES these honest folks at the Hall (whose simplicity and sweet rural purity surely show the advantage of a country life over a town one), we must introduce the reader to their relatives and neighbours at the Rectory, Bute Crawley and his wife.

The Reverend Bute Crawley was a tall, stately, jolly, shovel-hatted man, far more popular in his county than the Baronet his brother. At college he pulled stroke-oar in the Christchurch boat, and had thrashed all the best bruisers of the "town". He carried his taste for boxing and athletic exercises into private life; there was not a fight within twenty miles at which he was not present, nor a race, nor a coursing match, nor a regatta, nor a ball, nor an election, nor a visitation dinner, nor indeed a good dinner in the whole county, but he found means to attend it.

Mrs. Crawley, the Rector's wife, was a smart little body, who wrote this worthy divine's sermons. Being of a domestic turn, and keeping the house a great deal with her daughters, she ruled absolutely within the Rectory, wisely giving her husband full liberty without. He was welcome to come and go, and dine abroad as many days as his fancy dictated, for Mrs. Crawley was a saving woman and knew the price of port wine. Ever since Mrs. Bute carried off the young Rector of Queen's Crawley (she was of a good family, daughter of the late Lieut.-Colonel Hector MacTavish, and she and her mother played for Bute and won him at Harrogate) she had been a prudent and thrifty wife to him. In spite of her care, however, he was always in debt.

It cannot be supposed that the arrival of such a personage as Rebecca at Queen's Crawley, and her gradual establishment in the good graces of all people there, could be unremarked by Mrs. Bute Crawley. Mrs. Bute, who knew how many days the sirloin of beef lasted at the Hall; how much linen was got ready at the great wash; how many peaches were on the south wall; how many doses her ladyship took when she was ill—for such points are matters of intense interest to certain persons in the country—Mrs. Bute, I say, could not pass over the Hall governess without making every inquiry respecting her history and character. There was always the best understanding between the servants at the Rectory and the Hall.

Very soon then after her arrival, Rebecca began to take a regular place in Mrs. Crawley's bulletin from the Hall. It was to this effect: "The black porker's killed—weighed x stone—salted the sides—pig's pudding and leg of pork for dinner. Mr. Cramp from Mudbury, over with Sir Pitt about putting John Blackmore in jail—Mr. Pitt at meeting (with all the names of the people who attended)—my lady as usual—young ladies with the governess."

Then the report would come—The new governess be a rare manager—Sir Pitt be very sweet on her—Mr. Crawley too—He be reading tracts to her. "What an abandoned wretch!" said little, eager, active, black-faced Mrs. Bute Crawley.

Finally, the reports were that the governess had "come round" everybody—wrote Sir Pitt's letters, did his business, managed his accounts—had the upper hand of the whole house, my lady, Mr. Crawley, the girls and all; at which Mrs. Crawley declared she was an artful hussy, and had some dreadful designs in view. Thus the doings at the Hall were the great food for conversation at the Rectory, and Mrs. Bute's bright eyes spied out everything that took place in the enemy's camp—everything and a great deal besides.

"MRS. BUTE CRAWLEY TO MISS PINKERTON, THE MALL, CHISWICK.
"RECTORY, QUEEN'S CRAWLEY, *December*—.

"MY DEAR MADAM,—Although it is so *many* years since I profited by your *delightful* and *invaluable* instructions, yet I have *ever* retained the *fondest* and *most reverential* regard for Miss Pinkerton, and *dear* Chiswick. I hope your health is *good*. The world and *the cause of education* cannot afford to lose Miss Pinkerton for *many many years*. When my friend, Lady Fuddleston, mentioned that her dear girls required an instructress (I am *too poor* to engage a governess for mine, but was I not educated at Chiswick?—'Who,' I exclaimed, 'can we consult but the excellent, the incomparable Miss Pinkerton?' In a word, have you, dear madam, any ladies on your list, whose services might be made available to my kind friend and neighbour? I assure you she will take no governess *but of your choosing*.

"My dear husband is pleased to say that he likes *everything which comes from Miss Pinkerton's school*. How I wish I could present him and my beloved girls to the friend of my youth, and the *admired* of the great lexicographer of our country! If you ever travel into Hampshire, Mr. Crawley begs me to say, he hopes you will adorn our *rural rectory* with your presence. 'Tis the humble but happy home of
"Your affectionate
"MARTHA CRAWLEY.

"*P.S.*—Mr. Crawley's brother, the baronet, with whom we are not, alas, upon those terms of *unity* in which it *becomes brethren to dwell*, has a governess for his little girls, who, I am told, had the good fortune to be educated at Chiswick. I hear various reports of her; and as I have the tenderest interest in my dearest little nieces, whom I wish, in spite of family differences, to see among my own children—and as I long to be attentive to *any pupil of yours*—do, my dear Miss Pinkerton, tell me *the history* of this young lady, whom, for *your sake*, I am most anxious to befriend.—M.C."

"Miss Pinkerton to Mrs. Bute Crawley.

"Johnson House, Chiswick, *Dec.* 18—.

"Dear Madam,—I have the honour to acknowledge your polite communication, to which I promptly reply. 'Tis most gratifying to one in my most arduous position to find that my maternal cares have elicited a responsive affection; and to recognize in the amiable Mrs. Bute Crawley my excellent pupil of former years, *the sprightly and accomplished* Miss Martha MacTavish. I am happy to have under my charge now the daughters of many of those who were your contemporaries at my establishment—what pleasure it would give me if your own beloved young ladies had need of my instructive superintendence!

"Presenting my respectful compliments to Lady Fuddleston, I have the honour (epistolarily) to introduce to her ladyship my two friends, Miss Tuffin and Miss Hawky.

"Either of these young ladies is *perfectly qualified* to instruct in Greek, Latin, and the rudiments of Hebrew; in mathematics and history; in Spanish, French, Italian, and geography; in music, vocal and instrumental; in dancing, without the aid of a master; and in the elements of natural sciences. In the use of the globes both are proficients. In addition to these Miss Tuffin, who is daughter of the late Reverend Thomas Tuffin (Fellow of Corpus College, Cambridge), can instruct in the Syriac language, and the elements of Constitutional law. But as she is only eighteen years of age, and of exceedingly pleasing personal appearance, perhaps this young lady may be objectionable in Sir Huddleston Fuddleston's family.

"Miss Letitia Hawky, on the other hand, is not personally well-favoured. She is twenty-nine; her face is much pitted with the small-pox. She has a halt in her gait, red hair, and a trifling obliquity of vision. Both ladies are endowed with *every moral and religious virtue.* Their terms, of course, are such as their accomplishments merit. With my most grateful respects to the Reverend Bute Crawley, I have the honour to be, dear Madam,

"Your most faithful and obedient servant,

"Barbara Pinkerton.

"*P.S.*—The Miss Sharp, whom you mention as governess to Sir Pitt Crawley, Bart., M.P., was a pupil of mine, and I have nothing to say in her disfavour. Though her appearance is disagreeable—we cannot control the operations of nature—and though her parents were disreputable (her father being a painter, several times bankrupt, and her mother, as I have since learned, with horror, a dancer at the Opera), yet her talents are considerable, and I cannot regret that I received her *out of charity.* My dread is, lest the principles of the mother—who was represented to me as a French Countess, forced to emigrate in the late revolutionary horrors; but who, as I have since found, was a person of the *very lowest order and morals*—should at any time prove to be *hereditary* in the unhappy young woman whom I took as *an out-*

cast. But her principles have *hitherto* been correct (I believe), and I am sure nothing will occur to injure them in the elegant and refined circle of the eminent Sir Pitt Crawley."

When Mrs. Bute Crawley (whose artifices our ingenious Rebecca had so soon discovered) had procured from Miss Sharp the promise of a visit, she induced the all-powerful Miss Crawley to make the necessary application to Sir Pitt; and the good-natured old lady, who loved to be gay herself, and to see every one gay and happy round about her, was quite charmed, and ready to establish a reconciliation and intimacy between her two brothers. It was therefore agreed that the young people of both families should visit each other frequently for the future, and the friendship of course lasted as long as the jovial old mediatrix was there to keep the peace.

Miss Crawley had not long been established at the Hall before Rebecca's fascinations had won the heart of that good-natured London rake, as they had of the country innocents whom we have been describing. Taking her accustomed drive one day, she thought fit to order that "that little governess" should accompany her to Mudbury. Before they had returned Rebecca had made a conquest of her, having made her laugh four times, and amused her during the whole of the little journey.

"Not let Miss Sharp dine at table!" said she to Sir Pitt, who had arranged a dinner of ceremony, and asked all the neighbouring baronets. "My dear creature, do you suppose I can talk about the nursery with Lady Fuddleston or discuss justices' business with that goose, old Sir Giles Wapshot? I insist upon Miss Sharp appearing. Let Lady Crawley remain upstairs, if there is no room. But little Miss Sharp! Why, she's the only person fit to talk to in the county!"

Of course, after such a peremptory order as this, Miss Sharp, the governess, received commands to dine with the illustrious company below stairs. And when Sir Huddleston had, with great pomp and ceremony, handed Miss Crawley in to dinner, and was preparing to take his place by her side, the old lady cried out, in a shrill voice, "Becky Sharp! Miss Sharp! Come you and sit by me and amuse me; and let Sir Huddleston sit by Lady Wapshot."

When the parties were over, and the carriages had rolled away, the insatiable Miss Crawley would say, "Come to my dressing-room, Becky, and let us abuse the company,"—which, between them, this pair of friends did perfectly.

When Miss Rebecca Sharp wrote to her beloved friend the account of the little ball at Queen's Crawley, and the manner in which, for the first time, Captain Crawley had distinguished her, she did not, strange to relate, give an altogether accurate account of the transaction. The Captain had distinguished her a great number of times before. The Captain had met her in a half-score of walks. The Captain had lighted upon her in a half-hundred of corridors and passages. The Captain had hung over her piano twenty times of an evening (my Lady was now upstairs, being ill, and nobody heeded her) as Miss Sharp sang. The Captain had written her notes (the best that the great, blundering dragoon could devise and spell; but dullness gets on as well as any other quality with women). But when he put the first of the notes into the leaves of the song she was singing, the little governess, rising and looking him steadily in the face, took up the triangular missive daintly and waved it about as if it were a cocked-hat, and she, advancing to the enemy, popped the note into the fire, and made him a very low curtsy, and went back to her place, and began to sing away again more merrily than ever.

"What's that?" said Miss Crawley, interrupted in her after-dinner doze by the stoppage of the music.

"It's a false note," Miss Sharp said with a laugh; and Rawdon Crawley fumed with rage and mortification.

Seeing the evident partiality of Miss Crawley for the new governess, how good it was of Mrs. Bute Crawley not to be jealous, and to welcome the young lady to the Rectory, and not only her, but Rawdon Crawley, her husband's rival in the Old Maid's five per cents! They became very fond of each other's society, Mrs. Crawley and her nephew. He gave up hunting; he declined entertainments at Fuddleston; he would not dine with the mess of the depôt at Mudbury: his great pleasure was to stroll over to Crawley parsonage—whither Miss Crawley came too; and as their mamma was ill, why not the children with Miss Sharp? So the children (little dears!) came with Miss Sharp; and of an evening some of the party would walk back together. Not Miss Crawley—she preferred her carriage—but the walk over the Rectory fields, and in at the little park wicket, and through the dark plantation, and up the checkered avenue to Queen's Crawley, was charming in the moonlight to two such lovers of the picturesque as the Captain and Miss Rebecca.

CHAPTER XII

QUITE A SENTIMENTAL CHAPTER

WE must now take leave of Arcadia, and those amiable people practising the rural virtues there, and travel back to London, to inquire what has become of Miss Amelia.

While Becky Sharp was on her own wing in the country, hopping on all sorts of twigs, and amid a multiplicity of traps, and pecking up her food quite harmless and successful, Amelia lay snug in her home of Russell Square: if she went into the world, it was under the guidance of the elders; nor did it seem that any evil could befall her or that opulent, cheery comfortable home in which she was affectionately sheltered.

We have talked of shift, self, and poverty, as those dismal instructors under whom poor Miss Becky Sharp got her education. Now, love was Miss Amelia Sedley's last tutoress, and it was amazing what progress our young lady made under that popular teacher. In the course of fifteen or eighteen months' daily and constant attention to this eminent finishing governess, what a deal of secrets Amelia learned, which Miss Wirt and the black-eyed young ladies over the way, which old Miss Pinkerton of Chiswick herself, had no cognizance of!

This young person (perhaps it was very imprudent in her parents to encourage her, and abet her in such idolatry and silly romantic ideas) loved, with all her heart, the young officer in His Majesty's service with whom we have made a brief acquaintance. She thought about him the very first moment on waking, and his was the very last name mentioned in her prayers. She never had seen a man so beautiful or so clever; such a figure on horseback, such a dancer, such a hero in general! Talk of the Prince's bow! what was it to George's? She had seen Mr. Brummell, whom everybody praised so. Compare such a person as that to her George! Not amongst all the beaux at the Opera (and there were beaux in those days with actual opera hats) was there any one to equal him. He was only good enough to be a fairy prince; and oh, what magnanimity to stoop to such a humble Cinderella! Miss Pinkerton would have tried to check this blind devotion very likely, had she been Amelia's confidante; but not with much success, depend upon it. It is in the nature and instinct of some women. Some are made to scheme, and some to love; and I wish any respected bachelor that reads this may take the sort that best likes him.

What were her parents doing not to keep this little heart from beating so fast? Old Sedley did not seem much to notice matters. He was graver of late, and his City affairs absorbed him. Mrs. Sedley was of so easy and uninquisitive a nature that she wasn't even jealous. Mr. Jos was away, being besieged by an Irish widow at Cheltenham. Amelia had the house to herself—ah! too much to herself sometimes: not that she ever doubted, for, to be sure, George must be at the Horse Guards; and he can't always get leave from Chatham; and he must see his friends and sisters, and mingle in society when in town (he, such an ornament to every society!); and when he is with the regiment, he is too tired to write long letters.

CHAPTER XIII

SENTIMENTAL AND OTHERWISE

I FEAR the gentleman to whom Miss Amelia's letters were addressed was rather an obdurate critic. Such a number of notes followed Lieutenant Osborne about the country, that he became almost ashamed of the jokes of his mess-room companions regarding them, and ordered his servant never to deliver them except at his private apartment. He was seen lighting his cigar with one, to the horror of Captain Dobbin, who, it is my belief, would have given a bank-note for the document.

For some time George strove to keep the *liaison* a secret. There *was* a woman in the case, that he admitted. "And not the first either," said Ensign Spooney to Ensign Stubble. "That Osborne's a devil of a fellow. There was a judge's daughter at Demerara went almost mad about him; then there was that beautiful quadroon girl, Miss Pye, at St. Vincent's, you know; and since he's been home, they say he's a regular Don Giovanni, by Jove."

Stubble and Spooney thought that to be a "regular Don Giovanni, by Jove," was one of the finest qualities a man could possess; and Osborne's reputation was prodigious amongst the young men of the regiment.

Well, Stubble and Spooney and the rest indulged in most romantic conjectures regarding this female correspondent of Osborne's, and the real state of the case would never have been known at all in the regiment but for Captain Dobbin's indiscretion. The Captain was eating his breakfast one day in the mess-room, while Cackle, the assistant-surgeon, and the two above-named worthies were speculating upon Osborne's intrigue—Stubble holding out that the lady was a duchess about Queen Charlotte's court, and Cackle vowing she was an opera-singer of the worst reputation. At this idea Dobbin became so moved that, though his mouth was full of eggs and bread-and-butter at the time, and though he ought not to have spoken at all, yet he couldn't help blurting out, "Cackle, you're a stupid fool. You're always talking nonsense and scandal. Osborne is not going to run off with a duchess or ruin a milliner. Miss Sedley is one of the most charming young women that ever lived. He's been engaged to her ever so long; and the man who calls her names had better not do so in my hearing." With which, turning exceedingly red, Dobbin ceased speaking and almost choked himself with a cup of tea. The story was over the regiment in half-an-hour; and that evening Mrs. Major O'Dowd wrote off to her sister Glorvina at O'Dowdstown not to hurry from Dublin—young Osborne being prematurely engaged already.

She complimented the Lieutenant in an appropriate speech over a glass of whisky-toddy that evening, and he went home perfectly furious to quarrel with Dobbin (who had declined Mrs. Major O'Dowd's party, and sat in his own room playing the flute, and, I believe, writing poetry in a very melancholy manner)—to quarrel with Dobbin for betraying his secret.

"Who the deuce asked you to talk about my affairs?" Osborne shouted indignantly. "Why the devil is all the regiment to know that I am going to be married? Why is that tattling old harridan, Peggy O'Dowd, to make free with my name at her d——d supper-table, and advertise my engagement over the three kingdoms? After all, what ight have you to say I *am* engaged, or to meddle in my business at all, Dobbin?"

"Are you engaged?" Captain Dobbin interposed.

"What the devil's that to you or any one here if I am?"

"Are you ashamed of it?" Dobbin resumed.

"What right have you to ask me that question, sir, I should like to know?" George said.

"Good God, you don't mean to say you want to break off?" asked Dobbin, starting up.

"In other words, you ask me if I'm a man of honour," said Osborne fiercely; "is that what you mean? You've adopted such a tone regarding me lately that I'm —— if I'll bear it any more."

"What have I done? I've told you you were neglecting a sweet girl, George. I've told you that when you go to town you ought to go to her, and not to the gambling-houses about St. James's."

"You want your money back, I suppose," said George with a sneer.

"Of course I do—I always did, didn't I?" says Dobbin. "You speak like a generous fellow."

"No, hang it, William, I beg your pardon"—here George interposed in a fit of remorse—"you *have* been my friend in a hundred ways, Heaven knows. You've got me out of a score of scrapes. When Crawley of the Guards won that sum of money of me, I should have been done but for you; I know I should. But you shouldn't deal so hardly with me; you shouldn't be always catechizing me. I *am* very fond of Amelia; I adore her, and that sort of thing. Don't look angry. She's faultless; I know she is. But you see there's no fun in winning a thing unless you play for it. Hang it! the regiment's just back from the West Indies; I must have a little fling, and then when I'm married I'll reform; I will, upon my honour, now. And—I say—Dob—don't be angry with me, and I'll give you a hundred next month, when I know my father will stand something handsome; and I'll ask Heavytop for leave, and I'll go to town and see Amelia to-morrow—there now, will *that* satisfy you?"

The day after the little conversation at Chatham barracks, young Osborne, to show that he would be as good as his word, prepared to go to town, thereby incurring Captain Dobbin's applause. "I should have liked to make her a little present." Osborne said to his friend in confidence, "only I am quite out of cash until my father tips up." But Dobbin would not allow this good-nature and generosity to be baulked, and so accommodated Mr. Osborne with a few pound notes, which the latter took after a little faint scruple.

And I daresay he would have bought something very handsome for Amelia, only, getting off the coach in Fleet Street, he was attracted by a handsome shirt-pin in a jeweller's window, which he could not resist; and having paid for that, had very little money to spare for indulging in any further exercise of kindness. Never mind; you may be sure it was not his presents Amelia wanted. When he came to Russell Square, her face lighted up as if he had been sunshine. The little cares, fears, tears, timid misgivings, sleepless fancies of I don't know how many days and nights, were forgotten, under one moment's influence of that familiar, irresistible smile. He beamed on her from the drawing-room door—magnificent, with ambrosial whiskers, like a god. Sambo, whose face as he announced Captain Osbin (having conferred a brevet rank on that young officer) blazed with a sympathetic grin, saw the little girl start, and flush, and jump up from her watching-place in the window, and Sambo retreated; and as soon as the door was shut, she went fluttering to Lieutenant George Osborne's heart, as if it was the only natural home for her to nestle in. O thou poor panting little soul! The very finest tree in the whole forest, with the straightest stem and the strongest arms, and the thickest foliage, wherein you choose to build and coo, may be marked, for what you know, and may be down with a crash ere long. What an old, old simile that is, between man and timber.

In the meanwhile, George kissed her very kindly on her forehead and glistening eyes, and was very gracious and good; and she thought his diamond shirt-pin (which she had not known him to wear before) the prettiest ornament ever seen.

Building numberless castles in the air (which Amelia adorned with all sorts of flower-gardens, rustic walks, country churches, Sunday schools, and the like; while George had his mind's eye directed to the stables, the kennel, and the cellar), this young pair passed away a couple of hours very pleasantly; and as the Lieutenant had only that single day in town, and a great deal of most important business to transact, it was proposed that Miss Emmy should dine with her future sisters-in-law. This invitation was accepted joyfully. He conducted her to his sisters—where he left her talking and prattling in a way that astonished those ladies, who thought that George might make something of her—and he then went off to transact his business.

In a word, he went out and ate ices at a pastry-cook's shop in Charing Cross; tried a new coat in Pall Mall; dropped in at the Old Slaughters', and called for Captain Cannon; played eleven games at billiards with the Captain, of which he won eight; and returned to Russell Square half-an-hour late for dinner, but in very good humour.

CHAPTER XIV

MISS CRAWLEY AT HOME

ABOUT this time there drove up to an exceedingly snug and well-appointed house in Park Lane a travelling chariot with a lozenge on the panels, a discontented female in a green veil and crimpled curls on the rumble, and a large and confidential man on the box. It was the equipage of our friend Miss Crawley, returning from Hants. When the vehicle stopped, a large round bundle of shawls was taken out of the carriage by the aid of various domestics and a young lady who accompanied the heap of cloaks. That bundle contained Miss Crawley, who was conveyed upstairs forthwith, and put into a bed and chamber warmed properly as for the reception of an invalid. Messengers went off for her physician and medical man. They came, consulted, prescribed, vanished. The young companion of Miss Crawley, at the conclusion of their interview, came in to receive their instructions, and administered those antiphlogistic medicines which the eminent men ordered.

Captain Crawley of the Life Guards rode up from Knightsbridge Barracks the next day; his black charger pawed the straw before his invalid aunt's door. He was most affectionate in his inquiries regarding that amiable relative. There seemed to be much source of apprehension. He found Miss Crawley's maid (the discontented female) unusually sulky and despondent; he found Miss Briggs, her *dame de compagnie*, in tears alone in the drawing-room. She had hastened home, hearing of her beloved friend's illness.

Rawdon Crawley sent up his name by the sulky *femme de chambre*, and Miss Crawley's new companion, coming tripping down from the sick-room, put a little hand into his as he stepped forward eagerly to meet her, gave a glance of great scorn at the bewildered Briggs, and beckoning the young Guardsman out of the back drawing-room, led him downstairs into that now desolate dining-parlour, where so many a good dinner had been celebrated.

Here these two talked for ten minutes, discussing, no doubt, the symptoms of the old invalid above stairs; at the end of which period the parlour bell was rung briskly, and answered on that instant by Mr. Bowls, Miss Crawley's large confidential butler (who, indeed, happened to be at the key-hole during the most part of the interview); and the Captain coming out, curling his mustachios, mounted the black charger pawing among the straw, to the admiration of the little blackguard boys collected in the street. He looked in at the dining-room window, managing his horse, which curvetted and capered beautifully: for one instant the young person might be seen at the window, when her figure vanished, and, doubtless, she went upstairs again to resume the affecting duties of benevolence.

Who could this young woman be, I wonder? That evening a little dinner for two persons was laid in the dining-room—when Mrs. Firkin, the lady's-maid, pushed into her mistress's apartment, and bustled about there, during the vacancy occasioned by the departure of the new nurse—and the latter and Miss Briggs sat down to the neat little meal.

"It is a pity you take on so, Miss Briggs," the young lady said, with a cool, slightly sarcastic air.

"Have I not tended that dear couch for years?" Miss Briggs said, "and now——"

"Now she prefers somebody else. Well, sick people have these fancies, and must be humoured. When she's well I shall go."

"Never, never," Miss Briggs exclaimed, madly inhaling her salts-bottle.

"Never be well or never go, Miss Briggs?" the other said, with the same provoking good-nature. "Pooh—she will be well in a fortnight, when I shall go back to my little pupils at Queen's Crawley, and to their mother, who is a great deal more sick than our friend. You need not be jealous about me, my dear Miss Briggs. I am a poor little girl without any friends, or any harm in me. I don't want to supplant you in Miss Crawley's good graces. She will forget me a week after I am gone; and her affection for you has been the work of years. Give me a little wine if you please, my dear Miss Briggs, and let us be friends. I'm sure I want friends."

At the end of half-an-hour, the meal over, Miss Rebecca Sharp (for such, astonishing to state, is the name of her who has been described ingeniously as "the person" hitherto) went upstairs again to her patient's rooms, from which, with the most engaging politeness, she eliminated poor Firkin. "Thank you, Mrs. Firkin, that will quite do; how nicely you make it! I will ring when anything is wanted." "Thank you;" and Firkin came downstairs in a tempest of jealousy, only the more dangerous because she was forced to confine it in her own bosom.

Could it be the tempest which, as she passed the landing of the first floor, blew open the drawing-room door? No; it was stealthily opened by the hand of Briggs. Briggs had been on the watch. Briggs too well heard the creaking Firkin descend the stairs, and the clink of the spoon and gruel-basin the neglected female carried.

"Well, Firkin?" says she, as the other entered the apartment. "Well, Jane?"

"Wuss and wuss, Miss B.," Firkin said, wagging her head.

"Is she not better then?"

"She never spoke but once, and I asked her if she felt a little more easy, and she told me to hold my stupid tongue. O Miss B., I never thought to have seen *this* day!" And the waterworks again began to play.

"What sort of a person is this Miss Sharp, Firkin? I little thought, while enjoying my Christmas revels in the elegant home of my firm friends, the Reverend Lionel Delamere and his amiable lady, to find a stranger had taken my place in the affections of my dearest, my still dearest Matilda!" Miss Briggs, it will be seen by her language, was of a literary and sentimental turn, and had once published a volume of poems—*Trills of the Nightingale*—by subscription.

"Miss B., they are all infatyated about that young woman," Firkin replied. "Sir Pitt wouldn't have let her go, but he daredn't refuse Miss Crawley anything. Mrs. Bute at the Rectory jist as bad—never happy out of her sight. The Capting quite wild about her. Mr. Crawley mortial jealous. Since Miss C. was took ill, she won't have nobody near her but Miss Sharp, I can't tell for where nor for why; and I think somethink has bewidged everybody."

Rebecca passed that night in constant watching upon Miss Crawley; the next night the old lady slept so comfortably, that Rebecca had time for several hours' comfortable repose herself on the sofa, at the foot of her patroness's bed; very soon Miss Crawley was so well that she sat up and laughed heartily at a perfect imitation of Miss Briggs and her grief, which Rebecca described to her.

Captain Crawley came every day, and received bulletins from Miss Rebecca respecting his aunt's health. This improved so rapidly, that poor Briggs was allowed to see her patroness; and persons with tender hearts may imagine the smothered emotions of that sentimental female, and the affecting nature of the interview.

The causes which had led to the deplorable illness of Miss Crawley, and her departure from her brother's house in the country, were of such an unromantic nature that they are hardly fit to be explained in this genteel and sentimental novel. For how is it possible to hint of a delicate female, living in good society, that she ate and drank too much, and that a hot supper of lobsters profusely enjoyed at the Rectory was the reason of an indisposition which Miss Crawley herself persisted was solely attributable to the dampness of the weather? The attack was so sharp that Matilda—as his Reverence expressed it—was very nearly "off the hooks;" all the family were in a fever of expectation regarding the will, and Rawdon Crawley was making sure of at least forty thousand pounds before the commencement of the London season. Mr. Crawley sent over a choice parcel of tracts, to prepare her for the change from Vanity Fair and Park Lane for another world; but a good doctor from Southampton being called in in time, vanquished the lobster which was so nearly fatal to her, and gave her sufficient strength to enable her to return to London. The Baronet did not disguise his exceeding mortification at the turn which affairs took.

While everybody was attending on Miss Crawley, and messengers every hour from the Rectory were carrying news of her health to the affectionate folks there, there was a lady in another part of the house, being exceedingly ill, of whom no one took any notice at all; and this was the lady of Crawley herself. The good doctor shook his head after seeing her—to which visit Sir Pitt consented, as it could be paid without a fee—and she was left fading away in her lonely chamber, with no more heed paid to her than to a weed in the park.

Captain Rawdon got an extension of leave on his aunt's illness, and remained dutifully at home. He was always in her ante-chamber. (She lay sick in the state bedroom, into which you entered by the little blue saloon.) His father was always meeting him there; or if he came down the corridor ever so quietly, his father's door was sure to open, and the hyæna face of the old gentleman to glare out. What was it set one to watch the other so? A generous rivalry, no doubt, as to which should be most attentive to the dear sufferer in the state bedroom. Rebecca used to come out and comfort both of them—or one or the

other of them rather. Both of these worthy gentlemen were most anxious
to have news of the invalid from her little confidential messenger.

At dinner—to which meal she descended for half-an-hour—she kept
the peace between them; after which she disappeared for the night,
when Rawdon would ride over to the depot of the 150th at Mudbury,
leaving his Papa to the society of Mr. Horrocks and his rum and water.
She passed as weary a fortnight as ever mortal spent in Miss Crawley's
sick-room; but her little nerves seemed to be of iron, as she was quite
unshaken by the duty and the tedium of the sick-chamber.

If the Baronet of Queen's Crawley had not had the fear of losing
his sister's legacy before his eyes, he never would have permitted his
dear girls to lose the educational blessings which their invaluable
governess was conferring upon them. The old house at home seemed
a desert without her, so useful and pleasant had Rebecca made herself
there. Sir Pitt's letters were not copied and corrected; his books not
made up; his household business and manifold schemes neglected, now
that his little secretary was away. And it was easy to see how necessary
such an amanuensis was to him, by the tenor and spelling of the
numerous letters which he sent to her, entreating her and commanding
her to return. Almost every day brought a frank from the Baronet,
enclosing the most urgent prayers to Becky for her return, or conveying pathetic statements to Miss Crawley regarding the neglected
state of his daughter's education; of which documents Miss Crawley
took very little heed.

Well, meanwhile, Becky was the greatest comfort and convenience
to her. When Miss Crawley was convalescent and descended to the
drawing-room, Becky sang to her, and otherwise amused her; when
she was well enough to drive out, Becky accompanied her. And
amongst the drives which they took, whither, of all places in the world,
did Miss Crawley's admirable good-nature and friendship actually
induce her to penetrate, but to Russell Square, Bloomsbury, and the
house of John Sedley Esquire.

Ere that event many notes had passed, as may be imagined, between
the two dear friends. During the months of Rebecca's stay in Hampshire, the eternal friendship had (must it be owned?) suffered considerable diminution, and grown so decrepit and feeble with old age as to
threaten demise altogether. The fact is, both girls had their own real
affairs to think of—Rebecca her advance with her employers, Amelia
her own absorbing topic. When the two girls met, and flew into each
other's arms with that impetuosity which distinguishes the behaviour
of young ladies towards each other, Rebecca performed her part of
the embrace with the most perfect briskness and energy. Poor little
Amelia blushed as she kissed her friend, and thought she had been
guilty of something very like coldness towards her.

Their first interview was but a very short one. Amelia was just ready
to go out for a walk. Miss Crawley was waiting in her carriage below,

her people wondering at the locality in which they found themselves, and gazing upon honest Sambo, the black footman of Bloomsbury, as one of the queer natives of the place. But when Amelia came down, with her kind smiling looks (Rebecca must introduce her to her friend, Miss Crawley was longing to see her, and was too ill to leave her carriage)—when, I say, Amelia came down, the Park Lane shoulder-knot aristocracy wondered more and more that such a thing could come out of Bloomsbury; and Miss Crawley was fairly captivated by the sweet blushing face of the young lady who came forward so timidly and so gracefully to pay her respects to the protector of her friend.

"What a complexion, my dear! What a sweet voice!" Miss Crawley said, as they drove away westward after the little interview. "My dear Sharp, your young friend is charming. Send for her to Park Lane, do you hear?" Miss Crawley had a good taste. She liked natural manners—a little timidity only set them off. She liked pretty faces near her—as she liked pretty pictures and nice china. She talked of Amelia with rapture half-a-dozen times that day. She mentioned her to Rawdon Crawley, who came dutifully to partake of his aunt's chicken.

Of course, on this Rebecca instantly stated that Amelia was engaged to be married—to a Lieutenant Osborne—a very old flame.

"Is he a man in a line regiment?" Captain Crawley asked, remembering after an effort, as became a Guardsman, the number of the regiment, the —th.

Rebecca thought that was the regiment. "The Captain's name," she said, "was Captain Dobbin."

"A lanky, gawky fellow," said Crawley—"tumbles over everybody. I know him; and Osborne's a goodish-looking fellow, with large black whiskers?"

"Enormous," Miss Rebecca Sharp said, "and enormously proud of them, I assure you."

Captain Rawdon Crawley burst into a horse-laugh by way of reply; and being pressed by the ladies to explain, did so when the explosion of hilarity was over. "He fancies he can play at billiards," said he. "I won two hundred of him at the Cocoa-Tree. *He* play, the young flat! He'd have played for anything that day, but his friend Captain Dobbin carried him off, hang him!"

"Rawdon, Rawdon, don't be so wicked," Miss Crawley remarked, highly pleased. "Is he a presentable sort of a person?"

"Presentable?—oh, very well. You wouldn't see any difference," Captain Crawley answered. "Do let's have him, when you begin to see a few people; and his whatdyecallem—his inamorato—eh, Miss Sharp; that's what you call it—comes. Gad, I'll write him a note, and have him; and I'll try if he can play piquet as well as billiards. Where does he live, Miss Sharp?"

Miss Sharp told Crawley the Lieutenant's town address; and a few days after this conversation, Lieutenant Osborne received a letter in

Captain Rawdon's schoolboy hand, and enclosing a note of invitation
from Miss Crawley.

Rebecca dispatched also an invitation to her darling Amelia, who,
you may be sure, was ready enough to accept it when she heard that
George was to be of the party. It was arranged that Amelia was to
spend the morning with the ladies of Park Lane, where all were very
kind to her. Rebecca patronized her with calm superiority: she was
so much the cleverer of the two, and her friend so gentle and unassuming, that she always yielded when anybody chose to command, and
so took Rebecca's orders with perfect meekness and good-humour.
Miss Crawley's graciousness was also remarkable. She continued her
raptures about little Amelia, talked about her before her face as if she
were a doll, or a servant, or a picture, and admired her with the most
benevolent wonder possible. I admire that admiration which the
genteel world sometimes extends to the commonalty.

George came to dinner—a repast *en garçon* with Captain Crawley.
The great family coach of the Osbornes transported him to Park
Lane from Russell Square; where the young ladies, who were not themselves invited, and professed the greatest indifference at that slight,
nevertheless looked at Sir Pitt Crawley's name in the baronetage, and
learned everything which that work had to teach about the Crawley
family and their pedigree, and the Binkies, their relatives, etc., etc.
Rawdon Crawley received George Osborne with great frankness and
graciousness; praised his play at billiards; asked him when he would
have his revenge; was interested about Osborne's regiment; and would
have proposed piquet to him that very evening, but Miss Crawley
absolutely forbade any gambling in her house, so that the young
Lieutenant's purse was not lightened by his gallant patron, for that
day at least. However, they made an engagement for the next, somewhere: to look at a horse that Crawley had to sell, and to try him in
the Park; and to dine together, and to pass the evening with some jolly
fellows. "That is, if you're not on duty to that pretty Miss Sedley,"
Crawley said, with a knowing wink. "Monstrous nice girl, 'pon my
honour, though, Osborne," he was good enough to add. "Lots of tin,
I suppose, eh?"

Osborne wasn't on duty; he would join Crawley with pleasure; and
the latter, when they met the next day, praised his new friend's horse-
manship—as he might with perfect honesty—and introduced him to
three or four young men of the first fashion, whose acquaintance
immensely elated the simple young officer.

Some short period after the above events, and Miss Rebecca Sharp
still remaining at her patroness's house in Park Lane, one more hatchment might have been seen in Great Gaunt Street, figuring amongst the
many which usually ornament that dismal quarter. It was over Sir
Pitt Crawley's house, but it did not indicate the worthy baronet's
demise. It was a feminine hatchment, and indeed, a few years back,

had served as a funeral compliment to Sir Pitt's old mother, the late Dowager Lady Crawley. Its period of service over, the hatchment had come down from the front of the house, and lived in retirement somewhere in the back premises of Sir Pitt's mansion. It reappeared now for poor Rose Dawson. Sir Pitt was a widower again. The arms quartered on the shield along with his own were not, to be sure, poor Rose's. She had no arms. But the cherubs painted on the scutcheon answered as well for her as for Sir Pitt's mother, and *Resurgam* was written under the coat, flanked by the Crawley Dove and Serpent. Arms and Hatchments, Resurgam.—Here is an opportunity for moralizing.

Mr. Crawley had tended that otherwise friendless bedside. She went out of the world strengthened by such words and comfort as he could give her. For many years his was the only kindness she ever knew, the only friendship that solaced in any way that feeble, lonely soul. Her heart was dead long before her body. She had sold it to become Sir Pitt Crawley's wife.

When the demise took place, her husband was in London attending to some of his innumerable schemes, and busy with his endless lawyers.

The news of Lady Crawley's death provoked no more grief or comment than might have been expected in Miss Crawley's family circle. "I suppose I must put off my party for the 3rd," Miss Crawley said; and added, after a pause, "I hope my brother will have the decency not to marry again."

On the morrow, as Rebecca was gazing from the window, she startled Miss Crawley, who was placidly occupied with a French novel, by crying out, in an alarmed tone, "Here's Sir Pitt, Ma'am!" and the Baronet's knock followed this announcement.

"My dear, I can't see him—I won't see him. Tell Bowls not at home; or go downstairs and say I'm too ill to receive any one. My nerves really won't bear my brother at this moment," cried out Miss Crawley, and resumed the novel.

"She's too ill to see you, sir," Rebecca said, tripping down to Sir Pitt, who was preparing to ascend.

"So much the better," Sir Pitt answered. "I want to see *you*, Miss Becky. Come along a me into the parlour," and they entered that apartment together.

"I wawnt you back at Queen's Crawley, Miss," the Baronet said, fixing his eyes upon her, and taking off his black gloves and his hat with its great crape hat-band. His eyes had such a strange look, and fixed upon her so steadfastly, that Rebecca Sharp began almost to tremble.

"I hope to come soon," she said in a low voice, "as soon as Miss Crawley is better—and return to—to the dear children."

"You've said so these three months, Becky," replied Sir Pitt, "and still you go hanging on to my sister, who'll fling you off like an old shoe when she's wore you out. I tell you I *want* you. I'm going back to the Vuneral. Will you come back? Yes or no?"

"I daren't—I don't think—it would be right—to be alone—with you, sir," Becky said, seemingly in great agitation.

"I say agin, I want you," Sir Pitt said, thumping the table. "I can't git on without you. I didn't see what it was till you went away. The house all goes wrong. It's not the same place. All my accounts has got muddled agin. You *must* come back. Do come back. Dear Becky, do come."

"Come—as what, sir?" Rebecca gasped out.

"Come as Lady Crawley, if you like," the Baronet said, grasping his crape hat. "There! will that zatusfy you? Come back and be my wife. Your vit vor't. Birth be hanged! You're as good a lady as ever I see. You've got more brains in your little vinger than any baronet's wife in the county. Will you come? Yes or no?"

"O Sir Pitt!" Rebecca said, very much moved.

"Say yes, Becky," Sir Pitt continued. "I'm an old man, but a good'n. I'm good for twenty years. I'll make you happy, zee if I don't. You shall do what you like; spend what you like; and 'av it all your own way. I'll make you a zettlement."

Rebecca started back a picture of consternation. In the course of this history we have never seen her lose her presence of mind; but she did now, and wept some of the most genuine tears that ever fell from her eyes.

"O Sir Pitt!" she said—"O sir—I—I'm *married already*."

CHAPTER XV

IN WHICH REBECCA'S HUSBAND APPEARS FOR A SHORT TIME

Sir Pitt bounced up from his attitude of humility on the carpet, uttering exclamations which caused poor Rebecca to be more frightened than she was when she made her avowal. "Married! you're joking," the Baronet cried, after the first explosion of rage and wonder. "You're making vun of me, Becky. Who'd ever go to marry you without a shilling to your vortune?"

"Married! married!" Rebecca said, in an agony of tears—her voice choking with emotion, her handkerchief up to her ready eyes, fainting against the mantelpiece—a figure of woe fit to melt the most obdurate heart. "O Sir Pitt, dear Sir Pitt, do not think me ungrateful for all your goodness to me. It is only your generosity that has extorted my secret."

"Generosity be hanged!" Sir Pitt roared out. "Who is it tu, then, you're married? Where was it?"

"Let me come back with you to the country, sir! Let me watch over you as faithfully as ever! Don't, don't separate me from dear Queen's Crawley!"

"The feller has left you, has he?" the Baronet said, beginning, as he fancied, to comprehend. "Well, Becky—come back if you like. You can't eat your cake and have it. Anyways I made you a vair offer. Coom back as governess; you shall have it all your own way." She held out one hand. She cried fit to break her heart; her ringlets fell over her face, and over the marble mantelpiece where she laid it.

"So the rascal ran off, eh?" Sir Pitt said, with a hideous attempt at consolation. "Never mind, Becky, *I'll* take care of 'ee."

"O sir! it would be the pride of my life to go back to Queen's Crawley, and take care of the children, and of you as formerly, when you said you were pleased with the services of your little Rebecca. When I think of what you have just offered me, my heart fills with gratitude—indeed it does. I can't be your wife, sir; let me—let me be your daughter!"

Saying which, Rebecca went down on *her* knees in a most tragical way, and, taking Sir Pitt's horny black hand between her own two (which were very pretty and white, and as soft as satin), looked up in his face with an expression of exquisite pathos and confidence, when —when the door opened, and Miss Crawley sailed in.

Mrs. Firkin and Miss Briggs, who happened by chance to be at the parlour door soon after the Baronet and Rebecca entered the apartment, had also seen accidentally, through the keyhole, the old gentleman prostrate before the governess, and had heard the generous proposal which he made to her. It was scarcely out of his mouth when Mrs. Firkin and Miss Briggs had streamed up the stairs, had rushed into the drawing-room where Miss Crawley was reading the French novel, and had given that old lady the astounding intelligence that Sir Pitt was on his knees, proposing to Miss Sharp. And if you calculate the time for the above dialogue to take place—the time for Briggs and Firkin to fly to the drawing-room—the time for Miss Crawley to be astonished, and to drop her volume of Pigault le Brun—and the time for her to come downstairs—you will see how exactly accurate this history is, and how Miss Crawley *must* have appeared at the very instant when Rebecca had assumed the attitude of humility.

"It is the lady on the ground, and not the gentleman," Miss Crawley said, with a look and voice of great scorn. "They told me that *you* were on your knees, Sir Pitt: do kneel once more, and let me see this pretty couple!"

"I have thanked Sir Pitt Crawley, Ma'am," Rebecca said, rising, "and have told him that—that I never can become Lady Crawley."

"Refused him!" Miss Crawley said, more bewildered than ever. Briggs and Firkin at the door opened the eyes of astonishment and the lips of wonder.

"Yes—refused," Rebecca continued, with a sad, tearful voice.

"And am I to credit my ears that you absolutely proposed to her, Sir Pitt?" the old lady asked.

"Ees," said the Baronet, "I did."

"And she refused you, as she says?"

C

"Ees," Sir Pitt said, his features on a broad grin.

"It does not seem to break your heart at any rate," Miss Crawley remarked.

"Nawt a bit," answered Sir Pitt, with a coolness and good-humour which set Miss Crawley almost mad with bewilderment.

"I'm glad you think it good sport, brother," she continued, groping wildly through this amazement.

"Vamous," said Sir Pitt. "Who'd ha' thought it! what a sly little devil, what a little fox it waws!" he muttered to himself, chuckling with pleasure.

"Who'd have thought what?" cries Miss Crawley, stamping with her foot. "Pray, Miss Sharp, are you waiting for the Prince Regent's divorce, that you don't think our family good enough for you?"

"My attitude," Rebecca said, "when you came in, Ma'am, did not look as if I despised such an honour as this good—this noble man has deigned to offer me. Do you think I have no heart? Have you all loved me, and been so kind to the poor orphan—deserted—girl, and am *I* to feel nothing? O my friends! O my benefactors! may not my love, my life, my duty, try to repay the confidence you have shown me? Do you grudge me even gratitude, Miss Crawley? It is too much—my heart is too full:" and she sank down in a chair so pathetically, that most of the audience present were perfectly melted with her sadness.

"Whether you marry me or not, you're a good little girl, Becky, and I'm your friend, mind," said Sir Pitt, and putting on his crape-bound hat, he walked away—greatly to Rebecca's relief; for it was evident that her secret was unrevealed to Miss Crawley, and she had the advantage of a brief reprieve.

Putting her handkerchief to her eyes, and nodding away honest Briggs, who would have followed her upstairs, she went up to her apartment; while Briggs and Miss Crawley, in a high state of excitement, remained to discuss the strange event.

But Rebecca was a young lady of too much resolution and energy of character to permit herself much useless and unseemly sorrow for the irrevocable past; so, having devoted only the proper portion of regret to it, she wisely turned her whole attention towards the future, which was now vastly more important to her. And she surveyed her position, and its hopes, doubts, and chances.

In the first place, she was *married*;—that was a great fact. Sir Pitt knew it. She was not so much surprised into the avowal, as induced to make it by a sudden calculation. It must have come some day; and why not now as at a later period? He who would have married her himself must at least be silent with regard to her marriage. How Miss Crawley would bear the news—was the great question. Misgivings Rebecca had: but she remembered all Miss Crawley had said—the old lady's avowed contempt for birth; her daring liberal opinions; her general romantic propensities; her almost doting attachment to her nephew, and her repeatedly expressed fondness for Rebecca herself.

She is so fond of him, Rebecca thought, that she would forgive him anything; she is so used to me that I don't think she could be comfortable without me: when the *éclaircissement* comes there will be a scene, and hysterics, and a great quarrel, and then a great reconciliation. At all events, what use was there in delaying? the die was thrown, and now or to-morrow the issue must be the same. And so, resolved that Miss Crawley should have the news, the young person debated in her mind as to the best means of conveying it to her, and whether she should face the storm that must come, or fly and avoid it until its first fury was blown over. In this state of meditation she wrote the following letter:

"DEAREST FRIEND,—The great crisis which we have debated about so often is *come*. Half of my secret is known; and I have thought and thought, until I am quite sure that now is the time to reveal *the whole of the mystery*. Sir Pitt came to me this morning, and made—what do you think?—*a declaration in form*. Think of that! Poor little me! I might have been Lady Crawley. How pleased Mrs. Bute would have been; and *ma tante*, if I had taken precedence of her! I might have been somebody's mamma, instead of—Oh, I tremble, I tremble, when I think how soon we must tell all!—

"Sir Pitt knows I am married, and not knowing to whom is not very much displeased as yet. *Ma tante* is *actually angry* that I should have refused him. But she is all kindness and graciousness. She condescends to say I would have made him a good wife, and vows that she will be a mother to your little Rebecca. She will be shaken when she first hears the news. But need we fear anything beyond a momentary anger? I think not. *I am sure* not. She dotes upon you so (you naughty, good-for-nothing man), that she would pardon you *anything*; and, indeed, I believe, the next place in her heart is mine, and that she would be miserable without me. Dearest! something *tells me* we shall conquer. You shall leave that odious regiment—quit gaming, racing, and *be a good boy*; and we shall all live in Park Lane, and *ma tante* shall leave us all her money.

"I shall try and walk to-morrow at 3 in the usual place. If Miss B. accompanies me, you must come to dinner, and bring an answer, and put it in the third volume of Porteus's sermons. But, at all events, come to your own   R.

"To Miss Eliza Styles,
    "At Mr. Barnet's, Saddler, Knightsbridge."

And I trust there is no reader of this little story who has not discernment enough to perceive that the Miss Eliza Styles (an old schoolfellow, Rebecca said, with whom she had resumed an active correspondence of late, and who used to fetch these letters from the saddler's), wore brass spurs, and large curling mustachios, and was indeed no other than Captain Rawdon Crawley.

CHAPTER XVI

THE LETTER ON THE PINCUSHION

How they were married is not of the slightest consequence to anybody. What is to hinder a Captain who is a major, and a young lady
who is of age, from purchasing a licence, and uniting themselves at
any church in this town?

When, then, Becky told him that the great crisis was near and the
time for action had arrived, Rawdon expressed himself as ready to
act under her orders, as he would be to charge with his troop at the
command of his colonel. There is no need for him to put his letter
into the third volume of Porteus. Rebecca easily found a means to
get rid of Briggs, her companion, and met her faithful friend in "the
usual place" on the next day. She had thought over matters at night,
and communicated to Rawdon the result of her determinations.

It consisted simply in the hiring of quiet lodgings at Brompton, or
in the neighbourhood of the barracks, for Captain and Mrs. Crawley.
For Rebecca had determined, and very prudently, we think, to fly.
Rawdon was only too happy at her resolve; he had been entreating
her to take this measure any time for weeks past. He pranced off to
engage the lodgings with all the impetuosity of love. He agreed to pay
two guineas a week so readily, that the landlady regretted she had
asked him so little. He ordered in a piano, and half a nursery-house
full of flowers; and a heap of good things. As for shawls, kid gloves,
silk stockings, gold French watches, bracelets, and perfumery, he sent
them in with the profusion of blind love and unbounded credit. And
having relieved his mind by this outpouring of generosity, he went and
dined nervously at the club, waiting until the great moment of his life
should come.

On the second day after Sir Pitt Crawley's offer to Miss Sharp, the
sun rose as usual, and at the usual hour Betty Martin, the upstairs
maid, knocked at the door of the governess's bedchamber.

No answer was returned, and she knocked again. Silence was still
uninterrupted; and Betty, with the hot water, opened the door and
entered the chamber.

The little white dimity bed was as smooth and trim as on the day
previous, when Betty's own hands had helped to make it. Two little
trunks were corded in one end of the room; and on the table before the
window—on the pincushion—the great fat pincushion lined with pink
inside, and twilled like a lady's nightcap—lay a letter. It had been
reposing there probably all night.

Betty advanced towards it on tiptoe, as if she were afraid to awake
it; looked at it, and round the room, with an air of great wonder and
satisfaction; took up the letter, and grinned intensely as she turned
it round and over, and finally carried it into Miss Briggs's room below.

"La, Miss Briggs," the girl exclaimed, "O Miss, something must have happened—there's nobody in Miss Sharp's room; the bed ain't been slep in, and she've run away, and left this letter for you, Miss."

"*What!*" cried Briggs, dropping her comb, the thin wisp of faded hair falling over her shoulders; "an elopement! Miss Sharp a fugitive! What, what is this?" and she eagerly broke the neat seal, and, as they say, "devoured the contents" of the letter addressed to her.

"Dear Miss Briggs," the refugee wrote, "the kindest heart in the world, as yours is, will pity and sympathize with me and excuse me. With tears, and prayers, and blessings, I leave the home where the poor orphan has ever met with kindness and affection. Claims even superior to those of my benefactress call me hence. I go to my duty— to my *husband.* Yes, I am married. My husband *commands* me to seek the *humble home* which we call ours. Dearest Miss Briggs, break the news as your delicate sympathy will know how to do it—to my dear, my beloved friend and benefactress. Tell her, ere I went, I shed tears on her dear pillow—that pillow that I have so often soothed in sickness—that I long *again* to watch—Oh, with what joy shall I return to dear Park Lane! How I tremble for the answer which is to *seal my fate!* When Sir Pitt deigned to offer me his hand—an honour of which my beloved Miss Crawley said I was *deserving* (my blessings go with her for judging the poor orphan worthy to be *her sister!*)—I told Sir Pitt that I was *already a wife.* Even he forgave me. But my courage failed me, when I should have told him all—that I could not be his wife, for *I was his daughter!* I am wedded to the best and most generous of men—Miss Crawley's Rawdon is *my* Rawdon. At his *command* I open my lips, and follow him to our humble home, as I would *through the world.* O my excellent and kind friend intercede with my Rawdon's beloved aunt for him and the poor girl to whom all *his noble race* have shown such *unparalleled affection.* Ask Miss Crawley to receive *her children.* I can say no more, but blessings, blessings on all in the dear house I leave, prays

                    "Your affectionate and *grateful*
     "Midnight."   "REBECCA CRAWLEY.

Just as Briggs had finished reading this affecting and interesting document, which reinstated her in her position as first confidante of Miss Crawley, Mrs. Firkin entered the room. "Here's Mrs. Bute Crawley just arrived by mail from Hampshire, and wants some tea; will you come down and make breakfast, Miss?"

And to the surprise of Firkin, clasping her dressing-gown around her, the wisp of hair floating dishevelled behind her, the little curl-papers still sticking in bunches round her forehead, Briggs sailed down to Mrs. Bute with the letter in her hand containing the wonderful news.

"O Mrs. Firkin," gasped Betty, "sech a business. Miss Sharp have a gone and run away with the Capting, and they're off to Gretney

Green!" We would devote a chapter to describe the emotions of Mrs. Firkin, did not the passions of her mistresses occupy our genteeler muse.

When Mrs. Bute Crawley, numbed with midnight travelling, and warming herself at the newly crackling parlour fire, heard from Miss Briggs the intelligence of the clandestine marriage, she declared that it was quite providential that she should have arrived at such a time to assist poor dear Miss Crawley in supporting the shock.

It was not until the old lady was fairly ensconced in her usual armchair in the drawing-room, and the preliminary embraces and inquiries had taken place between the ladies, that the conspirators thought it advisable to submit her to the operation. Who has not admired the artifices and delicate approaches with which women "prepare" their friends for bad news? Miss Crawley's two friends made such an apparatus of mystery before they broke the intelligence to her, that they worked her up to the necessary degree of doubt and alarm.

Miss Crawley gave a scream and fell back in a faint. They were forced to take her back to the room which she had just quitted. One fit of hysterics succeeded another. The doctor was sent for—the apothecary arrived. Mrs. Bute took up the post of nurse by her bedside. "Her relations ought to be round about her," that amiable woman said.

She had scarcely been carried up to her room, when a new person arrived to whom it was also necessary to break the news. This was Sir Pitt. "Where's Becky?" he said, coming in. "Where's her traps? She's coming with me to Queen's Crawley."

"Have you not heard the astonishing intelligence regarding her surreptitious union?" Briggs asked

"What's that to me?" Sir Pitt asked. "I know she's married. That makes no odds. Tell her to come down at once, and not keep me."

"Are you not aware, sir," Miss Briggs asked, "that she has left our roof, to the dismay of Miss Crawley, who is nearly killed by the intelligence of Captain Rawdon's union with her?"

When Sir Pitt Crawley heard that Rebecca was married to his son, he broke out into a fury of language which it would do no good to repeat in this place, as indeed it sent poor Briggs shuddering out of the room; and with her we will shut the door upon the figure of the frenzied old man, wild with hatred and insane with baffled desire.

CHAPTER XVII

HOW CAPTAIN DOBBIN BOUGHT A PIANO

If there is any exhibition in all Vanity Fair which Satire and Sentiment can visit arm in arm together; where you light on the strangest contrasts, laughable and tearful; where you may be gentle and pathetic, or savage and cynical, with perfect propriety,—it is at one of those public assemblies, a crowd of which are advertised every day in the last page of *The Times* newspaper, and over which the late Mr. George Robins used to preside with so much dignity. There are very few London people, as I fancy, who have not attended at these meetings; and all with a taste for moralizing must have thought, with a sensation and interest not a little startling and queer, of the day when their turn shall come too, and Mr. Hammerdown will sell, by the orders of Diogenes's assignees, or will be instructed by the executors to offer to public competition, the library, furniture, plate, wardrobe, and choice cellar of wines of Epicurus deceased.

How changed the house is, though! The front is patched over with bills, setting forth the particulars of the furniture in staring capitals. They have hung a shred of carpet out of an upstairs window—a half-dozen of porters are lounging on the dirty steps—the halls swarms with dingy guests of Oriental countenance, who thrust printed cards into your hand, and offer to bid. Old women and amateurs have invaded the upper apartments, pinching the bed-curtains, poking into the feathers, shampooing the mattresses, and clapping the wardrobe drawers to and fro. O Dives! who would ever have thought, as we sat round the broad table sparkling with plate and spotless linen, to have seen such a dish at the head of it as that roaring auctioneer?

It was rather late in the sale. The excellent drawing-room furniture by the best makers; the rare and famous wines selected, regardless of cost, and with the well-known taste of the purchaser; the rich and complete set of family plate, had been sold on the previous days. Certain of the best wines (which all had a great character among amateurs in the neighbourhood) had been purchased for his master, who knew them very well, by the butler of our friend John Osborne, Esquire, of Russell Square. A small portion of the most useful articles of the plate had been bought by some young stockbrokers from the City.

Of all the other articles which Mr. Hammerdown had the honour to offer for public competition that day it is not our purpose to make mention, save of one only, a little square piano, which came down from the upper regions of the house (the state grand piano having been disposed of previously); this the young lady tried with a rapid and skilful hand (making the officer blush and start again), and for it, when its turn came, her agent began to bid.

But there was an opposition here. The Hebrew aide-de-camp in the service of the officer at the table bid against the Hebrew gentleman employed by another, and a brisk battle ensued over this little piano, the combatants being greatly encouraged by Mr. Hammerdown.

At last, when the competition had been prolonged for some time, the hammer came down and the auctioneer said: "Mr. Lewis, twenty-five," and Mr. Lewis's Chief thus became the proprietor of the little square piano. Having effected the purchase, he sate up as if he was greatly relieved, and the unsuccessful competitors catching a glimpse of him at this moment, the lady said to her friend:

"Why, Rawdon, it's Captain Dobbin."

The sale was at the old house in Russell Square, where we passed some evenings together at the beginning of this story. Good old John Sedley was a ruined man. His name had been proclaimed as a defaulter on the Stock Exchange, and his bankruptcy and commercial extermination had followed. With respect to the piano, as it had been Amelia's, and as she might miss it and want one now, and as Captain William Dobbin could no more play upon it than he could dance on the tight-rope it is probable that he did not purchase the instrument for his own use.

In a word, it arrived that evening at a wonderful small cottage in a street leading from the Fulham Road—one of those streets which have the finest romantic names—(this was called St. Adelaide Villas, Anna-Maria Road, West), where the houses looked like baby-houses; where the people, looking out of the first-floor windows, must infallibly, as you think, sit with their feet in the parlours; where the shrubs in the little gardens in front bloom with a perennial display of little children's pinafores, little red socks, caps, etc. (polyandria polygynia); whence you hear the sound of jingling spinets and women singing; where little porter pots hang on the railing sunning themselves; whither of evenings you see City clerks padding wearily: here it was that Mr. Clapp, the clerk of Mr. Sedley, had his domicile, and in this asylum the good old gentleman hid his head with his wife and daughter when the crash came.

I hope the reader has much too good an opinion of Captain and Mrs. Crawley to suppose that they ever would have dreamed of paying a visit to so remote a district as Bloomsbury, if they thought the family whom they proposed to honour with a visit were not merely out of fashion, but out of money, and could be serviceable to them in no possible manner. Rebecca was entirely surprised at the sight of the comfortable old house where she had met with no small kindness, ransacked by brokers and bargainers, and its quiet family treasures given up to public desecration and plunder. A month after her flight, she had bethought her of Amelia; and Rawdon, with a horse-laugh, had expressed a perfect willingness to see young George Osborne again. "He's a very agreeable acquaintance, Beck," the wag added. "I'd like to sell him another horse, Beck. I'd like to play a few more games at billiards with him. He'd be what I call *useful* just now, Mrs. C.—ha, ha!"

The old aunt was long in "coming to." A month had elapsed, Rawdon was denied the door by Mr. Bowls; his servants could not get a lodgment in the house at Park Lane; his letters were sent back unopened. Miss Crawley never stirred out—she was unwell—and Mrs. Bute remained still and never left her. Crawley and his wife both of them augured evil from the continued presence of Mrs. Bute.

That veteran rake, Rawdon Crawley, found himself converted into a very happy and submissive married man. His former haunts knew him not. They asked about him once or twice at his clubs, but did not miss him much; in those booths of Vanity Fair people seldom do miss each other. "My relations won't cry fie upon me," Becky said, with rather a bitter laugh; and she was quite contented to wait until the old aunt should be reconciled, before she claimed her place in society. So she lived at Brompton, and meanwhile saw no one, or only those few of her husband's male companions who were admitted into her little dining-room. These were all charmed with her.

There are gentlemen of very good blood and fashion in this city, who never have entered a lady's drawing-room; so that though Rawdon Crawley's marriage might be talked about in his county, where, of course, Mrs. Bute had spread the news, in London it was doubted, or not heeded, or not talked about at all. He lived comfortably on credit. He had a large capital of debts, which, laid out judiciously, will carry a man along for many years, and on which certain men about town contrive to live a hundred times better than even men with ready money can do.

Truth obliges us to confess that Rebecca had married a gentleman of this order. Everything was plentiful in his house but ready money, of which their *ménage* pretty early felt the want; and reading the Gazette one day, and coming upon the announcement of "Lieutenant G. Csborne to be Captain by purchase, vice Smith, who exchanges," Rawdon uttered that sentiment regarding Amelia's lover, which ended in the visit to Russell Square.

When Rawdon and his wife wished to communicate with Captain Dobbin at the sale, and to know particulars of the catastrophe which had befallen Rebecca's old acquaintances, the Captain had vanished; and such information as they got was from a stray porter or broker at the auction.

CHAPTER XVIII

WHO PLAYED ON THE PIANO CAPTAIN DOBBIN BOUGHT

"NAPOLEON has landed at Cannes." Such news might create a panic at Vienna, and cause Russia to drop his cards, and take Prussia into a corner, and Talleyrand and Metternich to wag their heads together, while Prince Hardenburg, and even the present Marquis of Londonderry, were puzzled; but how was this intelligence to affect a young lady in Russell Square, before whose door the watchman sang the hours when she was asleep; who, if she strolled in the square, was guarded there by the railing and the beadle; who, if she walked ever so short a distance to buy a ribbon in Southampton Row, was followed by black Sambo with an enormous cane; who was always cared for, dressed, put to bed, and watched over by ever so many guardian angels, with and without wages? *Bon Dieu*, I say, is it not hard that the fateful rush of the great Imperial struggle can't take place without affecting a poor little harmless girl of eighteen, who is occupied in billing and cooing, or working muslin collars in Russell Square? You, too, kindly, homely flower!—is the great roaring war tempest coming to sweep you down, here, although cowering under the shelter of Holborn? Yes, Napoleon is flinging his last stake, and poor little Emmy Sedley's happiness forms, somehow, part of it.

In the first place, her father's fortune was swept down with that fatal news. All his speculations had of late gone wrong with the luckless old gentleman. Ventures had failed; merchants had broken; funds had risen when he calculated they would fall. What need to particularize? If success is rare and slow, everybody knows how quick and easy ruin us.

Then Osborne had the intolerable sense of former benefits to goad and irritate him; these are always a cause of hostility aggravated. Finally, he had to break off the match between Sedley's daughter and his son; and as it had gone very far indeed, and as the poor girl's happiness and perhaps character were compromised, it was necessary to show the strongest reasons for the rupture, and for John Osborne to prove John Sedley to be a very bad character indeed.

If Amelia could have heard the comments regarding her which were made in the circle from which her father's ruin had just driven her, she would have seen what her own crimes were, and how entirely her character was jeopardized. Such criminal imprudence Mrs. Smith never knew of; such horrid familiarities Mrs. Brown had always condemned, and the end might be a warning to *her* daughters. "Captain Osborne, of course, could not marry a bankrupt's daughter," the Misses Dobbin said. "It was quite enough to have been swindled by the father. As for that little Amelia, her folly had really passed all——"

The French Emperor comes in to perform a part in this domestic comedy of Vanity Fair which we are now playing, and which would never have been enacted without the intervention of this august mute personage. It was he that ruined the Bourbons and Mr. John Sedley. It was he whose arrival in his capital called up all France in arms to defend him there, and all Europe to oust him. While the French nation and army were swearing fidelity round the eagles in the Champ de Mars, four mighty European hosts were getting in motion for the great *chasse à l'aigle*; and one of these was a British army, of which two heroes of ours, Captain Dobbin and Captain Osborne, formed a portion.

The agitation thrilling through the country and army in consequence of this news was so great, that private matters were little heeded; and hence probably George Osborne, just gazetted to his company, busy with preparations for the march, which must come inevitably, and panting for further promotion, was not so much affected by other incidents which would have interested him at a more quiet period. He was not, it must be confessed, very much cast down by good old Mr. Sedley's catastrophe. He tried his new uniform, which became him very handsomely, on the day when the first meeting of the creditors of the unfortunate gentleman took place. The bills were up in the Sedley house, where he had passed so many, many happy hours. He could see them as he walked from home that night (to the Old Slaughters', where he put up when in town) shining white in the moon. That comfortable home was shut then, upon Amelia and her parents: where had they taken refuge? The thought of their ruin affected him not a little. He was very melancholy that night in the coffee-room at the Slaughters'; and drank a good deal, as his comrades remarked there.

Dobbin came in presently, cautioned him about the drink—which he only took he said, because he was deuced low; but when his friend began to put to him clumsy inquiries, and asked him for news in a significant manner, Osborne declined entering into conversation with him; avowing, however, that he was devilish disturbed and unhappy.

Three days afterwards, Dobbin found Osborne in his room at the barracks—his head on the table, a number of papers about, the young Captain evidently in a state of great despondency. "She—she's sent me back some things I gave her—some damned trinkets. Look here!" There was a little packet directed in the well-known hand to Captain George Osborne, and some things lying about—a ring, a silver knife he had bought, as a boy, for her at a fair; a gold chain, and a locket with hair in it. "It's all over," said he, with a groan of sickening remorse. "Look, Will, you may read it if you like."

There was a little letter of a few lines, to which he pointed, which said:

"My papa has ordered me to return to you these presents, which you made in happier days to me; and I am to write to you for the last time. I think, I know you feel as much as I do the blow which has come upon us. It is I that absolve you from an engagement which is impossible in our present misery. I am sure you had no share in it, or in the cruel suspicions of Mr. Osborne, which are the hardest of all our griefs to bear. Farewell, Farewell. I pray God to strengthen me to bear this and other calamities, and to bless you always. A.

"I shall often play upon the piano—your piano. It was like you to send it."

"Where are they?" Osborne asked, after a long talk, and a long pause,—and, in truth, with no little shame at thinking that he had taken no steps to follow her. "Where are they? There's no address to the note."

Dobbin knew. He had not merely sent the piano, but had written a note to Mrs. Sedley, and asked permission to come and see her. And he had seen her, and Amelia too, yesterday, before he came down to Chatham; and, what is more, he had brought that farewell letter and packet which had so moved him.

The good-natured fellow had found Mrs. Sedley only too willing to receive him, and greatly agitated by the arrival of the piano, which, as she conjectured, *must* have come from George, and was a signal of

amity on his part. Captain Dobbin did not correct this error of the
worthy lady, but listened to all her story of complaints and misfortunes
with great sympathy—condoled with her losses and privations, and
agreed in reprehending the cruel conduct of Mr. Osborne towards his
first benefactor. When she had eased her overflowing bosom somewhat, and poured forth many of her sorrows, he had the courage to
ask actually to see Amelia, who was above in her room as usual, and
whom her mother led trembling downstairs.

Her appearance was so ghastly, and her look of despair so pathetic,
that honest William Dobbin was frightened as he beheld it, and read
the most fatal forebodings in that pale fixed face. After sitting in his
company a minute or two, she put the packet into his hand, and said,
"Take this to Captain Osborne, if you please, and—and I hope he's
quite well—and it was very kind of you to come and see us—and we
like our new house very much. And I—I think I'll go upstairs,
Mamma, for I'm not very strong." And with this, and a curtsy and
a smile, the poor child went her way. The mother, as she led her up,
cast black looks of anguish towards Dobbin. The good fellow wanted
no such appeal. He loved her himself too fondly for that. Inexpressible
grief, and pity, and terror pursued him, and he came away as if he
was a criminal after seeing her.

When Osborne heard that his friend had found her, he made hot
and anxious inquiries regarding the poor child. How was she? How
did she look? What did she say? His comrade took his hand, and
looked him in the face.

"George, she's dying," William Dobbin said, and could speak no
more.

There was a buxom Irish servant-girl, who performed all the duties
of the little house where the Sedley family had found refuge; and this
girl had in vain, on many previous days, striven to give Amelia aid
or consolation. Emmy was much too sad to answer, or even to be
aware of the attempts the other was making in her favour.

Four hours after the talk between Dobbin and Osborne, this servant-
maid came into Amelia's room, where she sat as usual, brooding
silently over her letters—her little treasures. The girl, smiling, and
looking arch and happy, made many trials to attract poor Emmy's
attention, who, however, took no heed of her.

"Miss Emmy," said the girl.

"I'm coming," Emmy said, not looking round.

"There's a message," the maid went on. "There's something—
somebody—sure, here's a new letter for you—don't be reading them
old ones any more." And she gave her a letter, which Emmy took, and
read.

"I must see you," the letter said. "Dearest Emmy—dearest love—
dearest wife, come to me."

George and her mother were outside, waiting until she had read the
letter.

CHAPTER XIX

MISS CRAWLEY AT NURSE

In the very best of moments, if anybody told Miss Crawley that she was, or looked ill, the trembling old lady sent off for her doctor; and I daresay she *was* very unwell after the sudden family event, which might serve to shake stronger nerves than hers. At least, Mrs. Bute thought it was her duty to inform the physician, and the apothecary, and the *dame de compagnie*, and the domestics, that Miss Crawley was in a most critical state, and that they were to act accordingly. She had the street laid knee-deep with straw, and the knocker put by with Mr. Bowls's plate. She insisted that the doctor should call twice a day; and deluged her patient with draughts every two hours. When anybody entered the room, she uttered a *shshshsh* so sibilant and ominous that it frightened the poor old lady in her bed, from which she could not look without seeing Mrs. Bute's beady eyes eagerly fixed on her, as the latter sate steadfast in the arm-chair by the bedside.

"If that poor man of mine had a head on his shoulders," Mrs. Bute Crawley thought to herself, "how useful he might be, under present circumstances, to this unhappy old lady! He might make her repent of her shocking free-thinking ways; he might urge her to do her duty, and cast off that odious reprobate who has disgraced himself and his family; and he might induce her to do justice to my dear girls and the two boys, who require and deserve, I am sure, every assistance which their relatives can give them."

And, as the hatred of vice is always a progress towards virtue, Mrs. Bute Crawley endeavoured to instil into her sister-in-law a proper abhorrence for all Rawdon Crawley's manifold sins; of which his uncle's wife brought forward such a catalogue as indeed would have served to condemn a whole regiment of young officers.

From Miss Pinkerton's the indefatigable Mrs. Bute followed the track of Sharp and his daughter back to the lodgings in Greek Street, which the defunct painter had occupied; and where portraits of the landlady in white satin, and of the husband in brass buttons, done by Sharp in lieu of a quarter's rent, still decorated the parlour walls. Mrs. Stokes was a communicative person, and quickly told all she knew about Mr. Sharp: how dissolute and poor he was; how good-natured and amusing; how he was always hunted by bailiffs and duns; how, to the landlady's horror, though she never could abide the woman he did not marry his wife till a short time before her death; and what a queer little wild vixen his daughter was; how she kept them all laughing with her fun and mimicry; how she used to fetch the gin from the public-house, and was known in all the studios in the quarter: in brief, Mrs. Bute got such a full account of her new niece's parentage, education, and behaviour as would scarcely have pleased Rebecca, had the latter known that such inquiries were being made concerning her.

Of all these industrious researches Miss Crawley had the full benefit. Mrs. Rawdon Crawley was the daughter of an opera-girl. She had danced herself. She had been a model to the painters. She was brought up as became her mother's daughter. She drank gin with her father, etc., etc. It was a lost woman who was married to a lost man; and the moral to be inferred from Mrs. Bute's tale was, that the knavery of the pair was irremediable and that no properly-conducted person should ever notice them again.

These were the materials which prudent Mrs. Bute gathered together in Park Lane—the provisions and ammunition, as it were, with which she fortified the house against the siege which she knew that Rawdon and his wife would lay to Miss Crawley.

Having the old lady under her hand, in bed, with nobody near, Mrs. Bute had made more than one assault upon her, to induce her to alter her will. But Miss Crawley's usual terrors regarding death increased greatly when such dismal propositions were made to her, and Mrs. Bute saw that she must get her patient into cheerful spirits and health before she could hope to attain the pious object which she had in view. Whither to take her was the next puzzle. The only place where she is not likely to meet those odious Rawdons is at church, and that won't amuse her, Mrs. Bute justly felt. "We must go and visit our beautiful suburbs of London," she then thought. "I hear they are the most picturesque in the world;" and so she had a sudden interest for Hampstead and Hornsey, and found that Dulwich had great charms for her, and getting her victim into her carriage, drove her to those rustic spots, beguiling the little journeys with conversations about Rawdon and his wife, and telling every story to the old lady which could add to her indignation against this pair of reprobates.

Perhaps Mrs. Bute pulled the string unnecessarily tight; for though she worked up Miss Crawley to a proper dislike of her disobedient nephew, the invalid had a great hatred and secret terror of her victimizer, and panted to escape from her. After a brief space, she rebelled against Highgate and Hornsey utterly. She would go into the Park. Mrs. Bute knew they would meet the abominable Rawdon there, and she was right. One day in the ring, Rawdon's stanhope came in sight; Rebecca was seated by him. In the enemy's equipage Miss Crawley occupied her usual place, with Mrs. Bute on her left, the poodle and Miss Briggs on the back seat. It was a nervous moment, and Rebecca's heart beat quick as she recognized the carriage; and as the two vehicles crossed each other in a line, she clasped her hands, and looked towards the spinster with a face of agonized attachment and devotion. Rawdon himself trembled, and his face grew purple behind his dyed mustachios. Only old Briggs was moved in the other carriage, and cast her great eyes nervously towards her old friends. Miss Crawley's bonnet was resolutely turned towards the Serpentine. Mrs. Bute happened to be in ecstasies with the poodle, and was calling him a little darling, and a sweet little zoggy, and a pretty pet. The carriages moved on, each in his line.

"Done, by Jove!" Rawdon said to his wife.

"Try once more, Rawdon," Rebecca answered. "Could not you lock your wheels into theirs, dearest?"

Rawdon had not the heart for that manœuvre. When the carriages met again, he stood up in his stanhope; he raised his hand ready to doff his hat; he looked with all his eyes. But this time Miss Crawley's face was not turned away; she and Mrs. Bute looked him full in the face, and cut their nephew pitilessly. He sank back in his seat with an oath, and, striking out of the ring, dashed away desperately homewards.

It was gallant and decided triumph for Mrs. Bute. But she felt the danger of many such meetings, as she saw the evident nervousness of Miss Crawley; and she determined that it was most necessary for her dear friend's health that they should leave town for a while, and recommended Brighton very strongly.

CHAPTER XX

IN WHICH CAPTAIN DOBBIN ACTS AS THE MESSENGER OF HYMEN

Without knowing how, Captain William Dobbin found himself the great promoter, arranger, and manager of the match between George Osborne and Amelia.

I forbear to enter into minute particulars of the interview between George and Amelia, when the former was brought back to the feet (or should we venture to say the arms?) of his young mistress by the intervention of his friend, honest William. A much harder heart than George's would have melted at the sight of that sweet face so sadly ravished by grief and despair, and at the simple, terder accents in which she told her little broken-hearted story; but as she did not faint when her mother, trembling, brought Osborne to her, and as she only gave relief to her overcharged grief by laying her head on her lover's shoulders and there weeping for a while the most tender, copious, and refreshing tears—old Mrs. Sedley, too greatly relieved, thought it was best to leave the young persons to themselves, and so quitted Emmy crying over George's hand, and kissing it humbly, as if he were her supreme chief and master, and as if she were quite a guilty and unworthy person needing every favour and grace from him.

You would scarcely have recognized the beaming little face upon Amelia's pillow that night as the one that was laid there the night before, so wan, so lifeless, so careless of all round about.

"He will be here again to-day," Amelia thought. "He is the greatest and best of men." And the fact is, that George thought he was one of the generousest creatures alive, and that he was making a tremendous sacrifice in marrying this young creature.

While she and Osborne were having their delightful *tête-à-tête* above stairs, old Mrs. Sedley and Captain Dobbin were conversing below upon the state of the affairs, and the chances and future arrangements of the young people. Mrs. Sedley having brought the two lovers together, and left them embracing each other with all their might, like a true woman, was of opinion that no power on earth would induce Mr. Sedley to consent to the match between his daughter and the son of a man who had so shamefully, wickedly, and monstrously treated him.

"My sisters say she has diamonds as big as pigeon's eggs," George said, laughing. "How they must set off her complexion! A perfect illumination it must be when her jewels are on her neck. Her jet-black hair is as curly as Sambo's. I daresay she wore a nose-ring when she went to court; and with a plume of feathers in her top-knot she would look a perfect Belle Sauvage."

George, in conversation with Amelia, was rallying the appearance of a young lady of whom his father and sisters had lately made the acquaintance, and who was an object of vast respect to the Russell Square family. She was reported to have I don't know how many plantations in the West Indies, a deal of money in the funds, and three stars to her name in the East India stockholders' list. She had a mansion in Surrey, and a house in Portland Place. The name of the rich West India heiress had been mentioned with applause in *The Morning Post*. Mrs. Haggistoun, Colonel Haggistoun's widow, her relative, "chaperoned" her, and kept her house. She was just from school, where she had completed her education, and George and his sisters had met her at an evening party at old Hulker's house, Devonshire Place (Hulker, Bullock & Co. were long the correspondents of her house in the West Indies), and the girls had made the most cordial advances to her, which the heiress had received with great goodhumour. An orphan in her position—with her money—so interesting! the Misses Osborne said. They were full of their new friend when they returned from the Hulker ball to Miss Wirt, their companion; they had made arrangements for continually meeting, and had the carriage and drove to see her the very next day. Mrs. Haggistoun, Colonel Haggistoun's widow, a relation of Lord Binkie, and always talking of him, struck the dear, unsophisticated girls as rather haughty, and too much inclined to talk about her great relations; but Rhoda was everything they could wish—the frankest, kindest, most agreeable creature —wanting a little polish, but so good-natured. The girls Christiannamed each other at once.

"How old is she?" asked Emmy, to whom George was rattling away regarding this dark paragon, on the morning of their reunion—rattling away as no other man in the world surely could.

"Why, the Black Princess, though she has only just left school, must be two or three and twenty. And you should see the hand she writes! Mrs. Colonel Haggistoun usually writes her letters, but in a moment of confidence she put pen to paper for my sisters; she spelt satin satting, and Saint James's, Saint Jams."

"Why, surely it must be Miss Swartz. the parlour-boarder," Emmy said, remembering that good-natured young mulatto girl, who had been so hysterically affected when Amelia left Miss Pinkerton's academy.

"The very name," George said. "Her father was a German Jew—a slave-owner they say—connected with the Cannibal Islands in some way or other. He died last year, and Miss Pinkerton has finished her education. She can play two pieces on the piano; she knows three songs; she can write when Mrs. Haggistoun is by to spell for her; and Jane and Maria already have got to love her as a sister."

When Captain Dobbin came back in the afternoon to these people—which he did with a great deal of sympathy for them—it did his heart good to see how Amelia had grown young again; how she laughed, and chirped, and sang familiar old songs at the piano, which were only interrupted by the bell from without proclaiming Mr. Sedley's return from the City, before whom George received a signal to retreat.

Beyond the first smile of recognition—and even that was a hypocrisy, for she thought his arrival rather provoking—Miss Sedley did not once notice Dobbin during his visit. But he was content, so that he saw her happy; and thankful to have been the means of making her so.

CHAPTER XXI

A QUARREL ABOUT AN HEIRESS

LOVE may be felt for any young lady endowed with such qualities as Miss Swartz possessed; and a great dream of ambition entered into old Mr. Osborne's soul, which she was to realize. He encouraged, with the utmost enthusiasm and friendliness, his daughters' amiable attachment to the young heiress, and protested that it gave him the sincerest pleasure as a father to see the love of his girls so well disposed.

What a match for George she'd be (the sisters and Miss Wirt agreed), and how much better than that insignificant little Amelia! Such a dashing young fellow as he is, with his good looks, rank, and accomplishments, would be the very husband for her. Visions of balls in Portland Place, presentations at court, and introductions to half the peerage, filled the minds of the young ladies, who talked of nothing but George and his grand acquaintances to their beloved new friend.

When the elder Osborne gave what he called "a hint," there was no possibility for the most obtuse to mistake his meaning. He called kicking a footman downstairs a hint to the latter to leave his service. With his usual frankness and delicacy he told Mrs. Haggistoun that he would give her a cheque for five thousand pounds on the day his son was married to her ward; and called that proposal a hint, and considered it a very dexterous piece of diplomacy. He gave George finally such another hint regarding the heiress, and ordered him to marry out of hand, as he would have ordered his butler to draw a cork, or his clerk to write a letter.

The day after George had his hint from his father, and a short time before the hour of dinner, he was lolling upon a sofa in the drawing-room in a very becoming and perfectly natural attitude of melancholy.

The girls, after vain attempts to engage him in conversation, talked about fashions and the last drawing-room until he was perfectly sick of their chatter.

The sisters began to play the Battle of Prague. "Stop that d——thing!" George howled out in a fury from the sofa. "It makes me mad.—*You* play us something, Miss Swartz, do. Sing something, any-thing but the Battle of Prague."

"I can sing Fluvy du Tajy," Swartz said, in a meek voice, "if I had the words." It was the last of the worthy young woman's collection.

"Oh, Fleuve du Tage," Miss Maria cried; "we have the song," and went off to fetch the book in which it was.

Now it happened that this song, then in the height of the fashion, had been given to the young ladies by a young friend of theirs, whose name was on the title, and Miss Swartz, having concluded the ditty with George's applause (for he remembered that it was a favourite of Amelia's), was hoping for an encore perhaps, and fiddling with the leaves of the music, when her eye fell upon the title, and she saw "Amelia Sedley" written in the corner.

"Lor!" cried Miss Swartz, spinning swiftly round on the music-stool, "is it *my* Amelia—Amelia that was at Miss P.'s at Hammersmith? I know it is. It's her, and—Tell me about her—where is she?"

"Don't mention her," Miss Maria Osborne said hastily. "Her family has disgraced itself. Her father cheated papa; and as for her, she is never to be mentioned *here*." This was Miss Maria's return for George's rudeness about the Battle of Prague.

"Are you a friend of Amelia's?" George said, bouncing up. "God bless you for it, Miss Swartz. Don't believe what the girls say. *She's* not to blame, at any rate. She's the best——"

"You know you're not to speak about her, George," cried Jane. "Papa forbids it."

"Who's to prevent me?" George cried out. "I *will* speak of her. I say she's the best, the kindest, the gentlest, the sweetest girl in England; and that, bankrupt or no, my sisters are not fit to hold candles to her.—If you like her, go and see her, Miss Swartz; she wants friends now; and I say, God bless everybody who befriends her. Anybody who speaks kindly of her is my friend; anybody who speaks against her is my enemy. Thank you, Miss Swartz;" and he went up and wrung her hand.

"George! George!" one of the sisters cried imploringly.

"I say," George said fiercely. "I thank everybody who loves Amelia Sed——" He stopped. Old Osborne was in the room, with a face livid with rage and eyes like hot coals.

Though George had stopped in his sentence, yet his blood being up, he was not to be cowed by all the generations of Osborne; rallying instantly, he replied to the bullying look of his father with another so indicative of resolution and defiance, that the elder man quailed in his turn, and looked away. He felt that the tussle was coming. "Mrs. Haggistoun, let me take you down to dinner," he said.—"Give your arm to Miss Swartz, George," and they marched.

"Miss Swartz, I love Amelia, and we've been engaged almost all our lives," Osborne said to his partner; and during all the dinner, George rattled on with a volubility which surprised himself, and made his father doubly nervous for the fight which was to take place as soon as the ladies were gone.

The old man also took a supply of ammunition, but his decanter clinked against the glass as he tried to fill it.

After giving a great heave, and with a purple choking face, he then began. "How dare you, sir, mention that person's name before Miss Swartz to-day, in my drawing-room? I ask you, sir, how dare you do it?"

"Stop, sir," said George, "don't say 'dare,' sir. 'Dare' isn't a word to be used to a Captain in the British Army."

"I shall say what I like to my son, sir. I can cut him off with a shilling if I like. I can make him a beggar if I like. I *will* say what I like," the elder said.

"I know very well that you give me plenty of money," said George (fingering a bundle of notes which he had got in the morning from Mr. Chopper). "You tell it me often enough, sir. There's no fear of my forgetting it."

"I wish you'd remember other things as well, sir," the sire answered. "I wish you'd remember that in this house—so long as you choose to *honour* it with your *company*, Captain—I'm the master, and that name, and that that—that you—that I say——"

"That what, sir?" George asked, with scarcely a sneer, filling another glass of claret.

"——!" burst out his father, with a screaming oath—"that the name of those Sedleys never be mentioned here, sir—not one of the whole damned lot of 'em, sir."

"It wasn't I, sir, that introduced Miss Sedley's name. It was my sisters who spoke ill of her to Miss Swartz; and by Jove I'll defend her wherever I go. Nobody shall speak lightly of that name in my presence. Our family has done her quite enough injury already, I think, and may leave off reviling her now she's down. I'll shoot any man but you who says a word against her."

"Go on, sir, go on," the old gentleman said, his eyes starting out of his head.

"Go on about what, sir? about the way in which we've treated that angel of a girl? Who told me to love her? It was your doing. I might have chosen elsewhere, and looked higher, perhaps, than your society; but I obeyed you. And now that her heart's mine you give me orders to fling it away, and punish her—kill her perhaps—for the faults of other people. It's a shame, by heavens," said George, working himself up into passion and enthusiasm as he proceeded, "to play at fast and loose with a young girl's affections—and with such an angel as that—one so superior to the people amongst whom she lived that she might have excited envy, only she was so good and gentle that it's a wonder anybody dared to hate her. If I desert her, sir, do you suppose she forgets me?"

"I ain't going to have any of this damn sentimental nonsense and humbug here, sir," the father cried out. "There shall be no beggar-marriages in my family. If you choose to fling away eight thousand a year, which you may have for the asking, you may do it; but by Jove you take your pack and walk out of this house, sir."

"I've done it," said George, coming into the Slaughters' an hour afterwards, looking very pale.

"What, my boy?" says Dobbin.

George told what had passed between his father and himself.

"I'll marry her to-morrow," he said, with an oath. "I love her more every day, Dobbin."

CHAPTER XXII

A MARRIAGE AND PART OF A HONEYMOON

ONE gusty, raw day at the end of April—the rain whipping the pavement of that ancient street where the old Slaughters' Coffee House was once situated—George Osborne came into the coffee-room, looking very haggard and pale; although dressed rather smartly in a blue coat and brass buttons, and a neat buff waistcoat of the fashion of those days. Here was his friend Captain Dobbin in blue and brass too, having abandoned the military frock and French grey trousers, which were the usual coverings of his lanky person.

He shook hands with Dobbin, looked at the clock, and told John, the waiter, to bring him some curaçoa. Of this cordial he swallowed off a couple of glasses with nervous eagerness. His friend asked with some interest about his health.

"Couldn't get a wink of sleep till daylight, Dob," said he. "Infernal headache and fever. Got up at nine, and went down to the Hummums for a bath. I say, Dob, I feel just as I did on the morning I went out with Rocket at Quebec."

"So do I," William responded. "I was a deuced deal more nervous than you were that morning. You made a famous breakfast, I remember. Eat something now."

"You're a good old fellow, Will. I'll drink your health, old boy, and farewell to——"

"No, no; two glasses are enough," Dobbin interrupted him.—"Here,.

take away the liqueurs, John.—Have some cayenne pepper with your fowl. Make haste though, for it is time we were there."

It was about half an hour from twelve when this brief meeting and colloquy took place between the two captains. A coach, into which Captain Osborne's servant put his master's desk and dressing-case, had been in waiting for some time; and into this the two gentlemen hurried under an umbrella, and the valet mounted on the box, cursing the rain and the dampness of the coachman who was steaming beside him. "We shall find a better trap than this at the church door," says he; "that's a comfort."

In a word, George had thrown the great cast. He was going to be married. Hence his pallor and nervousness—his sleepless night and agitation in the morning. I have heard people who have gone through the same thing own to the same emotion. After three or four ceremonies you get accustomed to it, no doubt; but the first dip, everybody allows, is awful.

The bride was dressed in a brown silk pelisse (as Captain Dobbin has since informed me), and wore a straw bonnet with a pink ribbon; over the bonnet she had a veil of white Chantilly lace, a gift from Mr. Joseph Sedley, her brother. Captain Dobbin himself had asked leave to present her with a gold chain and watch, which she sported on this occasion; and her mother gave her her diamond brooch—almost the only trinket which was left to the old lady. As the service went on, Mrs. Sedley sat and whimpered a great deal in a pew, consoled by the Irish maid-servant and Mrs. Clapp from the lodgings. Old Sedley would not be present. Jos acted for his father, giving away the bride, whilst Captain Dobbin stepped up as groomsman to his friend George.

When the service was completed, Jos Sedley came forward and kissed his sister, the bride, for the first time for many months. George's look of gloom had gone, and he seemed quite proud and radiant. "It's your turn, William," says he, putting his hand fondly upon Dobbin's shoulder; and Dobbin went up and touched Amelia on the cheek.

Then they went into the vestry and signed the register. "God bless you, old Dobbin," George said, grasping him by the hand, with something very like moisture glistening in his eyes. William replied only by nodding his head; his heart was too full to say much.

Our young bride and bridegroom had chosen Brighton as the place where they would pass the first few days after their marriage; and having engaged apartments at the Ship Inn, enjoyed themselves there in great comfort and quietude, until Jos presently joined them. Nor was he the only companion they found there. As they were coming into the hotel from a seaside walk one afternoon, on whom should they light but Rebecca and her husband. The recognition was immediate. Rebecca flew into the arms of her dearest friend. Crawley and Osborne shook hands together cordially enough; and Becky, in the course of a very few hours, found means to make the latter forget that little unpleasant passage of words which had happened between them. "Do you remember the last time we met at Miss Crawley's, when I was so rude to you, dear Captain Osborne? I thought you seemed careless about dear Amelia. It was that made me angry, and so pert, and so unkind, and so ungrateful. Do forgive me!" Rebecca said, and she held out her hand with so frank and winning a grace that Osborne could not but take it.

The two wedding parties met constantly in each other's apartments. After two or three nights the gentlemen of an evening had a little piquet, as their wives sate and chatted apart. This pastime, and the arrival of Jos Sedley, who made his appearance in his grand open carriage, and who played a few games at billiards with Captain Crawley, replenished Rawdon's purse somewhat, and gave him the benefit of that ready money for which the greatest spirits are sometimes at a standstill.

The three gentlemen walked down to see the Lightning coach come in. Punctual to the minute, the coach crowded inside and out, the guard blowing his accustomed tune on the horn, the Lightning came tearing down the street, and pulled up at the coach-office.

"Hallo! there's old Dobbin," George cried, quite delighted to see his old friend perched on the roof; and whose promised visit to Brighton had been delayed until now. "How are you, old fellow? Glad you're come down. Emmy'll be delighted to see you," Osborne said, shaking his comrade warmly by the hand as soon as his descent from the vehicle was effected; and then he added, in a lower and agitated voice, "What's the news? Have you been in Russell Square? What does the governor say? Tell me everything."

Dobbin looked very pale and grave. "I've seen your father," said he. "How's Amelia—Mrs. George? I'll tell you all the news presently; but I've brought the great news of all, and that is——"

"Out with it, old fellow," George said.

"We're ordered to Belgium. All the army goes—Guards and all. Heavytop's got the gout, and is mad at not being able to move. O'Dowd goes in command, and we embark from Chatham next week." This news of war could not but come with a shock upon our lovers, and caused all these gentlemen to look very serious.

CHAPTER XXIII

CAPTAIN DOBBIN PROCEEDS ON HIS CANVASS

WHILST our friend George and his young wife were enjoying the first blushing days of the honeymoon at Brighton, honest William was left as George's plenipotentiary in London, to transact all the business part of the marriage. His duty it was to call upon old Sedley and his wife, and to keep the former in good humour; to draw Jos and his brother-in-law nearer together, so that Jos's position and dignity, as Collector of Boggley Wollah, might compensate for his father's loss of station, and tend to reconcile old Osborne to the alliance; and finally, to communicate it to the latter in such a way as should least irritate the old gentleman.

Now, before he faced the head of the Osborne house with the news which it was his duty to tell, Dobbin bethought him that it would be politic to make friends of the rest of the family, and, if possible, have the ladies on his side. They can't be angry in their hearts, thought he. No woman ever was really angry at a romantic marriage. A little crying out, and they must come round to their brother, when the three of us will lay siege to old Mr. Osborne. So this Machiavellian captain of infantry cast about him for some happy means or stratagem by which he could gently and gradually bring the Misses Osborne to a knowledge of their brother's secret.

By a little inquiry regarding his mother's engagements he was pretty soon able to find out by whom of her ladyship's friends parties were given at this season, where he would be likely to meet Osborne's sisters; and, though he had that abhorrence of routs and evening parties which many sensible men, alas, entertain, he soon found one where the Misses Osborne were to be present. Making his appearance at the ball, where he danced a couple of sets with both of them, and was prodigiously polite, he actually had the courage to ask Miss Osborne for a few minutes' conversation at an early hour the next day, when he had, he said, to communicate to her news of the very greatest interest.

The next day he was scarcely out of the house when Miss Maria and Miss Wirt rushed in to Miss Osborne, and the whole wonderful secret was imparted to them by that lady. To do them justice, neither of the sisters was very much displeased. There is something about a runaway match with which few ladies can be seriously angry, and Amelia rather rose in their estimation from the spirit which she had displayed in consenting to the union. As they debated the story, and prattled about it, and wondered what papa would do and say, came a loud knock, as of an avenging thunder-clap, at the door, which made these conspirators start. It must be papa, they thought. But it was not he. It was only Mr. Frederick Bullock, who had come from the City according to appointment, to conduct the ladies to a flower-show.

This gentleman, as may be imagined, was not kept long in ignorance of the secret. But his face, when he heard it, showed an amazement which was very different from that look of sentimental wonder which the countenances of the sisters wore. Mr. Bullock was a man of the world, and a junior partner of a wealthy firm. He knew what money was, and the value of it, and a delightful throb of expectation lighted up his little eyes, and caused him to smile on his Maria, as he thought that by this piece of folly of Mr. George's she might be worth thirty thousand pounds more than he had ever hoped to get with her.

CHAPTER XXIV

IN WHICH MR. OSBORNE TAKES DOWN THE FAMILY BIBLE

So having prepared the sisters, Dobbin hastened away to the City to perform the rest and more difficult part of the task which he had undertaken. The idea of facing old Osborne rendered him not a little nervous, and more than once he thought of leaving the young ladies to communicate the secret, which, as he was aware, they could not long retain. But he had promised to report to George upon the manner in which the elder Osborne bore the intelligence; so going into the City to the paternal counting-house in Thames Street, he dispatched thence a note to Mr. Osborne begging for a half-hour's conversation relative to the affairs of his son George. Dobbin's messenger returned from Mr. Osborne's house of business, with the compliments of the latter, who would be very happy to see the Captain immediately, and away accordingly Dobbin went to confront him.

The Captain, with a half-guilty secret to confess, and with the prospect of a painful and stormy interview before him, entered Mr. Osborne's offices with a most dismal countenance and abashed gait, and, passing through the outer room where Mr. Chopper presided, was greeted by that functionary from his desk with a waggish air which further discomfited him. Mr. Chopper winked and nodded, and pointed his pen towards his patron's door, and said, "You'll find the governor all right," with the most provoking good-humour.

Osborne rose too, and shook him heartily by the hand, and said, "How do, my dear boy?" with a cordiality that made poor George's ambassador feel doubly guilty. His hand lay as if dead in the old gentleman's grasp. He felt that he, Dobbin, was more or less the cause of all that had happened. It was he had brought back George to Amelia; it was he had applauded, encouraged, transacted almost the marriage which he was come to reveal to George's father: and the latter was receiving him with smiles of welcome; patting him on the shoulder, and calling him "Dobbin, my dear boy." The envoy had indeed good reason to hang his head.

Osborne fully believed that Dobbin had come to announce his son's surrender. Mr. Chopper and his principal were talking over the matter between George and his father, at the very moment when Dobbin's messenger arrived. Both had been expecting it for some days—and, "Lord! Chopper, what a marriage we'll have!" Mr. Osborne said to his clerk, snapping his big fingers, and jingling all the guineas and shillings in his great pocket as he eyed his subordinate with a look of triumph.

At last Dobbin summoned courage to begin. "Sir," said he, "I've brought you some very grave news. I have been at the Horse Guards this morning, and there's no doubt that our regiment will be ordered abroad, and on its way to Belgium before the week is over. And you know, sir, that we shan't be home again before a tussle which may be fatal to many of us."

"What are you driving at, Dobbin?" his interlocutor said, uneasy and with a scowl. "I suppose no Briton's afraid of any d—— Frenchman, hey?"

"I only mean, that before we go, and considering the great and certain risk that hangs over every one of us—if there are any differences between you and George—it would be as well, sir, that—that you should shake hands: wouldn't it? Should anything happen to him, I think you would never forgive yourself if you hadn't parted in charity."

"You are a good fellow, William," said Mr. Osborne in a softened voice; "and me and George shouldn't part in anger, that is true. Look here. Am *I* wrong? Is the quarrel of *my* making? What do I seek but his good, for which I've been toiling like a convict ever since he was born? Nobody can say there's anything selfish in *me*. Let him come back. I say, here's my hand. I say, forget and forgive. As for marrying now, it's out of the question. Let him and Miss S. make it up, and make out the marriage afterwards, when he comes back a Colonel; for he shall be a Colonel, by G—— he shall, if money can do it. I'm glad you've brought him round. I know it's you, Dobbin. You've took him out of many a scrape before. Let him come. *I* shan't be hard. Come along, and dine in Russell Square to-day—both of you. The old shop, the old hour. You'll find a neck of venison and no questions asked."

This praise and confidence smote Dobbin's heart very keenly. Every moment the colloquy continued in this tone he felt more and more guilty. "Sir," said he, "I fear you deceive yourself. I am sure you do. George is much too high-minded a man ever to marry for money. A threat on your part that you would disinherit him in case of disobedience would only be followed by resistance on his."

"Why, hang it, man, you don't call offering eight or ten thousand a year threatening him?" Mr. Osborne said, with still provoking good-humour. "'Gad, if Miss S. will have me, I'm her man. *I* ain't particular about a shade or so of tawny." And the old gentleman gave his knowing grin and coarse laugh.

"You forget, sir, previous engagements into which Captain Osborne had entered," the ambassador said gravely.

"What engagements? What the devil do you mean? You don't mean," Mr. Osborne continued, gathering wrath and astonishment as the thought now first came upon him—"you don't mean that he's such a d—— fool as to be still hankering after that swindling old bankrupt's daughter? You've not come here for to make me suppose that he wants to marry *her*? Marry her, that *is* a good one. My son and heir marry a beggar's girl out of a gutter. D—— him, if he does, let him buy a broom and sweep a crossing. She was always dangling and ogling after him, I recollect now; and I've no doubt she was put on by her old sharper of a father."

"Sir," said Dobbin, starting up in undisguised anger, "no man shall abuse that lady in my hearing, and you least of all."

"Oh, you're a going to call me out, are you? Stop, let me ring the bell for pistols for two. Mr. George sent you here to insult his father, did he?" Osborne said, pulling at the bell-cord.

"Mr. Osborne," said Dobbin, with a faltering voice, "it's you who are insulting the best creature in the world. You had best spare her, sir, for she's your son's wife."

And with this, feeling that he could say no more, Dobbin went away, Osborne sinking back in his chair, and looking wildly after him. A clerk came in, obedient to the bell; and the Captain was scarcely out of the court where Mr. Osborne's offices were, when Mr. Chopper, the chief clerk, came rushing hatless after him.

"For God's sake, what is it?" Mr. Chopper said, catching the Captain by the skirt. "The governor's in a fit. What has Mr. George been doing?"

"He married Miss Sedley five days ago," Dobbin replied. "I was his groomsman, Mr. Chopper, and you must stand his friend."

The old clerk shook his head. "If that's your news, Captain, it's bad. The governor will never forgive him."

Dobbin begged Chopper to report progress to him at the hotel where he was stopping, and walked off moodily westwards, greatly perturbed as to the past and the future.

When the Russell Square family came to dinner that evening, they found the father of the house seated in his usual place, but with that air of gloom on his face, which, whenever it appeared there, kept the whole circle silent. The ladies, and Mr. Bullock who dined with them, felt that the news had been communicated to Mr. Osborne. His dark looks affected Mr. Bullock so far as to render him still and quiet; but he was unusually bland and attentive to Miss Maria, by whom he sat, and to her sister, presiding at the head of the table.

Mr. Osborne's countenance, when he arrived in the City at his usual time, struck those dependants who were accustomed, for good reasons, to watch its expression, as peculiarly ghastly and worn. At twelve o'clock Mr. Higgs (of the firm of Higgs & Blatherwick, solicitors, Bedford Row), called by appointment, and was ushered into the governor's private room, and closeted there for more than an hour. At about one Mr. Chopper received a note brought by Captain Dobbin's man, and containing an enclosure for Mr. Osborne, which the clerk went in and delivered. A short time afterwards Mr. Chopper and Mr. Birch, the next clerk, were summoned, and requested to witness a paper. "I've been making a new will." Mr. Osborne said, to which these gentlemen appended their names accordingly.

Osborne took a letter, and giving it to the clerk, requested the latter to deliver it into Dobbin's own hands immediately.

"And now, Chopper," says he, taking his hat, and with a strange look, "my mind will be easy." Exactly as the clock struck two (there was no doubt an appointment between the pair), Mr. Frederick Bullock called, and he and Mr. Osborne walked away together.

The Colonel of the —th regiment, in which Messieurs Dobbin and Osborne had companies, was an old General who had made his first campaign under Wolfe at Quebec, and was long since quite too old and feeble for command: but he took some interest in the regiment of which he was the nominal head, and made certain of his young officers welcome at his table, a kind of hospitality which I believe is not now common amongst his brethren. Captain Dobbin was an especial favourite of this old General. Dobbin was versed in the literature of his profession, and could talk about the great Frederick, and the Empress Queen, and their wars, almost as well as the General himself, who was indifferent to the triumphs of the present day, and whose heart was with the tacticians of fifty years back. This officer sent a summons to Dobbin to come and breakfast with him, on the morning when Mr. Osborne altered his will and Mr. Chopper put on his best shirt-frill, and then informed his young favourite, a couple of days in advance, of that which they were all expecting—a marching order to go to Belgium. The order for the regiment to hold itself in readiness would leave the Horse Guards in a day or two; and as transports were in plenty, they would get their route before the week was over.

This news made Dobbin grave, and he thought of our friends at Brighton; and then he was ashamed of himself that Amelia was always the first thing in his thoughts (always before anybody—before father and mother, sisters and duty—always at waking and sleeping indeed, and all day long); and returning to his hotel, he sent off a brief note to Mr. Osborne acquainting him with the information which he had received, and which might tend further, he hoped, to bring about a reconciliation with George.

This note, dispatched by the same messenger who had carried the invitation to Chopper on the previous day, alarmed the worthy clerk not a little. It was enclosed to him, and as he opened the letter he trembled lest the dinner should be put off on which he was calculating. His mind was inexpressibly relieved when he found that the envelope was only a reminder for himself. ("I shall expect you at half-past five," Captain Dobbin wrote.) He was very much interested about his employer's family; but, *que voulez-vous?* a grand dinner was of more concern to him than the affairs of any other mortal.

The Captain and Mr. Chopper dined together in the same box. Chopper brought the letter from Mr. Osborne, in which the latter briefly presented his compliments to Captain Dobbin, and requested him to forward the enclosed to Captain George Osborne. Chopper knew nothing further.

CHAPTER XXV

IN WHICH ALL THE PRINCIPAL PERSONAGES THINK FIT TO LEAVE BRIGHTON

CONDUCTED to the ladies, at the Ship Inn, Dobbin assumed a jovial and rattling manner, which proved that this young officer was becoming a more consummate hypocrite every day of his life.

The hypocritical Dobbin saluted Mrs. George Osborne quite gaily, tried to pay her one or two compliments relative to her new position as a bride (which compliments, it must be confessed, were exceedingly clumsy and hung fire woefully), and then fell to talking about Brighton, and the séa air, and the gaieties of the place, and the beauties of the road and the merits of the Lightning coach and horses,—all in a manner quite incomprehensible to Amelia, and very amusing to Rebecca, who was watching the Captain, as indeed she watched every one near whom she came.

When George and Dobbin were alone in the latter's room, to which George had followed him, Dobbin took from his desk the letter which he had been charged by Mr. Osborne to deliver to his son. "It's not in my father's handwriting," said George, looking rather alarmed. Nor was it: the letter was from Mr. Osborne's lawyer, and to the following effect:

"BEDFORD ROW, *May* 7, 1815.

"SIR,—I am commissioned by Mr. Osborne to inform you, that he abides by the determination which he before expressed to you, and that in consequence of the marriage which you have been pleased to contract, he ceases to consider you henceforth as a member of his family. This determination is final and irrevocable.

"Although the moneys expended upon you in your minority, and the bills which you have drawn upon him so unsparingly of late years, far exceed in amount the sum to which you are entitled in your own right (being the third part of the fortune of your mother, the late Mrs. Osborne, and which reverted to you at her decease, and to Miss Jane Osborne and Miss Maria Frances Osborne); yet I am instructed by Mr. Osborne to say, that he waives all claim upon your estate, and that the sum of £2,000, 4 per cent. annuities, at the value of the day (being your one-third share of the sum of £6,000), shall be paid over to yourself or your agents upon your receipt for the same, by

"Your obedient Servt.,

"S. HIGGS.

"*P.S.*—Mr. Osborne desires me to say, once for all, that he declines to receive any messages, letters, or communications from you on this or any other subject."

George was too humane or too much occupied with the tie of his neckcloth to convey at once all the news to Amelia which his comrade had brought with him from London. He came into her room, however, holding the attorney's letter in his hand, and with so solemn and important an air that his wife, always ingeniously on the watch for calamity, thought the worst was about to befall, and running up to her husband, besought her dearest George to tell her everything—he was ordered abroad—there would be a battle next week—she knew there would.

Dearest George parried the question about foreign service, and with a melancholy shake of the head said, "No, Emmy; it isn't that. It's not myself I care about; it's you. I have had bad news from my father. He refuses any communication with me; he has flung us off, and leaves us to poverty. *I* can rough it well enough; but you, my dear, how will you bear it? Read here." And he handed her over the letter.

"But he can't be angry with you long," she said after reading the letter; "nobody could, I'm sure. He must forgive you, my dearest, kindest husband. Oh, I shall never forgive myself if he does not."

"What vexes me, my poor Emmy, is not *my* misfortune, but yours," George said. "I don't care for a little poverty; and I think, without vanity, I've talents enough to make my own way."

"That you have," interposed his wife, who thought that war should cease, and her husband should be made a general instantly.

"Yes, I shall make my way as well as another," Osborne went on; "but you, my dear girl, how can I bear your being deprived of the comforts and station in society which my wife has a right to expect? My dearest girl in barracks; the wife of a soldier in a marching regiment; subject to all sorts of annoyance and privation! It makes me miserable."

Emmy, quite at ease, as this was her husband's only cause of disquiet, took his hand, and with a radiant face and smile began to warble that stanza from the favourite song of *Wapping Old Stairs.*

George laughed at her *naïveté;* and finally they went down to dinner, Amelia clinging to George's arm, still warbling the tune of *Wapping Old Stairs,* and more pleased and light of mind than she had been for some days past.

Thus the repast, which at length came off, instead of being dismal, was an exceedingly brisk and merry one. The excitement of the campaign counteracted in George's mind the depression occasioned by the disinheriting letter. Dobbin still kept up his character of rattle. He amused the company with accounts of the army in Belgium, where nothing but *fêtes* and gaiety and fashion were going on. Then, having a particular end in view, this dexterous Captain proceeded to describe Mrs. Major O'Dowd packing her own and her Major's wardrobe, and how his best epaulets had been stowed into a tea canister, whilst her own famous yellow turban, with the bird of paradise wrapped in brown paper, was locked up in the Major's tin cocked-hat case, and wondered what effect it would have at the French king's court at Ghent, or the great military balls at Brussels.

"Ghent! Brussels!" cried out Amelia, with a sudden shock and start. "Is the regiment ordered away, George—is it ordered away? " A look of terror came over the sweet, smiling face, and she clung to George as by an instinct.

"Don't be afraid, dear," he said good-naturedly; "it is but a twelve-hours' passage. It won't hurt you. You shall go too, Emmy."

"*I* intend to go," said Becky. "I'm on the staff. General Tufto is a great flirt of mine. Isn't he, Rawdon? "

Rawdon laughed out with his usual roar. William Dobbin flushed up quite red. "She can't go," he said; "think of the——" of the danger, he was going to add; but had not all his conversation during the dinner-time tended to prove there was none? He became very confused and silent.

"I must and will go," Amelia cried with the greatest spirit; and George, applauding her resolution, patted her under the chin, and asked all the persons present if they ever saw such a termagent of a wife, and agreed that the lady should bear him company.

Putting her arm round her friend's waist, Rebecca at length carried Amelia off from the dinner-table, where so much business of importance had been discussed, and left the gentlemen in a highly exhilarated state, drinking and talking very gaily.

In the course of the evening Rawdon got a little family note from his wife, which, although he crumpled it up and burnt it instantly in the candle, we had the good luck to read over Rebecca's shoulder. "Great news," she wrote. "Mrs. Bute is gone. Get the money from Cupid to-night, as he'll be off to-morrow most likely. Mind this.—R." So when the little company was about adjourning to coffee in the women's apartment, Rawdon touched Osborne on the elbow, and said gracefully, "I say, Osborne, my boy, if quite convenient, I'll trouble you for that 'ere small trifle." It was not quite convenient, but nevertheless George gave him a considerable present instalment in bank-notes from his pocket-book, and a bill on his agents at a week's date for the remaining sum.

This matter arranged, George, and Jos, and Dobbin held a council of war over their cigars and agreed that a general move should be made for London in Jos's open carriage the next day.

Besides these characters who are coming and going away, we must remember that there were some other old friends of ours at Brighton —Miss Crawley, namely, and the suite in attendance upon her. Now, although Rebecca and her husband were but a few stones' throw of the lodgings which the invalid Miss Crawley occupied, the old lady's door remained as pitilessly closed to them as it had been heretofore in London. As long as she remained by the side of her sister-in-law, Mrs. Bute Crawley took care that her beloved Matilda should not be agitated by a meeting with her nephew. When the spinster took her drive, the faithful Mrs. Bute sate beside her in the carriage. When

Miss Crawley took the air in a chair, Mrs. Bute marched on one side of the vehicle, while honest Briggs occupied the other wing. And if they met Rawdon and his wife by chance—although the former constantly and obsequiously took off his hat—the Miss Crawley party passed him by with such a frigid and killing indifference, that Rawdon began to despair.

Through Rawdon's valet, who still kept up a trifling acquaintance with the male inhabitants of Miss Crawley's servants' hall, and was instructed to treat the coachman to drink whenever they met, old Miss Crawley's movements were pretty well known by our young couple; and Rebecca luckily bethought herself of being unwell, and of calling in the same apothecary who was in attendance upon the spinster, so that their information was on the whole tolerably complete. Nor was Miss Briggs, although forced to adopt a hostile attitude, secretly inimical to Rawdon and his wife. She was naturally of a kindly and forgiving disposition. Now that the cause of jealousy was removed, her dislike for Rebecca disappeared also, and she remembered the latter's invariable good words and good-humour. And indeed, she and Mrs. Firkin, the lady's-maid, and the whole of Miss Crawley's household, groaned under the tyranny of the triumphant Mrs. Bute.

The Reverend Bute Crawley, her husband, riding home one night, fell from his horse and broke his collar-bone. Fever and inflammatory symptoms set in, and Mrs. Bute was forced to leave Sussex for Hampshire. As soon as ever Bute was restored, she promised to return to her dearest friend, and departed, leaving the strongest injunctions with the household regarding their behaviour to their mistress; and as soon as she got into the Southampton coach, there was such a jubilee and sense of relief in all Miss Crawley's house, as the company of persons assembled there had not experienced for many a week before. That very day Miss Crawley left off her afternoon dose of medicine; that afternoon Bowls opened an independent bottle of sherry for himself and Mrs. Firkin; that night Miss Crawley and Miss Briggs indulged in a game of piquet instead of one of Porteus's sermons. It was as in the old nursery-story, when the stick forgot to beat the dog, and the whole course of events underwent a peaceful and happy revolution.

At a very early hour in the morning, twice or thrice a week, Miss Briggs used to betake herself to a bathing-machine, and disport in the water in a flannel gown and an oilskin cap. Rebecca was aware of this circumstance, and though she did not attempt to storm Briggs, and actually dive into that lady's presence and surprise her under the sacredness of the awning, Mrs. Rawdon determined to attack Briggs as she came away from her bath, refreshed and invigorated by her dip, and likely to be in good-humour.

So getting up very early the next morning, Becky brought the telescope in their sitting-room, which faced the sea, to bear upon the bathing-machines on the beach; saw Briggs arrive, enter her box, and put out to sea; and was on the shore just as the nymph of whom she came in quest stepped out of the little caravan on to the shingles. It was a pretty picture: the beach, the bathing-women's faces, the long line of rocks and building were blushing and bright in the sunshine. Rebecca wore a kind, tender smile on her face, and was holding out her pretty white hand as Briggs emerged from the box. What could Briggs do but accept the salutation?

"Miss Sh——, Mrs. Crawley," she said.

Mrs. Crawley seized her hand, pressed it to her heart, and with a sudden impulse, flinging her arms round Briggs, kissed her affectionately. "Dear, dear friend!" she said, with a touch of such natural feeling that Miss Briggs of course at once began to melt, and even the bathing-woman was mollified.

Rebecca found no difficulty in engaging Briggs in a long, intimate, and delightful conversation. Everything that had passed since the morning of Becky's sudden departure from Miss Crawley's house in Park Lane up to the present day, and Mrs. Bute's happy retreat, was discussed and described by Briggs. Rebecca, after an hour's chat with her recovered friend, left her with the most tender demonstrations of regard, and quite assured that the conversation they had had together would be reported to Miss Crawley before many hours were over.

This interview ended, it became full time for Rebecca to return to her inn, where all the party of the previous day were assembled at a farewell breakfast. Rebecca took such a tender leave of Amelia as became two women who loved each other as sisters; and having used her handkerchief plentifully, and hung on her friend's neck as if they were parting for ever, and waved the handkerchief (which was quite dry, by the way) out of window, as the carriage drove off, she came back to the breakfast table and ate some prawns, with a good deal of appetite, considering her emotion; and while she was munching these delicacies, explained to Rawdon what had occurred in her morning walk between herself and Briggs. Her hopes were very high; she made her husband share them. She generally succeeded in making her husband share all her opinions, whether melancholy or cheerful.

"You will now, if you please, my dear, sit down at the writing-table and pen me a pretty little letter to Miss Crawley, in which you'll say that you are a good boy, and that sort of thing." So Rawdon sate down, and wrote off, "Brighton, Thursday," and "My dear Aunt," with great rapidity; but there the gallant officer's imagination failed him. He mumbled the end of his pen, and looked up in his wife's face. She could not help laughing at his rueful countenance, and marching up and down the room, with her hands behind her, the little woman began to dictate a letter, which he took down.

"Before quitting the country and commencing a campaign, which very possibly may be fatal——"

"What?" said Rawdon, rather surprised, but took the humour of the phrase, and presently wrote it down with a grin.

"Which very possibly may be fatal, I have come hither——"

"Why not say come here, Becky? come here's grammar," the dragoon interposed.

"I have come hither," Rebecca insisted, with a stamp of her foot, "to say farewell to my dearest and earliest friend. I beseech you before I go, not perhaps to return, once more to let me press the hand from which I have received nothing but kindnesses all my life."

"Kindnesses all my life," echoed Rawdon, scratching down the words, and quite amazed at his own facility of composition.

"I ask nothing from you but that we should part not in anger. I have the pride of my family on some points, though not on all. I married a painter's daughter, and am not ashamed of the union."

"No, run me through the body if I am!" Rawdon ejaculated.

"You old booby," Rebecca said, pinching his ear and looking over to see that he made no mistakes in spelling—"beseech is not spelt with an *a*, and earliest is." So he altered these words, bowing to the superior knowledge of his little Missis.

"I thought that you were aware of the progress of my attachment," Rebecca continued; "I know that Mrs. Bute Crawley confirmed and encouraged it. But I make no reproaches. I married a poor woman, and am content to abide by what I have done. Leave your property, dear Aunt, as you will. *I* shall never complain of the way in which you dispose of it. I would have you believe that I love you for yourself, and not for money's sake. I want to be reconciled to you ere I leave England. Let me, let me see you before I go. A few weeks or months hence it may be too late, and I cannot bear the notion of quitting the country without a kind word of farewell from you."

"She won't recognize my style in *that*," said Becky. "I made the sentences short and brisk on purpose." And this authentic missive was dispatched under cover to Miss Briggs.

Old Miss Crawley laughed when Briggs, with great mystery, handed her over this candid and simple statement. "We may read it now Mrs. Bute is away," she said. "Read it to me, Briggs."

When Briggs had read the epistle out, her patroness laughed more. "Don't you see, you goose," she said to Briggs, who professed to be much touched by the honest affection which pervaded the composition —"don't you see that Rawdon never wrote a word of it? He never wrote to me without asking for money in his life, and all his letters are full of bad spelling, and dashes, and bad grammar. It is that little serpent of a governess who rules him." They are all alike, Miss Crawley thought in her heart. They all want me dead, and are hankering for my money.

"I don't mind seeing Rawdon," she added, after a pause, and in a tone of perfect indifference. "I had just as soon shake hands with him as not. Provided there is no scene, why shouldn't we meet? I don't mind. But human patience has its limits; and mind, my dear, I respectively decline to receive Mrs. Rawdon; I can't support *that*

D

quite." And Miss Briggs was fain to be content with this half-message of conciliation; and thought that the best method of bringing the old lady and her nephew together, was to warn Rawdon to be in waiting on the Cliff, when Miss Crawley went out for her air in her chair.

There they met. I don't know whether Miss Crawley had any private feeling of regard or emotion upon seeing her old favourite; but she held out a couple of fingers to him with as smiling and good-humoured an air, as if they had met only the day before. And as for Rawdon, he turned as red as scarlet, and wrung off Briggs's hand, so great was his rapture and his confusion at the meeting.

"The old girl has always acted like a trump to me," he said to his wife, as he narrated the interview; "and I felt, you know, rather queer, and that sort of thing. I walked by the side of that whatdyecallem—you know, and to her own door, where Bowls came to help her in. And I wanted to go in very much, only——"

"*You didn't go in*, Rawdon?" screamed his wife.

"No, my dear; I'm hanged if I wasn't afraid when it came to the point."

"Well, dearest, to-morrow you must be on the look-out, and go and see her, mind, whether she asks you or no," Rebecca said, trying to soothe her angry yoke-mate. On which he replied, that he would do exactly as he liked, and would just thank her to keep a civil tongue in her head; and the wounded husband went away, and passed the forenoon at the billiard-room, sulky, silent, and suspicious.

But before the night was over he was compelled to give in, and own as usual, to his wife's superior prudence and foresight, by the most melancholy confirmation of the presentiments which she had regarding the consequences of the mistake which he had made. Miss Crawley *must* have had some emotion upon seeing him and shaking hands with him after so long a rupture. She mused upon the meeting a considerable time. "Rawdon is getting very fat and old, Briggs," she said to her companion. "His nose has become red, and he is exceedingly coarse in appearance. His marriage to that woman has hopelessly vulgarized him. Mrs. Bute always said they drank together; and I have no doubt they do. Yes; he smelt of gin abominably. I remarked it. Didn't you?"

"He was very much affected at seeing you, ma'am," the companion said; "and I am sure, when you remember that he is going to the field of danger——"

"How much money has he promised you, Briggs?" the old spinster cried out, working herself into a nervous rage;—"there now, of course you begin to cry. I hate scenes. Why am I always to be worried? Go and cry up in your own room, and send Firkin to me,—no, stop, sit down and blow your nose, and leave off crying, and write a letter to Captain Crawley." Poor Briggs went and placed herself obediently at the writing-book.

"Begin 'My dear sir,' or 'Dear sir,' that will be better, and say you are desired by Miss Crawley—no, by Miss Crawley's medical man, by Mr. Creamer, to state, that my health is such that all strong emotions would be dangerous in my present delicate condition; and that I must decline any family discussions or interviews whatever. And thank him for coming to Brighton and so forth, and beg him not to stay any longer on my account. And, Miss Briggs, you may add that I wish him a *bon voyage*; and that if he will take the trouble to call upon my lawyers in Gray's Inn Square, he will find there a communication for him. Yes, that will do; and that will make him leave Brighton." The benevolent Briggs penned this sentence with the utmost satisfaction.

"To seize upon me the very day after Mrs. Bute was gone," the old lady prattled on; "it was too indecent. Briggs, my dear, write to Mrs. Crawley, and say *she* needn't come back. No—she needn't—and she shan't—and I won't be a slave in my own house—and I won't be starved and choked with poison. They all want to kill me—all—all" —and with this the lonely old woman burst into a scream of hysterical tears.

That final paragraph which referred Rawdon to Miss Crawley's solicitor in London, and which Briggs had written so good-naturedly, consoled the dragoon and his wife somewhat, after their first blank disappointment on reading the spinster's refusal of a reconciliation. And it effected the purpose for which the old lady had caused it to be written, by making Rawdon very eager to get to London.

Out of Jos's losings and George Osborne's bank-notes he paid his bill at the inn, the landlord whereof does not probably know to this day how doubtfully his account once stood.

"I should have liked to see the old girl before we went," Rawdon said. "She looks so cut up and altered that I'm sure she can't last long. I wonder what sort of a cheque I shall have at Waxy's. Two hundred —it can't be less than two hundred,—hey, Becky?"

In consequence of the repeated visits of the aides-de-camp of the Sheriff of Middlesex, Rawdon and his wife did not go back to their lodgings at Brompton, but put up at an inn. Early the next morning, Rebecca had an opportunity of seeing them as she skirted that suburb on her road to old Mrs. Sedley's house at Fulham, whither she went to look for her dear Amelia and her Brighton friends. They were all off to Chatham, thence to Harwich, to take shipping for Belgium with the regiment—kind old Mrs. Sedley very much depressed and tearful, solitary. Returning from this visit, Rebecca found her husband, who had been off to Gray's Inn, and learned his fate. He came back furious.

"By Jove, Becky," says he, "she's only given me twenty pounds!"

Though it told against themselves, the joke was too good, and Becky burst out laughing at Rawdon's discomfiture.

CHAPTER XXVI

BETWEEN LONDON AND CHATHAM

ON quitting Brighton, our friend George, as became a person of rank and fashion travelling in a barouche with four horses, drove in state to a fine hotel in Cavendish Square, where a suite of splendid rooms and a table magnificently furnished with plate and surrounded by a half-dozen of black and silent waiters, was ready to receive the young gentleman and his bride. George did the honours of the place with a princely air to Jos and Dobbin; and Amelia, for the first time and with exceeding shyness and timidity, presided at what George called her own table.

A while after dinner, Amelia timidly expressed a wish to go and see her mamma, at Fulham; which permission George granted her with some grumbling.

Mrs. Sedley, you may be sure, clasped her daughter to her heart with all maternal eagerness and affection, running out of the door, as the carriage drew up before the little garden-gate, to welcome the weeping, trembling young bride. Old Mr. Clapp, who was in his shirt-sleeves, trimming the garden-plot, shrank back alarmed. The Irish servant-lass rushed up from the kitchen and smiled a "God bless you." Amelia could hardly walk along the flags and up the steps into the parlour.

In honour of the young bride's arrival, her mother thought it necessary to prepare I don't know what festive entertainment, and after the first ebullition of talk, took leave of Mrs. George Osborne for a while, and dived down to the lower regions of the house to a sort of kitchen-parlour (occupied by Mr. and Mrs. Clapp, and in the evening, when her dishes were washed and her curl-papers removed, by Miss Flannigan, the Irish servant), there to take measures for the preparing of a magnificent ornamented tea. All people have their ways of expressing kindness, and it seemed to Mrs. Sedley that a muffin and a quantity of orange marmalade spread out in a little cut-glass saucer would be peculiarly agreeable refreshments to Amelia in her most interesting situation.

While these delicacies were being transacted below, Amelia, leaving the drawing-room, walked upstairs, and found herself, she scarce knew how, in the little room which she had occupied before her marriage, and in that very chair in which she had passed so many bitter hours. She sank back in its arms as if it were an old friend, and fell to thinking over the past week and the life beyond it. Already to be looking sadly and vaguely back, always to be pining for something which when obtained brought doubt and sadness rather than pleasure—here was the lot of our poor little creature and harmless lost wanderer in the great struggling crowds of Vanity Fair.

But this may be said, that when the tea was finally announced, our young lady came downstairs a great deal more cheerful; that she did not despond, or deplore her fate, or think about George's coldness, or Rebecca's eyes, as she had been wont to do of late. She went downstairs, and kissed her father and mother, and talked to the old gentleman, and made him more merry than he had been for many a day. She sate down at the piano which Dobbin had bought for her, and sang over all her father's favourite old songs. She pronounced the tea to be excellent, and praised the exquisite taste in which the marmalade was arranged in the saucers. And in determining to make everybody else happy, she found herself so; and was sound asleep in the great funereal pavilion, and only woke up with a smile when George arrived from the theatre.

For the next day George had more important "business" to transact than that which took him to see Mr. Kean in Shylock. Immediately on his arrival in London he had written off to his father's solicitors, signifying his royal pleasure that an interview should take place between them on the morrow. His hotel bill, losses at billiards and cards to Captain Crawley, had almost drained the young man's purse, which wanted replenishing before he set out on his travels, and he had no resource but to infringe upon the two thousand pounds which the attorneys were commissioned to pay over to him. He had a perfect belief in his own mind that his father would relent before very long. How could any parent be obdurate for a length of time against such a paragon as he was? If his mere past and personal merits did not succeed in mollifying his father, George determined that he would distinguish himself so prodigiously in the ensuing campaign that the old gentleman must give in to him. And if not? Bah! the world was before him. His luck might change at cards, and there was a deal of spending in two thousand pounds.

So he sent off Amelia once more in a carriage to her mamma, with strict orders and *carte blanche* to the two ladies to purchase everything requisite for a lady of Mrs. George Osborne's fashion, who was going on a foreign tour. Well, in a word, she and her mother performed a great day's shopping, and she acquitted herself with considerable liveliness and credit on this her first appearance in the genteel world of London.

George meanwhile, with his hat on one side, his elbows squared, and his swaggering martial air, made for Bedford Row, and stalked into the attorney's offices as if he was lord of every pale-faced clerk who was scribbling there. He ordered somebody to inform Mr. Higgs that Captain Osborne was waiting, in a fierce and patronizing way, as if the *pékin* of an attorney, who had thrice his brains, fifty times his money, and a thousand times his experience, was a wretched underling who should instantly leave all his business in life to attend on the Captain's pleasure.

Perhaps George expected, when he entered Mr. Higgs's apartment, to find that gentleman commissioned to give him some message of compromise or conciliation from his father; perhaps his haughty and cold demeanour was adopted as a sign of his spirit and resolution; but if so, his fierceness was met by a chilling coolness and indifference on the attorney's part that rendered swaggering absurd. He pretended to be writing at a paper when the Captain entered. "Pray sit down, sir," said he, "and I will attend to your little affair in a moment.—Mr. Poe, get the release papers, if you please;" and then he fell to writing again.

Poe having produced those papers, his chief calculated the amount of two thousand pounds stock at the rate of the day, and asked Captain Osborne whether he would take the sum in a cheque upon the bankers, or whether he should direct the latter to purchase stock to that amount. "One of the late Mrs. Osborne's trustees is out of town," he said indifferently, "but my client wishes to meet your wishes, and have done with the business as quick as possible."

"Give me a cheque, sir," said the Captain very surlily. "Damn the shillings and halfpence, sir," he added, as the lawyer was making out the amount of the draft; and flattering himself that by this stroke of magnanimity he had put the old quiz to the blush, he stalked out of the office with the paper in his pocket.

"That chap will be in jail in two years," Mr. Higgs said to Mr. Poe.

"Won't O. come round, sir, don't you think?"

"Won't the monument come round?" Mr. Higgs replied.

"He's going it pretty fast," said the clerk. "He's only married a week, and I saw him and some other military chaps handing Mrs. Highflyer to her carriage after the play." And then another case was called, and Mr. George Osborne thenceforth dismissed from these worthy gentlemen's memory.

The draft was upon our friends Hulker & Bullock of Lombard Street, to whose house, still thinking he was doing business, George bent his way, and from whom he received his money. Frederick Bullock, Esq., whose yellow face was over a ledger, at which sate a demure clerk, happened to be in the banking-room when George entered. His yellow face turned to a more deadly colour when he saw the Captain, and he slunk back guiltily into the inmost parlour. George was too busy gloating over the money (for he had never had such a sum before) to mark the countenance or flight of the cadaverous suitor of his sister.

Fred Bullock told old Osborne of his son's appearance and conduct. "He came in as bold as brass," said Frederick. "He has drawn out every shilling. How long will a few hundred pounds last such a chap as that?" Osborne swore with a great oath that he little cared when or how soon he spent it. Fred dined every day in Russell Square now. But altogether George was highly pleased with his day's business. All his own baggage and outfit was put into a state of speedy preparation, and he paid Amelia's purchases with cheques on his agents, and with the splendour of a lord.

CHAPTER XXVII

IN WHICH AMELIA JOINS HER REGIMENT

WHEN Jos's fine carriage drove up to the inn door at Chatham, the first face which Amelia recognized was the friendly countenance of Captain Dobbin, who had been pacing the street for an hour past in expectation of his friend's arrival.

Along with the Captain was Ensign Stubble, who, as the barouche neared the inn, burst out with an exclamation of, "By Jove, what a pretty girl!" highly applauding Osborne's choice.

In the sitting-room which was awaiting the travellers, Amelia, to her surprise, found a letter addressed to Mrs. Captain Osborne. It was a triangular billet, on pink paper, and sealed with a dove and an olive branch, and a profusion of light blue sealing-wax, and it was written in a very large though undecided female hand.

"It's Peggy O'Dowd's fist," said George, laughing. "I know it by the kisses on the seal." And, in fact, it was a note from Mrs. Major O'Dowd, requesting the pleasure of Mrs. Osborne's company that very evening to a small friendly party.

But they had not been for many minutes in the enjoyment of Mrs. O'Dowd's letter when the door was flung open, and a stout, jolly lady, in a riding habit, followed by a couple of officers of Ours, entered the room.

"Sure, I couldn't stop till tay-time. Present me, Garge, my dear fellow, to your lady.—Madam, I'm deloighted to see ye, and to present to you me husband, Meejer O'Dowd;" and with this the jolly lady in the riding habit grasped Amelia's hand very warmly, and the latter knew at once that the lady was before her whom her husband had so often laughed at. "You've often heard of me from that husband of yours," said the lady, with great vivacity.

"You've often heard of her," echoed her husband, the Major.

Amelia answered, smiling, "that she had."

"And small good he's told you of me," Mrs. O'Dowd replied; adding that "George was a wicked divvle."

"That I'll go bail for," said the Major, trying to look knowing, at which George laughed; and Mrs. O'Dowd, with a tap of her whip, told the Major to be quiet, and then requested to be presented in form to Mrs. Captain Osborne.

"This, my dear," said George, with great gravity, "is my very good, kind, and excellent friend Auralia Margaretta, otherwise called Peggy."

"Faith, you're right," interposed the Major.

"Otherwise called Pegg, lady of Major Michael O'Dowd, of our regiment, and daughter of Fitzjurld Ber'sford de Burgo Malony of Glenmalony, County Kildare."

"And Muryan Squeer, Dobblin," said the lady with calm superiority.

"And Muryan Squeer, sure enough," the Major whispered.

" 'Twas there ye coorted me, Meejor dear," the lady said; and the

Major assented to this as to every other proposition which was made generally in company.

Major O'Dowd, who had served his sovereign in every quarter of the world, and had paid for every step in his profession by some more than equivalent act of daring and gallantry, was the most modest, silent, sheepfaced, and meek of little men, and as obedient to his wife as if he had been her tay-boy.

Peggy was one of five sisters, and eleven children, of the noble house of Glenmalony; but her husband, though her own cousin, was of the mother's side, and so had not the inestimable advantage of being allied to the Malonys, whom she believed to be the most famous family in the world.

Before Mrs. O'Dowd was half an hour in Amelia's (or indeed in anybody else's) company, this amiable lady told all her birth and pedigree to her new friend. "My dear," said she good-naturedly, "it was my intention that Garge should be a brother of my own, and my sister Glorvina would have suited him entirely. But as bygones are bygones, and he was engaged to yourself, why, I'm determined to take you as a sister instead, and to look upon you as such, and to love you as one of the family. Faith, you've got such a nice good-natured face and way widg you, that I'm sure we'll agree, and that you'll be an addition to our family anyway."

" 'Deed and she will," said O'Dowd, with an approving air, and Amelia felt herself not a little amused and grateful to be thus suddenly introduced to so large a party of relations.

The regiment indeed adopted her with acclamation. The Captains approved, the Lieutenants applauded, the Ensigns admired.

CHAPTER XXVIII

IN WHICH AMELIA INVADES THE LOW COUNTRIES

THE regiment with its officers was to be transported in ships provided by His Majesty's Government for the occasion; and in two days after the festive assembly at Mrs. O'Dowd's apartments, in the midst of cheering from all the East India ships, in the river and the military on shore, the band, playing "God save the King," the officers waving their hats, and the crews hurrahing gallantly, the transports went down the river and proceeded under convoy to Ostend. Meanwhile the gallant Jos had agreed to escort his sister and the Major's wife, the bulk of whose goods and chattels, including the famous bird of paradise and turban, were the regimental baggage; so that our two heroines drove pretty much unencumbered to Ramsgate, where there were plenty of packets plying, in one of which they had a speedy passage to Ostend.

Since Amelia's introduction to the regiment, George began to be rather ashamed of some of the company to which he had been forced to present her, and determined, as he told Dobbin (with what satisfaction to the latter it need not be said), to exchange into some better regiment soon, and to get his wife away from those damned vulgar women. Mrs. O'Dowd had a cock's plume in her hat, and a very large "repayther" on her stomach, which she used to ring on all occasions, narrating how it had been presented to her by her fawther, as she stipt into the car'ge after her mar'ge; and these ornaments, with other outward peculiarities of the Major's wife, gave excruciating agonies to Captain Osborne when his wife and the Major's came in contact; whereas Amelia was only amused by the honest lady's eccentricities, and not in the least ashamed of her company.

Those who like to lay down the History-book, and to speculate upon what *might* have happened in the world, but for the fatal occurrence of what actually did take place (a most puzzling, amusing, ingenious, and profitable kind of meditation), have no doubt often thought to themselves what a specially bad time Napoleon took to come back from Elba, and to let loose his eagle from Gulf San Juan to Notre Dame. The historians on our side tell us that the armies of the allied powers were all providentially on a war footing, and ready to bear down at a moment's notice upon the Elban Emperor. The august jobbers assembled at Vienna, and carving out the kingdoms of Europe according to their wisdom, had such causes of quarrel among themselves as might have set the armies which had overcome Napoleon to fight against each other, but for the return of the object of unanimous hatred and fear. This monarch had an army in full force because he had jobbed to himself Poland, and was determined to keep it; another had robbed half Saxony, and was bent upon maintaining his acquisition; Italy was the object of a third's solicitude. Each was protesting against the rapacity of the other; and could the Coriscan but have waited in prison until all these parties were by the ears, he might have returned and reigned unmolested.

In the meanwhile the business of life and living, and the pursuits of pleasure, especially, went on as if no end were to be expected to them, and no enemy in front. When our travellers arrived at Brussels, in which their regiment was quartered—a great piece of good fortune, as all said—they found themselves in one of the gayest and most brilliant little capitals in Europe, and where all the Vanity Fair booths were laid out with the most tempting liveliness and splendour. Gambling was here in profusion, and dancing in plenty; feasting was there to fill with delight that great gourmand of a Jos; there was a theatre where a miraculous Catalani was delighting all hearers, beautiful rides, all enlivened with martial splendour; a rare old city, with strange costumes and wonderful architecture, to delight the eyes of little Amelia, who had never before seen a foreign country, and fill her with charming surprises: so that now and for a few weeks' space in a fine handsome lodging, whereof the expenses were borne by Jos and Osborne, who

was flush of money and full of kind attentions to his wife—for about
a fortnight, I say, during which her honeymoon ended, Mrs. Amelia
was as pleased and happy as any little bride out of England.

One night, at a party given by the General of the division to which
George's regiment belonged, he had the honour of dancing with Lady
Blanche Thistlewood, Lord Bareacres' daughter. He bustled for ices
and refreshments for the two noble ladies; he pushed and squeezed
for Lady Bareacres' carriage; he bragged about the Countess when he
got home in a way which his own father could not have surpassed. He
called upon the ladies the next day; he rode by their side in the Park;
he asked their party to a great dinner at a restaurateur's, and was quite
wild with exultations when they agreed to come.

"I hope there will be no women besides our own party," Lady
Bareacres said.

"Gracious Heaven, Mamma, you don't suppose the man would bring
his wife!" shrieked Lady Blanche, who had been languishing in George's
arms in the newly-imported waltz for hours the night before. "The
men are bearable, but their women——"

"Wife, just married, dev'lish pretty woman, I hear," the old Earl said.

"Well, my dear Blanche," said the mother, "I suppose, as Papa
wants to go, we must go; but we needn't know them in England, you
know." And so, determined to cut their new acquaintance in Bond
Street, these great folks went to eat his dinner at Brussels, and condescending to make him pay for their pleasure, showed their dignity
by making his wife uncomfortable, and carefully excluding her from
the conversation. This is a species of dignity in which the high-bred
British female reigns supreme. To watch the behaviour of a fine lady
to other and humbler women is a very good sport for a philosophical
frequenter of Vanity Fair.

This festival, on which honest George spent a great deal of money,
was the very dismallest of all the entertainments which Amelia had in
her honeymoon. She wrote the most piteous accounts of the feast home
to her mamma: how the Countess of Bareacres would not answer when
spoken to; how Lady Blanche stared at her with her eye-glass; and
what a rage Captain Dobbin was in at their behaviour; and how my
lord, as they came away from the feast, asked to see the bill, and pronounced it a d—— bad dinner and d—— dear. But though Amelia
told all these stories, and wrote home regarding her guests' rudeness
and her own discomfiture, old Mrs. Sedley was mightily pleased nevertheless, and talked about Emmy's friend, the Countess of Bareacres,
with such assiduity that the news how his son was entertaining Peers
and Peeresses actually came to Osborne's ears in the City.

Those who know the present Lieutenant-General, Sir George Tufto,
K.C.B., and have seen him, as they may on most days in the season,
padded and in stays, strutting down Pall Mall with a rickety swagger
on his high-heeled lacquered boots, leering under the bonnets of passers-
by, or riding a showy chestnut, and ogling broughams in the Park—

those who know the present Sir George Tufto would hardly recognize
the daring Peninsular and Waterloo officer. He has thick, curling
brown hair and black eyebrows now, and his whiskers are of the
deepest purple. He was light-haired and bald in 1815, and stouter in
the person and in the limbs, which especially have shrunk very much
of late. When he was about seventy years of age (he is now nearly
eighty), his hair, which was very scarce and quite white, suddenly
grew thick and brown and curly, and his whiskers and eyebrows took
their present colour. Ill-natured people say that his chest is all wool,
and that his hair, because it never grows, is a wig. Tom Tufto, with
whose father he quarrelled ever so many years ago, declares that
Mademoiselle de Jaisey, of the French theatre, pulled his grandpa's
hair off in the green-room; but Tom is notoriously spiteful and jealous
and the General's wig has nothing to do with our story.

One day, as some of our friends of the —th were sauntering in the
flower-market of Brussels, having been to see the Hôtel de Ville, which
Mrs. Mauor O'Dowd declared was not near so large or handsome as her
fawther's mansion of Glenmalony, an officer of rank, with an orderly
behind him, rode up to the market, and descending from his horse,
came amongst the flowers, and selected the very finest bouquet which
money could buy.

"Dev'lish fine horse; who is it?" George asked.

"You should see me brother Molloy Malony's horse, Molasses, that
won the cup at the Curragh," the Major's wife was explaining, and was
continuing the family history, when her husband interrupted her by
saying,—

"It's General Tufto, who commands the —— cavalry division:"
adding quietly, "He and I were both shot in the same leg at Talavera."

"Where you got your step," said George, with a laugh. "General
Tufto! Then, my dear, the Crawleys are come."

Amelia's heart fell, she knew not why. The sun did not seem to
shine so bright. The tall old roofs and gables looked less picturesque
all of a sudden, though it was a brilliant sunset, and one of the brightest
and most beautiful days at the end of May.

CHAPTER XXIX

BRUSSELS

MR. Jos had hired a pair of horses for his open carriage, with which
cattle and the smart London vehicle he made a very tolerable figure
in the drives about Brussels. George purchased a horse for his private
riding, and he and Captain Dobbin would often accompany the
carriage in which Jos and his sister took daily excursions of pleasure.
They went out that day in the Park for their accustomed diversion,
and there, sure enough, George's remark with regard to the arrival
of Rawdon Crawley and his wife proved to be correct. In the midst

of a little troop of horsemen, consisting of some of the very greatest persons in Brussels, Rebecca was seen in the prettiest and tightest of riding habits, mounted on a beautiful little Arab, which she rode to perfection (having acquired the art at Queen's Crawley, where the baronet, Mr. Pitt, and Rawdon himself had given her many lessons), and by the side of the gallant General Tufto.

Rebecca did not make for the carriage; but as soon as she perceived her old acquaintance Amelia seated in it, acknowledged her presence by a gracious nod and smile, and by kissing and shaking her fingers playfully in the direction of the vehicle. Then she resumed her conversation with General Tufto, who asked "who the fat officer was in the gold-laced cap?" on which Becky replied, "that he was an officer in the East Indian service." But Rawdon Crawley rode out of the ranks of his company and came up and shook hands heartily with Amelia and said to Jos, "Well, old boy, how are you?" and stared in Mrs. O'Dowd's face and at the blackcock's feathers until she began to think she had made a conquest of him.

George, who had been delayed behind, rode up almost immediately with Dobbin, and they touched their caps to the august personages, among whom Osborne at once perceived Mrs. Crawley. He was delighted to see Rawdon leaning over his carriage familiarly and talking to Amelia, and met the aide-de-camp's cordial greeting with more than corresponding warmth. The nods between Rawdon and Dobbin were of the very faintest specimen of politeness.

Crawley told George where they were stopping, with General Tufto at the Hotel du Parc, and George made his friend promise to come speedily to Osborne's own residence. "Sorry I hadn't seen you three days ago," George said. "Had a dinner at the restaurateur's—rather a nice thing. Lord Bareacres, and the Countess, and Lady Blanche were good enough to dine with us—wish we'd had you." Having thus let his friend know his claims to be a man of fashion, Osborne parted from Rawdon, who followed the august squadron down an alley into which they cantered, while George and Dobbin resumed their places, one on each side of Amelia's carriage.

The apparition of the great personages held them all in talk during the drive, and at dinner, and until the hour came when they were all to go to the Opera. It was almost like old England.

At the end of the act George was out of the box in a moment, and he was even going to pay his respects to Rebecca in her *loge*. He met Crawley in the lobby, however, where they exchanged a few sentences upon the occurrences of the last fortnight.

"You found my cheque all right at the agent's?" George said, with a knowing air.

"All right, my boy," Rawdon answered. "Happy to give you your revenge. Governor come round?"

"Not yet," said George, "but he will; and you know I've some private fortune through my mother. Has aunty relented?"

"Sent me twenty pound, damned old screw. When shall we have a meet? The General dines out on Tuesday. Can't you come Tuesday? I say, make Sedley cut off his moustache. What the devil does a civilian mean with a moustache and those infernal frogs to his coat! By-bye. Try and come on Tuesday;" and Rawdon was going off with two brilliant young gentlemen of fashion, who were, like himself, on the staff of a general officer.

"When do you intend to give up play, George, as you have promised me—any time these hundred years?" Dobbin said to his friend a few days after the night at the Opera.

"When do you intend to give up sermonizing?" was the other's reply. "What the deuce, man, are you alarmed about? We play low; I won last night. You don't suppose Crawley cheats? With fair play it comes to pretty much the same thing at the year's end."

"But I don't think he could pay if he lost," Dobbin said; and his advice met with the success which advice usually commands. Osborne and Crawley were repeatedly together now. General Tufto dined abroad almost constantly. George was always welcome in the apartments (very close indeed to those of the General) which the aide-de-camp and his wife occupied in the hotel.

Amelia's manners were such when she and George visited Crawley and his wife at these quarters, that they had very nearly come to their first quarrel—that is, George scolded his wife violently for her evident unwillingness to go, and the high and mighty manner in which she comported herself towards Mrs. Crawley, her old friend; and Amelia did not say one single word in reply, but with her husband's eye upon her, and Rebecca scanning her as she felt, was, if possible, more bashful and awkward on the second visit which she paid to Mrs. Rawdon than on her first call.

Mr. Osborne, having a firm conviction in his own mind that he was a woman-killer and destined to conquer, did not run counter to his fate, but yielded himself up to it quite complacently. And as Emmy did not say much or plague him with her jealousy, but merely became unhappy and pined over it miserably in secret, he chose to fancy that she was not suspicious of what all his acquaintance were perfectly aware—namely, that he was carrying on a desperate flirtation with Mrs. Crawley. He rode with her whenever she was free. He pretended regimental business to Amelia (by which falsehood she was not in the least deceived), and consigning his wife to solitude or her brother's society, passed his evenings in the Crawleys' company—losing money to the husband, and flattering himself that the wife was dying of love for him. It is very likely that this worthy couple never absolutely conspired and agreed together in so many words—the one to cajole the young gentleman, whilst the other won his money at cards—but they understood each other perfectly well, and Rawdon let Osborne come and go with entire good-humour.

There never was, since the days of Darius, such a brilliant train of
camp-followers as hung round the Duke of Wellington's army in the
Low Countries in 1815, and led it, dancing and feasting as it were, up
to the very brink of battle. A certain ball which a noble Duchess gave
at Brussels on the 15th of June in the above-named year is historical.

On the appointed night, George, having commanded new dresses
and ornaments of all sorts for Amelia, drove to the famous ball, where
his wife did not know a single soul. After looking about for Lady
Bareacres—who cut him, thinking the card was quite enough—and
after placing Amelia on a bench, he left her to her own cogitations
there, thinking, on his own part, that he had behaved very handsomely
in getting her new clothes and bringing her to the ball, where she was
free to amuse herself as she liked. Her thoughts were not of the pleasantest, and nobody except honest Dobbin came to disturb them.

Whilst her appearance was an utter failure (as her husband felt with
a sort of rage), Mrs. Rawdon Crawley's *début* was, on the contrary,
very brilliant. She arrived very late. Her face was radiant, her dress
perfection. In the midst of the great persons assembled, and the eye-
glasses directed to her, Rebecca seemed to be as cool and collected
as when she used to marshal Miss Pinkerton's little girls to church.
Numbers of the men she knew already, and the dandies thronged
round her. Fifty would-be partners thronged round her at once, and
pressed to have the honour to dance with her. But she said she was
engaged, and only going to dance very little; and made her way at
once to the place where Emmy sate quite unnoticed, and dismally unhappy. And so, to finish the poor child at once, Mrs. Rawdon ran and
greeted affectionately her dearest Amelia, and began forthwith to
patronize her. She found fault with her friend's dress and her hair-
dresser, and wondered how she could be so *chaussée*, and vowed that
she must send her *corsetière* the next morning. She vowed that it was
a delightful ball; that there was everybody that every one knew, and
only a *very* few nobodies in the whole room. It is a fact that in a
fortnight, and after three dinners in general society, this young woman
had got up the genteel jargon so well that a native could not speak it
better, and it was only from her French being so good that you could
know she was not a born woman of fashion.

George, who had left Emmy on her bench on entering the ballroom,
very soon found his way back when Rebecca was by her dear friend's
side. Becky was just lecturing Mrs. Osborne upon the follies which her
husband was committing. "For God's sake, stop him from gambling,
my dear," she said, "or he will ruin himself. He and Rawdon are
playing at cards every night; and you know he is very poor, and
Rawdon will win every shilling from him if he does not take care.
Why don't you prevent him, you little, careless creature? Why don't
you come to us of an evening, instead of moping at home with that
Captain Dobbin? I daresay he is *très aimable* but how could one love
a man with feet of such size? Your husband's feet are darlings—here

he comes.—Where have you been, wretch? Here is Emmy crying her eyes out for you. Are you coming to fetch me for the quadrille?" And she left her bouquet and shawl by Amelia's side, and tripped off with George to dance.

George danced with Rebecca twice or thrice—how many times Amelia scarcely knew. She sate quite unnoticed in her corner, except when Rawdon came up with some words of clumsy conversation; and later in the evening, when Captain Dobbin made so bold as to bring her refreshments and sit beside her. He did not like to ask her why she was so sad; but as a pretext for the tears which were filling in her eyes, she told him that Mrs. Crawley had alarmed her by telling her that George would go on playing.

"It is curious, when a man is bent upon play, by what clumsy rogues he will allow himself to be cheated," Dobbin said; and Emmy said, "Indeed." She was thinking of something else. It was not the loss of the money that grieved her.

At last George came back for Rebecca's shawl and flowers. She was going away. She did not even condescend to come back and say good-bye to Amelia. The poor girl let her husband come and go without saying a word, and her head fell on her breast. Dobbin had been called away, and was whispering deep in conversation with the General of the division, his friend, and had not seen this last parting. George went away then with the bouquet; but when he gave it to the owner, there lay a note, coiled like a snake among the flowers. Rebecca's eye caught it at once; she had been used to deal with notes in early life. She put out her hand and took the nosegay. He saw by her eyes as they met that she was aware what she should find there. Her husband hurried her away, still too intent upon his own thoughts, seemingly, to take note of any marks of recognition which might pass between his friend and his wife. These were, however, but trifling. Rebecca gave George her hand with one of her usual quick, knowing glances, and made a curtsy and walked away. George bowed over the hand, said nothing in reply to a remark of Crawley's—did not hear it even, his brain was so throbbing with triumph and excitement—and allowed them to go away without a word.

His wife saw the one part at least of the bouquet-scene. It was quite natural that George should come at Rebecca's request to get her scarf and flowers—it was no more than he had done twenty times before in the course of the last few days; but now it was too much for her. "William," she said, suddenly clinging to Dobbin, who was near her, "you've always been very kind to me—I'm—I'm not well. Take me home." She did not know she called him by his Christian name, as George was accustomed to do. He went away with her quickly. Her lodgings were hard by; and they threaded through the crowd without, where everything seemed to be more astir than even in the ballroom within. George had been angry twice or thrice at finding his wife up on his return from the parties which he frequented, so she went straight to bed now; but although she did not sleep, and although the din and clatter and the galloping of horsemen were incessant, she never heard any of these noises, having quite other disturbances to keep her awake.

Osborne meanwhile, wild with elation, went off to a play table, and began to bet frantically. He won repeatedly. "Everything succeeds with me to-night," he said. But his luck at play even did not cure him of his restlessness, and he started up after a while, pocketing his winnings, and went to a buffet where he drank off many bumpers of wine.

Here, as he was rattling away to the people around, laughing loudly and wild with spirits, Dobbin found him. He had been to the card-tables to look there for his friend. Dobbin looked as pale and grave as his comrade was flushed and jovial.

"Hallo, Dob! Come and drink, old Dob! The Duke's wine is famous.—Give me some more, you sir;" and he held out a trembling glass for the liquor.

"Come out, George," said Dobbin, still gravely; "don't drink."

"Drink! there's nothing like it. Drink yourself, and light up your lantern jaws, old boy. Here's to you."

Dobbin went up and whispered something to him, at which George, giving a start and a wild hurray, tossed off his glass, clapped it on the table, and walked away speedily on his friend's arm. "The enemy has passed the Sambre," William said, "and our left is already engaged. Come away. We are to march in three hours."

Away went George, his nerves quivering with excitement at the news so long looked for, so sudden when it came. What were love and intrigue now? He thought about a thousand things but these in his rapid walk to his quarters—his past life and future chances—the fate which might be before him—the wife, the child perhaps, from whom unseen he might be about to part. Oh. how he wished that night's work undone, and that with a clear conscience at least he might say farewell to the tender and guileless being by whose love he had set such little store!

He thought over his brief married life. In those few weeks he had frightfully dissipated his little capital. How wild and reckless he had been! Should any mischance befall him, what was then left for her? How unworthy he was of her! Why had he married her? He was not fit for marriage. Why had he disobeyed his father, who had been always so generous to him? Hope, remorse, ambition, tenderness, and selfish regret filled his heart. He sate down and wrote to his father, remembering what he had said once before when he was engaged to fight a duel. Dawn faintly streaked the sky as he closed this farewell letter. He sealed it, and kissed the superscription. He thought how he had deserted that generous father, and of the thousand kindnesses which the stern old man had done him.

He had looked into Amelia's bedroom when he entered; she lay quiet, and her eyes seemed closed, and he was glad that she was asleep. On arriving at his quarters from the ball, he had found his regimental servant already making preparations for his departure; the man had understood his signal to be still, and these arrangements were very quickly and silently made. Should he go in and wake Amelia, he thought, or leave a note for her brother to break the news of departure to her? He went in to look at her once again.

She had been awake when he first entered her room, but had kept her eyes closed, so that even her wakefulness should not seem to reproach him. But when he had returned, so soon after herself too, this timid little heart had felt more at ease, and turning towards him as he stepped softly out of the room, she had fallen into a light sleep. George came in and looked at her again, entering still more softly. By the pale night-lamp he could see her sweet, pale face; the purple eyelids were fringed and closed, and one round arm, smooth and white, lay outside the coverlet. Good God! how pure she was; how gentle, how tender, and how friendless! and he—how selfish, brutal, and black with crime! Heart-stained and shame-stricken, he stood at the bed's foot and looked at the sleeping girl. How dared he—who was he, to pray for one so spotless! God bless her! God bless her! He came to the bedside, and looked at the hand, the little soft hand, lying asleep; and he bent over the pillow noiselessly towards the gentle, pale face.

Two fair arms closed tenderly round his neck as he stooped down. "I am awake, George," the poor child said, with a sob fit to break the little heart that nestled so closely by his own. She was awake, poor soul, and to what? At that moment a bugle from the Place of Arms began sounding clearly, and was taken up through the town; and amidst the drums of the infantry and the shrill pipes of the Scotch, the whole city awoke.

CHAPTER XXX

"THE GIRL I LEFT BEHIND ME"

WE do not claim to rank among the military novelists. Our place is with the non-combatants. When the decks are cleared for action, we go below, and wait meekly. We should only be in the way of the manœuvres that the gallant fellows are performing overhead. We shall go no further with the —th than to the city gate.

When the final news arrived that the campaign was opened, and the troops were to march, Rawdon's gravity became such that Becky rallied him about it in a manner which rather hurt the feelings of the Guardsman. "You don't suppose I'm afraid, Becky, I should think," he said, with a tremor in his voice. "But I'm a pretty good mark for a shot; and you see if it brings me down, why I leave one, and perhaps two, behind me, whom I should wish to provide for, as I brought 'em into the scrape. It is no laughing matter *that*, Mrs. C., anyways."

Rebecca by a hundred caresses and kind words tried to soothe the feelings of the wounded lover. It was only when her vivacity and sense of humour got the better of this sprightly creature (as they would do under most circumstances of life indeed) that she would break out with her satire, but she could soon put on a demure face. "Dearest love," she said, "do you suppose I feel nothing?" and hastily dashing something from her eyes, she looked up in her husband's face with a smile.

"Look here," said he. "If I drop, let us see what there is for you. I have had a pretty good run of luck here, and here's two hundred and thirty pounds. I have got ten napoleons in my pocket. That is as much as I shall want—for the General pays everything like a prince—and if I'm hit, why you know I cost nothing. Don't cry, little woman; I may live to vex you yet. Well, I shan't take either of my horses, but shall ride the General's grey charger; it's cheaper, and I told him mine was lame. If I'm done, those two ought to fetch you something."

He pleased himself by noting down with a pencil, in his big schoolboy handwriting, the various items of his portable property which might be sold for his widow's advantage—as, for example, "My double-barril by Manton, say 40 guineas; my driving cloak, lined with sable fur, £50; my duelling pistols in rosewood case (same which I shot Captain Marker), £20; my regulation saddle-holsters and housings; my Laurie ditto," and so forth, over all of which articles he made Rebecca the mistress.

And Rebecca, as we have said, wisely determined not to give way to unavailing sentimentality on her husband's departure. She waved him an adieu from the window, and stood there for a moment looking out after he was gone. The cathedral towers and the full gables of the quaint old houses were just beginning to blush in the sunrise. There had been no rest for her that night. She was still in her pretty ball-dress, her fair hair hanging somewhat out of curl on her neck, and the circles round her eyes dark with watching. "What a fright I seem," she said, examining herself in the glass; "and how pale this pink makes one look!" So she divested herself of this pink raiment; in doing which a note fell out from her corsage, which she picked up with a smile, and locked into her dressing-box. And then she put her bouquet of the ball into a glass of water, and went to bed, and slept very comfortably.

The town was quite quiet when she woke up at ten o'clock, and partook of coffee, very requisite and comforting after the exhaustion and grief of the morning's occurrences.

This meal over, she resumed honest Rawdon's calculations of the night previous, and surveyed her position. Should the worst befall, all things considered, she was pretty well-to-do. There were her own trinkets and trousseau, in addition to those which her husband had left behind. Rawdon's generosity, when they were first married, has already been described and lauded.

Every calculation made of these valuables, Mrs. Rebecca found, not without a pungent feeling of triumph and self-satisfaction, that should circumstances occur, she might reckon on six or seven hundred pounds at the very least, to begin the world with; and she passed the morning disposing, ordering, looking out, and locking up her properties in the most agreeable manner. Among the notes in Rawdon's pocket-book was a draft for twenty pounds on Osborne's banker. This made her think about Mrs. Osborne. "I will go and get the draft cashed," she said, "and pay a visit afterwards to poor little Emmy."

And there was another of our acquaintances who was also to be left behind, a non-combatant, and whose emotions and behaviour we have therefore a right to know. This was our friend, the ex-Collector of Boggley Wollah, whose rest was broken, like other people's, by the sounding of the bugles in the early morning. Being a great sleeper, and fond of his bed, it is possible he would have snoozed on until his usual hour of rising in the forenoon, in spite of all the drums, bugles, and bagpipes in the British army, but for an interruption, which did not come from George Osborne, who shared Jos's quarters with him, and was as usual occupied too much with his own affairs, or with grief at parting with his wife, to think of taking leave of his slumbering brother-in-law—it was not George, we say, who interposed between Jos Sedley and sleep, but Captain Dobbin, who came and roused him up, insisting on shaking hands with him before his departure.

"Very kind of you," said Jos, yawning, and wishing the Captain at the deuce.

"I—I didn't like to go off without saying good-bye, you know," Dobbin said in a very incoherent manner; "because you know some of us mayn't come back again, and I like to see you all well, and—and that sort of thing, you know."

Jos had always had rather a mean opinion of the Captain, and now began to think his courage was somewhat equivocal. "What is it I can do for you, Dobbin?" he said in a sarcastic tone.

If Captain Dobbin expected to get any personal comfort and satisfaction from having one more view of Amelia before the regiment marched away, his selfishness was punished just as such odious egotism deserved to be. The door of Jos's bedroom opened into the sitting-room which was common to the family party, and opposite this door was that of Amelia's chamber. The bugles had awakened everybody; there was no use in concealment now. George's servant was packing in this room, Osborne coming in and out of the contiguous bedroom, flinging to the man such articles as he thought fit to carry on the campaign. And presently Dobbin had the opportunity which his heart coveted, and he got sight of Amelia's face once more. But what a face it was! So white, so wild and despair-stricken, that the remembrance of it haunted him afterwards like a crime, and the sight smote him with inexpressible pangs of longing and pity. And there was no help; no means to soothe and comfort this helpless, speechless misery. He stood for a moment and looked at her, powerless and torn with pity, as a parent regards an infant in pain.

At last, George took Emmy's hand and led her back into the bed-

room, from whence he came out alone. The parting had taken place
in that moment, and he was gone.

"Thank Heaven that is over," George thought, bounding down the
stair, his sword under his arm, as he ran swiftly to the alarm ground,
where the regiment was mustered, and whither trooped men and
officers hurrying from their billets; his pulse was throbbing and his
cheeks flushed: the great game of war was going to be played, and
he one of the players.

The sun was just rising as the march began—it was a gallant sight
—the band led the column, playing the regimental march—then came
the Major in command, riding upon Pyramus, his stout charger—then
marched the grenadiers, their Captain at their head; in the centre were
the colours, borne by the senior and junior Ensigns—then George came
marching at the head of his company. He looked up, and smiled at
Amelia, and passed on; and even the sound of the music died away.

CHAPTER XXXI

IN WHICH JOS SEDLEY TAKES CARE OF HIS SISTER

THUS all the superior officers being summoned on duty elsewhere,
Jos Sedley was left in command of the little colony at Brussels, with
Amelia invalided, Isidor, his Belgian servant, and the *bonne* who was
maid-of-all work for the establishment, as a garrison under him.

About George's absence, his brother-in-law was very easy in mind.
Perhaps Jos was rather pleased in his heart that Osborne was gone;
for during George's presence, the other had played but a very secondary part in the household, and Osborne did not scruple to show his
contempt for the stout civilian. But Emmy had always been good and
attentive to him. It was she who ministered to his comforts, who
superintended the dishes that he liked, who walked or rode with him
(as she had many, too many opportunities of doing; for where was
George?), and who interposed her sweet face between his anger and
her husband's scorn.

"Put the Captain's hat into the anteroom," he said to Isidor, the
servant.

"Perhaps he won't want it again,' replied the lackey, looking knowingly at his master. He hated George too, whose insolence towards him
was quite of the English sort.

Amelia's attendant was much less selfishly disposed. Few dependants
could come near that kind and gentle creature without paying their
usual tribute of loyalty and affection to her sweet and affectionate
nature. And it is a fact that Pauline, the cook, consoled her mistress
more than anybody whom she saw on this wretched morning; for when
she found how Amelia remained for hours, silent, motionless, and
haggard, by the windows in which she had placed herself to watch the

last bayonets of the column as it marched away, the honest girl took the lady's hand, and said, "*Tenez, Madame, est-ce qu'il n'est pas aussi à l'armée, mon homme à moi?*" with which she burst into tears, and Amelia falling into her arms did likewise, and so each pitied and soothed the other.

Several times during the forenoon Mr. Jos's Isidor went from his lodging into the town, and to the gates of the hotels and lodging-houses round about the Parc, where the English were congregated, and there mingled with other valets, couriers, and lackeys, gathered such news as was abroad, and brought back bulletins for his master's information. Almost all these gentlemen were in heart partisans of the Emperor, and had their opinions about the speedy end of the campaign.

Jos was, if not seriously alarmed as yet, at least considerably disturbed in mind. "Give me my coat and cap, sir," said he, "and follow me. I will go myself and learn the truth of these reports." Isidor was furious as Jos put on the braided frock. "Milor had better not wear that military coat," said he; "the Frenchman have sworn not to give quarter to a single British soldier."

"Silence, sirrah!" said Jos, with a resolute countenance still, and thrust his arm into the sleeve with indomitable resolution, in the performance of which heroic act he was found by Mrs. Rawdon Crawley, who at this juncture came up to visit Amelia, and entered without ringing at the antechamber door.

Rebecca was dressed very neatly and smartly as usual. Her quiet sleep after Rawdon's departure had refreshed her; and her pink, smiling cheeks were quite pleasant to look at, in a town and on a day when everybody else's countenance wore the appearance of the deepest anxiety and gloom. She laughed at the attitude in which Jos was discovered, and the struggles and convulsions with which the stout gentleman thrust himself into the braided coat.

Rebecca's appearance struck Amelia with terror, and made her shrink back. It recalled her to the world, and the remembrance of yesterday. In the overpowering fears about to-morrow she had forgotten Rebecca,—jealousy,—everything except that her husband was gone and was in danger. Until this dauntless worldling came in and broke the spell, and lifted the latch, we too have forborne to enter into that sad chamber. How long had that poor girl been on her knees! what hours of speechless prayer and bitter prostration had she passed there!

After the first movement of terror in Amelia's mind—when Rebecca's green eyes lighted upon her, and, rustling in her fresh silks and brilliant ornaments, the latter tripped up with extended arms to embrace her— a feeling of anger succeeded; and from being deadly pale before, her face flushed up red, and she returned Rebecca's look after a moment with a steadiness which surprised and somewhat abashed her rival.

"Dearest Amelia, you are very unwell," the visitor said, putting forth her hand to take Amelia's. "What is it? I could not rest until I knew how you were."

Amelia drew back her hand; never since her life began had that gentle soul refused to believe or to answer any demonstration of good-will or affection. But she drew back her hand, and trembled all over. "Why are *you* here, Rebecca?" she said, still looking at her solemnly with her large eyes. These glances troubled her visitor.

"She must have seen him give me the letter at the ball," Rebecca thought. "Don't be agitated, dear Amelia," she said, looking down. "I came but to see if I could—if you were well."

"Are you well?" said Amelia. "I daresay you are. You don't love your husband. You would not be here if you did. Tell me, Rebecca, did I ever do you anything but kindness?"

"Indeed, Amelia, no," the other said, still hanging down her head.

"When you were quite poor, who was it that befriended you? Was I not a sister to you? You saw us all in happier days before he married me. I was all in all then to him; or would he have given up his fortune, his family, as he nobly did, to make me happy? Why did you come between my love and me? Who sent you to separate those whom God joined, and take my darling's heart from me—my own husband? Do you think you could love him as I did? His love was everything to me. You knew it, and wanted to rob me of it. For shame, Rebecca! bad and wicked woman—false friend and false wife!"

"Amelia, I protest before God, I have done my husband no wrong," Rebecca said, turning from her.

"Have you done *me* no wrong, Rebecca? You did not succeed, but you tried. Ask your heart if you did not."

She knows nothing, Rebecca thought.

"He came back to me. I knew he would. I knew that no falsehood, no flattery, could keep him from me long. I knew he would come. I prayed so that he should." The poor girl spoke these words with a spirit and volubility which Rebecca had never before seen in her, and before which the latter was quite dumb. "But what have I done to you," she continued, in a more pitiful tone, "that you should try and take him from me? I had him but for six weeks. You might have spared me those, Rebecca. And yet, from the very first day of our wedding, you came and blighted it. Now he is gone, are you come to see how unhappy I am?" she continued. "You made me wretched enough for the past fortnight; you might have spared me to-day."

"I—I never came here," interposed Rebecca, with unlucky truth.

"No, you didn't come. You took him away. Are you come to fetch him from me?" she continued in a wilder tone. "He was here, but he is gone now. There, on that very sofa, he sate. Don't touch it. We sate and talked there. I was on his knee, and my arms were round his neck, and we said, 'Our Father.' Yes, he was here: and they came and took him away, but he promised me to come back."

"He will come back, my dear," said Rebecca, touched in spite of herself.

"Look," said Amelia, "this is his sash—isn't it a pretty colour?" and she took up the fringe and kissed it. She had tied it round her waist at some part of the day. She had forgotten her anger, her jealousy, the very presence of her rival seemingly. For she walked silently and almost with a smile on her face towards the bed, and began to smooth down George's pillow.

Rebecca walked, too, silently away. "How is Amelia?" asked Jos, who still held his position in the chair.

"There should be somebody with her," said Rebecca. "I think she is very unwell." And she went away with a very grave face, refusing Mr. Sedley's entreaties that she would stay and partake of the early dinner which he had ordered.

Rebecca was of a good-natured and obliging disposition; and she liked Amelia rather than otherwise. Even her hard words, reproachful as they were, were complimentary—the groans of a person stinging under defeat. Meeting Mrs. O'Dowd, whom the Dean's sermons had by no means comforted, and who was walking very disconsolately in the Parc, Rebecca accosted the latter, rather to the surprise of the Major's wife, who was not accustomed to such remarks of politeness from Mrs. Rawdon Crawley, and informing her that poor little Mrs. Osborne was in a desperate condition, and almost mad with grief, sent off the good-natured Irishwoman straight to see if she could console her young favourite.

"I've cares of my own enough," Mrs. O'Dowd said gravely, "and I thought poor Amelia would be little wanting for company this day. But if she's so bad as you say, and you can't attend to her, who used to be so fond of her, faith I'll see if I can be of service. And so good-marning to ye, Madam;" with which speech and a toss of her head, the lady of the repayther took a farewell of Mrs. Crawley, whose company she by no means courted.

Becky watched her marching off, with a smile on her lips. She had the keenest sense of humour, and the Parthian look which the retreating Mrs. O'Dowd flung over her shoulder almost upset Mrs. Crawley's gravity. "My service to ye, me fine Madam, and I'm glad to see ye so cheerful," thought Peggy. "It's not *you* that will cry your eyes out with grief, any way." And with this she passed on, and speedily found her way to Mrs. Osborne's lodgings.

The poor soul was still at the bedside, where Rebecca had left her, and stood almost crazy with grief. The Major's wife, a strong-minded woman, endeavoured her best to comfort her young friend. "You must bear up, Amelia dear," she said kindly, "for he mustn't find you ill when he sends for you after the victory. It's not you are the only woman that are in the hands of God this day."

"I know that. I am very wicked, very weak," Amelia said. She knew her own weakness well enough. The presence of the more resolute friend checked it, however; and she was the better of this control and company. They went on till two o'clock; their hearts were with the column as it marched further and further away. Dreadful doubt and anguish—prayers and fears and griefs unspeakable—followed the regiment. It was the women's tribute to the war. It taxes both alike, and takes the blood of the men, and the tears of the women.

At half-past two, an event occurred of daily importance to Mr. Joseph—the dinner-hour arrived. Warriors may fight and perish, but he must dine. He came into Amelia's room to see if he could coax her to share that meal. "Try," said he; "the soup is very good. Do try, Emmy," and he kissed her hand. Except when she was married, he had not done so much for years before. "You are very good and kind, Joseph," she said. "Everybody is, but, if you please, I will stay in my room to-day."

The savour of the soup, however, was agreeable to Mrs. O'Dowd's nostrils, and she thought she would bear Mr. Jos company. So the two sate down to their meal. "God bless the meat," said the Major's wife solemnly: she was thinking of her honest Mick, riding at the head of the regiment. " 'Tis but a bad dinner those poor boys will get to-day," she said, with a sigh, and then, like a philosopher, fell to.

Jos's spirit rose with his meal. He would drink the regiment's health; or, indeed, take any other excuse to indulge in a glass of champagne. "We'll drink to O'Dowd and the brave —th," said he, bowing gallantly to his guest. "Hey, Mrs. O'Dowd? Fill Mrs. O'Dowd's glass, Isidor."

But all of a sudden Isidor started, and the Major's wife laid down her knife and fork. The windows of the room were open and looked southward, and a dull distant sound came over the sun-lighted roofs from that direction. "What is it?" said Jos. "Why don't you pour, you rascal?"

"*C'est le feu!*" said Isidor, running to the balcony.

"God defend us; it's cannon!" Mrs. O'Dowd cried, starting up, and followed too to the window. A thousand pale and anxious faces might have been seen looking from other casements. And presently it seemed as if the whole population of the city rushed into the streets.

CHAPTER XXXII

IN WHICH JOS TAKES FLIGHT, AND THE WAR IS BROUGHT TO A CLOSE

WHEN the noise of the cannonading was over, Mrs. O'Dowd issued out of Amelia's room into the parlour adjoining, where Jos sate with two emptied flasks, and courage entirely gone. Once or twice he had ventured into his sister's bedroom, looking very much alarmed, and as if he would say something. But the Major's wife kept her place, and he went away without disburthening himself of his speech. He was ashamed to tell her that he wanted to fly. But when she made her appearance in the dining-room, where he sate in the twilight in the cheerless company of his empty champagne bottles, he began to open his mind to her.

"Mrs. O'Dowd," he said, "hadn't you better get Amelia ready?"

"Are you going to take her out for a walk?" said the Major's lady; "sure she's too weak to stir."

"I—I've ordered the carriage," he said, "and—and post-horses; Isidor is gone for them," Jos continued.

"What do you want with driving to-night?" answered the lady. "Isn't she better on her bed? I've just got her to lie down."

"Get her up," said Jos; "she must get up, I say;" and he stamped his foot energetically. "I say the horses are ordered—yes, the horses are ordered. It's all over and——"

"And what?" asked Mrs. O'Dowd.

"I'm off for Ghent," Jos answered. "Everybody is going; there's a place for you! We shall start in half an hour."

The Major's wife looked at him with infinite scorn. "I don't move till O'Dowd gives me the route," said she. "You may go if you like, Mr. Sedley; but, faith, Amelia and I stop here."

"She *shall* go," said Jos, with another stamp of his foot.

Mrs. O'Dowd put herself with arms akimbo before the bedroom door.

"Is it her mother you're going to take her to?" she said; "or do you want to go to Mamma yourself, Mr. Sedley? Good-marning—a pleasant journey to ye, sir. *Bon voyage*, as they say; and take my counsel, and shave off them mustachios, or they'll bring you into mischief."

"D——n!" yelled out Jos, wild with fear, rage, and mortification; and Isidor came in at this juncture, swearing in his turn. "*Pas de chevaux, sacrebleu!*" hissed out the furious domestic. All the horses were gone. Jos was not the only man in Brussels seized with panic that day.

But Jos's fears, great and cruel as they were already, were destined to increase to an almost frantic pitch before the night was over. Pauline the *bonne*, had *son homme à elle* also in the ranks of the army that had gone out to meet the Emperor Napoleon. This lover was a native of Brussels, and a Belgian hussar. The troops of his nation signalized themselves in this war for anything but courage, and young Van Cutsum, Pauline's admirer, was too good a soldier to disobey his colonel's orders to run away. Whilst in garrison at Brussels young Regulus (he had been born in the revolutionary times) found his great comfort, and passed almost all his leisure moments, in Pauline's kitchen; and it was with pockets and holsters crammed full of good things from her larder, that he had taken leave of his weeping sweetheart, to proceed upon the campaign, a few days before.

At some ten o'clock the clinking of a sabre might have been heard up the stair of the house where the Osbornes occupied a storey in the Continental fashion. A knock might have been heard at the kitchen door; and poor Pauline, come back from church, fainted almost with terror as she opened it and saw before her her haggard hussar. He looked as pale as the midnight dragoon who came to disturb Leonora. Pauline would have screamed, but that her cry would have called her masters, and discovered her friend. She stifled her scream, then, and leading her hero into the kitchen, gave him beer, and the choice bits from the dinner.

His regiment had performed prodigies of courage, and had withstood for a while the onset of the whole French army. But they were overwhelmed at last, as was the whole British army by this time. Ney destroyed each regiment as it came up. The Belgians in vain interposed to prevent the butchery of the English. The Brunswickers were routed and had fled—their Duke was killed. It was a general *débâcle*. He sought to drown his sorrow for the defeat in floods of beer.

Isidor, who had come into the kitchen, heard the conversation, and rushed out to inform his master. "It is all over!" he shrieked to Jos. "Milor Duke is a prisoner—the Duke of Brunswick is killed—the British army is in full flight; there is only one man escaped, and he is in the kitchen now—come and hear him." So Jos tottered into that apartment, where Regulus still sate on the kitchen table, and clung fast to his flagon of beer. In the best French which he could muster, and which was in sooth of a very ungrammatical sort, Jos besought the hussar to tell his tale. The disasters deepened as Regulus spoke. He was the only man of his regiment not slain on the field. He had seen the Duke of Brunswick fall, the black hussars fly, the Ecossais pounded down by the cannon.

"And the —th?" gasped Jos.

"Cut in pieces," said the hussar; upon which Pauline cried out, "O my mistress, *ma bonne petite dame*," went off fairly into hysterics and filled the house with her screams.

Wild with terror, Mr. Sedley knew not how or where to seek for safety. He rushed from the kitchen back to the sitting-room, and cast an appealing look at Amelia's door, which Mrs. O'Dowd had closed and locked in his face; but he remembered how scornfully the latter had received him, and after pausing and listening for a brief space at the door, he left it, and resolved to go into the street, for the first time that day. So, seizing a candle, he looked about for his gold-laced cap, and found it lying in its usual place, on a console-table, in the anteroom, placed before a mirror at which Jos used to coquet, always giving his side-locks a twirl, and his cap the proper cock over his eye, before he went forth to make appearance in public. Such is the force of habit, that even in the midst of his terror he began mechanically to twiddle with his hair, and arrange the cock of his hat. Then he looked amazed at the pale face in the glass before him, and especially at his mustachios, which had attained a rich growth in the course of near seven weeks, since they had come into the world. They *will* mistake me for a military man, thought he, remembering Isidor's warning as to the massacre with which all the defeated British army was threatened; and staggering back to his bed-chamber, he began wildly pulling the bell which summoned his valet.

Isidor answered that summons. Jos had sunk in a chair—he had torn off his neckcloths, and turned down his collars, and was sitting with both his hands lifted to his throat.

"*Coupez-moi*, Isidor," shouted he; "*vite! coupez-moi!*"

Isidor thought for a moment he had gone mad, and that he wished his valet to cut his throat.

"*Les moustaches*," gasped Jos; "*les moustaches—coupy, rasy, vite!*"—his French was of this sort—voluble, as we have said, but not remarkable for grammar.

Isidor swept off the mustachios in no time with the razor, and heard with inexpressible delight his master's orders that he should fetch a hat and a plain coat. "*Ne porty ploo—habit militair—bonny—bonny a voo, prenny dehors*"—were Jos's words: the coat and cap were at last his property.

This gift being made, Jos selected a plain black coat and waistcoat from his stock, and put on a large white neckcloth and a plain beaver. If he could have got a shovel-hat he would have worn it. As it was, you would have fancied he was a flourishing, large parson of the Church of England.

"*Venny maintenong*," he continued, "*sweevy—ally—party—dong la roo.*" And so having said, he plunged swiftly down the stairs of the house, and passed into the street.

Although Regulus had vowed that he was the only man of his regiment, or of the allied army, almost, who had escaped being cut to pieces by Ney, it appeared that his statement was incorrect, and that a good number more of the supposed victims had survived the massacre. Many scores of Regulus's comrades had found their way back to Brussels, and—all agreeing that they had run away—filled the whole town with an idea of the defeat of the allies. The arrival of the French was expected hourly; the panic continued, and preparations for flight went on everywhere. No horses! thought Jos, in terror.

Almost all the hotels occupied by the English in Brussels face the Parc, and Jos wandered irresolutely about in this quarter, with crowds of other people, oppressed as he was by fear and curiosity.

Rebecca Crawley occupied apartments in this hotel, and had before this period had sundry hostile meetings with the ladies of the Bareacres family. My Lady Bareacres cut Mrs. Crawley on the stairs when they met by chance; and in all places where the latter's name was mentioned, spoke perseveringly ill of her neighbour.

Rebecca had her revenge now upon these insolent enemies. It became known in the hotel that Captain Crawley's horses had been left behind; and when the panic began, Lady Bareacres condescended to send her maid to the Captain's wife with her Ladyship's compliments, and a desire to know the price of Mrs. Crawley's horses. Mrs. Crawley returned the note with her compliments, and an intimation that it was not her custom to transact bargains with ladies'-maids.

This curt reply brought the Earl in person to Becky's apartment;

but he could get no more success than the first ambassador. "Send a lady's-maid to *me*!" Mrs. Crawley cried in great anger, "why didn't my Lady Bareacres tell me to go and saddle the horses? Is it her Ladyship that wants to escape, or her Ladyship's *femme de chambre*?" And this was all the answer that the Earl bore back to his Countess.

What will not necessity do? The Countess herself actually came to wait upon Mrs. Crawley on the failure of her second envoy. She entreated her to name her own price; she even offered to invite Becky to Bareacres House, if the latter would but give her the means of returning to that residence. Mrs. Crawley sneered at her.

"I don't want to be waited on by bailiffs in livery," she said; "you will never get back though most probably—at least not you and your diamonds together. I would not sell you my horses, no, not for the two largest diamonds that your Ladyship wore at the ball." Lady Bareacres trembled with rage and terror. The diamonds were sewed into her habit, and secreted in my Lord's padding and boots. "Woman, the diamonds are at the banker's, and I *will* have the horses," she said. Rebecca laughed in her face. The infuriated Countess went below, and sat in her carriage; her maid, her courier, and her husband, were sent once more through the town, each to look for cattle: and woe betide those who came last! Her Ladyship was resolved on departing the very instant the horses arrived from any quarter—with her husband or without him.

Rebecca had the pleasure of seeing her Ladyship in the horseless carriage, and keeping her eyes fixed upon her, and bewailing, in the loudest tone of voice, the Countess's perplexities. "Not to be able to get horses!" she said, "and to have all those diamonds sewed into the carriage cushions! What a prize it will be for the French when they come!—the carriage and the diamonds, I mean; not the lady!" She gave this information to the landlord, to the servants, to the guests, and the innumerable stragglers about the courtyard. Lady Bareacres could have shot her from the carriage window. It was while enjoying the humiliation of her enemy that Rebecca caught sight of Jos, who made towards her directly he perceived her.

That altered, frightened, fat face told his secret well enough. He too wanted to fly, and was on the look-out for the means of escape. "*He* shall buy my horses," thought Rebecca, "and I'll ride the mare."

Jos walked up to his friend, and put the question for the hundredth time during the past hour, " Did she know where horses were to be had?"

"What, *you* fly?" said Rebecca with a laugh. "I thought you were the champion of all the ladies, Mr. Sedley."

"I—I'm not a military man," gasped he.

"And Amelia?—Who is to protect that poor little sister of yours?" asked Rebecca. "You surely would not desert her?"

"What good can I do her, suppose—suppose the enemy arrive?" Jos answered. "They'll spare the women; but my man tells me that they have taken an oath to give no quarter to the men—the dastardly cowards."

"Horrid!" cried Rebecca, enjoying his perplexity.

"Besides, I don't want to desert her," cried the brother. "She *shan't* be deserted. There is a seat for her in my carriage, and one for you, dear Mrs. Crawley, if you will come, and if we can get horses"— sighed he——

"I have two to sell," the lady said. Jos could have flung himself into her arms at the news. "Get the carriage, Isidor," he cried; "we've found them—we have found them!"

"My horses never were in harness," added the lady. "Bullfinch would kick the carriage to pieces, if you put him in the traces."

"But he is quiet to ride?" asked the civilian.

"As quiet as a lamb, and as fast as a hare," answered Rebecca.

"Do you think he is up to my weight?" Jos said. He was already on his back, in imagination, without ever so much as a thought for poor Amelia. What person who loved a horse-speculation could resist such a temptation?

In reply, Rebecca asked him to come into her room, whither he followed her quite breathless to conclude the bargain. Jos seldom spent a half-hour in his life which cost him so much money. Rebecca, measuring the value of the goods which she had for sale by Jos's eagerness to purchase as well as by the scarcity of the article, put upon her horses a price so prodigious as to make even the civilian draw back. "She would sell both, or neither," she said resolutely.

Jos ended by agreeing, as might be supposed of him. The sum he had to give her was so large that he was obliged to ask for time— so large as to be a little fortune to Rebecca, who rapidly calculated that with this sum and the sale of the residue of Rawdon's effects, and her pension as a widow should he fall, she would now be absolutely independent of the world, and might look her weeds steadily in the face.

Jos and Isidor went off to the stables to inspect the newly-purchased cattle. Jos bade his man saddle the horses at once. He would ride away that very night—that very hour. And he left the valet busy in getting the horses ready, and went homewards himself to prepare for his departure. It must be secret. He would go to his chamber by the back entrance. He did not care to face Mrs. O'Dowd and Amelia, and own to them that he was about to run.

By the time Jos's bargain with Rebecca was completed, and his horses had been visited and examined, it was almost morning once more. But though midnight was long past, there was no rest for the city: the people were up, the lights in the houses flamed, crowds were still about the doors, and the streets were busy. Rumours of various natures went still from mouth to mouth: one report averred that the Prussians had been utterly defeated; another that it was the English who had been attacked and conquered; a third that the latter had

held their ground. This last rumour gradually got strength. No
Frenchmen had made their appearance. Stragglers had come in from
the army bringing reports more and more favourable. At last an aide-
de-camp actually reached Brussels with dispatches for the Commandant of the place, who placarded presently through the town an official
announcement of the success of the allies at Quatre Bras, and the
entire repulse of the French under Ney after a six hours' battle. The
aide-de-camp must have arrived some time while Jos and Rebecca were
making their bargain together, or the latter was inspecting his purchase. When he reached his own hotel, he found a score of its numerous inhabitants on the threshold discoursing of the news; there was
no doubt as to its truth. And he went up to communicate it to the
ladies under his charge. He did not think it was necessary to tell
them how he had intended to take leave of them, how he had bought
horses, and what a price he had paid for them.

But success or defeat was a minor matter to them, who had only
thought for the satefy of those they loved. Amelia, at the news of
the victory, became still more agitated even than before. She was for
going that moment to the army. She besought her brother with tears
to conduct her thither. Her doubts and terrors reached their paroxysm;
and the poor girl, who for many hours had been plunged into stupor,
raved and ran hither and thither in hysteric insanity—a piteous sight.
No man writhing in pain on the hard-fought field fifteen miles off,
where lay, after their struggles, so many of the brave—no man suffered
more keenly than this poor harmless victim of the war. Jos could not
bear the sight of her pain. He left his sister in the charge of her stouter
female companion, and descended once more to the threshold of the
hotel, where everybody still lingered, and talked, and waited for more
news.

It grew to be broad daylight as they stood here, and fresh news
began to arrive from the war, brought by men who had been actors
in the scene. Wagons and long country carts laden with wounded came
rolling into the town: ghastly groans came from within them, and
haggard faces looked up sadly from out of the straw. Jos Sedley was
looking at one of these carriages with a painful curiosity. The moans
of the people within were frightful; the wearied horses could hardly
pull the cart. "Stop! Stop!" a feeble voice cried from the straw, and
the carriage stopped opposite Mr. Sedley's hotel.

"It is George! I know it is!" cried Amelia, rushing in a moment
to the balcony, with a pallid face and loose flowing hair. It was not
George, however, but it was the next best thing—it was news of him.
It was poor Tom Stubble, who had marched out of Brussels so gallantly
twenty-four hours before, bearing the colours of the regiment, which
he had defended very gallantly upon the field. A French lancer had
speared the young Ensign in the leg, who fell, still bravely holding to
his flag. At the conclusion of the engagement, a place had been found
for the poor boy in a cart, and he had been brought back to Brussels.

"Mr. Sedley, Mr. Sedley!" cried the boy faintly, and Jos came up almost frightened at the appeal. He had not at first distinguished who it was that called him.

Little Tom Stubble held out his hot and feeble hand. "I'm to be taken in here," he said. "Osborne—and—and Dobbin said I was; and you are to give the man two napoleons; my mother will pay you." This young fellow's thoughts during the long feverish hours passed in the cart, had been wandering to his father's parsonage which he had quitted only a few months before, and he had sometimes forgotten his pain in that delirium.

The hotel was large, and the people kind, and all the inmates of the cart were taken in and placed on various couches. The young Ensign was conveyed upstairs to Osborne's quarters. Amelia and the Major's wife had rushed down to him, when the latter had recognized him from the balcony. You may fancy the feelings of these women when they were told that the day was over, and both their husbands were safe; in what mute rapture Amelia fell on her good friend's neck, and embraced her; in what a grateful passion of prayer she fell on her knees, and thanked the Power which had saved her husband.

Our young lady, in her fevered and nervous condition, could have had no more salutary medicine prescribed for her by any physician than that which chance put in her way. She and Mrs. O'Dowd watched incessantly by the wounded lad, whose pains were very severe; and in the duty thus forced upon her, Amelia had no time to brood over her personal anxieties, or to give herself up to her own fears and forebodings after her wont. The young patient told in his simple fashion the events of the day, and the actions of our friends of the gallant —th. They had suffered severely. They had lost very many officers and men. The Major's horse had been shot under him as the regiment charged, and they all thought that O'Dowd was gone, and that Dobbin had got his majority, until, on their return from the charge to their own ground, the Major was discovered seated on Pyramus's carcass, refreshing himself from a case-bottle. It was Captain Osborne that cut down the French lancer who had speared the Ensign. Amelia turned so pale at the notion, that Mrs. O'Dowd stopped the young Ensign in his story. And it was Captain Dobbin who, at the end of the day, though wounded himself, took up the lad in his arms and carried him to the surgeon, and thence to the cart which was to bring him back to Brussels. And it was he who promised the driver two louis if he would make his way to Mr. Sedley's hotel in the city, and tell Mrs. Captain Osborne that the action was over, and that her husband was unhurt and well.

"Indeed, but he has a good heart that William Dobbin," Mrs. O'Dowd said, "though he is always laughing at me."

When Jos, on the afternoon of the 17th of June, went to Rebecca's hotel, he found that the great Bareacres carriage had at length rolled away from the *porte cochère*. The Earl had produced a pair of horses

somehow, in spite of Mrs. Crawley, and was rolling on the road to
Ghent. Louis the Desired was getting ready his portmanteau in that
city too. It seemed as if Misfortune was never tired of worrying into
motion that unwieldy exile.

Jos felt that the delay of yesterday had been only a respite, and that
his dearly-bought horses must of a surety be put into requisition. His
agonies were very severe all this day. As long as there was an English
army between Brussels and Napoleon, there was no need of immediate
flight; but he had his horses brought from their distant stables to the
stables in the courtyard of the hotel where he lived, so that they might
be under his own eyes, and beyond the risk of violent abduction. Isidor
watched the stable-door constantly, and had the horses saddled, to be
ready for the start. He longed intensely for that event.

After the reception of the previous day, Rebecca did not care to
come near her dear Amelia. She clipped the bouquet which George
had brought her, and gave fresh water to the flowers, and read over
the letter which he had sent her. "Poor wretch," she said, twirling
round the little bit of paper in her fingers, "how I could crush her with
this!—And it is for a thing like this that she must break her heart,
forsooth—for a man who is stupid—a coxcomb—and who does not
care for her! My poor good Rawdon is worth ten of this creature."
And then she fell to thinking what she should do if—if anything
happened to poor good Rawdon, and what a great piece of luck it was
that he had left his horses behind.

In the course of this day too, Mrs. Crawley, who saw not without
anger the Bareacres party drive off, bethought her of the precaution
which the Countess had taken, and did a little needlework for her own
advantage. She stitched away the major part of her trinkets, bills,
and bank-notes about her person; and so prepared, was ready for any
event—to fly if she thought fit, or to stay and welcome the conqueror,
were he Englishman or Frenchman.

The next day was a Sunday. And Mrs. Major O'Dowd had the satisfaction of seeing both her patients refreshed in health and spirits by
some rest which they had taken during the night. She herself had
slept in a great chair in Amelia's room, ready to wait upon her poor
friend or the Ensign, should either need her nursing. When morning
came, this robust woman went back to the house where she and her
Major had their billet, and here performed an elaborate and splendid
toilette befitting the day. And it is very possible that whilst alone in
that chamber, which her husband had inhabited, and where his cap
still lay on the pillow, and his cane stood in the corner, one prayer at
least was sent up to Heaven for the welfare of the brave soldier, Michael
O'Dowd.

When she returned she brought her prayer-book with her, and her
uncle the Dean's famous book or sermons, out of which she never failed
to read every Sabbath; not understanding all, haply, not pronouncing
many of the words aright, which were long and abstruse—for the Dean

was a learned man, and loved long Latin words—but with great gravity, vast emphasis, and with tolerable correctness in the main. How often has my Mick listened to these sermons, she thought, and me reading in the cabin of a calm! She proposed to resume this exercise on the present day, with Amelia and the wounded Ensign for a congregation. The same service was read on that day in twenty thousand churches at the same hour; and millions of British men and women, on their knees, implored protection of the Father of all.

They did not hear the noise which disturbed our little congregation at Brussels. Much louder than that which had interrupted them two days previously, as Mrs. O'Dowd was reading the service in her best voice, the cannon of Waterloo began to roar.

When Jos heard that dreadful sound, he made up his mind that he would bear this perpetual recurrence of terrors no longer, and would fly at once. He rushed into the sick man's room, where our three friends had paused in their prayers, and further interrupted them by a passionate appeal to Amelia.

"I can't stand it any more, Emmy," he said; "I won't stand it; and you must come with me. I have bought a horse for you—never mind at what price—and you must dress and come with me, and ride behind Isidor."

"God forgive me, Mr. Sedley! but you are no better than a coward," Mrs. O'Dowd said, laying down the book.

"I say come, Amelia," the civilian went on; "never mind what she says. Why are we to stop here and be butchered by the Frenchmen?"

"You forget the —th, my boy," said the little Stubble, the wounded hero, from his bed—"and—and you won't leave me, will you, Mrs. O'Dowd?"

"No, my dear fellow," said she, going up and kissing the boy. "No harm shall come to you while I stand by. I don't budge till I get word from Mick. A pretty figure I'd be, wouldn't I, stuck behind that chap on a pillion?"

This image caused the young patient to burst out laughing in his bed, and even made Amelia smile. "I don't ask her," Jos shouted out—"I don't ask that—that Irishwoman, but you, Amelia; once for all, will you come?"

"Without my husband, Joseph?" Amelia said, with a look of wonder, and gave her hand to the Major's wife. Jos's patience was exhausted.

"Good-bye, then," he said, shaking his fist in a rage, and slamming the door by which he retreated. And this time he really gave his order for march, and mounted in the courtyard. Mrs. O'Dowd heard the clattering hoofs of the horses as they issued from the gate; and looking on, made many scornful remarks on poor Joseph as he rode down the street with Isidor after him in the laced cap.

All that day, from morning until past sunset, the cannon never ceased to roar. It was dark when the cannonading stopped all of a sudden.

E

All of us have read of what occurred during that interval.

All our friends took their share and fought like men in the great field. All day long, whilst the women were praying ten miles away, the lines of the dauntless English infantry were receiving and repelling the furious charges of the French horsemen. Guns which were heard at Brussels were ploughing up their ranks, and comrades falling, and the resolute survivors closing in. Towards evening, the attack of the French, repeated and resisted so bravely, slackened in its fury. They had other foes besides the British to engage, or were preparing for a final onset. It came at last: the columns of the Imperial Guard marched up the hill of Saint Jean, at length and at once to sweep the English from the height which they had maintained all day, and spite of all. Unscared by the thunder of the artillery, which hurled death from the English line, the dark rolling column pressed on and up the hill. It seemed almost to crest the eminence, when it began to wave and falter. Then it stopped, still facing the shot. Then at last the English troops rushed from the post from which no enemy had been able to dislodge them, and the Guard turned and fled.

No more firing was heard at Brussels—the pursuit rolled miles away. Darkness came down on the field and city; and Amelia was praying for George, who was lying on his face, dead, with a bullet through his heart.

CHAPTER XXXIII

IN WHICH MISS CRAWLEY'S RELATIONS ARE VERY ANXIOUS ABOUT HER

THE kind reader must please to remember—while the army is marching from Flanders, and, after its heroic actions there, is advancing to take the fortifications on the frontiers of France, previous to an occupation of that country—that there are a number of persons living peaceably in England who have to do with the history at present in hand, and must come in for their share of the chronicle. During the time of these battles and dangers old Miss Crawley was living at Brighton, very moderately moved by the great events that were going on. The great events rendered the newspapers rather interesting, to be sure; and Briggs read out the Gazette, in which Rawdon Crawley's gallantry was mentioned with honour, and his promotion was presently recorded.

"What a pity that young man has taken such an irretrievable step in the world!" his aunt said. "With his rank and distinction he might have married a brewer's daughter with a quarter of a million—like Miss Grains—or have looked to ally himself with the best families in England. He would have had my money some day or other, or his children would—for I'm not in a hurry to go, Miss Briggs, although you may be in a hurry to be rid of me; and instead of that, he is a doomed pauper, with a dancing-girl for a wife."

Whatever individual differences there might be between them all,

Miss Crawley's dear nephews and nieces were unanimous in loving her and sending her tokens of affection. Thus Mrs. Bute sent guinea-fowls, and some remarkably fine cauliflowers, and a pretty purse or pincushion worked by her darling girls, who begged to keep a *little* place in the recollection of their dear aunt, while Mr. Pitt sent peaches and grapes and venison from the Hall. The Southampton coach used to carry these tokens of affection to Miss Crawley at Brighton; it used sometimes to convey Mr. Pitt thither too, for his differences with Sir Pitt caused Mr. Crawley to absent himself a good deal from home now; and besides, he had an attraction at Brighton in the person of Lady Jane Sheepshanks, whose engagement to Mr. Crawley has been formerly mentioned in this history. Her Ladyship and her sisters lived at Brighton with their mamma, the Countess Southdown, that strong-minded woman so favourably known in the serious world.

CHAPTER XXXIV

PITT CRAWLEY'S VISIT

The amiable behaviour of Mr. Crawley, and Lady Jane's kind reception of her, highly flattered Miss Briggs, who was enabled to speak a good word for the latter after the cards of the Southdown family had been presented to Miss Crawley.

As she got well Miss Crawley was pining for society. Mr. Creamer, her medical man, would not hear of her returning to her old haunts and dissipation in London. The old spinster was too glad to find any companionship at Brighton, and not only were the cards acknowledged the very next day, but Pitt Crawley was graciously invited to come and see his aunt. He came, bringing with him Lady Southdown and her daughter. The dowager did not say a word about the state of Miss Crawley's soul, but talked with much discretion about the weather, about the war and the downfall of the monster Bonaparte, and above all, about doctors, quacks, and the particular merits of Dr. Podgers, whom she then patronized.

"Don't let Lady Southdown come again, Pitt," said the old lady. "She is stupid and pompous, like all your mother's family, whom I never could endure. But bring that nice good-natured little Jane as often as ever you please." Pitt promised that he would do so. He did not tell the Countess of Southdown what opinion his aunt had formed of her Ladyship, who, on the contrary, thought that she had made a most delightful and majestic impression on Miss Crawley.

And so, nothing loth to comfort a sick lady, and perhaps not sorry in her heart to be freed now and again from the dreary spouting of the Reverend Bartholomew Irons, and the serious toadies who gathered round the footstool of the pompous Countess, her mamma, Lady Jane became a pretty constant visitor to Miss Crawley, accompanied her in her drives, and solaced many of her evenings.

In the autumn evenings (when Rebecca was flaunting in Paris, the gayest among the gay conquerors there, and our Amelia, our dear wounded Amelia, ah! where was she?) Lady Jane would be sitting in Miss Crawley's drawing-room, singing sweetly to her, in the twilight, her little simple songs and hymns, while the sun was setting, and the sea was roaring on the beach. The old spinster used to wake up when these ditties ceased, and ask for more. As for Briggs, and the quantity of tears of happiness which she now shed as she pretended to knit, and looked out at the splendid ocean darkling before the windows, and the lamps of heaven beginning more brightly to shine—who, I say, can measure the happiness and sensibility of Briggs?

Pitt meanwhile in the dining-room, with a pamphlet on the Corn Laws or a Missionary Register by his side, took that kind of recreation which suits romantic and unromantic men after dinner. He sipped Madeira, built castles in the air, thought himself a fine fellow, felt himself much more in love with Jane than he had been any time these seven years, during which their *liaison* had lasted without the slightest impatience on Pitt's part—and slept a good deal. When the time for coffee came, Mrs. Bowls used to enter in a noisy manner, and summon Squire Pitt, who would be found in the dark very busy with his pamphlet.

Where meanwhile was he who had been once first favourite for the race for money? Becky and Rawdon, as we have seen, were come together after Waterloo, and were passing the winter of 1815 at Paris in great splendour and gaiety. Rebecca was a good economist, and the price poor Jos Sedley had paid for her two horses was in itself sufficient to keep their little establishment afloat for a year at the least; there was no occasion to turn into money "my pistols, the same which I shot Captain Marker," or the gold dressing-case, or the cloak lined with sable. Becky had it made into a pelisse for herself, in which she rode in the Bois de Boulogne to the admiration of all; and you should have seen the scene between her and her delighted husband, whom she rejoined after the army had entered Cambray, and when she unsewed herself, and let out of her dress all those watches, nicknacks, banknotes, cheques, and valuables which she had secreted in the wadding previous to her meditated flight from Brussels! Tufto was charmed, and Rawdon roared with delightful laughter, and swore that she was better than any play he ever saw, by Jove. And in the way in which she jockeyed Jos, and which she described with infinite fun, carried up his delight to a pitch of quite insane enthusiasm. He believed in his wife as much as the French soldiers in Napoleon.

Her success in Paris was remarkable. All the French ladies voted her charming. She spoke their language admirably. She adopted at once their grace, their liveliness, their manner. Her husband was stupid certainly—all English are stupid—and, besides, a dull husband at Paris is always a point in a lady's favour.

So in *fêtes*, pleasures, and prosperity the winter of 1815–16 passed away with Mrs. Rawdon Crawley, who accommodated herself to polite life as if her ancestors had been people of fashion for centuries past, and who, from her wit, talent, and energy, indeed merited a place of honour in Vanity Fair. In the early spring of 1816, *Galignani's Journal* contained the following announcement in an interesting corner of the paper: "On the 26th of March, the Lady of Lieutenant-Colonel Crawley, of the Life Guards Green, of a son and heir."

This event was copied into the London papers, out of which Miss Briggs read the statement to Miss Crawley, at breakfast, at Brighton. The intelligence, expected as it might have been, caused a crisis in the affairs of the Crawley family. The spinster's rage rose to its height, and sending instantly for Pitt her nephew, and for the Lady Southdown from Brunswick Square, she requested an immediate celebration of the marriage which had been so long pending between the two families. And she announced that it was her intention to allow the young couple a thousand a year during her lifetime, at the expiration of which the bulk of her property would be settled upon her nephew and her dear niece Lady Jane Crawley. Waxy came down to ratify the deeds. Lord Southdown gave away his sister. She was married by a Bishop.

When they were married, Pitt would have liked to take a hymeneal tour with his bride, as became people of their condition. But the affection of the old lady towards Lady Jane had grown so strong that she fairly owned she could not part with her favourite. Pitt and his wife came therefore and lived with Miss Crawley, and (greatly to the annoyance of poor Pitt, who conceived himself a most injured character —being subject to the humours of his aunt on one side, and of his mother-in-law on the other) Lady Southdown, from her neighbouring house, reigned over the whole family—Pitt, Lady Jane, Miss Crawley, Briggs, Bowls, Firkin, and all. She pitilessly dosed them with her tracts and her medicine, she dismissed Creamer, she installed Rodgers, and soon stripped Miss Crawley of even the semblance of authority. The poor soul grew so timid that she actually left off bullying Briggs any more, and clung to her niece, more fond and terrified every day. Peace to thee, kind and selfish, vain and generous old heathen! We shall see thee no more. Let us hope that Lady Jane supported her kindly, and led her with gentle hand out of the busy struggle of Vanity Fair.

CHAPTER XXXV

WIDOW AND MOTHER

THE news of the great fights of Quatre Bras and Waterloo reached England at the same time. The Gazette first published the result of the two battles; at which glorious intelligence all England thrilled with triumph and fear. Particulars then followed, and after the announcement of the victories came the list of the wounded and the slain.

The news which that famous Gazette brought to the Osbornes gave a dreadful shock to the family and its chief. The girls indulged un-restrained in their grief. The gloom-stricken old father was still more borne down by his fate and sorrow. He strove to think that a judgment was on the boy for his disobedience. He dared not own that the severity of the sentence frightened him, and that its fulfilment had come too soon upon his curses. Sometimes a shuddering terror struck him, as if he had been the author of the doom which he had called down on his son. There was a chance before of reconciliation. The boy's wife might have died, or he might have come back and said, Father, I have sinned. But there was no hope now. He stood on the other side of the gulf impassable, haunting his parent with sad eyes.

Whatever his sensations might have been, however, the stern old man would have no confidant. He never mentioned his son's name to his daughters, but ordered the elder to place all the females of the establishment in mourning, and desired that the male servants should be similarly attired in deep black. All parties and entertainments, of course, were to be put off. No communications were made to his future son-in-law, whose marriage-day had been fixed; but there was enough in Mr. Osborne's appearance to prevent Mr. Bullock from making any inquiries or in any way pressing forward that ceremony. He and the ladies whispered about it under their voices in the drawing-room some-times, whither the father never came. He remained constantly in his own study; the whole front part of the house being closed until some time after the completion of the general mourning.

About three weeks after the 18th of June, Mr. Osborne's acquaintance, Sir William Dobbin, called at Mr. Osborne's house in Russell Square, with a very pale and agitated face, and insisted upon seeing that gentleman. Ushered into his room, and after a few words which neither the speaker nor the host understood, the former produced from an enclosure a letter sealed with a large red seal. "My son, Major Dobbin," the Alderman said, with some hesitation, "dispatched me a letter by an officer of the —th, who arrived in town to-day. My son's letter contains one for you, Osborne." The Alderman placed the letter on the table, and Osborne stared at him for a moment or two in silence. His looks frightened the ambassador, who, after looking guiltily for a little time at the grief-stricken man, hurried away without another word.

The letter was in George's well-known bold handwriting. It was that one which he had written before daybreak on the 16th of June, and just before he took leave of Amelia. The great red seal was emblazoned with the sham coat of arms which Osborne had assumed from the Peerage, with "Pax in bello" for a motto—that of the ducal house with which the vain old man tried to fancy himself connected. The hand that signed it would never hold pen or sword more. The very seal that sealed it had been robbed from George's dead body as it lay on the field of battle. The father knew nothing of this, but sat and looked at the letter in a terrified vacancy. He almost fell when he went to open it.

Have you ever had a difference with a dear friend? How his letters, written in the period of love and confidence, sicken and rebuke you! What a dreary mourning it is to dwell upon these vehement protests of dead affection! What lying epitaphs they make over the corpse of Love! What dark, cruel comments upon Life and Vanities! Most of us have got or written drawers full of them. They are closet-skeletons which we keep and shun. Osborne trembled long before the letter from his dead son.

The poor boy's letter did not say much. He had been too proud to acknowledge the tenderness which his heart felt. He only said that on the eve of a great battle he wished to bid his father farewell, and solemnly to implore his good offices for the wife—it might be for the child—whom he left behind him. He owned with contrition that his irregularities and extravagance had already wasted a large part of his mother's little fortune. He thanked his father for his former generous conduct, and promised him that, if he fell on the field or survived it, he would act in a manner worthy of the name of George Osborne.

His English habit, pride, awkwardness perhaps, had prevented him from saying more. His father could not see the kiss George had placed on the superscription of his letter. Mr. Osborne dropped it with the bitterest, deadliest pang of balked affection and revenge. His son was still beloved and unforgiven.

About two months afterwards, however, as the young ladies of the family went to church with their father, they remarked how he took a different seat from that which he usually occupied when he chose to attend divine worship, and that from his cushion opposite he looked up at the wall over their heads. This caused the young women likewise to gaze in the direction towards which their father's gloomy eyes pointed; and they saw an elaborate monument upon the wall, where Britannia was represented weeping over an urn, and a broken sword and a couchant lion indicated that the piece of sculpture had been erected in honour of a deceased warrior.

Under the memorial in question was emblazoned the well-known and pompous Osborne arms, and the inscription said that the monument was "Sacred to the Memory of George Osborne, Junior, Esq., late a Captain in His Majesty's —th regiment of foot, who fell on the 18th of June, 1815, aged 28 years, while fighting for his king and country in the glorious victory of Waterloo. *Dulce et decorum est pro patriâ mori.*"

If the sisters had any anxiety regarding the possible recognition of Amelia as a daughter of the family, it was increased presently, and towards the end of the autumn, by their father's announcement that he was going abroad. He did not say whither, but they knew at once that his steps would be turned towards Belgium, and were aware that George's widow was still in Brussels. They had pretty accurate news indeed of poor Amelia from Lady Dobbin and her daughters. Our honest Captain had been promoted in consequence of the death of the second Major of the regiment on the field; and the brave O'Dowd, who had distinguished himself greatly here, as upon all occasions where he had a chance to show his coolness and valour, was a Colonel and Companion of the Bath.

Very many of the brave —th, who had suffered severely upon both days of action, were still at Brussels in the autumn recovering of their wounds. The city was a vast military hospital for months after the great battles; and as men and officers began to rally from their hurts, the gardens and places of public resort swarmed with maimed warriors, old and young, who, just rescued out of death, fell to gambling, and gaiety, and love-making, as people of Vanity Fair will do. Mr. Osborne found out some of the —th easily. He knew their uniform quite well, and had been used to follow all the promotions and exchanges in the regiment, and loved to talk about it and its officers as if he had been one of the number. On the day after his arrival at Brussels, and as he issued from his hotel, which faced the Parc, he saw a soldier in the well-known facings, reposing on a stone bench in the garden, and went and sate down trembling by the wounded convalescent man.

"Were you in Captain Osborne's company?" he said, and added, after a pause, "He was my son, sir."

The man was not of the Captain's company, but he lifted up his wounded arm and touched his cap sadly and respectfully to the haggard, broken-spirited gentleman who questioned him. "The whole army didn't contain a finer or a better officer," the soldier said. "The Sergeant of the Captain's company (Captain Raymond had it now) was in town, though, and was just well of a shot in the shoulder. His honour might see him if he liked, who could tell him anything he wanted to know about—about the —th's actions. But his honour had seen Major Dobbin, no doubt, the brave Captain's great friend; and Mrs. Osborne, who was here, too, and had been very bad, he heard everybody say. They say she was out of her mind like for six weeks or more. But your honour knows all about that—and asking your pardon——" the man added.

Osborne put a guinea into the soldier's hand, and told him he should have another if he would bring the Sergeant to the Hôtel du Parc; a promise which very soon brought the desired officer to Mr. Osborne's presence. And the first soldier went away; and after telling a comrade or two how Captain Osborne's father was arrived, and what a free-handed, generous gentleman he was, they went and made good cheer with drink and feasting, as long as the guineas lasted which had come from the proud purse of the mourning old father.

In the Sergeant's company, who was also just convalescent, Osborne made the journey of Waterloo and Quatre Bras—a journey which thousands of his countrymen were then taking. He took the Sergeant with him in his carriage, and went through both fields under his guidance. He saw the point of the road where the regiment marched into action on the sixteenth, and the slope down which they drove the French cavalry who were pressing on the retreating Belgians. There was the spot where the noble Captain cut down the French officer who was grappling with the young Ensign for the colours, the Colour-Sergeants having been shot down. Along this road they retreated on the next day, and here was the bank at which the regiment bivouacked under the rain of the night of the seventeenth. Farther on was the position which they took and held during the day, forming time after time to receive the charge of the enemy's horsemen, and lying down under the shelter of the bank from the furious French cannonade. And it was at this declivity, when at evening the whole English line received the order to advance as the enemy fell back after his last charge, that the Captain, hurrahing and rushing down the hill waving his sword, received a shot and fell dead. "It was Major Dobbin who took back the Captain's body to Brussels," the Sergeant said, in a low voice, "and had him buried, as your honour knows." The peasants and relic-hunters about the place were screaming round the pair as the soldier told his story, offering for sale all sorts of mementoes of the fight—crosses, and epaulets, and shattered cuirasses, and eagles.

Osborne gave a sumptuous reward to the Sergeant when he parted with him, after having visited the scenes of his son's last exploits. His burial-place he had already seen. Indeed, he had driven thither immediately after his arrival at Brussels. George's body lay in the pretty burial-ground of Laeken, near the city, in which place, having once visited it on a party of pleasure, he had lightly expressed a wish to have his own grave made. And there the young officer was laid by his friend, in the unconsecrated corner of the garden, separated by a little hedge from the temples and towers and plantations of flowers and shrubs under which the Roman Catholic dead repose.

As, after the drive to Waterloo, Mr. Osborne's carriage was nearing the gates of the city at sunset, they met another open barouche, in which were a couple of ladies and a gentleman, and by the side of which an officer was riding. Osborne gave a start back, and the Sergeant, seated with him, cast a look of surprise at his neighbour as he touched his cap to the officer, who mechanically returned his salute. It was Amelia, with the lame young Ensign by her side, and opposite to her her faithful friend Mrs. O'Dowd. It was Amelia, but how changed from the fresh and comely girl Osborne knew! Her face was white and thin. Her pretty brown hair was parted under a widow's cap—the poor child. Her eyes were fixed, and looked nowhere. They stared blank in the face of Osborne as the carriages crossed each other, but she did not know him, nor did he recognize her, until, looking up, he saw Dobbin riding by her, and then he knew who it was. He hated her. He did not know how much until he saw her there. When her carriage had passed on, he turned and stared at the Sergeant, with a curse and defiance in his eye cast at his companion, who could not help looking at him—as much as to say, "How dare *you* look at me? Damn you! I *do* hate her. It is she who has tumbled my hopes and all my pride down." "Tell the scoundrel to drive on quick," he shouted, with an oath, to the lackey on the box. A minute afterwards a horse came clattering over the pavement behind Osborne's carriage, and Dobbin rode up. His thoughts had been elsewhere as the carriages passed each other, and it was not until he had ridden some paces forward that he remembered it was Osborne who had just passed him. Then he turned to examine if the sight of her father-in-law had made any impression on Amelia; but the poor girl did not know who had passed. Then William, who daily used to accompany her on her drives, taking out his watch, made some excuse about an engagement which he suddenly recollected, and so rode off. She did not remark that either, but sate looking before her, over the homely landscape towards the woods in the distance by which George had marched away.

"Mr. Osborne, Mr. Osborne!" cried Dobbin, as he rode up and held out his hand. Osborne made no motion to take it, but shouted out once more, and with another curse, to his servant to drive on.

Dobbin laid his hand on the carriage side. "I will see you, sir," he said. "I have a message for you."

"From that woman?" said Osborne fiercely.

"No," replied the other, "from your son;" at which Osborne fell back into the corner of his carriage, and Dobbin allowing it to pass on, rode close behind it, and so through the town until they reached Mr. Osborne's hotel, and without a word. There he followed Osborne up to his apartments. George had often been in the rooms; they were the lodgings which the Crawleys had occupied during their stay in Brussels.

"Pray, have you any commands for me, Captain Dobbin? or, I beg your pardon, I should say *Major* Dobbin, since better men than you are dead, and you step into their *shoes*," said Mr. Osborne, in that sarcastic tone which he sometimes was pleased to assume.

"Better men *are* dead," Dobbin replied. "I want to speak to you about one."

"Make it short, sir," said the other with an oath, scowling at his visitor.

"I am here as his closest friend," the Major resumed, "and the executor of his will. He made it before he went into action. Are you aware how small his means are, and of the straitened circumstances of his widow?"

"I don't know his widow, sir," Osborne said. "Let her go back to her father." But the gentleman whom he addressed was determined to remain in good temper, and went on without heeding the interruption.

"Do you know, sir, Mrs. Osborne's condition? Her life and her reason almost have been shaken by the blow which has fallen on her. It is very doubtful whether she will rally. There is a chance left for her, however, and it is about this I came to speak to you. She will be a mother soon. Will you visit the parent's offence upon the child's head? or will you forgive the child for poor George's sake?"

Osborne broke out into a rhapsody of self-praise and imprecations—

by the first, excusing himself to his own conscience for his conduct; by the second, exaggerating the undutifulness of George. No father in all England could have behaved more generously to a son who had rebelled against him wickedly. He had died without even so much as confessing he was wrong. Let him take the consequences of his undutifulness and folly. As for himself, Mr. Osborne, he was a man of his word. He had sworn never to speak to that woman, or to recognize her as his son's wife. "And that's what you may tell her," he concluded, with an oath; "and that's what I will stick to to the last day of my life."

There was no hope from that quarter then. The widow must live on her slender pittance, or on such aid as Jos could give her. "I might tell her, and she would not heed it," thought Dobbin sadly; for the poor girl's thoughts were not here at all since her catastrophe, and, stupefied under the pressure of her sorrow, good and evil were alike indifferent to her.

So, indeed, were even friendship and kindness. She received them both uncomplainingly, and having accepted them, relapsed into her grief.

Suppose some twelve months after the above conversation took place to have passed in the life of our poor Amelia. She has spent the first portion of that time in a sorrow so profound and pitiable that we who have been watching and describing some of the emotions of that weak and tender heart must draw back in the presence of the cruel grief under which it is bleeding. Tread silently round the hapless couch of the poor prostrate soul. Shut gently the door of the dark chamber wherein she suffers, as those kind people did who nursed her through the first months of her pain, and never left her until Heaven had sent her consolation. A day came, of almost terrified delight and wonder, when the poor widowed girl pressed a child upon her breast—a child, with the eyes of George who was gone—a little boy, as beautiful as a cherub. What a miracle it was to hear its first cry! How she laughed and wept over it! how love, and hope, and prayer woke again in her bosom as the baby nestled there! She was safe.

It was our friend Dobbin who brought her back to England and to her mother's house, where Mrs. O'Dowd, receiving a peremptory summons from her Colonel, had been forced to quit her patient. To see Dobbin holding the infant, and to hear Amelia's laugh of triumph as she watched him, would have done any man good who had a sense of humour. William was the godfather of the child, and exerted his ingenuity in the purchase of cups, spoons, papboats, and corals for this little Christian.

How his mother nursed him, and dressed him, and lived upon him; how she drove away all nurses, and would scarce allow any hand but her own to touch him; how she considered that the greatest favour she could confer upon his godfather, Major Dobbin, was to allow the Major occasionally to dandle him, need not be told here. This child was her being. Her existence was a maternal caress.

I suppose Amelia's father and mother saw through the intentions of the Major, and were not ill-disposed to encourage him; for Dobbin visited their house daily, and stayed for hours with them, or with Amelia, or with the honest landlord, Mr. Clapp. and his family. He brought, on one pretext or another, presents to everybody, and almost every day; and went, with the landlord's little girl, who was rather a favourite with Amelia, by the name of Major Sugarplums. It was this little child who commonly acted as mistress of the ceremonies to introduce him to Mrs. Osborne. She laughed one day when Major Sugarplums' cab drove up to Fulham, and he descended from it, bringing out a wooden horse, a drum, a trumpet, and other warlike toys, for little Georgy, who was scarcely six months old, and for whom the articles in question were entirely premature.

The child was asleep. "Hush!" said Amelia, annoyed perhaps at the creaking of the Major's boots; and she held out her hand, smiling because William could not take it until he had rid himself of his cargo of toys. "Go downstairs, little Mary," said he presently to the child; "I want to speak to Mrs. Osborne." She looked up rather astonished, and laid down the infant on its bed.

"I am come to say good-bye, Amelia," said he, taking her slender little white hand gently.

"Good-bye? and where are you going?" she said, with a smile.

"Send the letters to the agents," he said—"they will forward them; for you will write to me, won't you? I shall be away a long time."

"I'll write to you about Georgy," she said. "Dear William, how good you have been to him and to me! Look at him. Isn't he like an angel?"

The little pink hands of the child closed mechanically round the honest soldier's finger, and Amelia looked up in his face with bright maternal pleasure. The cruellest looks could not have wounded him more than that glance of hopeless kindness. He bent over the child and mother. He could not speak for a moment. And it was only with all his strength that he could force himself to say a God bless you. "God bless you," said Amelia, and held up her face and kissed him.

"Hush! don't wake Georgy!" she added, as William Dobbin went to the door with heavy steps. She did not hear the noise of his cab wheels as he drove away; she was looking at the child, who was laughing in his sleep.

CHAPTER XXXVI

HOW TO LIVE WELL ON NOTHING A YEAR

I suppose there is no man in this Vanity Fair of ours so little observant as not to think sometimes about the worldly affairs of his acquaintances, or so extremely charitable as not to wonder how his neighbour Jones or his neighbour Smith can make both ends meet at

the end of the year. Many a glass of wine have we all of us drunk,
I have very little doubt, hob-and-nobbing with the hospitable giver,
and wondering how the deuce he paid for it.

Some three or four years after his stay in Paris, when Rawdon
Crawley and his wife were established in a very small, comfortable
house in Curzon Street, Mayfair, there was scarcely one of the numerous
friends whom they entertained at dinner that did not ask the above
question regarding them.

On nothing per annum then, and during a course of some two or
three years, of which we can afford to give but a very brief history,
Crawley and his wife lived very happily and comfortably at Paris. It
was in this period that he quitted the Guards, and sold out in the army.
When we find him again, his mustachios, and the title of Colonel on
his card, are the only relics of his military profession.

Now, our friend the Colonel had a great aptitude for all games of
chance; and exercising himself, as he continually did, with the cards,
the dice-box, or the cue, it is natural to suppose that he attained a
much greater skill in the use of these articles than men can possess
who only occasionally handle them. To use a cue at billiards well is
like using a pencil, or a German flute, or a small-sword: you cannot
master any one of these implements at first, and it is only by repeated
study and perseverence, joined to a natural taste, that a man can
excel in the handling of either. Now Crawley, from being only a
brilliant amateur, had grown to be a consummate master of billiards.
Like a great general, his genius used to rise with the danger; and
when the luck had been unfavourable to him for a whole game, and the
bets were consequently against him, he would, with consummate skill
and boldness, make some prodigious hits which would restore the
battle, and come in a victor at the end, to the astonishment of everybody—of everybody, that is, who was a stranger to his play. Those
who were accustomed to see it were cautious how they staked their
money against a man of such sudden resources and brilliant and overpowering skill.

At games of cards he was equally skilful; for though he would
constantly lose money at the commencement of an evening, playing
so carelessly and making such blunders that newcomers were often inclined to think meanly of his talent, yet when roused to action, and
awakened to caution by repeated small losses, it was remarked that
Crawley's play became quite different, and that he was pretty sure
of beating his enemy thoroughly before the night was over. Indeed,
very few men could say that they ever had the better of him.

His successes were so repeated that no wonder the envious and the
vanquished spoke sometimes with bitterness regarding them. And as
the French say of the Duke of Wellington, who never suffered a defeat,
that only an astonishing series of lucky accidents enabled him to be an
invariable winner—yet even they allow that he cheated at Waterloo,
and was enabled to win the last great trick—so it was hinted at head-

quarters in England that some foul play must have taken place in order to account for the continued successes of Colonel Crawley.

At this juncture news arrived which was spread among the many creditors of the Colonel at Paris, and which caused them great satisfaction. Miss Crawley, the rich aunt from whom he expected his immense inheritance, was dying; the Colonel must haste to her bedside. Mrs. Crawley and her child would remain behind until he came to reclaim them. He departed for Calais, and having reached that place in safety, it might have been supposed that he went to Dover; but instead he took the diligence to Dunkirk, and thence travelled to Brussels, for which place he had a former predilection. The fact is, he owed more money at London than at Paris, and he preferred the quiet little Belgian city to either of the more noisy capitals.

Her aunt was dead. Mrs. Crawley ordered the most intense mourning for herself and little Rawdon. The Colonel was busy arranging the affairs of the inheritance. They could take the premier now instead of the little *entresol* of the hotel which they occupied. Mrs. Crawley and the landlord had a consultation about the new hangings, an amicable wrangle about the carpets, and a final adjustment of everything except the bill. She went off in one of his carriages, her French *bonne* with her, the child by her side, the admirable landlord and landlady smiling farewell to her from the gate. He *serréd* the trunks which she left in his charge with the greatest care. They had been especially recommended to him by Madame Crawley. They were not, however, found to be particularly valuable when opened some time after.

But before she went to join her husband in the Belgic capital, Mrs. Crawley made an expedition into England, leaving behind her her little son upon the Continent, under the care of her French maid.

Rebecca's object in her journey to London was to effect a kind of compromise with her husband's numerous creditors, and by offering them a dividend of ninepence or a shilling in the pound to secure a return for him into his own country. It does not become us to trace the steps which she took in the conduct of this most difficult negotiation; but having shown them to their satisfaction that the sum which she was empowered to offer was all her husband's available capital, and having convinced them that Colonel Crawley would prefer a perpetual retirement on the Continent to a residence in this country with his debts unsettled; having proved to them that there was no possibility of money accruing to him from other quarters, and no earthly chance of their getting a larger dividend than that which she was empowered to offer, she brought the Colonel's creditors unanimously to accept her proposals, and purchased, with fifteen hundred pounds of ready money, more than ten times that amount of debts.

Mrs. Crawley employed no lawyer in the transaction. The matter was so simple, to have or to leave, as she justly observed, that she made the lawyers of the creditors themselves do the business. And Mr. Lewis, representing Mr. Davids of Red Lion Square, and Mr. Moss, acting for Mr. Manesseh of Cursitor Street (chief creditors of the Colonel's), complimented his lady upon the brilliant way in which she did business, and declared that there was no professional man who could beat her.

Rebecca received their congratulations with perfect modesty; ordered a bottle of sherry and a bread cake to the little dingy lodgings where she dwelt, while conducting the business, to treat the enemy's lawyers; shook hands with them at parting, in excellent good humour, and returned straightway to the Continent, to rejoin her husband and son, and acquaint the former with the glad news of his entire liberation.

And so Colonel and Mrs. Crawley came to London, and it is at their house in Curzon Street, Mayfair, that they really showed the skill which must be possessed by those who would live on the resources above named.

CHAPTER XXXVII

THE SUBJECT CONTINUED

In the first place, and as a matter of the greatest necessity, we are bound to describe how a house may be got for nothing a year. These mansions are to be had either unfurnished, where, if you have credit with Messrs. Gillows or Bantings, you can get them splendidly *montées* and decorated entirely according to your own fancy; or they are to be let furnished—a less troublesome and complicated arrangement to most parties. It was so that Crawley and his wife preferred to hire their house.

Before Mr. Bowls came to preside over Miss Crawley's house and cellar in Park Lane, that lady had had for a butler a Mr. Raggles, who was born on the family estate of Queen's Crawley, and indeed was a younger son of a gardener there. By good conduct, a handsome person and calves, and a grave demeanour, Raggles rose from the knife-board to the footboard of the carriage, from the footboard to the butler's pantry. When he had been a certain number of years at the head of Miss Crawley's establishment, where he had had good wages, fat' perquisites, and plenty of opportunities of saving, he announced that he was about to contract a matrimonial alliance with a late cook of Miss Crawley's, who had subsisted in an honourable manner by the exercise of a mangle, and the keeping of a small greengrocer's shop in the neighbourhood. The truth is, that the ceremony had been clandestinely performed some years back, although the news of Mr. Raggles' marriage was first brought to Miss Crawley by a little boy and girl of seven and eight years of age, whose continual presence in the kitchen had attracted the attention of Miss Briggs.

Mr. Raggles then retired, and personally undertook the superintendence of the small shop and the greens. He added milk and cream, eggs and country-fed pork to his stores, contenting himself, whilst other retired butlers were vending spirits in public-houses, by dealing in the simplest country produce. And having a good connection amongst the butlers in the neighbourhood, and a snug back parlour where he and Mrs. Raggles received them, his milk, cream, and eggs got to be adopted by many of the fraternity, and his profits increased every year. Year after year he quietly and modestly amassed money, and when at length that snug and complete bachelor's residence at No. 201 Curzon Street, Mayfair, lately the residence of the Honourable Frederick Deuceace, gone abroad, with its rich and appropriate furniture by the first makers, was brought to the hammer, who should go in and purchase the lease and furniture of the house but Charles Raggles? A part of the money he borrowed, it is true, and at rather a high interest, from a brother butler, but the chief part he paid down; and it was with no small pride that Mrs. Raggles found herself sleeping in a bed of carved mahogany, with silk curtains, with a prodigious cheval-glass opposite to her, and a wardrobe which would contain her, and Raggles, and all the family.

Of course, they did not intend to occupy permanently an apartment so splendid. It was in order to let the house again that Raggles purchased it. As soon as a tenant was found, he subsided into the greengrocer's shop once more; but a happy thing it was for him to walk out of that tenement and into Curzon Street, and there survey his house —his own house—with geraniums in the window and a carved bronze knocker. The footman, occasionally lounging at the area railings, treated him with respect; the cook took her green stuff at his house, and called him Mr. Landlord; and there was not one thing the tenants did, or one dish which they had for dinner, that Raggles might not know of, if he liked.

He was a good man, good and happy. The house brought him in so handsome a yearly income that he was determined to send his children to good schools, and accordingly, regardless of expense, Charles was sent to boarding at Dr. Swishtail's, Sugarcane Lodge, and little Matilda to Miss Peckover's, Laurentinum House, Clapham.

Raggles loved and adored the Crawley family as the author of all his prosperity in life. He had a silhouette of his mistress in his back shop, and a drawing of the Porter's Lodge at Queen's Crawley, done by that spinster herself in India ink; and the only addition he made to the decorations of the Curzon Street house was a print of Queen's Crawley in Hampshire, the seat of Sir Walpole Crawley, Paronet, who was represented in a gilded car drawn by six white horses, and passing by a lake covered with swans, and barges containing ladies in hoops, and musicians with flags and periwigs. Indeed Raggles thought there was no such palace in all the world, and no such august family.

As luck would have it, Raggles' house in Curzon Street was to let when Rawdon and his wife returned to London. The Colonel knew it and its owner quite well; the latter's connection with the Crawley family had been kept up constantly, for Raggles helped Mr. Bowls whenever Miss Crawley received friends. And the old man not only let his house to the Colonel, but officiated as his butler whenever he had company; Mrs. Raggles operated in the kitchen below, and sending up dinners of which old Miss Crawley herself might have approved. This was the way, then, Crawley got his house for nothing: for though Raggles had to pay taxes and rates, and the interest of the mortgage to the brother butler, and the insurance of his life, and the charges for his children at school, and the value of the meat and drink which his own family—and for a time that of Colonel Crawley too—consumed; and though the poor wretch was utterly ruined by the transaction, his children being flung on the streets, and himself driven into the Fleet Prison, yet somebody must pay even for gentlemen who live for nothing a year; and so it was this unlucky Raggles was made the representative of Colonel Crawley's defective capital.

Rebecca's wit, cleverness, and flippancy made her speedily the vogue in London among a certain class. You saw demure chariots at her door, out of which stepped very great people. You beheld her carriage in the Park, surrounded by dandies of note. The little box in the third tier of the Opera was crowded with heads constantly changing: but it must be confessed that the ladies held aloof from her, and that their doors were shut to our little adventurer.

Now the few female acquaintances whom Mrs. Crawley had known abroad not only declined to visit her when she came to this side of the Channel, but cut her severely when they met in public places.

Rawdon at first felt very acutely the slights which were passed upon his wife, and was inclined to be gloomy and savage. He talked of calling out the husbands or brothers of every one of the insolent women who did not pay a proper respect to his wife, and it was only by the strongest commands and entreaties on her part that he was brought into keeping a decent behaviour. "You can't shoot me into society," she said good-naturedly. "Remember, my dear, that I was but a governess, and you, you poor silly old man, have the worst reputation for debt, and dice, and all sorts of wickedness. We shall get quite as many friends as we want by-and-by, and in the meanwhile you must be a good boy, and obey your schoolmistress in everything she tells you to do. When your father dies, Queen's Crawley will be a pleasant house for you and me to pass the winter in. If we are ruined, you can carve and take charge of the stable, and I can be a governess to Lady Jane's children. Ruined! fiddlededee! I will get you a good place before that; or Pitt and his little boy will die, and we will be Sir Rawdon and my lady. While there is life there is hope, my dear, and I intend to make a man of you yet. Who sold your horses for you? who paid your debts for you?" Rawdon was obliged to confess that he owed all these benefits to his wife, and to trust himself to her guidance for the future.

Indeed, when Miss Crawley quitted the world, and that money for which all her relatives had been fighting so eagerly was finally left to Pitt, Bute Crawley, who found that only five thousand pounds had

been left to him instead of the twenty upon which he calculated, was
in such a fury at his disappointment that he vented it in savage abuse
upon his nephew, and the quarrel always rankling between them
ended in an utter breach of intercourse. Rawdon Crawley's conduct,
on the other hand, who got but a hundred pounds, was such as to
astonish his brother and delight his sister-in-law, who was disposed
to look kindly upon all the members of her husband's family. He
wrote to his brother a very frank, manly, good-humoured letter from
Paris. He was aware, he said, that by his own marriage he had for-
feited his aunt's favour; and though he did not disguise his disappointment that she should have been so entirely relentless towards him, he
was glad that the money was still kept in their branch of the family,
and heartily congratulated his brother on his good fortune.

An article as necessary to a lady in this position as her brougham
or her bouquet is her companion. I have always admired the way
in which the tender creatures, who cannot exist without sympathy, hire
an exceedingly plain friend of their own sex from whom they are
almost inseparable. And you will hardly see them in any public place
without a shabby companion in a dyed silk, sitting somewhere in the
shade close behind them.

"Rawdon," said Becky, very late one night, as a party of gentlemen
were seated round her crackling drawing-room fire (for the men came
to her house to finish the night, and she had ice and coffee for them,
the best in London), "I must have a sheep-dog."

"A what?" said Rawdon, looking up from an *écarté* table.

"A dog to keep the wolves off me," Rebecca continued—"a companion."

About the little Rawdon, if nothing has been said all this while, it
is because he is hidden upstairs in a garret somewhere, or has crawled
below into the kitchen for companionship. His mother scarcely ever took
notice of him. He passed the days with his French *bonne* as long as that
domestic remained in Mr. Crawley's family, and when the Frenchwoman
went away, the little fellow, howling in the loneliness of the night, had
compassion taken on him by a housemaid, who took him out of his
solitary nursery into her bed in the garret hard by and comforted him.
Rebecca, by Lord Steyne, and one or two more were in the drawing-
room taking tea after the Opera when this shouting was heard over-
head. "It's my cherub crying for his nurse," she said. She did not
offer to move to go and see the child. "Don't agitate your feelings by
going to look for him," said Lord Steyne sardonically. "Bah!" replied
the other, with a sort of blush, "he'll cry himself to sleep;" and they
fell to talking about the Opera.

Rawdon had stolen off though, to look after his son and heir, and
came back to the company when he found that honest Dolly was con-
soling the child.

Now Rawdon Crawley, rascal as the Colonel was, had certain manly tendencies of affection in his heart and could love a child and a woman still. For Rawdon minor he had a great secret tenderness then, which did not escape Rebecca, though she did not talk about it to her husband. It did not annoy her—she was too good-natured—it only increased her scorn for him. He felt somehow ashamed of his paternal softness, and hid it from his wife, only indulging in it when alone with the boy.

Rebecca was fond of her husband. She was always perfectly good-humoured and kind to him. She did not even show her scorn much for him; perhaps she liked him the better for being a fool. He was her upper servant and *maître d'hôtel*. He went on her errands, obeyed her orders without question, drove in the carriage in the ring with her without repining, took her to the opera-box, solaced himself at his club during the performance, and came punctually back to fetch her when due. He would have liked her to be a little fonder of the boy, but even to that he reconciled himself. "Hang it, you know, she's so clever," he said, "and I'm not literary and that, you know." For, as we have said before, it requires no great wisdom to be able to win at cards and billiards, and Rawdon made no pretensions to any other sort of skill.

When the companion came, his domestic duties became very light. His wife encouraged him to dine abroad; she would let him off duty at the Opera. "Don't stay and stupefy yourself at home to-night, my dear," she would say. "Some men are coming who will only bore you. I would not ask them but you know it's for your good; and now I have a sheep-dog, I need not be afraid to be alone."

"A sheep-dog—a companion! Becky Sharp with a companion! Isn't it good fun?" thought Mrs. Crawley to herself. The notion tickled hugely her sense of humour.

One Sunday morning, as Rawdon Crawley, his little son, and the pony were taking their accustomed walk in the Park, they passed by an old acquaintance of the Colonel's, Corporal Clink of the regiment, who was in conversation with a friend, an old gentleman, who held a boy in his arms about the age of little Rawdon. This other youngster had seized hold of the Waterloo medal which the Corporal wore, and was examining it with delight.

"Good-morning, your honour," said Clink, in reply to the "How do, Clink?" of the Colonel. "This 'ere young gentleman is about the young Colonel's age, sir," continued the Corporal.

"His father was a Waterloo man, too," said the old gentleman, who carried the boy. "Wasn't he, Georgy?"

"Yes," said Georgy. He and the little chap on the pony were looking at each other with all their might, solemnly scanning each other as children do.

"In a line regiment," Clink said, with a patronizing air.

"He was a Captain in the —th regiment," said the old gentleman, rather pompously—"Captain George Osborne, sir; perhaps you knew him. He died the death of a hero, sir, fighting against the Corsican tyrant."

Colonel Crawley blushed quite red. "I knew him very well, sir," he said; "and his wife, his dear little wife, sir, how is she?"

"She is my daughter, sir," said the old gentleman, putting down the boy, and taking out a card with great solemnity, which he handed to the Colonel. On it was written:

"Mr. Sedley, Sole Agent for the Black Diamond and Anti-Cinder Coal Association, Bunker's Wharf, Thames Street, and Anna-Maria Cottages, Fulham Road West."

Little Georgy went up and looked at the Shetland pony.

"Should you like to have a ride?" said Rawdon minor from the saddle.

"Yes," said Georgy. The Colonel, who had been looking at him with some interest, took up the child and put him on the pony behind Rawdon minor.

"Take hold of him, Georgy," he said—"take my little boy round the waist; his name is Rawdon." And both the children began to laugh.

"You won't see a prettier pair, I think, *this* summer's day, sir," said the good-natured Corporal; and the Colonel, the Corporal, and old Mr. Sedley with his umbrella, walked by the side of the children.

CHAPTER XXXVIII

A FAMILY IN A SMALL WAY

WE must suppose little George Osborne has ridden from Knightsbridge towards Fulham, and will stop and make inquiries at that village regarding some friends whom we have left there. How is Mrs. Amelia after the storm of Waterloo? Is she living and thriving? What has become of Major Dobbin, whose cab was always hankering about her premises? and is there any news of the Collector of Boggley Wollah? The facts concerning the latter are briefly these.

Our worthy fat friend Joseph Sedley returned to India not long after his escape from Brussels. Either his furlough was up, or he dreaded to meet any witnesses of his Waterloo flight. However it might be, he went back to his duties in Bengal very soon after Napoleon had taken up his residence at St. Helena, where Jos saw the ex-Emperor.

Jos's London agents had orders to pay one hundred and twenty pounds yearly to his parents at Fulham. It was the chief support of the old couple, for Mr. Sedley's speculations in life subsequent to his bankruptcy did not by any means retrieve the broken old gentleman's fortune. He tried to be a wine-merchant, a coal-merchant, a commission lottery agent, etc., etc. He sent round prospectuses to his friends whenever he took a new trade, and ordered a new brass plate for the door, and talked pompously about making his fortune still. But Fortune never came back to the feeble and stricken old man.

On Sundays, for "business" prevented him on weekdays from taking such a pleasure, it was old Sedley's delight to take out his little grandson Georgy to the neighbouring parks or Kensington Gardens, to see the soldiers or to feed the ducks. Georgy loved the redcoats, and his grandpa told him how his father had been a famous soldier, and introduced him to many sergeants and others with Waterloo medals on their breasts, to whom the old grandfather pompously presented the child as the son of Captain Osborne of the —th, who died gloriously on the glorious eighteenth.

Between Mrs. Sedley and her daughter there was a sort of coolness about this boy, and a secret jealously; for one evening in George's very early days, Amelia, who had been seated at work in their little parlour, scarcely remarking that the old lady had quitted the room, ran upstairs instinctively to the nursery at the cries of the child, who had been asleep until that moment, and there found Mrs. Sedley in the act of surreptitiously administering Daffy's Elixir to the infant. Amelia, the gentlest and sweetest of everyday mortals, when she found this meddling with her maternal authority, thrilled and trembled all over with anger. Her cheeks, ordinarily pale, now flushed up, until they were as red as they used to be when she was a child of twelve years old. She seized the baby out of her mother's arms, and then grasped at the bottle, leaving the old lady gaping at her, furious, and holding the guilty teaspoon.

Amelia flung the bottle crashing into the fireplace. "I will *not* have baby poisoned, mamma!" cried Emmy, rocking the infant about violently with both her arms round him, and turning with flashing eyes at her mother.

"Poisoned, Amelia!" said the old lady; "this language to me?"

"He shall not have any medicine but that which Mr. Pestler sends for him. He told me that Daffy's Elixir was poison."

"Very good; you think I'm a murderess then," replied Mrs. Sedley. "This is the language you use to your mother. I have met with misfortunes; I have sunk low in life; I have kept my carriage, and now walk on foot; but I did not know I was a murderess before, and thank you for the *news*."

"Mamma," said the poor girl, who was always ready for tears, "you shouldn't be hard upon me. I—I didn't mean—I mean, I did not wish to say you would do any wrong to this dear child; only——"

"Oh, no, my love,—only that I was a murderess; in which case, I had better go to the Old Bailey. Though I didn't poison *you* when you were a child, but gave you the best of education and the most expensive masters money could procure. Yes; I've nursed five children, and buried three; and the one I loved the best of all, and tended through croup, and teething, and measles, and whooping-cough, and brought up with foreign masters, regardless of expense, and with accomplishments at Minerva House—which I never had when I was a girl, when I was too glad to honour my father and mother, that I might live long in the land, and to be useful, and not to mope all day in my rooms and act the fine lady—says I'm a murderess. Ah, Mrs. Osborne! may *you* never nourish a viper in your bosom, that's *my* prayer."

"Mamma, mamma!" cried the bewildered girl; and the child in her arms set up a frantic chorus of shouts.

"A murderess, indeed! Go down on your knees and pray to God to cleanse your wicked, ungrateful heart, Amelia; and may He forgive you as I do!" and Mrs. Sedley tossed out of the room, hissing out the word poison once more, and so ending her charitable benediction.

Till the termination of her natural life, this breach between Mrs. Sedley and her daughter was never thoroughly mended.

Besides Amelia's pension of fifty pounds a year, there had been five hundred pounds, as her husband's executor stated, left in the agents' hands at the time of Osborne's demise, which sum, as George's guardian, Dobbin proposed to put out at 8 per cent. in an Indian house of agency. Mr. Sedley, who thought the Major had some roguish intentions of his own about the money, was strongly against this plan; and he went to the agents to protest personally against the employment of the money in question, when he learned, to his surprise, that there had been no such sum in their hands, that all the late Captain's assets did not amount to a hundred pounds, and that the five hundred pounds in question must be a separate sum, of which Major Dobbin knew the particulars. More than ever convinced that there was some roguery, old Sedley pursued the Major. As his daughter's nearest friend, he demanded, with a high hand, a statement of the late Captain's accounts, Dobbin's stammering, blushing, and awkwardness added to the other's convictions that he had a rogue to deal with; and in a majestic tone he told that officer a piece of his mind, as he called it, simply stating his belief that the Major was unlawfully detaining his late son-in-law's money.

Dobbin at this lost all patience, and if his accuser had not been so old and so broken, a quarrel might have ensued between them at the Slaughters' Coffee-House, in a box of which place of entertainment the gentlemen had their colloquy. "Come upstairs, sir," lisped out the Major. "I insist on your coming up the stairs, and I will show which is the injured party, poor George or I;" and, dragging the old gentleman up to his bedroom, he produced from his desk Osborne's accounts, and a bundle of IOU's which the latter had given, who, to do him justice, was always ready to give an IOU. "He paid his bills in England," Dobbin added; " but he had not a hundred pounds in the world when he fell. I and one or two of his brother officers made up the little sum, which was all that we could spare; and you dare tell us that we are trying to cheat the widow and the orphan!" Sedley was very contrite and humbled; though the fact is, that William Dobbin had told a great falsehood to the old gentleman, having himself given every shilling of the money, having buried his friend, and paid all the fees and charges incident upon the calamity and removal of poor Amelia.

About these expenses old Osborne had never given himself any trouble to think, nor any other relative of Amelia, nor Amelia herself, indeed. She trusted to Major Dobbin as an accountant; took his somewhat confused calculations for granted; and never once suspected how much she was in his debt.

Twice or thrice in the year, according to her promise, she wrote him letters to Madras, letters all about little Georgy. How he treasured these papers! Whenever Amelia wrote he answered, and not until then. But he sent over endless remembrances of himself to his godson and to her.

Amidst such humble scenes and associates George's early youth was passed, and the boy grew up delicate, sensitive, imperious, woman-bred—domineering the gentle mother whom he loved with passionate affection. He ruled all the rest of the little world round about him. As he grew, the elders were amazed at his haughty manner and his constant likeness to his father. He asked questions about everything, as inquiring youth will do. The profundity of his remarks and interrogatories astonished his old grandfather, who perfectly bored the club at the tavern with stories about the little lad's learning and genius. He suffered his grandmother with a good-humoured indifference. The small circle round about him believed that the equal of the boy did not exist upon the earth. Georgy inherited his father's pride, and perhaps thought they were not wrong.

When he grew to be about six years old, Dobbin began to write to him very much. The Major wanted to hear that Georgy was going to a school, and hoped he would acquit himself with credit there; or would he have a good tutor at home? it was time that he should begin to learn, and his godfather and guardian hinted that he hoped to be allowed to defray the charges of the boy's education, which would fall heavily upon his mother's straitened income. The Major, in a word, was always thinking about Amelia and her little boy, and by orders to his agents kept the latter provided with picture-books, paint-boxes, desks, and all conceivable implements of amusement and instruction. Three days before George's sixth birthday a gentlemen in a gig, accompanied by a servant, drove up to Mr. Sedley's house, and asked to see Master George Osborne. It was Mr. Woolsey, military tailor, of Conduit Street, who came at the Major's order to measure the young gentleman for a suit of clothes. He had had the honour of making for the Captain, the young gentleman's father. Sometimes, too, and by the Major's desire no doubt, his sisters, the Misses Dobbin, would call in the family carriage to take Amelia and the little boy a drive if they were so inclined. The patronage and kindness of these ladies was very uncomfortable to Amelia; but she bore it meekly enough, for her nature was to yield, and, besides, the carriage and its splendours gave little Georgy immense pleasure. The ladies begged occasionally that the child might pass a day with them; and he was always glad to go to that fine garden-house at Denmark Hill, where they lived, and where there were such fine grapes in the hot-houses and peaches on the walls.

One day they kindly came over to Amelia with news which they were *sure* would delight her—something *very* interesting about their dear William.

"What was it? was he coming home?" she asked, with pleasure beaming in her eyes.

"Oh, no—not the least—but they had very good reason to believe that dear William was about to be married—and to a relation of a very dear friend of Amelia's—to Miss Glorvina O'Dowd, Sir Michael O'Dowd's sister, who had gone out to join Lady O'Dowd at Madras—a very beautiful and accomplished girl, everybody said."

Amelia said, "Oh!" Amelia was very, *very* happy indeed. But she supposed Glorvina could not be like her old acquaintance, who was most kind—but—but she was very happy indeed. And by some impulse of which I cannot explain the meaning, she took George in her arms and kissed him with an extraordinary tenderness. Her eyes were quite moist when she put the child down, and she scarcely spoke a word during the whole of the drive—though she was so very happy indeed.

CHAPTER XXXIX

A CYNICAL CHAPTER

OUR duty now takes us back for a brief space to some old Hampshire acquaintances of ours, whose hopes respecting the disposal of their rich kinswoman's property were so woefully disappointed. After counting upon thirty thousand pounds from his sister, it was a heavy blow to Bute Crawley to receive but five; out of which sum, when he had paid his own debts and those of Jim, his son at college, a very small fragment remained to portion off his four plain daughters.

So Mrs. Bute, after the first shock of rage and disappointment, began to accommodate herself as best she could to her altered fortunes, and to save and retrench with all her might. She instructed her daughters how to bear poverty cheerfully, and invented a thousand notable methods to conceal or evade it. She took them about to balls and public places in the neighbourhood, with praiseworthy energy; nay, she entertained her friends in a hospitable, comfortable manner at the Rectory, and much more frequently than before dear Miss Crawley's legacy had fallen in.

Mrs. Bute certainly thought herself one of the most virtuous women in England, and the sight of her happy family was an edifying one to strangers. They were so cheerful, so loving, so well-educated, so simple! Martha painted flowers exquisitely, and furnished half the charity bazaars in the county. Emma was a regular County Bulbul, and her verses in *The Hampshire Telegraph* were the glory of its Poet's Corner. Fanny and Matilda sang duets together, mamma playing the piano, and the other two sisters sitting with their arms round each other's waists and listening affectionately. Nobody saw the poor girls drumming at the duets in private. No one saw mamma drilling them rigidly hour after hour. In a word, Mrs. Bute put a good face against fortune, and kept up appearances in the most virtuous manner.

Between such a woman and her brother-in-law, the odious Baronet at the Hall, it is manifest that there could be very little in common. The rupture between Bute and his brother Sir Pitt was complete; indeed, between Sir Pitt and the whole county, to which the old man was a scandal. His dislike for respectable society increased with age, and the lodge-gates had not opened to a gentleman's carriage-wheels since Pitt and Lady Jane came to pay their visit of duty after their marriage.

That was an awful and unfortunate visit, never to be thought of by the family without horror. Pitt begged his wife, with a ghastly countenance, never to speak of it; and it was only through Mrs. Bute herself, who still knew everything which took place at the Hall, that the circumstances of Sir Pitt's reception of his son and daughter-in-law were ever known at all.

As they drove up the avenue of the park in their neat and well-appointed carriage, Pitt remarked with dismay and wrath great gaps among the trees—his trees—which the old Baronet was felling entirely without licence. The park wore an aspect of utter dreariness and ruin. The drives were ill-kept, and the neat carriage splashed and floundered in muddy pools along the road. The great sweep in front of the terrace and entrance stair was black and covered with mosses, the once trim flower-beds rank and weedy. Shutters were up along almost the whole line of the house; the great hall door was unbarred after much ringing of the bell; an individual in ribbons was seen flitting up the black oak stair, as Horrocks at length admitted the heir of Queen's Crawley and his bride into the halls of their fathers. He led the way into Sir Pitt's "Library," as it was called, the fumes of tobacco growing stronger as Pitt and Lady Jane approached that apartment. "Sir Pitt ain't very well," Horrocks remarked apologetically, and hinted that his master was afflicted with lumbago.

The library looked out on the front walk and park. Sir Pitt had opened one of the windows, and was bawling out thence to the postilion and Pitt's servant, who seemed to be about to take the baggage down.

"Don't move none of them trunks!" he cried, pointing with a pipe which he held in his hand. "It's only a morning visit, Tucker, you fool. Lor, what cracks that off hoss has in his heels! Ain't there no one at the King's Head to rub 'em a little?—How do, Pitt? How do, my dear? Come to see the old man, hey? 'Gad, you've a pretty face, too. You ain't like that old horse-god-mother, your mother. Come and give old Pitt a kiss, like a good little gal."

The embrace disconcerted the daughter-in-law somewhat, as the caresses of the old gentleman, unshorn and perfumed with tobacco, might well do. But she remembered that her brother Southdown had mustachios, and smoked cigars, and submitted to the Baronet with a tolerable grace.

"Pitt has got vat," said the Baronet, after this mark of affection. "Does he read ee very long zermons, my dear? Hundredth Psalm, Evening Hymn, hey, Pitt? Go and get a glass of Malmsey and a cake for my Lady Jane, Horrocks, you great big booby, and don't stand stearing there like a fat pig. I won't ask you to stop, my dear; you'll find it too stoopid, and so should I too along a Pitt. I'm an old man now, and like my own ways, and my pipe and backgammon of a night."

"I can play at backgammon, sir," said Lady Jane, laughing. "I used to play with Papa and Miss Crawley, didn't I, Mr. Crawley?"

"Lady Jane can play, sir, at the game to which you state that you are so partial," Pitt said haughtily.

"But she wawn't stop for all that. Naw, naw; goo back to Mudbury, and give Mrs. Rincer a benefit; or drive down to the Rectory, and ask Buty for a dinner. He'll be charmed to see you, you know; he's so much obliged to you for gettin' the old woman's money. Ha, ha! Some of it will do to patch up the Hall when I'm gone!"

"I perceive, sir," said Pitt, with a heightened voice, "that your people will cut down the timber."

"Yees, yees; very fine weather and seasonable for the time of year," Sir Pitt answered, who had suddenly grown deaf. "But I'm gittin' old, Pitt, now. Law bless you, you ain't far from fifty yourself. But he wears well, my pretty Lady Jane, don't he? It's all godliness, sobriety, and a moral life. Look at me, I'm not very fur from fowr-score—he, he!" and he laughed, and took snuff, and leered at her and pinched her hand.

The horror of Pitt Crawley may be imagined, as reports of his father's dotage reached the most exemplary and correct of gentlemen. After that first and last visit, his father's name was never mentioned in Pitt's polite and genteel establishment. It was the skeleton in his house, and all the family walked by it in terror and silence.

Miss Horrocks was installed as housekeeper at Queen's Crawley, and ruled all the domestics there with great majesty and rigour. All the servants were instructed to address her as "Mum," or "Madam"; and there was one little maid, on her promotion, who persisted in calling her "My Lady," without any rebuke on the part of the house-keeper. "There has been better ladies, and there has been worser, Hester," was Miss Horrocks's reply to this compliment of her inferior.

One day the Baronet surprised "her Ladyship," as he jocularly called her, seated at that old and tuneless piano in the drawing-room, which has scarcely been touched since Becky Sharp played quadrilles upon it—seated at the piano with the utmost gravity, and squalling to the best of her power in imitation of the music which she had some-times heard. The little kitchen-maid on her promotion was standing at her mistress's side, quite delighted during the operation, and wag-ging her head up and down, and crying, "Lor, Mum, 'tis bittiful,"— ust like a genteel sycophant in a real drawing-room.

This incident made the old Baronet roar with laughter, as usual. He narrated the circumstance a dozen times to Horrocks in the course of the evening, and greatly to the discomfiture of Miss Horrocks. He thrummed on the table as if it had been a musical instrument, and squalled in imitation of her manner of singing. He vowed that such a beautiful voice ought to be cultivated, and declared she ought to have singing-masters, in which proposals she saw nothing ridiculous. He was in great spirits that night, and drank with his friend and butler an extraordinary quantity of rum-and-water. At a very late hour the faithful friend and domestic conducted his master to his bedroom.

Half an hour afterwards there was a great hurry and bustle in the house. Lights went about from window to window in the lonely desolate old Hall, whereof but two or three rooms were ordinarily occupied by its owner. Presently, a boy on a pony went galloping off to Mudbury, to the doctor's house there. And in another hour (by which fact we ascertain how carefully the excellent Mrs. Bute Crawley had always kept up an understanding with the great house), that lady in her clogs and calash, the Reverend Bute Crawley, and James Crawley her son, had walked over from the Rectory through the park, and had entered the mansion by the open hall door.

They passed through the hall and the small oak parlour, on the table of which stood the three tumblers and the empty rum-bottle which had served for Sir Pitt's carouse, and through that apartment into Sir Pitt's study, where they found Miss Horrocks, with a wild air, trying at the presses and escritoires with a bunch of keys. She dropped them with a scream of terror, as little Mrs. Bute's eyes flashed out at her from under her black calash.

"Look at that, James and Mr. Crawley," cried Mrs. Bute, pointing at the scared figure of the black-eyed, guilty wench.

"He gave 'em me; he gave 'em me!" she cried.

"Gave them you, you abandoned creature!" screamed Mrs. Bute. "Bear witness, Mr. Crawley, we found this good-for-nothing woman in the act of stealing your brother's property; and she will be hanged, as I always said she would."

Betsy Horrocks, quite daunted, flung herself down on her knees, bursting into tears. But those who know a really good woman are aware that she is not in a hurry to forgive, and that the humiliation of an enemy is a triumph to her soul.

"Ring the bell, James," Mrs. Bute said. "Go on ringing it till the people come." The three or four domestics resident in the deserted old house came presently at that jangling and continued summons.

"Put that woman in the strong-room," she said. "We caught her in the act of robbing Sir Pitt. Mr. Crawley, you'll make out her committal—and, Beddoes, you'll drive her over in the spring-cart, in the morning, to Southampton Jail."

"My dear," interposed the Magistrate and Rector—"she's only——"

"Are there no handcuffs?" Mrs. Bute continued, stamping in her clogs. "There used to be handcuffs. Where's the creature's abominable father?"

"He *did* give 'em me," still cried poor Betsy; "didn't he, Hester? You saw Sir Pitt—you know you did—give 'em me, ever so long ago —the day after Mudbury fair. Not that I want 'em. Take 'em if you think they ain't mine." And here the unhappy wretch pulled out from her pocket a large pair of paste shoe-buckles which had excited her admiration, and which she had just appropriated out of one of the book-cases in the study, where they had lain.

"Law, Betsy, how could you go for to tell such a wicked story!" said Hester, the little kitchenmaid late on her promotion—"and to Madame Crawley, so good and kind, and his Rev'rince (with a curtsy); and you may search all *my* boxes, Mum, I'm sure, and here's my keys, as I'm an honest girl though of pore parents and workhouse bred—and if you find so much as a beggarly bit of lace or a silk stocking out of all the gownds as *you've* had the picking of, may I never go to church again."

"Give up your keys, you hardened hussy!" hissed out the virtuous little lady in the calash.

"And here's a candle, Mum; and if you please, Mum, I can show you her room, Mum, and the press in the housekeeper's room, Mum, where she keeps heaps and heaps of things, Mum," cried out the eager little Hester with a profusion of curtsies.

"Hold your tongue, if you please. I know the room which the creature occupies perfectly well. Mrs. Brown, have the goodness to come with me—and, Beddoes, don't you lose sight of that woman," said Mrs. Bute, seizing the candle. "Mr. Crawley, you had better go upstairs and see that they are not murdering your unfortunate brother" —and the calash, escorted by Mrs. Brown, walked away to the apartment which, as she said truly, she knew perfectly well.

Bute went upstairs, and found the doctor from Mudbury, with the frightened Horrocks over his master in a chair. They were trying to bleed Sir Pitt Crawley.

With the early morning an express was sent off to Mr. Pitt Crawley by the Rector's lady, who assumed the command of everything, and had watched the old Baronet through the night. He had been brought back to a sort of life; he could not speak, but seemed to recognize people. Mrs. Bute kept resolutely by his bedside. She never seemed to want to sleep, that little woman, and did not close her fiery black eyes once, though the doctor snored in the arm-chair. Horrocks made some wild efforts to assert his authority and assist his master; but Mrs. Bute called him a tipsy old wretch, and bade him never show his face again in that house, or he should be transported, like his abominable daughter.

Terrified by her manner, he slunk down to the oak parlour where Mr. James was, who, having tried the bottle standing there and found no liquor in it, ordered Mr. Horrocks to get another bottle of rum, which he fetched, with clean glasses, and to which the Rector and his son sat down—ordering Horrocks to put down the keys at that instant, and never to show his face again. Cowed by this behaviour, Horrocks gave up the keys; and he and his daughter slunk off silently through the night, and gave up possession of the house of Queen's Crawley.

CHAPTER XL

IN WHICH BECKY IS RECOGNIZED BY THE FAMILY

The heir of Crawley arrived at home, in due time, after this catastrophe, and henceforth may be said to have reigned in Queen's Crawley. For though the old Baronet survived many months, he never recovered the use of his intellect or his speech completely, and the government of the estate devolved upon his elder son. In a strange condition Pitt found it. Sir Pitt was always buying and mortgaging; he had twenty men of business, and quarrels with each; quarrels with all his tenants, and lawsuits with them; lawsuits with the lawyers; lawsuits with the Mining and Dock Companies in which he was proprietor; and with every person with whom he had business. To unravel these difficulties, and to set the estate clear, was a task worthy of the orderly and persevering diplomatist of Pumpernickel; and he set himself to work with prodigious assiduity. His whole family, of course, was transported to Queen's Crawley, whither Lady Southdown, of course, came too; and she set about converting the parish under the Rector's nose, and brought down her irregular clergy, to the dismay of the angry Mrs. Bute. Sir Pitt had concluded no bargain for the sale of the living of Queen's Crawley; when it should drop, her Ladyship proposed to take the patronage into her own hands, and present a young *protégé* to the Rectory; on which subject the diplomatic Pitt said nothing.

Mrs. Bute's intentions with regard to Miss Betsy Horrocks were not carried into effect, and she paid no visit to Southampton Jail. She and her father left the Hall, when the latter took possession of the Crawley Arms in the village, of which he had got a lease from Sir Pitt. The ex-butler had obtained a small freehold there likewise, which gave him a vote for the borough. The Rector had another of these votes, and these and four others formed the representative body which returned the two members for Queen's Crawley.

Early one morning, as Pitt Crawley was at his steward's and bailiff's books in the study, a knock came to the door, and Hester presented herself, dropping a curtsy, and said—

"If you please, Sir Pitt, Sir Pitt died this morning, Sir Pitt. I was a-making of his toast, Sir Pitt, for his gruel, Sir Pitt, which he took every morning regular at six, Sir Pitt, and—I thought I heard a moan-like, Sir Pitt—and—and—and——" She dropped another curtsy.

What was it that made Pitt's pale face flush quite red? Was it because he was Sir Pitt at last, with a seat in Parliament, and perhaps future honours in prospect? "I'll clear the estate now with the ready money," he thought, and rapidly calculated its encumbrances, and the improvements which he would make. He would not use his aunt's money previously lest Sir Pitt should recover, and his outlay be in vain.

All the blinds were pulled down at the Hall and Rectory; the church bell was tolled, and the chancel hung in black; and Bute Crawley didn't go to a coursing meeting, but went and dined quietly at Fuddleston, where they talked about his deceased brother and young Sir Pitt over their port. Miss Betsy, who was by this time married to a saddler at Mudbury, cried a good deal. The family surgeon rode over and paid his respectful compliments, and inquiries for the health of their ladyships. The death was talked about at Mudbury and at the Crawley Arms; the landlord whereof had become reconciled with the Rector of late, who was occasionally known to step into the parlour and taste Mr. Horrocks's mild beer.

When the faithful Lord Steyne arrived in the evening, he found Becky and her companion, who was no other than our friend Briggs, busy cutting, ripping, snipping, and tearing all sorts of black stuffs available for the melancholy occasion.

"Miss Briggs and I are plunged in grief and despondency for the death of our papa," Rebecca said. "Sir Pitt Crawley is dead, my Lord. We have been tearing our hair all the morning, and now we are tearing up our old clothes."

"O Rebecca, how can you!" was all that Briggs could say, as she turned up her eyes.

"O Rebecca, how can you!" echoed my Lord. "So that old scoundrel's dead, is he? He might have been a Peer if he had played his cards better. Mr. Pitt had very nearly made him; but he rattled always at the wrong time. What an old Silenus it was!"

"I might have been Silenus's widow," said Rebecca. "Don't you remember, Miss Briggs, how you peeped in at the door, and saw old Sir Pitt on his knees to me?" Miss Briggs, our old friend, blushed very much at this reminiscence, and was glad when Lord Steyne ordered her to go downstairs and make him a cup of tea.

Briggs was the house-dog whom Rebecca had provided as guardian of her innocence and reputation. Miss Crawley had left her a little annuity. She would have been content to remain in the Crawley family with Lady Jane, who was good to her and to everybody; but Lady Southdown dismissed poor Briggs as quickly as decency permitted, and Mr. Pitt (who thought himself much injured by the uncalled-for generosity of his deceased relative towards a lady who had only been Miss Crawley's faithful retainer a score of years) made no objection to that exercise of the Dowager's authority. Bowls and Firkin likewise received their legacies, and their dismissals; and married and set up a lodging-house, according to the custom of their kind.

Briggs tried to live with her relations in the country, but found that attempt was vain after the better society to which she had been accustomed. Brigg's friends, small tradesmen in a country town, quarrelled over Miss Briggs's forty pound a year as eagerly and more openly than Miss Crawley's kinsfolk had for that lady's inheritance. Briggs's brother, a radical hatter and grocer, called his sister a purse-proud aristocrat, because she would not advance a part of her capital to stock his shop; and she would have done so most likely, but that their sister, a dissenting shoemaker's lady, at variance with the hatter and grocer, who went to another chapel, showed how their brother was on the verge of bankruptcy, and took possession of Briggs for a while. The dissenting shoemaker wanted Miss Briggs to send his son to college, and make a gentleman of him. Between them the two families got a great portion of her private savings out of her; and finally she fled to London, followed by the anathemas of both, and determined to seek for servitude again, as infinitely less onerous than liberty. And advertising in the papers that a "Gentlewoman of agreeable manners, and accustomed to the best society, was anxious to," etc., she took up her residence with Mr. Bowls in Half Moon Street, and waited the result of the advertisement.

So it was that she fell in with Rebecca. Mrs. Rawdon's dashing little carriage and ponies was whirling down the street one day, just as Miss Briggs, fatigued, had reached Mr. Bowls' door, after a weary walk to *The Times* office in the City, to insert her advertisement for the sixth time. Rebecca was driving, and at once recognized the gentlewoman with agreeable manners; and being a perfectly good-humoured woman, as we have seen, and having a regard for Briggs, she pulled up the ponies at the door-steps, gave the reins to the groom, and jumping out, had hold of both Briggs's hands, before she of the agreeable manners had recovered from the shock of seeing an old friend.

When she found how her friend was situated, and how, having a snug legacy from Miss Crawley, salary was no object to our gentlewoman, Becky instantly formed some benevolent little domestic plans concerning her. This was just such a companion as would suit her establishment, and she invited Briggs to come to dinner with her that very evening, when she should see Becky's dear little darling Rawdon.

CHAPTER XLI

IN WHICH BECKY REVISITS THE HALLS OF HER ANCESTORS

So the mourning being ready, and Sir Pitt Crawley warned of their arrival, Colonel Crawley and his wife took a couple of places in the same old Highflyer coach by which Rebecca had travelled in the defunct Baronet's company, on her first journey into the world some nine years before.

They were going through the lodge-gates kept by old Mrs. Lock, whose hand Rebecca insisted upon shaking, as she flung open the creaking old iron gate, and the carriage passed between the two moss-grown pillars surmounted by the dove and serpent.

"The governor has cut into the timber," Rawdon said, looking about, and then was silent; so was Becky. Both of them were rather agitated, and thinking of old times. He about Eton, and his mother, whom he remembered, a frigid demure woman, and a sister who died, of whom he had been passionately fond; and how he used to thrash Pitt; and about little Rawdy at home. And Rebecca thought about her own youth, and the dark secrets of those early tainted days; and of her entrance into life by yonder gates; and of Miss Pinkerton, and Jos, and Amelia.

The gravel walk and terrace had been scraped quite clean. A grand painted hatchment was already over the great entrance, and two very solemn and tall personages in black flung open each a leaf of the door as the carriage pulled up at the familiar steps. Rawdon turned red, and Becky somewhat pale, as they passed through the old hall arm-in-arm. She pinched her husband's arm as they entered the oak parlour, where Sir Pitt and his wife were ready to receive them—Sir Pitt in black, Lady Jane in black, and my Lady Southdown with a large black headpiece of bugles and feathers, which waved on her Ladyship's head like an undertaker's tray.

Sir Pitt had judged correctly, that she would not quit the premises. She contented herself by preserving a solemn and stony silence when in company of Pitt and his rebellious wife, and by frightening the children in the nursery by the ghastly gloom of her demeanour. Only a very faint bending of the head-dress and plumes welcomed Rawdon and his wife, as those prodigals returned to their family.

To say the truth, they were not affected very much one way or other by this coolness. Her Ladyship was a person only of secondary consideration in their minds just then: they were intent upon the reception which the reigning brother and sister would afford them.

Pitt, with rather a heightened colour, went up and shook his brother by the hand, and saluted Rebecca with a handshake and a very low bow. But Lady Jane took both the hands of her sister-in-law, and kissed her affectionately. The embrace somehow brought tears into the eyes of the little adventuress—which ornaments, as we knew, she wore very seldom. The artless mark of kindness and confidence touched and pleased her; and Rawdon, encouraged by this demonstration on his sister's part, twirled up his mustachios, and took leave to salute Lady Jane with a kiss, which caused her Ladyship to blush exceedingly.

"Dev'lish nice little woman, Lady Jane," was his verdict, when he and his wife were together again. "Pitt's got fat, too, and is doing the thing handsomely." "He can afford it," said Rebecca; and agreed in her husband's further opinion, "that the mother-in-law was a tremendous old guy, and that the sisters were rather well-looking young women."

Lady Jane conducted Rebecca to the apartments prepared for her —which, with the rest of the house, had assumed a very much improved appearance of order and comfort during Pitt's regency—and here, beholding that Mrs. Rawdon's modest little trunks had arrived, and were placed in the bedroom and dressing-room adjoining, helped her to take off her neat black bonnet and cloak, and asked her sister-in-law in what more she could be useful.

"What I should like best," said Rebecca, "would be to go to the nursery, and see your dear little children." On which the two ladies looked very kindly at each other, and went to that apartment hand-in-hand.

Becky admired little Matilda, who was not quite four years old, as the most charming little love in the world; and the boy, a little fellow of two years—pale, heavy-eyed, and large-headed—she pronounced to be a perfect prodigy in point of size, intelligence, and beauty.

And so having easily won the daughter's good-will, the indefatigable little woman bent herself to conciliate the august Lady Southdown. As soon as she found her Ladyship alone, Rebecca attacked her on the nursery question at once, and said that her own little boy was saved, actually saved, by calomel, freely administered, when all the physicians in Paris had given the dear child up. And then she mentioned how often she had heard of Lady Southdown from that excellent man, the Reverend Lawrence Grills, minister of the chapel in Mayfair, which she frequented; and how her views were very much changed by circumstances and misfortunes; and how she hoped that a past life spent in worldliness and error might not incapacitate her from *more serious* thought for the future. She described how, in former days, she had been indebted to Mr. Crawley for religious instruction; touched upon the "Washerwoman of Finchley Common," which she had read with the greatest profit; and asked about Lady Emily, its gifted author, now Lady Emily Hornblower, at Cape Town, where her husband had strong hopes of becoming Bishop of Caffraria.

But she crowned all, and confirmed herself in Lady Southdown's favour, by feeling very much agitated and unwell after the funeral, and requesting her Ladyship's medical advice, which the Dowager not only gave, but, wrapped up in a bed-gown, and looking more like Lady Macbeth than ever, came privately in the night to Becky's room, with a parcel of favourite tracts, and a medicine of her own composition, which she insisted that Mrs. Rawdon should take.

Becky first accepted the tracts, and began to examine them with great interest engaging the Dowager in a conversation concerning them and the welfare of her soul, by which means she hoped that her body might escape medication. But after the religious topics were exhausted, Lady Macbeth would not quit Becky's chamber until her cup of night-drink was emptied too; and poor Mrs. Rawdon was compelled actually to assume a look of gratitude, and to swallow the medicine under the unyielding old Dowager's nose, who left her victim finally with a benediction.

It did not much comfort Mrs. Rawdon. Her countenance was very queer when Rawdon came in and heard what had happened; and his explosions of laughter were as loud as usual, when Becky, with a fun which she could not disguise, even though it was at her own expense, described the occurrence, and how she had been victimized by Lady Southdown.

Sir Pitt remembered the testimonies of respect and veneration which Rebecca had paid personally to himself in early days, and was tolerably well disposed towards her. The marriage, ill-advised as it was, had improved Rawdon very much—that was clear from the Colonel's altered habits and demeanour—and had it not been a lucky union as regarded Pitt himself? The cunning diplomatist smiled inwardly as he owned that he owed his fortune to it, and acknowledged that he at least ought not to cry out against it. His satisfaction was not removed by Rebecca's own statements, behaviour and conversation.

She doubled the deference which before had charmed him, calling out his conversational powers in such a manner as quite to surprise Pitt himself, who, always inclined to respect his own talents, admired them the more when Rebecca pointed them out to him. With her sister-in-law, Rebecca was satisfactorily able to prove that it was Mrs. Bute Crawley who brought about the marriage which she afterwards so calumniated; that it was Mrs. Bute's avarice—who hoped to gain all Miss Crawley's fortune, and deprive Rawdon of his aunt's favour —which caused and invented all the wicked reports against Rebecca. "She succeeded in making us poor," Rebecca said, with an air of angelical patience; "but how can I be angry with a woman who has given me one of the best husbands in the world? And has not her own avarice been sufficiently punished by the ruin of her own hopes, and the loss of the property by which she set so much store? Poor!" she cried. "Dear Lady Jane, what care we for poverty? I am used to it from childhood; and I am often thankful that Miss Crawley's money has gone to restore the splendour of the noble old family of which I am so proud to be a member. I am sure Sir Pitt will make a much better use of it than Rawdon would."

All these speeches were reported to Sir Pitt by the most faithful of wives, and increased the favourable impression which Rebecca made; so much so, that when, on the third day after the funeral, the family party were at dinner, Sir Pitt Crawley, carving fowls at the head of the table, actually said to Mrs. Rawdon, "Ahem! *Rebecca*, may I give you a wing?"—a speech which made the little woman's eyes sparkle with pleasure.

While Rebecca was prosecuting the above schemes and hopes, and Pitt Crawley arranging the funeral ceremonial and other matters connected with his future progress and dignity, and Lady Jane busy with her nursery, as far as her mother would let her, and the sun rising and setting, and the clock-tower bell of the Hall ringing to dinner and to prayers as usual, the body of the late owner of Queen's Crawley lay in the apartment which he had occupied, watched unceasingly by the professional attendants who were engaged for that rite. A woman or two, and three or four undertaker's men, the best whom Southampton could furnish, dressed in black, and of a proper stealthy and tragical demeanour, had charge of the remains, which they watched turn about, having the housekeeper's room for their place of rendezvous when off duty, where they played at cards in privacy and drank their beer.

The members of the family and servants of the house kept away from the gloomy spot, where the bones of the descendant of an ancient line of knights and gentlemen lay, awaiting their final consignment to the family crypt.

Those who will may follow his remains to the grave, whither they were borne on the appointed day, in the most becoming manner, the family in black coaches, with their handkerchiefs up to their noses, ready for the tears which did not come; the undertaker and his gentlemen in deep tribulation; the select tenantry mourning out of compliment to the new landlord; the neighbouring gentry's carriages at three miles an hour, empty, and in profound affliction; the parson speaking out the formula about "our dear brother departed."

As the birds were pretty plentiful, and partridge-shooting is as it were the duty of an English gentleman of statesmanlike propensities, Sir Pitt Crawley, the first shock of grief over, went out a little and partook of that diversion in a white hat with crape round it. The sight of those fields of stubble and turnips, now his own, gave him many secret joys. Sometimes, and with an exquisite humility, he took no gun, but went out with a peaceful bamboo cane; Rawdon, his big brother, and the keepers blazing away at his side. Pitt's money and acres had a great effect upon his brother. The penniless Colonel became quite obsequious and respectful to the head of his house, and despised the milksop Pitt no longer.

Rebecca, during her stay at Queen's Crawley, made as many friends of the Mammon of Unrighteousness as she could possibly bring under control. Lady Jane and her husband bade her farewell with the warmest demonstrations of goodwill. They looked forward with pleasure to the time when, the family house in Gaunt Street being repaired and beautified, they were to meet again in London. Lady Southdown made her up a packet of medicine, and sent a letter by her to the Rev. Lawrence Grills, exhorting that gentleman to save the brand who "honoured" the letter from the burning. Pitt accompanied them with four horses in the carriage to Mudbury, having sent on their baggage in a cart previously, accompanied with loads of game.

"How happy you will be to see your darling little boy again!" Lady Crawley said, taking leave of her kinswoman.

"Oh, so happy!" said Rebecca, throwing up the green eyes. She was immensely happy to be free of the place, and yet loth to go. Queen's Crawley was abominably stupid; and yet the air there was somehow purer than that which she had been accustomed to breathe. Everybody had been dull, but had been kind in their way. "It is all the influence of a long course of Three per Cents.," Becky said to herself, and was right very likely.

However, the London lamps flashed joyfully as the stage rolled into Piccadilly, and Briggs had made a beautiful fire in Curzon Street, and little Rawdon was up to welcome back his papa and mamma.

CHAPTER XLII

WHICH TREATS OF THE OSBORNE FAMILY

CONSIDERABLE time has elapsed since we have seen our respectable friend, old Mr. Osborne of Russell Square. He has not been the happiest of mortals since last we met him. Events have occurred which have not improved his temper, and in more instances than one he has not been allowed to have his own way. To be thwarted in this reasonable desire was always very injurious to the old gentleman; and resistance became doubly exasperating when gout, age, loneliness, and the force of many disappointments, combined to weigh him down. His stiff black hair began to grow white soon after his son's death; his face grew redder; his hands trembled more and more as he poured out his glass of port wine. He led his clerks a dire life in the City; his family at home were not much happier.

Frederick Bullock, Esq., of the house of Bullock, Hulker & Bullock, had married Maria Osborne, not without a great deal of difficulty and grumbling on Mr. Bullock's part.

It was a grand affair—the bridegroom's relatives giving the breakfast, their habitations being near St. George's, Hanover Square, where the business took place. The "nobs of the West End" were invited, and many of them signed the book.

The young couple had a house near Berkeley Square, and a small villa at Roehampton, among the banking colony there. Fred was considered to have made rather a *mésalliance* by the ladies of his family, whose grandfather had been in a Charity School, and who were allied through the husbands with some of the best blood in England. And Maria was bound, by superior pride and great care in the composition of her visiting-book, to make up for the defects of birth, and felt it her duty to see her father and sister as little as possible.

One can fancy the pangs with which Miss Osborne in her solitude in Russell Square read *The Morning Post*, where her sister's name occurred every now and then, in the articles headed "Fashionable Réunions," and where she had an opportunity of reading a description of Mrs. F. Bullock's costume, when presented at the Drawing-room by Lady Frederica Bullock. Jane's own life, as we have said, admitted of no such grandeur. It was an awful existence. She had to get up of black winter's mornings to make breakfast for her scowling old father, who would have turned the whole house out of doors if his tea had not been ready at half-past eight. She remained silent opposite to him, listening to the urn hissing, and sitting in tremor while the parent read his paper, and consumed his accustomed portion of muffins and tea. At half-past nine he rose and went to the City, and she was almost free till dinner-time, to make visitations in the kitchen, and to scold the servants; to drive abroad and descend upon the tradesmen, who were prodigiously respectful; to leave her cards and her papa's at the great, glum, respectable houses of their City friends; or to sit alone in the large drawing-room, expecting visitors, and working at a huge piece of worsted by the fire, on the sofa hard by the great Iphigenia clock, which ticked and tolled with mournful loudness in the dreary room. The great glass over the mantelpiece, faced by the other great console glass at the opposite end of the room, increased and multiplied between them the brown holland bag in which the chandelier hung; until you saw these brown holland bags fading away in endless perspectives, and this apartment of Miss Osborne's seemed the centre of a system of drawing-rooms. When she removed the cordovan leather from the grand piano, and ventured to play a few notes on it, it sounded with a mournful sadness, startling the dismal echoes of the house. George's picture was gone, and laid upstairs in a lumber-room in the garret; and though there was a consciousness of him, and father and daughter often instinctively knew that they were thinking of him, no mention was ever made of the brave and once darling son.

At five o'clock Mr. Osborne came back to his dinner, which he and his daughter took in silence (seldom broken, except when he swore and was savage, if the cooking was not to his liking), or which they shared twice a month with a party of dismal friends of Osborne's rank and age. Old Dr. Gulp and his lady from Bloomsbury Square; old Mr. Frowser, the attorney, from Bedford Row, a very great man, and, from his business, hand-in-glove with the "nobs at the West End"; old Colonel Livermore, of the Bombay Army, and Mrs. Livermore, from Upper Bedford Place; old Serjeant Toffy and Mrs. Toffy; and sometimes old Sir Thomas Coffin and Lady Coffin, from Bedford Square. Sir Thomas was celebrated as a hanging judge, and the particular tawny port was produced when he dined with Mr. Osborne.

These people and their like gave the pompous Russell Square merchant pompous dinners back again. They had solemn rubbers of whist, when they went upstairs after drinking, and their carriages were called at half-past ten. Many rich people, whom we poor devils are in the habit of envying, lead contendly an existence like that above described. Jane Osborne scarcely ever met a man under sixty and almost the only bachelor who appeared in their society was Mr. Smirk, the celebrated ladies' doctor.

It has been described how the Misses Dobbin lived with their father at a fine villa at Denmark Hill, where there were beautiful graperies and peach-trees which delighted little Georgy Osborne. The Misses Dobbin, who drive often to Brompton to see our dear Amelia, came sometimes to Russell Square too, to pay a visit to their old acquaintance Miss Osborne. I believe it was in consequence of the commands of their brother the Major in India (for whom their papa had a prodigious respect), that they paid attention to Mrs. George; for the Major, the godfather and guardian of Amelia's little boy, still hoped that the child's grandfather might be induced to relent towards him, and acknowledge him for the sake of his son. The Misses Dobbin kept Miss Osborne acquainted with the state of Amelia's affairs: how she was living with her father and mother; how poor they were; how they wondered what men, and such men as their brother and dear Captain Osborne, could find in such an insignificant little chit; how she was still, as heretofore, a namby-pamby, milk-and-water, affected creature; but how the boy was really the noblest little boy ever seen—for the hearts of all women warm towards young children, and the sourest spinster is kind to them.

One day, after great entreaties on the part of the Misses Dobbin, Amelia allowed little George to go and pass a day with them at Denmark Hill—a part of which day she spent herself in writing to the Major in India. She congratulated him on the happy news which his sisters had just conveyed to her. She prayed for his prosperity and that of the bride he had chosen. She thanked him for a thousand thousand kind offices and proofs of steadfast friendship to her in her affliction. She told him the last news about little Georgy, and how he was gone to spend that very day with his sisters in the country. She underlined the letter a great deal, and she signed herself affectionately his friend, Amelia Osborne. She forgot to send any message of kindness to Lady O'Dowd, as her wont was; and did not mention Glorvina by name, and only in italics, as the Major's *bride*, for whom she begged *blessings*. But the news of the marriage removed the reserve which she had kept up towards him. She was glad to be able to own and feel how warmly and gratefully she regarded him; and as for the idea of being jealous of Glorvina (Glorvina, indeed!), Amelia would have scouted it, if an angel from heaven had hinted it to her.

That night, when Georgy came back in the pony-carriage in which he rejoiced, and in which he was driven by Sir William Dobbin's old coachman, he had round his neck a fine gold chain and watch. He said an old lady, not pretty, had given it to him, who cried and kissed him a great deal. But he didn't like her. He liked grapes very much. And he only liked his mamma. Amelia shrank and started: the timid soul felt a presentiment of terror when she heard that the relations of the child's father had seen him.

Miss Osborne came back to give her father his dinner. He had made a good speculation in the City, and was rather in a good-humour that day, and chanced to remark the agitation under which she laboured. "What's the matter, Miss Osborne?" he deigned to say.

The woman burst into tears. "O sir," she said, "I've seen little George. He is as beautiful as an angel—and so like him!" The old man opposite to her did not say a word, but flushed up, and began to tremble in every limb.

CHAPTER XLIII

IN WHICH THE READER HAS TO DOUBLE THE CAPE

THE astonished reader must be called upon to transport himself ten thousand miles to the military station of Bundlegunge, in the Madras division of our Indian Empire, where our gallant old friends of the —th regiment are quartered, under the command of the brave Colonel, Sir Michael O'Dowd. Time has dealt kindly with that stout officer, as it does ordinarily with men who have good stomachs and good tempers, and are not perplexed overmuch by fatigue of the brain. The Colonel plays a good knife and fork at tiffin, and resumes those weapons with great success at dinner. He smokes his hookah after both meals, and puffs as quietly while his wife scolds him as he did under the fire of the French at Waterloo. Age and heat have not diminished the activity or the eloquence of the descendant of the Malonys and the Molloys. Her Ladyship, our old acquaintance, is as much at home at Madras as at Brussels—in the cantonment as under the tents. On the march you saw her at the head of the regiment seated on a royal elephant—a noble sight. Mounted on that beast she has been into action with tigers in the jungle; she has been received by native princes who have welcomed her and Glorvina into the recesses of their zenanas, and offered her shawls and jewels which it went to her heart to refuse. The sentries of all arms salute her wherever she makes her appearance; and she touches her hat gravely to their salutation. Lady O'Dowd is one of the greatest ladies in the Presidency of Madras.

Among other points, she had made up her mind that Glorvina should marry our old friend Dobbin. Mrs. O'Dowd knew the Major's expectations, and appreciated his good qualities and the high character which he enjoyed in his profession. Glorvina, a very handsome, fresh-coloured, black-haired, blue-eyed young lady, who could ride a horse or play a sonata with any girl out of the County Cork, seemed to be the very person destined to ensure Dobbin's happiness—much more than that poor good little weak-spur'ted Amelia, about whom he used to take on so. "Look at Glorvina enter a room," Mrs. O'Dowd would say, "and compare her with that poor Mrs. Osborne, who couldn't say bo to a goose. She'd be worthy of you, Major; you're a quiet man yourself, and want some one to talk for ye. And though she does not come of such good blood as the Malonys or Molloys, let me tell ye, she's of an ancient family that any nobleman might be proud to marry into."

Well, although Lady O'Dowd and Glorvina quarrelled a great number of times every day, and upon almost every conceivable subject—indeed, if Mick O'Dowd had not possessed the temper of an angel, two such women constantly about his ears would have driven him out of his senses—yet they agreed between themselves on this point, that Glorvina should marry Major Dobbin, and were determined that the Major should have no rest until the arrangement was brought about. Undismayed by forty or fifty previous defeats, Glorvina laid siege to him. No wonder that public rumour assigned her to him, and that the Major's sisters in England should fancy they were about to have a sister-in-law.

But the truth is, neither beauty nor fashion could conquer him. Our honest friend had but one idea of a woman in his head, and that one did not in the least resemble Miss Glorvina O'Dowd in pink satin. A gentle little woman in black, with large eyes and brown hair, seldom speaking save when spoken to, and then in a voice not the least resembling Miss Glorvina's; a soft young mother tending an infant and beckoning the Major up with a smile to look at him; a rosy-cheeked lass coming singing into the room in Russell Square, or hanging on George Osborne's arm, happy and loving—there was but this image that filled our honest Major's mind by day and by night, and reigned over it always. Very likely Amelia was not like the portrait the Major had formed of her. There was a figure in a book of fashions which his sisters had in England, and with which William had made away privately, pasting it into the lid of his desk, and fancying he saw some resemblance to Mrs. Osborne in the print; whereas I have seen it, and can vouch that it is but the picture of a high-waisted gown with an impossible doll's face simpering over it; and perhaps Mr. Dobbin's sentimental Amelia was no more like the real one than this absurd little print which he cherished. But what man in love, of us, is better informed? or is he much happier when he sees and owns his delusion? Dobbin was under this spell. He did not bother his friends and the public much about his feelings, or indeed lose his natural rest or appetite on account of them. His head has grizzled since we saw him last, and a line or two of silver may be seen in the soft brown hair likewise. But his feelings are not in the least changed or oldened, and his love remains as fresh as a man's recollections of boyhood are.

We have said how the two Misses Dobbin and Amelia, the Major's correspondents in Europe, wrote him letters from England—Mrs. Osborne congratulating him with great candour and cordiality upon his approaching nuptials with Miss O'Dowd.

"Your sister has just kindly visited me," Amelia wrote in her letter, "and informed me of an *interesting event*, upon which I beg to offer my *most sincere congratulations*. I hope the young lady to whom I hear you are to be *united* will in every respect prove worthy of one who is himself all kindness and goodness. The poor widow has only her prayers to offer, and her cordial, cordial wishes for *your prosperity!* Georgy sends his love to *his dear godpapa*, and hopes that you will not forget him. I tell him that you are about to form *other ties*, with one who I am sure merits *all your affection*, but that, although such ties must of course be the strongest and most sacred, and supersede *all others*, yet that I am sure the widow and the child whom you have ever protected and loved will always *have a corner in your heart*." The letter, which has been before alluded to, went on in this strain, protesting throughout as to the extreme satisfaction of the writer.

Sick and sorry felt poor William, more than ever wretched and lonely. He would like to have done with life and its vanity altogether, so bootless and unsatisfactory the struggle, so cheerless and dreary the prospect seemed to him. He lay all that night sleepless, and yearning to go home. Amelia's letter had fallen as a blank upon him. No fidelity, no constant truth and passion, could move her into warmth. She would not see that he loved her.

There came another ship from Europe bringing letters on board, and amongst them some more for the unhappy man. These were home letters bearing an earlier post-mark than that of the former packets, and Major Dobbin recognized among his the handwriting of his sister —who always crossed and recrossed her letters to her brother, gathered together all the possible bad news which she could collect, abused him and read him lectures with sisterly frankness, and always left him miserable for the day after "Dearest William" had achieved the perusal of one of her epistles. He took it up and prepared himself for a disagreeable hour's communings with that crabbed-handed absent relative. . . . It may have been an hour after the Major's departure from the Colonel's house. Sir Michael was sleeping the sleep of the just; Glorvina had arranged her black ringlets in the innumerable little bits of paper in which it was her habit to confine them; Lady O'Dowd, too, had gone to her bed in the nuptial chamber, on the ground floor, and had tucked her mosquito curtains round her fair form; when the guard at the gates of the commanding officer's compound beheld Major Dobbin in the moonlight rushing towards the house with a swift step and a very agitated countenance, and he passed the sentinel and went up to the windows of the Colonel's bedchamber.

"O'Dowd—Colonel!" said Dobbin, and kept up a great shouting.

"Heavens, Meejor!" said Glorvina of the curl-papers, putting out her head too from her window.

"What is it, Dob, me boy?" said the Colonel, expecting there was a fire in the station, or that the route had come from headquarters.

"I—I must have leave of absence. I must go to England—on the most urgent private affairs," Dobbin said.

"Good heavens, what has happened?" thought Glorvina, trembling with all the papillotes.

"I want to be off—now—to-night," Dobbin continued; and the Colonel getting up, came out to parley with him.

In the postscript of Miss Dobbins cross-letter the Major had just come upon a paragraph to the following effect: "I drove yesterday to see your old *acquaintance*, Mrs. Osborne. The wretched place they live at since they were bankrupts you know. Mr. S., to judge from a *brass-plate* on the door of his hut (it is little better) is a coal-merchant. The little boy, your godson, is certainly a fine child, though forward, and inclined to be saucy and self-willed. But we have taken notice of him as you wished it, and have introduced him to his aunt, Miss O., who was rather pleased with him. Perhaps his grandpapa—not the bankrupt one, who is almost doting, but Mr. Osborne of Russell Square—may be induced to relent towards the child of your friend, *his erring and self-willed son*. And Amelia will not be ill-disposed to give him up. The widow is *consoled*, and is about to marry a reverend gentleman, the Rev. Mr. Binny, one of the curates of Brompton. A poor match. But Mrs. O. is getting old, and I saw a great deal of grey in her hair—she was in very good spirits; and your little godson overate himself at our house. Mamma sends her love, with that of your affectionate, Ann Dobbin."

CHAPTER XLIV

A ROUNDABOUT CHAPTER BETWEEN LONDON AND HAMPSHIRE

OUR old friends the Crawley's family house, in Great Gaunt Street, still bore over its front the hatchment which had been placed there as a token of mourning for Sir Pitt Crawley's demise; yet this heraldic emblem was in itself a very splendid and gaudy piece of furniture, and all the rest of the mansion became more brilliant than it had ever been during the late baronet's reign. The black outer coating of the bricks was removed, and they appeared with a cheerful, blushing face streaked with white; the old bronze lions of the knocker were gilt handsomely, the railings painted, and the dismallest house in Great Gaunt Street became the smartest in the whole quarter, before the green leaves in Hampshire had replaced those yellowing ones which were on the trees in Queen's Crawley avenue when old Sir Pitt Crawley passed under them for the last time.

A little woman, with a carriage to correspond, was perpetually seen about this mansion; an elderly spinster, accompanied by a little boy, also might be remarked coming thither daily. It was Miss Biggs and little Rawdon, whose business it was to see to the inward renovation of Sir Pitt's house, to superintend the female band engaged in stitching the blinds and hangings, to poke and rummage in the drawers and cupboards crammed with the dirty relics and congregated trumperies of a couple of generations of Lady Crawleys, and to take inventories of the china, the glass, and other properties in the closets and store-rooms.

Mrs. Rawdon Crawley was general-in-chief over these arrangements, with full order from Sir Pitt to sell, barter, confiscate, or purchase furniture; and she enjoyed herself not a little in an occupation which gave full scope to her taste and ingenuity. The renovation of the house was determined upon when Sir Pitt came to town in November to see his lawyers, and when he passed nearly a week in Curzon Street, under the roof of his affectionate brother and sister.

He had put up at a hotel at first; but Becky, as soon as she heard of the Baronet's arrival, went off alone to greet him, and returned in an hour to Curzon Street with Sir Pitt in the carriage by her side.

A fire was blazing already in Sir Pitt's apartment (it was Miss Brigg's room, by the way, who was sent upstairs to sleep with the maid). "I knew I should bring you," she said, with pleasure beaming in her glance. Indeed, she was really sincerely happy at having him for a guest.

Becky made Rawdon dine out once or twice on business while Pitt stayed with them, and the Baronet passed the happy evening alone with her and Briggs.

Then when he had drunk up the bottle of *petit vin blanc*, she gave him her hand and took him up to the drawing-room, and made him snug on the sofa by the fire, and let him talk as she listened with the tenderest kindly interest, sitting by him, and hemming a shirt for her dear little boy. Whenever Mrs. Rawdon wished to be particularly humble and virtuous, this little shirt used to come out of her work-box. It had got to be too small for Rawdon long before it was finished.

Well, Rebecca listened to Pitt, she talked to him, she sang to him, she coaxed him, and cuddled him, so that he found himself more and more glad every day to get back from the lawyer's at Gray's Inn to the blazing fire in Curzon Street—a gladness in which the men of law likewise participated, for Pitt's harangues were of the longest—and so that when he went away he felt quite a pang at departing. How pretty she looked kissing her hand to him from the carriage, and waving her handkerchief when he had taken his place in the mail! She put her handkerchief to her eyes once. He pulled his sealskin cap over his as the coach drove away, and sinking back he thought to himself how she respected him and how he deserved it, and how Rawdon was a foolish, dull fellow, who didn't half appreciate his wife; and

how mum and stupid his own wife was compared to that brilliant little
Becky. Becky had hinted every one of these things herself, perhaps,
but so delicately and gently that you hardly knew when or where. And
before they parted it was agreed that the house in London should be
redecorated for the next season, and that the brother's families should
meet again in the country at Christmas.

Rawdon was a fine open-faced boy, with blue eyes and waving flaxen
hair, sturdy in limb, but generous and soft in heart, fondly attaching
himself to all who were good to him—to the pony; to Lord Southdown,
who gave him the horse (he used to blush and glow all over when he
saw that kind young nobleman); to the groom who had charge of the
pony; to Molly, the cook, who crammed him with ghost stories at
night, and with good things from the dinner; to Briggs, whom he
plagued and laughed at; and to his father especially, whose attachment
towards the lad was curious too to witness. Here, as he grew to be
about eight years old, his attachments may be said to have ended.
The beautiful mother-vision had faded away after a while. During near
two years she had scarcely spoken to the child. She disliked him. He
had the measles and the whooping-cough. He bored her. One day
when he was standing at the landing-place, having crept down from
the upper regions, attracted by the sound of his mother's voice, who
was singing to Lord Steyne, the drawing-room door opening suddenly
discovered the little spy, who but a moment before had been rapt in
delight, and listening to the music.

His mother came out and struck him violently a couple of boxes on
the ear. He heard a laugh from the Marquis in the inner room (who
was amused by this free and artless exhibition of Becky's temper), and
fled down below to his friends of the kitchen, bursting in an agony of
grief.

"It is not because it hurts me," little Rawdon gasped out—"only—
only"—sobs and tears wound up the sentence in a storm. It was the
little boy's heart that was bleeding. "Why mayn't I hear her singing?
Why don't she ever sing to me—as she does to that bald-headed man
with the large teeth?" He gasped out at various intervals these
exclamations of rage and grief. The cook looked at the housemaid,
the housemaid looked knowingly at the footman—the awful kitchen
inquisition, which sits in judgment in every house and knows everything, sate on Rebecca at that moment.

After this incident the mother's dislike increased to hatred; the
consciousness that the child was in the house was a reproach and a
pain to her. His very sight annoyed her. Fear, doubt, and resistance
sprang up, too, in the boy's own bosom. They were separated from
that day of the boxes on the ear.

A day or two before Christmas, Becky, her husband, and her son
made ready and went to pass the holidays at the seat of their ancestors
at Queen's Crawley. Becky would have liked to leave the little brat
behind, and would have done so but for Lady Jane's urgent invitation

to the youngster, and the symptoms of revolt and discontent which Rawdon manifested at her neglect of her son. "He's the finest boy in England," the father said in a tone of reproach to her, "and you don't seem to care for him, Becky, as much as you do for your spaniel. He shan't bother you much: at home he will be away from you in the nursery, and he shall go outside on the coach with me."

"Where you go yourself because you want to smoke those filthy cigars," replied Mrs. Rawdon.

"I remember when you liked 'em though," answered the husband.

Becky laughed; she was almost always good-humoured. "That was when I was on my promotion, Goosey," she said. "Take Rawdon outside with you, and give him a cigar too if you like."

It was dark again when little Rawdon was wakened up to enter his uncle's carriage at Mudbury, and he sate and looked out of it wondering as the great iron gates flew open, and at the white trunks of the limes as they swept by, until they stopped at length before the lighted windows of the Hall, which were blazing and comfortable with Christmas welcome. The hall-door was flung open; a big fire was burning in the great old fireplace; a carpet was down over the chequered black flags. "It's the old Turkey one that used to be in the Ladies' Gallery," thought Rebecca, and the next instant was kissing Lady Jane.

She and Sir Pitt performed the same salute with great gravity; but Rawdon having been smoking, hung back rather from his sister-in-law, whose two children came up to their cousin; and while Matilda held out her hand and kissed him, Pitt Binkie Southdown, the son and heir, stood aloof rather, and examined him as a little dog does a big dog.

Then the kind hostess conducted her guests to the snug apartments blazing with cheerful fires. Then the young ladies came and knocked at Mrs. Rawdon's door, under the pretence that they were desirous to be useful, but in reality to have the pleasure of inspecting the contents of her band and bonnet boxes, and her dresses, which though black were of the newest London fashion. And they told her how much the Hall was changed for the better, and how old Lady Southdown was gone, and how Pitt was taking his station in the county, as became a Crawley, in fact. Then the great dinner-bell having rung, the family assembled at dinner, at which meal Rawdon Junior was placed by his aunt, the good-natured lady of the house; Sir Pitt being uncommonly attentive to his sister-in-law at his own right hand.

Little Rawdon exhibited a fine appetite, and showed a gentlemanlike behaviour.

The brothers had good occupation for several mornings in examining the improvements which had been effected by Sir Pitt's genius and economy. And as they walked or rode and looked at them, they could talk without too much boring each other. And Pitt took care to tell Rawdon what a heavy outlay of money these improvements had occasioned, and that a man of landed and funded property was often very hard pressed for twenty pounds. "There is that new lodge gate," said Pitt, pointing to it humbly with the bamboo cane: "I can no more pay for it before the dividends in January than I can fly."

"I can lend you, Pitt, till then," Rawdon answered, rather ruefully; and they went in and looked at the restored lodge, where the family arms were just new scraped in stone, and where old Mrs. Lock, for the first time these many long years, had tight doors, sound roofs, and whole windows.

CHAPTER XLV

BETWEEN HAMPSHIRE AND LONDON

Sir Pitt Crawley had done more than repair fences and restore dilapidated lodges on the Queen's Crawley estate. Like a wise man, he had set to work to rebuild the injured popularity of his house, and stop up the gaps and ruins in which his name had been left by his disreputable and thriftless old predecessor.

A great part of the altered demeanour and popularity of Sir Pitt Crawley might have been traced to the counsels of that astute little lady of Curzon Street. "*You* remain a baronet—you consent to be a mere country gentleman!" she said to him, while he had been her guest in London. "No, Sir Pitt Crawley, I know you better. I know your talents and your ambition. You fancy you hide them both, but you can conceal neither from me. I showed Lord Steyne your pamphlet on Malt. He was familiar with it, and said it was in the opinion of the whole Cabinet the most masterly thing that had appeared on the subject. The Ministry has its eye upon you, and I know what you want. You want to distinguish yourself in Parliament; every one says you are the finest speaker in England (for your speeches at Oxford are still remembered). You want to be member for the county, where, with your own vote and your borough at your back, you can command anything. And you want to be Baron Crawley of Queen's Crawley, and will be before you die. I saw it all. I could read your heart, Sir Pitt. If I had a husband who possessed your intellect as he does your name, I sometimes think I should not be unworthy of him; but—but I am yours kinswoman now," she added, with a laugh. "Poor little penniless I have got a little interest; and who knows, perhaps the mouse may be able to aid the lion."

Pitt Crawley was amazed and enraptured with her speech. "How that woman comprehends me!" he said.

On Christmas Day a great family gathering took place. All the Crawleys from the Rectory came to dine. Rebecca was as frank and fond of Mrs. Bute as if the other had never been her enemy; she was affectionately interested in the dear girls, and surprised at the progress which they had made in music since her time, and insisted upon encoring one of the duets out of the great song-books which Jim, grumbling, had been forced to bring under his arm from the Rectory. Mrs. Bute, perforce, was obliged to adopt a decent demeanour towards the little adventuress—of course being free to discourse with her daughters afterwards about the absurd respect with which Sir Pitt treated his sister-in-law. But Jim, who had sat next to her at dinner, declared she was a trump; and one and all of the Rector's family agreed that little Rawdon was a fine boy. They respected a possible baronet in the boy, between whom and the title there was only the little sickly pale Pitt Binkie.

Also before this merry Christmas was over, the Baronet had screwed up courage enough to give his brother another draft on his bankers, and for no less a sum than a hundred pounds; an act which caused Sir Pitt cruel pangs at first, but which made him glow afterwards to think himself one of the most generous of men. Rawdon and his son went away with the utmost heaviness of heart. Becky and the ladies parted with some alacrity, however, and our friend returned to London to commence those avocations with which we find her occupied when this chapter begins. Under her care the Crawley house in Great Gaunt Street was quite rejuvenescent, and ready for the reception of Sir Pitt and his family when the Baronet came to London to attend his duties in Parliament, and to assume that position in the country for which his vast genius fitted him.

Lady Jane's sweetness and kindness had inspired Rebecca with such a contempt for her Ladyship as the little woman found no small difficulty in concealing. That sort of goodness and simplicity which Lady Jane possessed annoyed our friend Becky, and it was impossible for her at times not to show or to let the other divine her scorn. Her presence, too, rendered Lady Jane uneasy. Her husband talked constantly with Becky. Signs of intelligence seemed to pass between them, and Pitt spoke with her on subjects on which he never thought of discoursing with Lady Jane.

So these two ladies did not see much of each other except upon those occasions when the younger brother's wife, having an object to gain from the other, frequented her. They my-loved and my-deared each other assiduously, but kept apart generally; whereas Sir Pitt, in the midst of his multiplied avocations, found daily time to see his sister-in-law.

On the occasion of his first Speaker's dinner, Sir Pitt took the opportunity of appearing before his sister-in-law in his uniform—that old diplomatic suit which he had worn when *attaché* to the Pumpernickel legation.

Becky complimented him upon that dress, and admired him almost as much as his own wife and children, to whom he displayed himself before he set out. She said that it was only the thoroughbred gentleman who could wear the Court suit with advantage; it was only your men of ancient race whom the *culotte courte* became. Pitt looked down

with complacency at his legs, which had not, in truth, much more
symmetry or swell than the lean Court sword which dangled by his
side—looked down at his legs, and thought in his heart that he was
killing.

CHAPTER XLVI

STRUGGLES AND TRIALS

OUR friends at Brompton were meanwhile passing their Christmas
after their fashion, and in a manner by no means too cheerful.

Out of the hundred pounds a year which was about the amount of
her income the widow Osborne had been in the habit of giving up
nearly three-fourths to her father and mother, for the expenses of herself and her little boy. With £120 more, supplied by Jos, this family
of four people, attended by a single Irish servant, who also did for
Clapp and his wife, might manage to live in decent comfort through the
year, and hold up their heads yet, and be able to give a friend a dish
of tea still, after the storms and disappointments of their early life.
Sedley still maintained his ascendency over the family of Mr. Clapp,
his ex-clerk. Clapp remembered the time when, sitting on the edge of
the chair, he tossed off a bumper to the health of "Mrs. S——, Miss
Emmy, and Mr. Joseph in India," at the merchant's rich table in
Russell Square. Time magnified the splendour of those recollections in
the honest clerk's bosom.

Out of the small residue of her income, which Amelia kept back for
herself, the widow had need of all the thrift and care possible in order
to enable her to keep her darling boy dressed in such a manner as became George Osborne's son, and to defray the expenses of the little
school to which, after much misgiving and reluctance, and many secret
pangs and fears on her own part, she had been induced to send the lad.

Georgy made great progress in the school, which was kept by a
friend of his mother's constant admirer, the Rev. Mr. Binny. He
brought home numberless prizes and testimonials of ability. He told
his mother countless stories every night about his school companions;
and what a fine fellow Lyons was, and what a sneak Sniffin was.

In these quiet labours and harmless cares the gentle widow's life was
passing away, a silver hair or two marking the progress of time on her
head, and a line deepening ever so little on her fair forehead.

We have seen how one of George's grandfathers (Mr. Osborne), in
his easy-chair in Russell Square, daily grew more violent and moody,
and how his daughter, with her fine carriage, and her fine horses, and
her name on half the public charity lists of the town, was a lonely
miserable, persecuted old maid. She thought again and again of the
beautiful little boy, her brother's son, whom she had seen. She longed
to be allowed to drive in the fine carriage to the house in which he
lived; and she used to look out day after day as she took her solitary
drive in the Park, in hopes that she might see him.

On that night when Jane Osborne had told her father that she had seen his grandson, the old man had made her no reply; but he had shown no anger, and had bade her good-night on going himself to his room in rather a kindly voice. And he must have meditated on what she said, and have made some inquiries of the Dobbin family regarding her visit; for a fortnight after it took place, he asked her where was her little French watch and chain she used to wear?

"I bought it with my money, sir," she said, in a great fright.

"Go and order another like it, or a better if you can get it," said the old gentleman, and lapsed again into silence.

Of late the Misses Dobbin more than once repeated their entreaties to Amelia to allow George to visit them. His aunt had shown her inclination; perhaps his grandfather himself, they hinted, might be disposed to be reconciled to him. Surely Amelia could not refuse such advantageous chances for the boy.

Nor could she; but she acceded to their overtures with a very heavy and suspicious heart, was always uneasy during the child's absence from her, welcomed him back as if he was rescued out of some danger. He brought back money and toys, at which the widow looked with alarm and jealousy; she asked him always if he had seen any gentleman. "Only old Sir William, who drove him about in the four-wheeled chaise, and Mr. Dobbin, who arrived on the beautiful bay horse in the afternoon—in the green coat and pink neckcloth, with the gold-headed whip, who promised to show him the Tower of London and take him out with the Surrey hounds." At last he said, "There was an old gentleman, with thick eyebrows and a broad hat, and large chain and seals." He came one day as the coachman was lunging Georgy round the lawn on the grey pony. "He looked at me very much. He shook very much. I said, 'My name is Norval' after dinner. My aunt began to cry. She is always crying." Such was George's report on that night.

The Amelia knew that the boy had seen his grandfather, and looked out feverishly for a proposal which she was sure would follow, and which came, in fact, in a few days afterwards. Mr. Osborne formally offered to take the boy, and make him heir to the fortune which he had intended that his father should inherit. He would make Mrs. George Osborne an allowance, such as to assure her a decent competency. If Mrs. George Osborne proposed to marry again, as Mr. O. heard was her intention, he would not withdraw that allowance. But it must be understood that the child would live entirely with his grandfather in Russell Square, or at whatever other place Mr. O. should select, and that he would be occasionally permitted to see Mrs. George Osborne at her own residence. This message was brought or read to her in a letter one day, when her mother was from home, and her father absent as usual in the City.

She was never seen angry but twice or thrice in her life, and it was in one of these moods that Mr. Osborne's attorney had the fortune to behold her. She rose up trembling and flushing very much as soon as, after reading the letter, Mr. Poe handed it to her, and she tore the paper into a hundred fragments, which she trod on. " 'I marry again! I take money to part from my child! Who dares insult me by proposing such a thing? Tell Mr. Osborne it is a cowardly letter, sir—a cowardly letter; I will not answer it. I wish you good-morning, sir.' And she bowed me out of the room like a tragedy queen," said the lawyer who told the story.

Her parents never remarked her agitation on that day, and she never told them of the interview. They had their own affairs to interest them —affairs which deeply interested this innocent and unconscious lady. The old gentleman, her father, was always dabbling in speculation. We have seen how the Wine Company and the Coal Company had failed him. But prowling about the City always eagerly and restlessly still, he lighted upon some other scheme, of which he thought so well that he embarked in it in spite of the remonstrances of Mr. Clapp, to whom indeed he never dared to tell how far he had engaged himself in it. And as it was always Mr. Sedley's maxim not to talk about money matters before women, they had no inkling of the misfortunes that were in store for them until the unhappy old gentleman was forced to make gradual confessions.

The bills of the little household, which had been settled weekly, first fell into arrear. The remittances had not arrived from India, Mr. Sedley told his wife, with a disturbed face. As she had paid her bills very regularly hitherto, one or two of the tradesmen to whom the poor lady was obliged to go round asking for time were very angry at a delay to which they were perfectly used from more irregular customers. Emmy's contribution, paid over cheerfully without any questions, kept the little company in half-rations, however. And the first six months passed away pretty easily, old Sedley still keeping up with the notion that his shares must rise, and that all would be well.

No sixty pounds, however, came to help the household at the end of the half-year, and it fell deeper and deeper into trouble. Mrs. Sedley, who was growing infirm and was much shaken, remained silent, or wept a great deal with Mrs. Clapp in the kitchen. The butcher was particularly surly, the grocer insolent. Once or twice little Georgy had grumbled about the dinners, and Amelia, who still would have been satisfied with a slice of bread for her own dinner, could not but perceive that her son was neglected, and purchased little things out of her private purse to keep the boy in health.

At last they told her, or told her such a garbled story as people in difficulties tell. One day, her own money having been received, and Amelia about to pay it over, she, who had kept an account of the moneys expended by her, proposed to keep a certain portion back out of her dividend, having contracted engagements for a new suit for Georgy.

Then it came out that Jos's remittances were not paid; that the house was in difficulties, which Amelia ought to have seen before, her mother said, but she cared for nothing or nobody except Georgy. At this she passed all her money across the table, without a word, to her mother, and returned to her room to cry her eyes out. She had a great access of sensibility too that day when obliged to go and countermand the clothes, the darling clothes on which she had set her heart for Christmas Day, and the cut and fashion of which she had arranged in many conversations with a small milliner her friend.

Hardest of all, she had to break the matter to Georgy, who made a loud outcry. Everybody had new clothes at Christmas. The others would laugh at him. He *would* have new clothes. She had promised them to him. The poor widow had only kisses to give him. She darned the old suit in tears.

CHAPTER XLVII

GAUNT HOUSE

ALL the world knows that Lord Steyne's town palace stands in Gaunt Square, out of which Great Gaunt Street leads whither we first conducted Rebecca in the time of the departed Sir Pitt Crawley. Peering over the railings and through the black trees into the garden of the Square, you see a few miserable governesses with wan-faced pupils wandering round and round it, and round the dreary grass-plot, in the centre of which rises the statue of Lord Gaunt, who fought at Minden, in a three-tailed wig, and otherwise habited like a Roman emperor. Gaunt House occupies nearly a side of the Square. The remaining three sides are composed of mansions that have passed away into dowagerism —tall, dark houses, with window-frames of stone, or picked out of a lighter red.

A few score yards down New Gaunt Street, and leading into Gaunt Mews indeed, is a little modest back door, which you would not remark from that of any of the other stables. But many a little close carriage has stopped at that door, as my informant (little Tom Eaves, who knows everything, and who showed me the place) told me. "The Prince and Perdita have been in and out of that door, sir," he has often told me; "Madame Clarke has entered it with the Duke of ——. It conducts to the famous *petits appartements* of Lord Steyne—one, sir, fitted up all in ivory and white satin, another in ebony and black velvet; there is a little banqueting-room taken from Sallust's house at Pompeii, and painted by Cosway—a little private kitchen, in which every saucepan was silver and all the spits were gold. It was there that Egalité Orleans roasted partridges on the night when he and the Marquis of Steyne won a hundred thousand from a great personage at ombre. Half of the money went to the French Revolution, half to purchase Lord Gaunt's Marquisate and Garter; and the remainder" —but it forms no part of our scheme to tell what became of the remainder, for every shilling of which, and a great deal more, little Tom Eaves, who knows everybody's affairs, is ready to account.

Besides his town palace, the Marquis had castles and palaces in various quarters of the three kingdoms, whereof the descriptions may be found in the road-books—Castle Strongbow, with its woods, on the Shannon shore; Gaunt Castle, in Carmarthenshire, where Richard II was taken prisoner; Gauntly Hall in Yorkshire, where I have been informed there were two hundred silver teapots for the breakfasts of the guests of the house, with everything to correspond in splendour; and Stillbrook in Hampshire, which was my lord's farm, a humble place of residence, of which we all remember the wonderful furniture which was sold at my lord's demise by a late celebrated auctioneer.

My Lord Gaunt married, as every person who frequents the Peerage knows, the Lady Blanche Thistlewood, a daughter of the noble house of Bareacres, before-mentioned in this veracious history. A wing of Gaunt House was assigned to this couple; for the head of the family chose to govern it, and while he reigned to reign supreme: his son and heir, however, living little at home, disagreeing with his wife, and borrowing upon post-obits such moneys as he required beyond the very moderate sums which his father was disposed to allow him. The Marquis knew every shilling of his son's debts. At his lamented demise, he was found himself to be possessor of many of his heir's bonds, purchased for their benefit, and devised by his Lordship to the children of his younger son.

As, to my Lord Gaunt's dismay, and the chuckling delight of his natural enemy and father, the Lady Gaunt had no children, the Lord Gaunt was desired to return from Vienna, where he was engaged in waltzing and diplomacy, and to contract a matrimonial alliance with the Honourable Joan, only daughter of John Johnes, First Baron Helvellyn, and head of the firm of Jones, Brown & Robinson, of Threadneedle Street, Bankers; from which union sprang several sons and daughters, whose doings do not appertain to this story.

The marriage at first was a happy and prosperous one. My Lord George Gaunt could not only read, but write pretty correctly. He spoke French with considerable fluency, and was one of the finest waltzers in Europe. With these talents, and his interest at home, there was little doubt that his Lordship would rise to the highest dignities in his profession. The lady, his wife, felt that courts were her sphere; and her wealth enabled her to receive splendidly in those Continental towns whither her husband's diplomatic duties led him. There was talk of appointing him Minister, and bets were laid at the Travellers' that he would be ambassador ere long, when, of a sudden, rumours arrived of the secretary's extraordinary behaviour. At a grand diplomatic dinner given by his chief, he had started up, and declared that a *pâté de foie gras* was poisoned. He went to a ball at the hotel of the Bavarian envoy, the Count de Springbock-Hohenlaufen, with his head shaved, and dressed as a Capuchin friar. It was not a masked ball, as some folks wanted to persuade you. It was something queer, people whispered. His grandfather was so. It was in the family.

His wife and family returned to this country, and took up their abode at Gaunt House. Lord George gave up his post on the European continent, and was gazetted to Brazil. But people knew better: he never returned from that Brazil expedition—never died there—never lived there—never was there at all. He was nowhere; he was gone out altogether. "Brazil," said one gossip to another, with a grin—"Brazil is St. John's Wood. Rio Janeiro is a cottage surrounded by four walls; and George Gaunt is accredited to a keeper, who has invested him with the order of the Strait-Waistcoat." These are the kind of epitaphs which men pass over one another in Vanity Fair.

Twice or thrice in a week, in the earliest morning, the poor mother went for her sins and saw the poor invalid. Sometimes he laughed at her (and his laughter was more pitiful than to hear him cry); some-times she found the brilliant dandy diplomatist of the Congress of Vienna dragging about a child's toy, or nursing the keeper's baby's doll. Sometimes he knew her and Father Mole, her director and com-panion; oftener he forgot her, as he had done wife, children, love, ambition, vanity. But he remembered his dinner hour, and used to cry if his wine-and-water was not strong enough.

It was the mysterious taint of the blood: the poor mother had brought it from her own ancient race. The evil had broken out once or twice in the father's family, long before Lady Steyne's sins had begun, or her fasts and tears and penances had been offered in their expiation. The pride of the race was struck down as the first-born of Pharaoh. The dark mark of fate and doom was on the threshold,—the tall old threshold surmounted by coronets and carved heraldry.

So there was splendour and wealth, but no great happiness per-chance, behind the tall carved portals of Gaunt House with its smoky coronets and ciphers. The feasts there were of the grandest in London; but there was not overmuch content therewith, except among the guests who sat at my lord's table. Had he not been so great a prince very few possibly would have visited him, but in Vanity Fair the sins of very great personages are looked at indulgently. "*Nous regardons à deux fois*" (as the French Lady said) before we condemn a person of my lord's undoubted quality. Some notorious carpers and squeamish moralists might be sulky with Lord Steyne, but they were glad enough to come when he asked them.

CHAPTER XLVIII

IN WHICH THE READER IS INTRODUCED TO THE VERY BEST OF COMPANY

At last Becky's kindness and attention to the chief of her husband's family were destined to meet with an exceeding great reward; a reward which, though certainly somewhat unsubstantial, the little woman coveted with greater eagerness than more positive benefits. If she did not wish to lead a virtuous life, at least she desired to enjoy a character for virtue; and we know that no lady in the genteel world can possess this desideratum, until she has put on a train and feathers, and has been presented to her Sovereign at Court. From that august interview they come out stamped as honest women.

Well, there came a happy day in Mrs. Rawdon Crawley's existence when this angel was admitted into the paradise of a Court which she coveted; her sister-in-law acting as her godmother. On the appointed day, Sir Pitt and his lady, in their great family carriage (just newly built, and ready for the Baronet's assumption of the office of High Sheriff of his county), drove up to the little house in Curzon Street, to the edification of Raggles, who was watching from his greengrocer's shop, and saw fine plumes within, and enormous bunches of flowers in the breasts of the new livery-coats of the footmen.

Sir Pitt, in a glittering uniform, descended and went into Curzon Street, his sword between his legs. Little Rawdon stood with his face against the parlour window-panes, smiling and nodding with all his might to his aunt in the carriage within; and presently Sir Pitt issued forth from the house again, leading forth a lady with grand feathers, covered in a white shawl, and holding up daintily a train of magnificent brocade. She stepped into the vehicle as if she were a princess and accustomed all her life to go to Court, smiling graciously on the footman at the door, and on Sir Pitt, who followed her into the carriage.

Then Rawdon followed in his old Guards' uniform, which had grown woefully shabby, and was much too tight. He was to have followed the procession, and waited upon his Sovereign in a cab, but that his good-natured sister-in-law insisted that they should be a family party. The coach was large, the ladies not very big, they would hold their trains in their laps—finally, the four went fraternally together; and their carriage presently joined the line of royal equipages which was making its way down Piccadilly and St. James's Street, towards the old brick palace where the Star of Brunswick was in waiting to receive his nobles and gentlefolk.

We are authorized to state that Mrs. Rawdon Crawley's *costume de cour* on the occasion of her presentation to the Sovereign was of the most elegant and brilliant description.

And the diamonds—"Where the doose did you get the diamonds, Becky?" said her husband, admiring some jewels which he had never seen before, and which sparkled in her ears and on her neck with brilliance and profusion.

Becky blushed a little, and looked at him hard for a moment. Pitt Crawley blushed a little too, and looked out of window. The fact is, he had given her a very small portion of the brilliants—a pretty diamond clasp, which confined a pearl necklace which she wore—and the Baronet had omitted to mention the circumstance to his lady.

Becky looked at her husband, and then at Sir Pitt, with an air of saucy triumph—as much as to say, "Shall I betray you?"

"Guess!" she said to her husband. "Why, you silly man," she continued, "where do you suppose I got them?—all except the little clasp, which a dear friend of mine gave me long ago. I hired them, to be sure. I hired them at Mr. Polonius's, in Coventry Street. You don't suppose that all the diamonds which go to Court belong to the wearers; like those beautiful stones that Lady Jane has, and which are much handsomer than any which I have, I am certain."

"They are family jewels," said Sir Pitt, again looking uneasy. And in this family conversation the carriage rolled down the street, until its cargo was finally discharged at the gates of the palace where the Sovereign was sitting in state.

The diamonds, which had created Rawdon's admiration, never went back to Mr. Polonius, of Coventry Street, and that gentleman never applied for their restoration; but they retired into a little private repository, in an old desk, which Amelia Sedley had given her years and years ago, and in which Becky kept a number of useful and, perhaps, valuable things about which her husband knew nothing.

Thus Rawdon knew nothing about the brilliant diamond earrings, or the superb brilliant ornament which decorated the fair bosom of his lady; but Lord Steyne, who was in his place at Court, as Lord of the Powder Closet, and one of the great dignitaries and illustrious defences of the throne of England, and came up with all his stars, garters, collars, and cordons, and paid particular attention to the little woman, knew whence the jewels came, and who paid for them.

The particulars of Becky's costume were in the newspapers—feathers, lappets, superb diamonds, and all the rest. Lady Crackenbury read the paragraph in bitterness of spirit, and discoursed to her followers about the airs which that woman was giving herself. Mrs. Bute Crawley and her young ladies in the country had a copy of *The Morning Post* from town; and gave a vent to their honest indignation.

A few days after the famous presentation, another great and exceeding honour was vouchsafed to the virtuous Becky. Lady Steyne's carriage drove up to Mr. Rawdon Crawley's door, and the footman, instead of driving down the front of the house, as by his tremendous knocking he appeared to be inclined to do, relented, and only delivered in a couple of cards, on which were engraven the names of the Marchioness of Steyne and the Countess of Gaunt. If these bits of pasteboard had been beautiful pictures, or had had a hundred yards of Malines lace rolled round them worth twice the number of guineas, Becky could not have regarded them with more pleasure.

My Lord Steyne coming to call a couple of hours afterwards, and looking about him, and observing everything as was his wont, found his ladies' cards already ranged as the trumps of Becky's hand, and grinned, as this old cynic always did at any naïve display of human weakness.

She found him grinning over the cards. She was discovered, and she blushed a little. "Thank you, Monseigneur," she said. "You see your ladies have been here. How good of you!"

"Well," said the old gentleman, twiddling round his wife's card, "you are bent on becoming a fine lady. You pester my poor old life out to get you into the world. You won't be able to hold you own there, you silly little fool. You've got no money."

"You will get us a place," interposed Becky, "as quick as possible."

"You've got no money, and you want to compete with those who have. You poor little earthenware pipkin, you want to swim down the stream along with the great copper kettles. All women are alike. Everybody is striving for what is not worth the having!"

Briggs looked up from the work-table at which she was seated in the farther room, and gave a deep sigh as she heard the great Marquis speak so lightly of her sex.

"If you don't turn off that abominable sheep-dog," said Lord Steyne, with a savage look over his shoulder at her, "I will have her poisoned."

"I always give my dog dinner from my own plate," said Rebecca, laughing mischievously; and having enjoyed from some time the discomfiture of my lord, who hated poor Briggs for interrupting his *tête-à-tête* with the fair Colonel's wife, Mrs. Rawdon at length had pity upon her admirer, and calling to Briggs, praised the fineness of the weather to her, and bade her to take out the child for a walk.

"I can't send her away," Becky said presently, after a pause, and in a very sad voice. Her eyes filled with tears as she spoke, and she turned away her head.

"You owe her her wages, I suppose?" said the Peer.

"Worse than that," said Becky, still casting down her eyes; "I have ruined her."

"Ruined her!—then why don't you turn her out?" the gentleman asked.

"Men do that," Becky answered bitterly. "Women are not so bad as you. Last year, when we were reduced to our last guinea, she gave us everything. She shall never leave me, until we are ruined utterly ourselves, which does not seem far off, or until I can pay her the utmost farthing."

"—— it, how much is it?" said the Peer, with an oath. And Becky, reflecting on the largeness of his means, mentioned not only the sum which she had borrowed from Miss Briggs, but one of nearly double the amount.

This caused the Lord Steyne to break out in another brief and energetic expression of anger, at which Rebecca held down her head the more, and cried bitterly. "I could not help it. It was my only chance. I dare not tell my husband. He would kill me if I told him what I have done. I have kept it a secret from everybody but you— and you forced it from me. Ah, what shall I do, Lord Steyne? for I am very, very unhappy!"

Lord Steyne made no reply except by beating the devil's tattoo, and biting his nails. At last he clapped his hat on his head, and flung out of the room. Rebecca did not rise from her attitude of misery until the door slammed upon him, and his carriage whirled away. Then she rose up with the queerest expression of victorious mischief glittering in her green eyes. She burst out laughing once or twice to herself, as she sate at work; and sitting down at the piano, she rattled away a triumphant voluntary on the keys, which made the people pause under her window to listen to her brilliant music.

That night there came two notes from Gaunt House for the little woman, the one containing a card of invitation from Lord and Lady Steyne to a dinner at Gaunt House next Friday; while the other enclosed a slip of grey paper bearing Lord Steyne's signature and the address of Messrs. Jones, Brown & Robinson, Lombard Street.

Rawdon heard Becky laughing in the night once or twice. It was only her delight at going to Gaunt House and facing the ladies there, she said, which amused her so. But the truth was, that she was occupied with a great number of other thoughts. Should she pay off old Briggs and give her her congé? Should she astonish Raggles by settling his account? She turned over all these thoughts on her pillow; and on the next day, when Rawdon went out to pay his morning visit to the Club, Mrs. Crawley (in a modest dress with a veil on) whipped off in a hackney-coach to the City, and being landed at Messrs. Jones & Robinson's bank, presented a document there to the authority at the desk, who, in reply, asked her, "How she would take it?"

She gently said "she would take a hundred and fifty pounds in small notes, and the remainder in one note;" and passing through St. Paul's Churchyard, stopped there and bought the handsomest black silk gown for Briggs which money could buy, and which, with a kiss and the kindest speeches, she presented to the simple old spinster.

Then she walked to Mr. Raggles', inquired about his children affectionately, and gave him fifty pounds on account. Then she went to the liveryman from whom she jobbed her carriages, and gratified him with a similar sum. "And I hope this will be a lesson to you, Spavin," she said, "and that on the next Drawing-room day my brother, Sir Pitt, will not be inconvenienced by being obliged to take four of us in his carriage to wait upon His Majesty, because my *own* carriage is not forthcoming." It appears there had been a difference on the last Drawing-room day. Hence the degradation which the Colonel had almost suffered, of being obliged to enter the presence of his Sovereign in a hack cab.

These arrangements concluded, Becky paid a visit upstairs to the before-mentioned desk, which Amelia Sedley had given her years and years ago, and which contained a number of useful and valuable little things; in which private museum she placed the one note which Messrs. Jones & Robinson's cashier had given her.

CHAPTER XLIX

IN WHICH WE ENJOY THREE COURSES AND A DESSERT

WHEN the ladies of Gaunt House were at breakfast that morning, Lord Steyne, who took his chocolate in private, and seldom disturbed the females of his household, or saw them except upon public days, or when they crossed each other in the hall, or when from his pit-box at the Opera he surveyed them in their box on the grand tier—his Lordship, we say, appeared among the ladies and children who were assembled over the tea and toast, and a battle-royal ensued apropos of Rebecca.

"My Lady Steyne," he said, "I want to see the list for your dinner on Friday; and I want you, if you please, to write a card for Colonel and Mrs. Crawley."

"Blanche writes them," Lady Steyne said, in a flutter; "Lady Gaunt writes them."

"I will not write to that person," Lady Gaunt said, a tall and stately lady, who looked up for an instant and then down again after she had spoken. It was not good to meet Lord Steyne's eyes for those who had offended him.

"Send the children out of the room.—Go!" said he, pulling at the bell-rope. The urchins, always frightened before him, retired; their mother would have followed too. "Not you," he said; "you stop."

"My Lady Steyne," he said, "once more will you have the goodness to go to the desk and write that card for your dinner on Friday?"

"My Lord, I will not be present at it," Lady Gaunt said; "I will go home."

"I wish you would, and stay there. You will find the bailiffs at Bareacres very pleasant company, and I shall be freed from lending money to your relations, and from your own damned tragedy airs. Who are you to give orders here? You have no money; you've got no brains. You were here to have children and you have not had any. Gaunt's tired of you, and George's wife is the only person in the family who doesn't wish you were dead. Gaunt would marry again if you were."

"I wish I were," her Ladyship answered, with tears and rage in her eyes.

"You, forsooth, must give yourself airs of virtue; while my wife, who is an immaculate saint, as everybody knows, and never did wrong in her life, has no objection to meet my young friend Mrs. Crawley. My Lady Steyne knows that appearances are sometimes against the best of women; that lies are often told about the most innocent of them. Pray, Madam, shall I tell you some little anecdotes about my Lady Bareacres, your mamma?"

"You may strike me if you like, sir, or hit any cruel blow," Lady

Gaunt said. To see his wife and daughter suffering always put his Lordship into a good humour.

"My sweet Blanche," he said, "I am a gentleman, and never lay my hand upon a woman, save in the way of kindness. I only wish to correct little faults in your character. You women are too proud, and sadly lack humility, as Father Mole, I'm sure, would tell my Lady Steyne if he were here. You mustn't give yourselves airs; you must be meek and humble, my blessings. For all Lady Steyne knows, this calumniated, simple, good-humoured Mrs. Crawley is quite innocent— even more innocent than herself. Her husband's character is not good; but it is as good as Bareacres', who has played a little and not paid a great deal, who cheated you out of the only legacy you ever had, and left you a pauper on my hands. And Mrs. Crawley is not very well born; but she is not worse than Fanny's illustrious ancestor, the first De la Jones."

"The money which I brought into the family, sir," Lady George cried out—

"You purchased a contingent reversion with it," the Marquis said darkly. "If Gaunt dies, your husband may come to his honours; your little boys may inherit them, and who knows what besides? In the meanwhile, ladies, be as proud and virtuous as you like abroad, but don't give *me* any airs. As for Mrs. Crawley's character, I shan't demean myself or that most spotless and perfectly irreproachable lady by even hinting that it requires a defence. You will be pleased to receive her with the utmost cordiality, as you will receive all persons whom I present in this house. This house?" He broke out with a laugh. "Who is the master of it? and what is it? This Temple of Virtue belongs to me. And if I invite all Newgate or all Bedlam here, by —— they shall be welcome."

After this vigorous allocution, to one of which sort Lord Steyne treated his "Hareem" whenever symptoms of insubordination appeared in his household, the crestfallen women had nothing for it but to obey. Lady Gaunt wrote the invitation which his Lordship required, and she and her mother-in-law drove in person, and with bitter and humiliated hearts, to leave the cards on Mrs. Rawdon, the reception of which caused that innocent woman so much pleasure.

The ladies of Gaunt House called Lady Bareacres in to their aid, in order to repulse the common enemy. One of Lady Gaunt's carriages went to Hill Street for her Ladyship's mother, all whose equipages were in the hands of the bailiffs, whose very jewels and wardrobe, it was said, had been seized by those inexorable Israelites.

The Colonel's countenance on coming into this polite society wore as many blushes as the face of a boy of sixteen assumes when he is confronted with his sister's schoolfellows. It has been told before that honest Rawdon had not been much used at any period of his life to ladies' company. Indeed, Becky would have left him at home, but that virtue ordained that her husband should be by her side to protect the timid and fluttering little creature on her first appearance in polite society.

On her first appearance Lord Steyne stepped forward, taking her hand, and greeting her with great courtesy, and presenting her to Lady Steyne and their ladyships her daughters. Their ladyships made three stately curtsies, and the elder lady, to be sure, gave her hand to the newcomer, but it was as cold and lifeless as marble.

That night was a great triumph for Becky. She sang her very best, and it was so good that every one of the men came and crowded round the piano. The women, her enemies, were left quite alone. And Mr. Paul Jefferson Jones thought he had made a conquest of Lady Gaunt by going up to her Ladyship and praising her delightful friend's first-rate singing.

CHAPTER L

CONTAINS A VULGAR INCIDENT

THE muse, whoever she be, who presides over this Comic History must now descend from the genteel heights in which she has been soaring, and have the goodness to drop down upon the lowly roof of John Sedley at Brompton, and describe what events are taking place there. Here, too, in this humble tenement, live care, and distrust, and dismay. Mrs. Clapp in the kitchen is grumbling in secret to her husband about the rent, and urging the good fellow to rebel against his old friend and patron and his present lodger. Mrs. Sedley has ceased to visit her landlady in the lower regions now, and indeed is in a position to patronize Mrs. Clapp no longer. How can one be condescending to a lady to whom one owes a matter of forty pounds, and who is perpetually throwing out hints for the money? The Irish maid-servant has not altered in the least in her kind and respectful behaviour; but Mrs. Sedley fancies that she is growing insolent and ungrateful, and, as the guilty thief who fears each bush an officer, sees threatening innuendoes and hints of capture in all the girl's speeches and answers. Miss Clapp, grown quite a young woman now, is declared by the sour old lady to be an unbearable and impudent little minx. Why Amelia can be so fond of her, or have her in her room so much, or walk out with her so constantly, Mrs. Sedley cannot conceive. The bitterness of poverty has poisoned the life of the once cheerful and kindly woman. She is thankless for Amelia's constant and gentle bearing towards her; carps at her for her efforts at kindness or service; rails at her for her silly pride in her child, and her neglect of her parents. Georgy's house is not a very lively one since Uncle Jos's annuity has been withdrawn, and the little family are almost upon famine diet.

Amelia thinks, and thinks, and racks her brain to find some means of increasing the small pittance upon which the household is starving. At the beginning of the struggle she had written off a letter of tender supplication to her brother at Calcutta, imploring him not to withdraw the support which he had granted to their parents, and painting in terms of artless pathos their lonely and hapless condition. She did not know the truth of the matter. The payment of Jos's annuity was still regular, but it was a money-lender in the City who was receiving it; old Sedley had sold it for a sum of money wherewith to prosecute his bootless schemes. Emmy was calculating eagerly the time that would lapse before the letter would arrive and be answered. She had written down the date in her pocket-book of the day when she dispatched it. To her son's guardian, the good Major at Madras, she had not communicated any of her griefs and perplexities. She had not written to him since she wrote to congratulate him on his approaching marriage. She thought with sickening despondency that that friend—the only one, the one who had felt such a regard for her—was fallen away.

One day, when things had come to a very bad pass—when the creditors were pressing, the mother in hysteric grief, the father in more than usual gloom, the inmates of the family avoiding each other, each secretly oppressed with his private unhappiness and notion of wrong—the father and daughter happened to be left alone together; and Amelia thought to comfort her father by telling him what she had done. She had written to Joseph; an answer must come in three or four months. He was always generous though careless. He could not refuse when he knew how straitened were the circumstances of his parents.

Then the poor old gentleman revealed the whole truth to her—that his son was still paying the annuity, which his own imprudence had flung away. He had not dared to tell it sooner. He thought Amelia's ghastly and terrified look, when, with a trembling, miserable voice he made the confession, conveyed reproaches to him for his concealment. "Ah," said he, with quivering lips and turning away, "you despise your old father now!"

"O papa! it is not that," Amelia cried out, falling on his neck, and kissing him many times. "You are always good and kind. You did it for the best. It is not for the money; it is—O my God, my God! have mercy upon me, and give me strength to bear this trial;" and she kissed him again wildly, and went away.

Still the father did not know what that explanation meant, and the burst of anguish with which the poor girl left him. It was that she was conquered. The sentence was passed. The child must go from her—to others—to forget her. Her heart and her treasure—her joy, hope, love, worship—her God almost! She must give him up, and then—and then she would go to George; and they would watch over the child, and wait for him until he came to them in heaven.

She put on her bonnet, scarcely knowing what she did, and went out to walk in the lanes by which George used to come back from school, and where she was in the habit of going on his return to meet the boy. It was May, a half-holiday. The leaves were all coming out, the weather was brilliant. The boy came running to her flushed with

health, singing, his bundle of school-books hanging by a thong. There
he was. Both her arms were round him. No, it was impossible. They
could not be going to part. "What is the matter, mother?" said he;
"you look very pale."

"Nothing, my child," she said, and stooped down and kissed him.

Her mind being made up, the widow began to take such measures as
seemed right to her for advancing the end which she proposed. One
day Miss Osborne, in Russell Square—Amelia had not written the name
or number of the house for ten years; her youth, her early story came
back to her as she wrote the superscription—one day Miss Osborne got
a letter from Amelia which made her blush very much and look
towards her father, sitting glooming in his place at the other end of
the table.

In simple terms Amelia told her the reasons which had induced her
to change her mind respecting her boy. Her father had met with fresh
misfortunes, which had entirely ruined him. Her own pittance was so
small that it would barely enable her to support her parents, and would
not suffice to give George the advantages which were his due. Great as
her sufferings would be at parting with him, she would, by God's help,
endure them for the boy's sake. She knew that those to whom he was
going would do all in their power to make him happy. She described
his disposition, such as she fancied it—quick and impatient of control
or harshness, easily to be moved by love and kindness. In a postscript
she stipulated that she should have a written agreement that she should
see the child as often as she wished; she could not part with him under
any other terms.

"What! Mrs. Pride has come down, has she?" old Osborne said,
when with a tremulous, eager voice Miss Osborne read him the letter.
"Reg'lar starved out, hey? ha, ha! I knew she would." He tried to
keep his dignity and to read his paper as usual, but he could not follow
it. He chuckled and swore to himself behind the sheet.

At last he flung it down, and scowling at his daughter, as his wont
was, went out of the room into his study adjoining, from whence he
presently returned with a key. He flung it to Miss Osborne.

"Get the room over mine—his room that was—ready," he said.

"Yes, sir," his daughter replied in a tremble. It was George's room.
It had not be opened for more than ten years. Some of his clothes,
papers, handkerchiefs, whips and caps, fishing-rods and sporting gear,
were still there. An Army List of 1814, with his name written on the
cover, a little dictionary he was wont to use in writing, and the Bible
his mother had given him were on the mantelpiece, with a pair of
spurs, and a dried inkstand covered with the dust of ten years. Ah,
since that ink was wet, what days and people had passed away! The
writing-book, still on the table, was blotted with his hand.

Miss Osborne was much affected when she first entered this room
with the servants under her. She sank quite pale on the little bed.

"This is blessed news, mam—indeed, mam," the housekeeper said; "and the good old times is returning, mam. The dear little feller, to be sure, mam; how happy he will be! But some folks in Mayfair, mam, will owe him a grudge, mam;" and she clicked back the bolt which held the window-sash, and let the air into the chamber.

"You had better send that woman some money," Mr. Osborne said, before he went out. "She shan't want for nothing. Send her a hundred pound."

"And I'll go and see her to-morrow?" Miss Osborne asked.

"That's your look-out. She don't come in here, mind. No, by ——, not for all the money in London. But she mustn't want now. So look out and get things right." With which brief speeches Mr. Osborne took leave of his daughter, and went on his accustomed way into the City.

"Here, papa, is some money," Amelia said that night, kissing the old man, her father, and putting a bill for a hundred pounds into his hands.—"And—and, mamma, don't be harsh with Georgy; he—he is not going to stop with us long." She could say nothing more, and walked away silently to her room. Let us close it upon her prayers and her sorrow. I think we had best speak little about so much love and grief.

Miss Osborne came the next day, according to the promise contained in her note, and saw Amelia. The meeting between them was friendly. A look and a few words from Miss Osborne showed the poor widow that, with regard to this woman at least, there need be no fear lest she should take the first place in her son's affection. She was cold, sensible, not unkind. The mother had not been so well-pleased, perhaps, had the rival been better looking, younger, more affectionate, warmer-hearted. Miss Osborne, on the other hand, thought of old times, and memories, and could not but be touched with the poor mother's pitiful situation. She was conquered, and laying down her arms, as it were, she humbly submitted. That day they arranged together the preliminaries of the treaty of capitulation.

Georg : was kept from school the next day, and saw his aunt. Amelia left them alone together, and went to her room. She was trying the separation—as that poor gentle Lady Jane Grey felt the edge of the axe that was to come down and sever her slender life. Days were passed in parleys, visits, preparations. The widow broke the matter to Georgy with great caution; she looked to see him very much affected by the intelligence. He was rather elated than otherwise, and the poor woman turned sadly away. He bragged about the news that day to the boys at school; told them how he was going to live with his grand-papa, his father's father, not the one who comes here sometimes; and that he would be very rich, and have a carriage and a pony, and go to a much finer school, and when he was rich he would buy Leader's pencil-case, and pay the tart woman. The boy was the image of his father, as his fond mother thought.

Indeed I have no heart, on account of our dear Amelia's sake, to go through the story of George's last days at home.

At last the day came. The carriage drove up; the little humble packets containing tokens of love and remembrance were ready and disposed in the hall long since. George was in his new suit, for which the tailor had come previously to measure him. He had sprung up with the sun and put on the new clothes—his mother hearing him from the room close by, in which she had been lying, in speechless grief and watching. Days before she had been making preparations for the end—purchasing little stores for the boy's use; marking his books and linen; talking with him and preparing him for the change—fondly fancying that he needed preparation.

So that he had change, what cared he? He was longing for it. By a thousand eager declarations as to what he would do when he went to live with his grandfather, he had shown the poor widow how little the idea of parting had cast him down. "He would come and see his mamma often on the pony," he said; "he would come and fetch her in the carriage; they would drive in the Park; and she should have everything she wanted." The poor mother was fain to content herself with these selfish demonstrations of attachment, and tried to convince herself how sincerely her son loved her. He must love her. All children were so; a little anxious for novelty, and—no, not selfish, but self-willed. Her child must have his enjoyments and ambition in the world. She herself, by her own selfishness and imprudent love for him, had denied him his just rights and pleasures hitherto.

A few days are past, and the great event of Amelia's life is consummated. No angel has intervened. The child is sacrificed and offered up to fate, and the widow is quite alone.

The boy comes to see her often, to be sure. He rides on a pony with a coachman behind him, to the delight of his old grandfather, Sedley, who walks proudly down the lane by his side. She sees him, but he is not her boy any more. Why, he rides to see the boys at the little school, too, and to show off before them his new wealth and splendour. In two days he has adopted a slightly imperious air and pa·onizing manner. He was born to command, his mother thinks, as his father was before him.

CHAPTER LI

IN WHICH A CHARADE IS ACTED WHICH MAY OR MAY NOT PUZZLE THE READER

AFTER Becky's appearance at my Lord Steyne's private and select parties, the claims of that estimable woman as regards fashion were settled, and some of the very greatest and tallest doors in the metropolis were speedily opened to her—doors so great and tall that the beloved reader and writer hereof may hope in vain to enter at them.

The upshot of her visit to Lord Steyne was that His Highness the Prince of Peterwaradin took occasion to renew his acquaintance with

Colonel Crawley, when they met on the next day at the Club, and
to compliment Mrs. Crawley in the Ring of Hyde Park with a profound
salute of the hat. She and her husband were invited immediately to
one of the Prince's small parties at Levant House, then occupied by
His Highness during the temporary absence from England of its noble
proprietor. She sang after dinner to a very little *comité*. The Marquis
of Steyne was present, paternally superintending the progress of his
pupil.

Becky has often spoken in subsequent years of this season of her
life, when she moved among the very greatest circles of the London
fashion. Her success excited, elated, and then bored her.

How the Crawleys got the money which was spent upon the entertainments with which they treated the polite world was a mystery which
gave rise to some conversation at the time, and probably added zest to
these little festivities.

The truth is, that by economy and good management—by a sparing
use of ready money and by paying scarcely anybody—people can
manage, for a time at least, to make a great show with very little
means; and it is our belief that Becky's much-talked-of parties, which
were not, after all was said, very numerous, cost this lady very little
more than the wax candles which lighted the walls. Stillbrook and
Queen's Crawley supplied her with game and fruit in abundance. Lord
Steyne's cellars were at her disposal, and that excellent nobleman's
famous cooks presided over her little kitchen, or sent by my lord's
order the rarest delicacies from their own.

At the time whereof we are writing, though the Great George was on
the throne and ladies wore *gigots* and large combs like tortoiseshell
shovels in their hair, instead of the simple sleeves and lovely wreaths
which are actually in fashion, the manners of the very polite world
were not, I take it, essentially different from those of the present day,
and their amusements pretty similar.

At this time the amiable amusement of acting charades had come
among us from France, and was considerably in vogue in this country,
enabling the many ladies amongst us who had beauty to display their
charm, and the fewer number who had cleverness to exhibit their wit.
My Lord Steyne was incited by Becky, who perhaps believed herself
endowed with both the above qualifications, to give an entertainment at
Gaunt House which should include some of these little dramas; and we
must take leave to introduce the reader to this brilliant *réunion*, and
with a melancholy welcome too, for it will be among the very last of
the fashionable entertainments to which it will be our fortune to conduct him.

A portion of that splendid room, the picture gallery of Gaunt House,
was arranged as the charade theatre. It had been so used when George
III. was king; and one or two of the old properties were drawn out
of the garrets, where they had lain ever since, and furbished up anew
for the present festivities.

G

Servants brought in salvers covered with numerous cool dainties, and the performers disappeared to get ready for the first charade-tableau.

The three syllables of this charade were to be depicted in pantomime, and the performance took place in the following wise:

First Syllable. Colonel Rawdon Crawley, C.B., with a slouched hat and a staff, a greatcoat, and a lantern borrowed from the stables, passed across the stage, bawling out as if warning the inhabitants of the hour. In the lower window are seen two bagmen, playing apparently at the game of cribbage, over which they yawn much. To them enters one looking like Boots (the Honourable G. Ringwood, which character the young gentleman performed to perfection), and divests them of their lower coverings; and presently Chambermaid (the Right Honourable Lord Southdown), with two candlesticks and a warming-pan. She ascends to the upper apartment, and warms the bed. She uses the warming-pan as a weapon wherewith she wards off the attention of the bagmen. She exits. They put on their nightcaps and pull down the blinds. Boots comes out and closes the shutters of the ground-floor chamber. You hear him bolting and chaining the door within. All the lights go out. The music plays *Dormez, dormez, chers Amours*. A voice from behind the curtain says, "First syllable."

Second syllable. The lamps are lighted up all of a sudden. The music plays the old air from John de Paris, *Ah! quel plaisir d'etre voyage*. It is the same scene. Between the first and second floors of the house represented you behold a sign on which the Steyne arms are painted. All the bells are ringing all over the house. In the lower apartment you see a man with a long slip of paper presenting it to another, who shakes his fists, threatens, and vows that it is monstrous. "Ostler, bring round my gig," cries another at the door. He chucks Chambermaid (the Right Honourable Lord Southdown) under the chin; she seems to deplore his absence, as Calypso did that of that other eminent traveller Ulysses. Boots (the Honourable G. Ringwood) passes with a wooden box containing silver flagons, and cries "Pots" with such exquisite humour and naturalness that the whole house rings with applause, and a bouquet is thrown to him. Crack, crack, crack go the whips. Landlord, chambermaid, waiter rush to the door; but just as some distinguished guest is arriving, the curtains close, and the invisible theatrical manager cries out "Second syllable."

"I think it must be 'Hotel,' " says Captain Grigg of the Life Guards. There is a general laugh at the Captain's cleverness. He is not very far from the mark.

While the third syllable is in preparation, the band begins a nautical medley—"All in the Downs," "Cease, Rude Boreas," "Rule Britannia," "In the Bay of Biscay O!" Some maritime event is about to take place. A bell is heard ringing as the curtain draws aside. "Now, gents, for the shore!" a voice exclaims. People take leave of each other. They point anxiously as if towards the clouds, which are represented by a dark curtain, and nod their heads in fear. Lady Squeams (the Right Honourable Lord Southdown), her lap-dog, her bags, reticules, and husband sit down. and cling hold of some ropes. It is evidently a ship.

The Captain (Colonel Crawley, C.B.), with a cocked hat and a telescope, comes in, holding his hat on his head and looks out; his coat-tails fly about as if in the wind. When he leaves go of his hat to use his telescope, his hat flies off, with immense applause. It is blowing fresh. The music rises and whistles louder and louder; the mariners go across the stage staggering, as if the ship was in severe motion. The Steward (the Honourable G. Ringwood) passes reeling by, holding six basins. He put one rapidly by Lord Squeams. Lady Squeams, giving a pinch to her dog, which begins to howl piteously, puts her pocket-handkerchief to her face, and rushes away as for the cabin. The music rises up to the wildest pitch of stormy excitement, and the third syllable is concluded.

There was a little ballet, "Le Rossignol," in which Montessu and Noblet used to be famous in those days, and which Mr. Wagg transferred to the English stage as an opera, putting his verse, of which he was a skilful writer, to the pretty airs of the ballet. It was dressed in old French costume, and little Lord Southdown now appeared admirably attired in the disguise of an old woman hobbling about the stage with a faultless crooked stick.

Trills of melody were heard behind the scenes, and gurgling from a sweet pasteboard cottage covered with roses and trellis-work. "Philomèle, Philomèle," cries the old woman; and Philomèle comes out.

More applause: it is Mrs. Rawdon Crawley in powder and patches, the most *ravissante* little Marquise in the world.

She comes in laughing, humming, and frisks about the stage with all the innocence of theatrical youth; she makes a curtsy. Mamma says, "Why, child, you are always laughing and singing," and away she goes, with—

THE ROSE UPON MY BALCONY

The rose upon my balcony the morning air perfuming
   Was leafless all the winter time, and pining for the spring;
You ask me why her breath is sweet and why her cheek is blooming;
   It is because the sun is out and birds begin to sing.

The nightingale, whose melody is through the greenwood ringing,
   Was silent when the boughs were bare and winds were blowing keen;
And if, Mamma, you ask of me the reason of his singing,
   It is because the sun is out and all the leaves are green.

Thus each performs his part, Mamma: the birds have found their voices,
   The blowing rose a flush, Mamma, her bonny cheek to dye;
And there's sunshine in my heart, Mamma, which wakens and rejoices,
   And so I sing and blush, Mamma, and that's the reason why.

During the intervals of the stanzas of this ditty, the good-natured
personage addressed as mamma by the singer, and whose large whiskers
appeared under her cap, seemed very anxious to exhibit her maternal
affection by embracing the innocent creature who performed the
daughter's part. Every caress was received with loud acclamations of
laughter by the sympathizing audience. At its conclusion (while the
music was performing a symphony as if ever so many birds were
warbling) the whole house was unanimous for an *encore*, and applause
and bouquets without end were showered upon the NIGHTINGALE of the
evening. Lord Steyne's voice of applause was loudest of all. Becky,
the nightingale, took the flowers which he threw to her, and pressed
them to her heart with the air of a consummate comedian. Lord Steyne
was frantic with delight. His guests' enthusiasm harmonized with his
own. Where was the beautiful black-eyed Houri whose appearance in
the first charade had caused such delight? She was twice as handsome
as Becky, but the brilliancy of the latter had quite eclipsed her. All
voices were for her. Stephens, Caradori, Ronzi de Begnis—people
compared her to one or the other, and agreed, with good reason, very
likely, that had she been an actress none on the stage could have
surpassed her. She had reached her culmination; her voice rose trilling
and bright over the storm of applause, and soared as high and joyful
as her triumph. There was a ball after the dramatic entertainments,
and everybody pressed round Becky as the great point of attraction of
the evening. The Royal Personage declared, with an oath, that she was
perfection, and engaged her again and again in conversation.

The greatest triumph of all was at supper-time. She was placed at
the grand exclusive table with his Royal Highness, the exalted personage before-mentioned, and the rest of the great guests. She was
served on gold plate. She might have had pearls melted into her
champagne if she liked—another Cleopatra; and the potentate of Peterwaradin would have given half the brilliants off his jacket for a kind
glance from those dazzling eyes. Jabotière wrote home about her to
his government. The ladies at the other tables, who supped off mere
silver, and marked Lord Steyne's constant attention to her, vowed
it was a monstrous infatuation, a gross insult to ladies of rank. If
sarcasm could have killed, Lady Stunningham would have slain her
on the spot.

Rawdon Crawley was scared at these triumphs. They seemed to
separate his wife farther than ever from him somehow. He thought,
with a feeling very like pain, how immeasurably she was his superior.

When the hour of departure came, a crowd of young men followed
her to her carriage, for which the people without bawled, the cry
being taken up by the linkmen who were stationed outside the tall
gates of Gaunt House, congratulating each person who issued from
the gate and hoping his Lordship had enjoyed this noble party.

Mrs. Rawdon Crawley's carriage, coming up to the gate after due
shouting, rattled into the illuminated courtyard, and drove up to the

covered way. Rawdon put his wife into the carriage, which drove off. Mr. Wenham had proposed to him to walk home, and offered the Colonel the refreshment of a cigar.

They lighted their cigars by the lamp of one of the many linkboys outside, and Rawdon walked on with his friend Wenham. Two persons separated from the crowd and followed the two gentlemen; and when they had walked down Gaunt Square a few score of paces, one of the men came up, and touching Rawdon on the shoulder, said, "Beg your pardon, Colonel, I wish to speak to you most particular." This gentleman's acquaintance gave a loud whistle as the latter spoke, at which signal a cab came clattering up from those stationed at the gate of Gaunt House, and the aide-de-camp ran round and placed himself in front of Colonel Crawley.

That gallant officer at once knew what had befallen him. He was in the hands of bailiffs. He started back, falling against the man who had first touched him.

"We're three on us; it's no use bolting," the man behind said.

"It's you, Moss, it it?" said the Colonel, who appeared to know his interlocutor. "How much is it?"

"Only a small thing, whispered Mr. Moss of Cursitor Street, Chancery Lane, and assistant officer to the Sheriff of Middlesex—"one hundred and thirty-six, six and eightpence, at the suit of Mr. Nathan."

"Lend me a hundred, Wenham, for God's sake," poor Rawdon said; "I've got seventy at home."

"I've not got ten pounds in the world," said poor Mr. Wenham. "Good-night, my dear fellow."

"Good-night," said Rawdon ruefully. And Wenham walked away, and Rawdon Crawley finished his cigar as the cab drove under Temple Bar.

CHAPTER LII

IN WHICH LORD STEYNE SHOWS HIMSELF IN A MOST AMIABLE LIGHT

WHEN Lord Steyne was benevolently disposed, he did nothing by halves, and his kindness towards the Crawley family did the greatest honour to his benevolent discrimination. His Lordship extended his good-will to little Rawdon: he pointed out to the boy's parents the necessity of sending him to a public school; that he was of an age now when emulation, the first principles of the Latin language, pugilistic exercises, and the society of his fellow-boys would be of the greatest benefit to the boy. His father objected that he was not rich enough to send the boy to a good public school; his mother, that Briggs was a capital mistress for him, and had brought him on (as indeed was the fact) famously in English, the Latin rudiments, and in general learning; but all these objections disappeared before the generous perseverance of the Marquis of Steyne. His lordship was one of the governors of that

famous old collegiate institution called the Whitefriars. It had been a
Cistercian Convent in old days, when the Smithfield, which is contiguous to it, was a tournament ground. Obstinate heretics used to be
brought thither convenient for burning hard by. Henry VIII., the
Defender of the Faith, seized upon the monastry and its possessions,
and hanged and tortured some of the monks who could not accommodate themselves to the pace of his reform. Finally, a great merchant
bought the house and land adjoining, in which, and with the help of
other wealthy endowments of land and money, he established a famous
foundation hospital for old men and children. An extern school grew
round the old almost monastic foundation, which subsists still with its
Middle-Age costume and usages; and all Cistercians pray that it may
long flourish.

Rawdon Crawley, though the only book which he studied was the
Racing Calendar, and though his chief recollections of polite learning
were connected with the floggings which he received at Eton in his
early youth, had that decent and honest reverence for classical learning
which all English gentlemen feel, and was glad to think that his son
was to have a provision for life, perhaps, and a certain opportunity of
becoming a scholar. And although his boy was his chief solace and
companion, and endeared to him by a thousand small ties, about which
he did not care to speak to his wife, who had all along shown the
utmost indifference to their son, yet Rawdon agreed at once to part
with him, and to give up his own greatest comfort and benefit for the
sake of the welfare of the little lad. He did not know how fond he was
of the child until it became necessary to let him go away. When he
was gone, he felt more sad and downcast than he cared to own—far
sadder than the boy himself, who was happy enough to enter a new
career, and find companions of his own age. Becky burst out laughing
once or twice when the Colonel, in his clumsy, incoherent way, tried
to express his sentimental sorrow at the boy's departure.

The Colonel went to see his son a short time afterwards, and found
the lad sufficiently well and happy, grinning and laughing in his little
black gown and little breeches.

His father sagaciously tipped Blackball, his master, a sovereign, and
secured that young gentleman's goodwill towards his fag. As a *protégé*
of the great Lord Steyne, the nephew of a County member, and son of
a Colonel and C.B., whose name appeared in some of the most
fashionable parties in *The Morning Post*, perhaps the school authorities
were disposed not to look unkindly on the child. He had plenty of
pocket-money, which he spent in treating his comrades royally to
raspberry tarts; and he was often allowed to come home on Saturdays
to his father, who always made a jubilee of that day. When free,
Rawdon would take him to the play, or send him thither with the
footman; and on Sundays he went to church with Briggs and Lady
Jane and his cousins.

Little Rawdon being disposed of, Lord Steyne, who took such a

parental interest in the affairs of this amiable poor family, thought
that their expenses might be very advantageously curtailed by the
departure of Miss Briggs, and that Becky was quite clever enough to
take the management of her own house. It has been narrated in a
former chapter how the benevolent nobleman had given his *protégé*
money to pay off her little debt to Miss Briggs, who, however, still
remained behind with her friends; whence my lord came to the painful
conclusion that Mrs. Crawley had made some other use of the money
confided to her than that for which her generous patron had given the
loan. However, Lord Steyne was not so rude as to impart his suspicions
upon this head to Mrs. Becky, whose feelings might be hurt by any
controversy on the money question, and who might have a thousand
painful reasons for disposing otherwise of his Lordship's generous loan.
But he determined to satisfy himself of the real state of the case, and
instituted the necessary inquiries in a most cautious and delicate
manner.

In the first place, he took an early opportunity of pumping Miss
Briggs. That was not a difficult operation. A very little encouragement
would set that worthy woman to talk volubly, and pour out all within
her. And one day when Mrs. Rawdon had gone out to drive (as Mr.
Fiche his Lordship's confidential servant, easily learned at the livery
stables where the Crawleys kept their carriage and horses, or rather
where the liveryman kept a carriage and horses for Mr. and Mrs.
Crawley), my lord dropped in upon the Curzon Street house, asked
Briggs for a cup of coffee, told her that he had good accounts of the
little boy at school, and in five minutes found out from her that Mrs.
Rawdon had given her nothing except a black silk gown, for which
Miss Briggs was immensely grateful.

He laughed within himself at this artless story. For the truth is,
our dear friend Rebecca had given him a most circumstantial narration
of Briggs's delight at receiving her money—eleven hundred and twenty-
five pounds—and in what securities she had invested it, and what a
pang Becky herself felt in being obliged to pay away such a delightful
sum of money. "Who knows," the dear woman may have thought
within herself, "perhaps he may give me a little more?" My Lord,
however, made no such proposal to the little schemer—very likely
thinking that he had been sufficiently generous already.

He had the curiosity, then, to ask Miss Briggs about the state of
her private affairs, and she told his Lordship candidly what her position
was—how Miss Crawley had left her a legacy; how her relatives had
had part of it; how Colonel Crawley had put out another portion, for
which she had the best security and interest; and how Mr. and Mrs.
Rawdon had kindly busied themselves with Sir Pitt, who was to dispose
of the remainder most advantageously for her, when he had time. My
lord asked me how much the Colonel had already invested for her, and
Miss Briggs at once and truly told him that the sum was six hundred
and odd pounds.

But as soon as she had told her story, the voluble Briggs repented of her frankness, and besought my lord not to tell Mr. Crawley of the confessions which she had made. "The Colonel was so kind—Mr. Crawley might be offended and pay back the money, for which she could get no such good interest anywhere else." Lord Steyne, laughing, promised he never would divulge their conversation, and when he and Miss Briggs parted he laughed still more.

"What an accomplished little devil it is!" thought he; "what a splendid actress and manager! She had almost got a second supply out of me the other day with her coaxing ways. She beats all the women I have ever seen in the course of all my well-spent life. They are babies compared to her. I am a greenhorn myself, and a fool in her hands—an old fool. She is unsurpassable in lies." His Lordship's admiration for Becky rose immeasurably at this proof of her cleverness. Getting the money was nothing, but getting double the sum she wanted, and paying nobody—it was a magnificent stroke. And Crawley, my lord thought—Crawley is not such a fool as he looks and seems. He has managed the matter cleverly enough on his side. Nobody would ever have supposed from his face and demeanour that he knew anything about this money business; and yet he put her up to it, and has spent the money, no doubt. In this opinion my lord, we know, was mistaken; but it influenced a good deal his behaviour towards Colonel Crawley, whom he began to treat with even less than that semblance of respect which he had formerly shown towards that gentleman.

He taxed Becky upon the point on the very first occasion when he met her alone, and he complimented her good-humouredly on her cleverness in getting more than the money which she required. Becky was only a little taken aback. It was not the habit of this dear creature to tell falsehoods except when necessity compelled, but in these great emergencies it was her practice to lie very freely; and in an instant she was ready with another neat, plausible circumstantial story which she administered to her patron. The previous statement which she had made to him was a falsehood—a wicked falsehood—she owned it; but who had made her tell it? "Ah, my Lord," she said, "you don't know all I have to suffer and bear in silence. You see me gay and happy before you; you little know what I have to endure when there is no protector near me. It was my husband, by threats and the most savage treatment, forced me to ask for that sum about which I deceived you. It was he who, foreseeing that questions might be asked regarding the disposal of the money, forced me to account for it as I did. He took the money. He told me he had paid Miss Briggs; I did not want, I did not dare to doubt him. Pardon the wrong which a desperate man is forced to commit, and pity a miserable, miserable woman." She burst into tears as she spoke. Persecuted virtue never looked more bewitchingly wretched.

They had a long conversation, driving round and round the Regent's Park in Mrs. Crawley's carriage together—a conversation of which it is not necessary to repeat the details; but the upshot of it was, that when Becky came home she flew to her dear Briggs with a smiling face, and announced that she had some very good news for her. Lord Steyne had acted in the noblest and most generous manner. He was always thinking how and when he could do good. Now that little Rawdon was gone to school, a dear companion and friend was no longer necessary to her. She was grieved beyond measure to part with Briggs; but her means required that she should practise every retrenchment, and her sorrow was mitigated by the idea that her dear Briggs would be far better provided for by her generous patron than in her humble home. Mrs. Pilkington, the housekeeper at Gauntly Hall, was growing exceedingly old, feeble, and rheumatic: she was not equal to the work of superintending that vast mansion, and must be on the look-out for a successor. It was a splendid position. The family did not go to Gauntly once in two years. At other times the housekeeper was the mistress of the magnificent mansion: had four covers daily for her table; was visited by the clergy and the most respectable people of the county—was the lady of Gauntly, in fact; and the two last house-keepers before Mrs. Pilkington had married rectors of Gauntly, but Mrs. P. could not, being the aunt of the present Rector. The place was not to be hers yet; but she might go down on a visit to Mrs. Pilkington, and see whether she would like to succeed her.

What words can paint the ecstatic gratitude of Briggs! All she stipulated for was that little Rawdon should be allowed to come down and see her at the Hall. Becky promised this—anything. She ran up to her husband when he came home and told him the joyful news. Rawdon was glad, deuced glad; the weight was off his conscience about poor Briggs's money. She was provided for, at any rate, but—but his mind was disquiet. He did not seem to be all right somehow. He told little Southdown what Lord Steyne had done, and the young man eyed Crawley with an air which surpassed the latter.

He told Lady Jane of this second proof of Steyne's bounty, and she, too, looked odd and alarmed; so did Sir Pitt. "She is too clever and—and gay to be allowed to go from party to party without a companion," both said. "You must go with her, Rawdon, wherever she goes, and you *must* have somebody with her—one of the girls from Queen's Crawley, perhaps, though they were rather giddy guardians for her."

Somebody Becky should have. But in the meantime it was clear that honest Briggs must not lose her chance of settlement for life; and so she and her bags were packed and she set off on her journey. And so two of Rawdon's out-sentinels were in the hands of the enemy.

And it was while Rawdon's mind was agitated with doubts and perplexities that the incident occurred which was mentioned in the last chapter, and the unfortunate Colonel found himself a prisoner away from home.

CHAPTER LIII

A RESCUE AND A CATASTROPHE

FRIEND Rawdon drove on then to Mr. Moss's mansion in Cursitor
Street, and was duly inducted into that dismal place of hospitality.
Morning was breaking over the cheerful house-tops of Chancery Lane
as the rattling cab woke up the echoes there. A little, pink-eyed Jew-
boy, with a head as ruddy as the rising morn, let the party into the
house, and Rawdon was welcomed to the ground-floor apartments by
Mr. Moss, his travelling companion and host, who cheerfully asked
him if he would like a glass of something warm after his drive.

"I'll ring when I want anything," said Rawdon, and went quietly
to his bedroom. He was an old soldier, we have said, and not to be
disturbed by any little shocks of fate. A weaker man would have sent
off a letter to his wife on the instant of his capture. "But what is the
use of disturbing her night's rest?" thought Rawdon. "She won't know
whether I am in my room or not. It will be time enough to write to
her when she has had her sleep out, and I have had mine. It's only
a hundred-and-seventy, and the deuce is in it if we can't raise that."
And so, thinking about little Rawdon (whom he would not have known
that he was in such a queer place), the Colonel turned into the bed
and fell asleep. It was ten o'clock when he woke up, and the ruddy-
headed youth brought him, with conscious pride, a fine silver dressing-
case, wherewith he might perform the operation of shaving. Indeed,
Mr. Moss's house, though somewhat dirty, was splendid throughout.
There were dirty trays in wine-coolers *en permanence* on the sideboard, huge dirty gilt cornices, with dingy yellow satin hanging to
the barred windows, which looked into Cursitor Street—vast and dirty
gilt picture-frames surrounding pieces sporting and sacred, all of which
works were by the greatest masters; and fetched the greatest prices,
too, in the bill transactions, in the course of which they were sold and
bought over and over again. The Colonel's breakfast was served to
him in the same dingy and gorgeous plated ware. Miss Moss, a dark-
eyed maid in curl-papers, appeared with the teapot, and, smiling, asked
the Colonel how he had slep'?

After a lively chat with this lady (who sat on the edge of the breakfast table in an easy attitude, displaying the drapery of her stocking
and an ex-white satin shoe which was down at heel), Colonel Crawley
called for pens and ink, and paper; and being asked how many sheets,
chose one which was brought to him between Miss Moss's own finger
and thumb. Many a sheet had that dark-eyed damsel brought in;
many a poor fellow had scrawled and blotted hurried lines of entreaty,
and paced up and down that awful room until his messenger brought
back the reply. Poor men always use messengers instead of the post.
Who has not had their letters, with the wafers wet, and the announcement that a person is waiting in the hall?

Now on the score of his application, Rawdon had not many mis-givings.

"DEAR BECKY (Rawdon wrote),—*I hope you slept well.* Don't be *frightened* if I don't bring you in your *coffy.* Last night as I was coming home smoking, I met with an *accadent.* I was *nabbed* by Moss of Cursitor Street—from whose *gilt and splendid parler* I write this—the same that had me this time two years. Miss Moss brought in my tea—she is grown very *fat*, and, as usual, had *her stockens down at heal.*

"It's Nathan's business—a hundred-and-fifty—with costs, hundred-and-seventy. Please send me my desk and some *cloths*—I'm in pumps and a white tye (something like Miss M.'s stockings)—I've seventy in it. And as soon as you get this, Drive to Nathan's—offer him seventy-five down, and ask *him to renew*—say I'll take wine—we may as well have some dinner sherry; but not *picturs*, they're too dear.

"If he won't stand it. Take my ticker and such of your things as you can *spare*, and send them to Balls—we must, of coarse, have the sum to-night. It won't do to let it stand over, as to-morrow's Sunday; the beds here are not very *clean*, and there may be other things out against me—I'm glad it an't Rawdon's Satuřday for coming home. God bless you.

                    "Yours in haste,
                                                    "R.C.
"*P.S.*—Make haste and come."

This letter, sealed with a wafer, was dispatched by one of the messengers who are always hanging about Mr. Moss's establishment; and Rawdon, having seen him depart, went out in the courtyard, and smoked his cigar with a tolerably easy mind—in spite of the bars over-head; for Mr. Moss's courtyard is railed in like a cage, lest the gentle-men who are boarding with him should take a fancy to escape from his hospitality.

Three hours, he calculated, would be the utmost time required, before Becky should arrive and open his prison doors; and he passed these pretty cheerfully in smoking, in reading the paper, and in the coffee-room with an acquaintance, Captain Walker, who happened to be there, and with whom he cut for sixpences for some hours, with pretty equal luck on either side.

But the day passed away and no messenger returned—no Becky. Mr. Moss's tably-dy-hoty was served at the appointed hour of half-past five, when such of the gentlemen lodging in the house as could afford to pay for the banquet came and partook of it in the splendid front parlour before described, and with which Mr. Crawley's tem-porary lodging communicated, when Miss M. (Miss Hem, as her papa called her) appeared without the curl-papers of the morning, and Mrs. Hem did the honours of a prime boiled leg of mutton and turnips, of

which the Colonel ate with a very faint appetite. Asked whether he
would "stand" a bottle of champagne for the company, he consented,
and the ladies drank to his 'ealth, and Mr. Moss, in the most polite
manner "looked towards him."

In the midst of this repast, however, the door-bell was heard. Young
Moss, of the ruddy hair, rose up with the keys and answered the
summons; and coming back, told the Colonel that the messenger had
returned with a bag, a desk, and a letter, which he gave him. "No
ceramony, Colonel, I beg," said Mrs. Moss with a wave of her hand,
and he opened the letter rather tremulously. It was a beautiful letter,
highly scented, on a pink paper, and with a light green seal.

"MON PAUVRE CHER PETIT (Mrs. Crawley wrote), —I could not sleep
one wink for thinking of what had become of *my odious old monstre;*
and only got to rest in the morning after sending for Mr. Blench (for
I was in a fever), who gave me a composing draught, and left orders
with Finette that I should be disturbed *on no account.* So that my poor
old man's messenger, who had *bien mauvaise mine,* Finette says, and
sentoit le genièvre remained in the hall for some hours waiting my bell.
You may fancy my state when I read your poor dear old ill-spelt letter.

"Ill as I was, I instantly called for the carriage, and as soon as I was
dressed (though I couldn't drink a drop of chocolate—I assure you I
couldn't without my *monstre* to bring it to me), I drove *ventre à terre*
to Nathan's. I saw him—I wept—I cried—I fell at his odious knees.
Nothing would mollify the horrid man. He would have all the money,
he said, or keep my poor *monstre* in prison. I drove home with the
intention of paying that *triste visite chez mon oncle* (when every trinket
I have should be at your disposal, though they would not fetch a
hundred pounds, for some, you know, are with *ce cher oncle* already),
and found Milor there with the Bulgarian old sheep-faced monster, who
had come to compliment me upon last night's performances. Padding-
ton came in, too, drawling and lisping and twiddling his hair, so did
Champignac, and his chief—everybody with *foison* of compliments and
pretty speeches—plaguing poor me, who longed to be rid of them,
and was thinking *every moment of the time of mon pauvre prisonnier.*

"When they were gone, I went down on my knees to Milor; told
him we were going to pawn everything, and begged and prayed him
to give me two hundred pounds. He pish'd and psha'd in a fury—
told me not to be such a fool as to pawn—and said he would see
whether he could lend me the money. At last he went away, promising
that he would send it to me in the morning; when I will bring it to my
poor old monster with a kiss from his affectionate   BECKY.

"I am writing in bed. Oh, h a v e such a headache and such a
heartache!"

When Rawdon read over this letter, he turned so red and looked so
savage that the company at the *table d'hôte* easily perceived that bad

news had reached him. All his suspicions, which he had been trying to banish, returned upon him. She could not even go out and sell her trinkets to free him. She could laugh and talk about compliments paid to her, whilst he was in prison. Who had put him there? Wenham had walked with him. Was there . . . He could hardly bear to think of what he suspected. Leaving the room hurriedly, he ran into his own, opened his desk, wrote two hurried lines, which he directed to Sir Pitt or Lady Crawley, and bade the messenger carry them at once to Gaunt Street, bidding him to take a cab, and promising him a guinea if he was back in an hour.

In the note he besought his dear brother and sister, for the sake of God—for the sake of his dear child and his honour—to come to him and relieve him from his difficulty. He was in prison: he wanted a hundred pounds to set him free—he entreated them to come to him.

He went back to the dining-room after dispatching his messenger, and called for more wine. He laughed and talked with a strange boisterousness, as the people thought. Sometimes he laughed madly at his own fears, and went on drinking for an hour; listening all the while for the carriage which was to bring his fate back.

At the expiration of that time, wheels were heard whirling up to the gate. The young janitor went out with his gate-keys. It was a lady whom he let in at the bailiff's door.

"Colonel Crawley," she said, trembling very much. He, with a knowing look, locked the outer door upon her; then unlocked and opened the inner one, and calling out, "Colonel, you're wanted," led her into the back parlour which he occupied.

Rawdon came in from the dining-parlour where all those people were carousing, into his back room; a flare of coarse light following him into the apartment where the lady stood, still very nervous.

"It is I, Rawdon," she said in a timid voice, which she strove to render cheerful. "It is Jane." Rawdon was quite overcome by that kind of voice and presence. He ran up to her—caught her in his arms—gasped out some inarticulate words of thanks, and fairly sobbed on her shoulder. She did not know the cause of his emotion.

The bills of Mr. Moss were quickly settled, perhaps to the disappointment of that gentleman, who had counted on having the Colonel as his guest over Sunday at least; and Jane, with beaming smiles and happiness in her eyes, carried away Rawdon from the bailiff's house, and they went homewards in the cab in which she had hastened to his release. "Pitt was gone to a Parliamentary dinner," she said, "when Rawdon's note came, and so, dear Rawdon, I—I came myself;" and she put her kind hand in his. Perhaps it was well for Rawdon Crawley that Pitt was away at that dinner. Rawdon thanked his sister a hundred times, and with an ardour of gratitude which touched and almost alarmed that soft-hearted woman. "Oh," said he, in his rude, artless way, "you—you don't know how I'm changed since I've known you, and—and little Rawdy. I—I'd like to change somehow.

You see I want—I want—to be——" He did not finish the sentence, but she could interpret it. And that night after he left her, and as she sate by her own little boy's bed, she prayed humbly for that poor wayward sinner.

Rawdon left her and walked home rapidly. It was nine o'clock at night. He ran across the streets, and the great squares of Vanity Fair, and at length came up breathless opposite his own house. He started back and fell against the railings, trembling as he looked up. The drawing-room windows were blazing with light. She had said that she was in bed and ill. He stood there for some time, the light from the rooms on his pale face.

He took out his door-key and let himself into the house. He could hear laughter in the upper rooms. He was in the ball-dress in which he had been captured the night before. He went silently up the stairs, leaning against the banisters at the stair-head. Nobody was stirring in the house besides; all the servants had been sent away. Rawdon heard laughter within—laughter and singing. Becky was singing a snatch of the song of the night before; a hoarse voice shouted, "Brava! Brava!"—it was Lord Steyne's.

Rawdon opened the door and went in. A little table with a dinner was laid out—and wine and plate. Steyne was hanging over the sofa on which Becky sate. The wretched woman was in a brilliant full toilette, her arms and all her fingers sparkling with bracelets and rings, and the brilliants on her breast which Steyne had given her. He had her hand in his, and was bowing over it to kiss it, when Becky started up with a faint scream as she caught sight of Rawdon's white face. At the next instant she tried a smile, a horrid smile, as if to welcome her husband; and Steyne rose up, grinding his teeth, pale, and with fury in his looks.

He, too, attempted a laugh; and came forward, holding out his hand. "What, come back! How d'ye do, Crawley?" he said, the nerves of his mouth twitching as he tried to grin at the intruder.

There was that in Rawdon's face which caused Becky to fling herself before him. "I am innocent, Rawdon," she said; "before God, I am innocent!" She clung hold of his coat, of his hands; her own were all covered with serpents, and rings, and baubles. "I am innocent.—Say I am innocent!" she said to Lord Steyne.

He thought a trap had been laid for him, and was as furious with the wife as with the husband. "You innocent! Damn you," he screamed out. "You innocent! Why, every trinket you have on your body is paid for by me. I have given you thousands of pounds which this fellow has spent, and for which he has sold you. Innocent, by ——! You're as innocent as your mother, the ballet-girl, and your husband the bully. Don't think to frighten me as you have done others. Make way, sir, and let me pass;" and Lord Steyne seized up his hat, and, with flame in his eyes, and looking his enemy fiercely in the face, marched upon him, never for a moment doubting that the other would give way.

But Rawdon Crawley springing out, seized him by the neckcloth, until Steyne, almost strangled, writhed, and bent under his arm. "You lie, you dog!" said Rawdon. "You lie, you coward and villain!" And he struck the Peer twice over the face with his open hand, and flung him bleeding to the ground. It was all done before Rebecca could interpose. She stood there trembling before him. She admired her husband, strong, brave, and victorious.

"Come here," he said. She came up at once.

"Take off those things." She began, trembling, pulling the jewels from her arms, and the rings from her shaking fingers, and held them all in a heap, quivering and looking up at him. "Throw them down," he said, and she dropped them. He tore the diamond ornament out of her breast, and flung it at Lord Steyne. It cut him on his bald forehead. Steyne wore the scar to his dying day.

"Come upstairs," Rawdon said to his wife. "Don't kill me, Rawdon," she said. He laughed savagely. "I want to see if that man lies about the money as he has about me. Has he given you any?"

"No," said Rebecca, "that is——"

"Give me your keys," Rawdon answered, and they went out together.

Rebecca gave him all the keys but one; and she was in hopes that he would not have remarked the absence of that. It belonged to the little desk which Amelia had given her in early days, and which she kept in a secret place. But Rawdon flung open boxes and wardrobes, throwing the multifarious trumpery of their contents here and there, and at last he found the desk. The woman was forced to open it. It contained papers, love-letters many years old—all sorts of small trinkets and woman's memoranda. And it contained a pocket-book with bank-notes. Some of these were dated ten years back, too, and one was quite a fresh one—a note for a thousand pounds which Lord Steyne had given her.

"Did he give you this?" Rawdon said.

"Yes," Rebecca answered.

"I'll send it to him to-day," Rawdon said (for day had dawned again, and many hours had passed in this search), "and I will pay Briggs, who was kind to the boy, and some of the debts. You will let me know where I shall send the rest to you. You might have spared me a hundred pounds, Becky, out of all this; I have always shared with you."

"I am innocent," said Becky. And he left her without another word.

What were her thoughts when he left her? She remained for hours after he was gone, the sunshine pouring into the room, and Rebecca sitting alone on the bed's edge. The drawers were all opened and their contents scattered about—dresses and feathers, scarfs and trinkets, a heap of tumbled vanities lying in a wreck. Her hair was falling over her shoulders; her gown was torn where Rawdon had wrenched the brilliants out of it. She heard him go downstairs a few minutes after he left her, and the door slamming and closing on him. She knew he would never come back. He was gone for ever. Would he kill himself? she thought—not until after he had met Lord Steyne. She thought of her long past life, and all the dismal incidents of it. Ah, how dreary it seemed, how miserable, lonely, and profitless! Should she take laudanum, and end it, too—have done with all hopes, schemes, debts, and triumphs? The French maid found her in this position—sitting in the midst of her miserable ruins with clasped hands and dry eyes. The woman was her accomplice and in Steyne's pay. "*Mon Dieu*, Madame, what has happened?" she asked.

What *had* happened? Was she guilty or not? She said not; but who could tell what was truth which came from those lips, or if that corrupt heart was in this case pure? All her lies and her schemes, all her selfishness and her wiles, all her wit and genius had come to this bankruptcy. The woman closed the curtains, and with some entreaty and show of kindness persuaded her mistress to lie down on the bed. Then she went below and gathered up the trinkets which had been lying on the floor since Rebecca dropped them there at her husband's orders, and Lord Steyne went away.

CHAPTER LIV

SUNDAY AFTER THE BATTLE

THE mansion of Sir Pitt Crawley in Great Gaunt Street was just beginning to dress itself for the day, as Rawdon, in his evening costume, which he had now worn two days, passed by the scared female who was scouring the steps, and entered into his brother's study. Lady Jane, in her morning-gown, was up and above stairs in the nursery superintending the toilettes of her children, and listening to the morning prayers which the little creatures performed at her knee. Every morning she and they performed this duty privately, and before the public ceremonial at which Sir Pitt presided, and at which all the people of the household were expected to assemble. Rawdon sate down in the study before the Baronet's table, set out with the orderly blue books and the letters, the neatly-docketed bills and symmetrical pamphlets; the locked account-books, desks, and dispatch-boxes, the Bible, *The Quarterly Review*, and *The Court Guide*, which all stood as if on parade awaiting the inspection of their chief.

Punctually, as the shrill-toned bell of the black marble study clock began to chime nine, Sir Pitt made his appearance, fresh, neat, smugly shaved, with a waxy clean face, and stiff shirt collar, his scanty hair combed and oiled, trimming his nails as he descended the stairs majestically in a starched cravat and a grey flannel dressing-gown— a real old English gentleman, in a word—a model of neatness and every propriety. He started when he saw poor Rawdon in his study in tumbled clothes, with bloodshot eyes, and his hair over his face. He thought his brother was not sober, and had been out all night on some orgy. "Good gracious, Rawdon," he said, with a blank face, "what brings you here at this time of the morning? Why ain't you at home?"

"Home," said Rawdon, with a wild laugh. "Don't be frightened, Pitt. I'm not drunk. Shut the door; I want to speak to you."

Pitt closed the door and came up to the table, where he sate down in the other arm-chair—that one placed for the reception of the steward, agent, or confidential visitor who came to transact business with the Baronet—and trimmed his nails more vehemently than ever.

"Pitt, it's all over with me," the Colonel said, after a pause. "I'm done."

"I always said it would come to this," the Baronet cried peevishly, and beating a tune with his clean-trimmed nails. "I warned you a thousand times. I can't help you any more. Every shilling of my money is tied up. Even the hundred pounds that Jane took you last night were promised to my lawyer to-morrow morning, and the want of it will put me to great inconvenience. I don't mean to say that I won't assist you ultimately. But as for paying your creditors in full, I might as well hope to pay the National Debt. It is madness, sheer madness, to think of such a thing. You must come to a compromise. It's a painful thing for the family; but everybody does it. There was George Kitely, Lord Ragland's son, went through the Court last week, and was what they call whitewashed, I believe. Lord Ragland would not pay a shilling for him, and——"

"It's not money I want," Rawdon broke in. "I'm not come to you about myself. Never mind what happens to me——"

"What is the matter, then?" said Pitt, somewhat relieved.

"It's the boy," said Rawdon, in a husky voice. "I want you to promise me that you will take charge of him when I'm gone. That dear good wife of yours has always been good to him, and he's fonder of her than he is of his . . .—Damn it. Look here, Pitt: you know that I was to have had Miss Crawley's money. I wasn't brought up like a younger brother, but was always encouraged to be extravagant and kep' idle. But for this I might have been quite a different man. I didn't do my duty with the regiment so bad. You know how I was thrown over about the money, and who got it."

"After the sacrifices I have made, and the manner in which I have stood by you, I think this sort of reproach is useless," Sir Pitt said. "Your marriage was your own doing, not mine."

"That's over now," said Rawdon—"that's over now." And the words were wrenched from him with a groan, which made his brother start.

"Good God! is she dead?" Sir Pitt said, with a voice of genuine alarm and commiseration.

"I wish *I* was," Rawdon replied. "If it wasn't for little Rawdon, I'd have cut my throat this morning, and that damned villain's too."

Sir Pitt instantly guessed the truth, and surmised that Lord Steyne was the person whose life Rawdon wished to take. The Colonel told his senior briefly, and in broken accents, the circumstances of the case.

Then he took out of his pocket the little pocket-book which he had discovered in Becky's desk, and from which he drew a bundle of the notes which it contained. "Here's six hundred," he said—"you didn't know I was so rich. I want you to give the money to Briggs, who lent it to us—and who was kind to the boy—and I've always felt ashamed of having taken the poor old woman's money. And here's some more—I've only kept back a few pounds—which Becky may as well have, to get on with." As he spoke he took hold of the other notes to give to his brother; but his hands shook, and he was so agitated that the pocket-book fell from him, and out of it the thousand-pound note which had been the last of the unlucky Becky's winnings.

Pitt stooped and picked them up, amazed at so much wealth. "Not that," Rawdon said; "I hope to put a bullet into the man whom that belongs to." He had thought to himself, it would be a fine revenge to wrap a ball in the note, and kill Steyne with it.

After this colloquy the brothers once more shook hands and parted.

CHAPTER LV

IN WHICH THE SAME SUBJECT IS PURSUED

BECKY did not rally from the state of stupor and confusion in which the events of the previous night had plunged her intrepid spirit, until the bells of the Curzon Street chapels were ringing for afternoon service; and rising from her bed she began to ply her own bell, in order to summon the French maid who had left her some hours before.

Mrs. Rawdon Crawley rang many times in vain; and though, on the last occasion, she rang with such vehemence as to pull down the bell-rope, Mademoiselle Fifine did not make her appearance,—no not though her mistress, in a great pet, and with the bell-rope in her hand, came out to the landing-place with her hair over her shoulders, and screamed out repeatedly for her attendant.

The truth is, she had quitted the premises for many hours, and upon that permission which is called French leave among us. After picking up the trinkets in the drawing-room, Mademoiselle had ascended to her own apartments, packed and corded her own boxes there, tripped out and called a cab for herself, brought down her trunks with her own hand, and without ever so much as asking the aid of any of the other servants, who would probably have refused it, as they hated her cordially, and without wishing any one of them goodbye, had made her exit from Curzon Street.

The game, in her opinion, was over in that little domestic establishment. Fifine went off in a cab, as we have known more exalted persons of her nation to do under similar circumstances; but, more provident or lucky than these, she secured not only her own property, but some of her mistress's (if indeed that lady could be said to have any property at all), and not only carried off the trinkets before alluded to, and some favourite dresses on which she had long kept her eye, but four richly gilt Louis Quatorze candlesticks, six gilt Albums, Keepsakes, and Books of Beauty, a gold enamelled snuff-box which had once belonged to Madame du Barri, and the sweetest little inkstand and mother-of-pearl blotting-book, which Becky used when she composed her charming little pink notes, had vanished from the premises in Curzon Street together with Mademoiselle Fifine, and all the silver laid on the table for the little *festin* which Rawdon interrupted.

Rebecca dressed herself, this time without the aid of her French maid. She went into Rawdon's room, and there saw that a trunk and bag were packed ready for removal, with a pencil direction that they should be given when called for. Then she went into the Frenchwoman's garret: everything was clean, and all the drawers emptied there. She bethought herself of the trinkets which had been left on the ground, and felt certain that the woman had fled. "Good heavens! was ever such ill luck as mine?" she said; "to be so near, and to lose all. Is it all too late?"

Rawdon found some of the young fellows of the regiment seated in the mess-room at breakfast, and was induced without much difficulty to partake of that meal, and of the devilled legs of fowls and soda-water with which these young gentlemen fortified themselves.

The old bucks and habitués, who ordinarily stand gaping and grinning out of the great front window of the Club, had not arrived at their posts as yet; the newspaper-room was almost empty. One man was present whom Rawdon did not know; another to whom he owed a little score for whist, and whom, in consequence, he did not care to meet; a third was reading *The Royalist* (a periodical famous for its scandal and its attachment to Church and King) Sunday paper at the table, and looking up at Crawley with some interest, said, "Crawley, I congratulate you."

"What do you mean?" said the Colonel.

"It's in *The Observer* and *The Royalist* too," said Mr. Smith.

"What?" Rawdon cried, turning very red. He thought that the affair with Lord Steyne was already in the public prints. Smith looked up wondering and smiling at the agitation which the Colonel exhibited as he took up the paper, and trembling, began to read.

Mr. Smith and Mr. Brown (the gentleman with whom Rawdon had the outstanding whist account) had been talking about the Colonel just before he came in.

"It is come just in the nick of time," said Smith. "I suppose Crawley had not a shilling in the world."

"It's a wind that blows everybody good," Mr. Brown said. "He can't go away without paying me a pony he owes me."

"What's the salary?" asked Smith.

"Two or three thousand," answered the other. "But the climate's so infernal, they don't enjoy it long. Liverseege died after eighteen months of it; and the man before went off in six weeks, I hear."

"Some people say his brother is a very clever man. I always found him a d—— bore," Smith ejaculated. "He must have good interest, though. He must have got the Colonel the place,"

"*He!*" said Brown, with a sneer—"Pooh. It was Lord Steyne got it."

"How do you mean?"

"A virtuous woman is a crown to her husband," answered the other enigmatically, and went to read his papers.

Rawdon, for his part, read in *The Royalist* the following astonishing paragraph:

"GOVERNORSHIP OF COVENTRY ISLAND.—H.M.S. *Yellowjack*, Commander Jaunders, has brought letters and papers from Coventry Island. H.E. Sir Thomas Liverseege had fallen a victim to the prevailing fever at Swampton. His loss is deeply felt in the flourishing colony. We hear that the Governorship has been offered to Colonel Rawdon Crawley, C.B., a distinguished Waterloo officer. We need not only men of acknowledged bravery, but men of administrative talents to superintend the affairs of our colonies; and we have no doubt that the gentleman selected by the Colonial Office to fill the lamented vacancy which has occurred at Coventry Island is admirably calculated for the post which he is about to occupy."

"Coventry Island! where was it? who had appointed him to the government? You must take me out as your secretary, old boy," Captain Macmurdo said, laughing.

Rawdon Crawley resisted for some time the idea of taking the place which had been procured for him by so odious a patron; and was also for removing the boy from the school where Lord Steyne's interest had placed him. He was induced, however, to acquiesce in these benefits by the entreaties of his brother and Macmurdo; but mainly by the latter pointing out to him what a fury Steyne would be in, to think that his enemy's fortune was made through his means.

When the Marquis of Steyne came abroad after his accident, the Colonial Secretary bowed up to him, and congratulated himself and the Service upon having made so excellent an appointment. These congratulations were received with a degree of gratitude which may be imagined on the part of Lord Steyne.

The bailiffs and brokers seized upon poor Raggles in Curzon Street; and the late fair tenant of that poor little mansion was in the meanwhile—where? Who cared? Who asked after a day or two? Was she guilty or not? We all know how charitable the world is, and how the verdict of Vanity Fair goes when there is a doubt. Some people said she had gone to Naples in pursuit of Lord Steyne; whilst others averred that his Lordship quitted that city, and fled to Palermo on hearing of Becky's arrival; some said she was living in Bierstadt, and had become a *dame d'honneur* to the Queen of Bulgaria; some that she was at Boulogne; and others, at a boarding-house at Cheltenham.

Rawdon made her a tolerable annuity; and we may be sure that she was a woman who could make a little money go a great way, as the saying is. He would have paid his debts on leaving England, could he have got any insurance office to take his life; but the climate of Coventry Island was so bad that he could borrow no money on the strength of his salary. He remitted, however, to his brother punctually, and wrote to his little boy regularly every mail. He kept Macmurdo in cigars; and sent over quantities of shells, cayenne pepper, hot pickles, guava jelly, and colonial produce to Lady Jane. He sent his brother home *The Swamp Town Gazette*, in which the new Governor was praised with immense enthusiasm; whereas *The Swamp Town Sentinel*, whose wife was not asked to Government House, declared that His Excellency was a tyrant, compared to whom Nero was an enlightened philanthropist. Little Rawdon used to like to get the papers and read about His Excellency.

His mother never made any movement to see the child. He went home to his aunt for Sundays and holidays; he soon knew every bird's nest about Queen's Crawley, and rode out with Sir Huddleston's hounds, which he admired so on his first well-remembered visit to Hampshire.

CHAPTER LVI

GEORGY IS MADE A GENTLEMAN

GEORGY Osborne was now fairly established in his grandfather's mansion in Russell Square—occupant of his father's room in the house, and heir-apparent of all the splendours there. The good looks, gallant bearing, and gentleman-like appearance of the boy won the grand-sire's heart for him. Mr. Osborne was as proud of him as ever he had been of the elder George.

Though he was scarcely eleven years of age, Master George wore straps, and the most beautiful little boots like a man. He had gilt spurs, and a gold-headed whip, and a fine pin in his handkerchief, and the neatest little kid gloves which Lamb's, Conduit Street, could furnish. His mother had given him a couple of neckcloths, and care-fully hemmed and made some little shirts for him; but when her Samuel came to see the widow, they were replaced by much finer linen. He had little jewelled buttons in the lawn shirt-fronts. Her humble presents had been put aside—I believe Miss Osborne had given them to the coach-man's boy. Amelia tried to think she was pleased at the change. Indeed, she was happy and charmed to see the boy looking so beautiful.

She had had a little black profile of him done for a shilling, and
this was hung up by the side of another portrait over her bed. One
day the boy came on his accustomed visit, galloping down the little
street at Brompton, and bringing, as usual, all the inhabitants to the
windows to admire his splendour; and with great eagerness, and a
look of triumph in his face, he pulled a case out of his greatcoat—
(it was a natty white greatcoat, with a cape and a velvet collar)—
pulled out a red morocco case, which he gave her.

"I brought it with my own money, mamma," he said. "I thought
you'd like it."

Amelia opened the case, and giving a little cry of delighted affection,
seized the boy and embraced him a hundred times. It was a miniature
of himself, very prettily done (though not half handsome enough, we
may be sure the widow thought). His grandfather had wished to have
a picture of him by an artist whose works, exhibited in a shop-window
in Southampton Row, had caught the old gentleman's eyes; and
George, who had plenty of money, bethought him of asking the
painter how much a copy of the little portrait would cost, saying that
he would pay for it out of his own money, and that he wanted to give
it to his mother. The pleased painter executed it for a small price;
and old Osborne himself, when he heard of the incident, growled out
his satisfaction, and gave the boy twice as many sovereigns as he paid
for the miniature.

But what was the grandfather's pleasure compared to Amelia's
ecstasy? That proof of the boy's affection charmed her so, that she
thought no child in the world was like hers for goodness. For long
weeks after, the thought of his love made her happy. She slept better
with the picture under her pillow; and how many, many times did
she kiss it, and weep and pray over it! A small kindness from those
she loved made that timid heart grateful. Since her parting with
George she had had no such joy and consolation.

George's education was confided to a neighbouring scholar and
private pedagogue who "prepared young noblemen and gentlemen for
the Universities, the senate, and the learned professions; whose system
did not embrace the degrading corporal severities still practised at the
ancient places of education, and in whose family the pupils would find
the elegances of refined society and the confidence and affection of a
home." It was in this way that the Reverend Lawrence Veal of Hart
Street, Bloomsbury, and Domestic Chaplain to the Earl of Bareacres,
strove with Mrs. Veal his wife to entice pupils.

By thus advertising and pushing sedulously, the Domestic Chaplain
and his Lady generally succeeded in having one or two scholars by
them; who paid a high figure, and were thought to be in uncommonly
comfortable quarters.

In Russell Square everybody was afraid of Mr. Osborne, and Mr.
Osborne was afraid of Georgy. The boy's dashing manners, and off-
hand rattle about books and learning, his likeness to his father (dead

unreconciled in Brussels yonder), awed the old gentleman, and gave the young boy the mastery. The old man would start at some hereditary feature or tone unconsciously used by the little lad, and fancy that George's father was again before him. He tried by indulgence to the grandson to make up for harshness to the elder George. People were surprised at his gentleness to the boy. He growled and swore at Miss Osborne as usual, and would smile when George came down late for breakfast.

The broken-spirited, old maternal grandfather was likewise subject to the little tyrant. He could not help respecting the lad who had such fine clothes, and rode with a groom behind him. Georgy, on his side, was in the constant habit of hearing coarse abuse and vulgar satire levelled at John Sedley by his pitiless old enemy, Mr. Osborne. Osborne used to call the other the old pauper, the old coalman, the old bankrupt, and by many other such names of brutal contumely. How was little George to respect a man so prostrate? A few months after he was with his paternal grandfather, Mrs. Sedley died. There had been little love between her and the child. He did not care to show much grief. He came down to visit his mother in a fine new suit of mourning, and was very angry that he could not go to a play upon which he had set his heart.

The illness of that old lady had been the occupation and perhaps the safeguard of Amelia. What do men know about women's martyrdoms? We should go mad had we to endure the hundredth part of those daily pains which are meekly borne by many women. Ceaseless slavery, meeting with no reward; constant gentleness and kindness, met by cruelty as constant; love, labour, patience, watchfulness, without even so much as the acknowledgement of a good word,—all this how many of them have to bear in quiet, and appear abroad with cheerful faces, as if they felt nothing. Tender slaves that they are, they must needs be hypocrites and weak.

From her chair Amelia's mother had taken to her bed, which she had never left; and from which Mrs. Osborne herself was never absent, except when she ran to see George. The old lady grudged her even those rare visits; she, who had been a kind, smiling, good-natured mother once, in the days of her prosperity, but whom poverty and infirmities had broken down. Her illness or estrangement did not affect Amelia. They rather enabled her to support the other calamity under which she was suffering, and from the thoughts of which she was kept by the ceaseless calls of the invalid. Amelia bore her harshness quite gently; smoothed the uneasy pillow; was always ready with a soft answer to the watchful, querulous voice; soothed the sufferer with words of hope, such as her pious simple heart could best feel and utter; and closed the eyes that had once looked so tenderly upon her.

One day, as the young gentlemen were assembled in the study at the Rev. Mr. Veal's, and the domestic chaplain to the Right Honourable

the Earl of Bareacres was spouting away as usual, a smart carriage
drove up to the door decorated with the statue of Athene, and two
gentlemen stepped out. The young Masters. Bangles rushed to the
window, with a vague notion that their father might have arrived
from Bombay. The great hulking scholar of three-and-twenty, who was
crying secretly over a passage of Eutropius, flattened his neglected
nose against the panes, and looked at the drag, as the *laquais de place*
sprang from the box and let out the persons in the carriage.

"It's a fat one and a thin one," Mr. Bluck said, as a thundering
knock came to the door.

Everybody was interested, from the domestic chaplain himself, who
hoped he saw the fathers of some future pupils, down to Master Georgy,
glad of any pretext for laying his book down.

The boy in the shabby livery with the faded copper buttons, who
always thrust himself into the tight coat to open the door, came into
the study and said, "Two gentlemen want to see Master Osborne."
The professor had had a trifling altercation in the morning with that
young gentleman, owing to a difference about the introduction of
crackers in school-time; but his face resumed its habitual expression
of bland courtesy, as he said, "Master Osborne, I give you full permission to go and see your carriage friends, to whom I beg you to
convey the respectful compliments of myself and Mrs. Veal."

Georgy went into the reception-room, and saw two strangers, whom
he looked at with his head up, in his usual haughty manner. One was
fat, with mustachios, and the other was lean and long, in a blue frock-
coat, with a brown face and a grizzled head.

"My God, how like he is!" said the long gentleman, with a start.
"Can you guess who we are, George?"

The boy's face flushed up, as it did usually when he was moved,
and his eyes brightened. "I don't know the other," he said, "but I
should think you must be Major Dobbin."

Indeed it was our old friend. His voice trembled with pleasure as he
greeted the boy, and taking both the other's hands in his own, drew
the lad to him.

"Your mother has talked to you about me—has she?" he said.

"That she has," Georgy answered, "hundreds and hundreds of
times."

CHAPTER LVII

EOTHEN

It was one of the many causes for personal pride with which old
Osborne chose to recreate himself, that Sedley, his ancient rival,
enemy, and benefactor, was in his last days so utterly defeated and
humiliated as to be forced to accept pecuniary obligations at the hands
of the man who had most injured and insulted him. The successful
man of the world cursed the old pauper, and relieved him from time

to time. As he furnished George with money for his mother, he gave
the boy to understand by hints, delivered in his brutal, coarse way,
that George's maternal grandfather was but a wretched old bankrupt
and dependant, and that John Sedley might thank the man to whom
he already owed ever so much money for the aid which his generosity
now chose to administer. George carried the pompous supplies to his
mother and the shattered old widower whom it was now the main
business of her life to tend and comfort. The little fellow patronized
the feeble and disappointed old man.

Old Sedley grew very fond of his daughter after his wife's death,
and Amelia had her consolation in doing her duty by the old man.

But we are not going to leave these two people long in such a low
and ungenteel station of life. Better days, as far as worldly prosperity
went, were in store for both. Perhaps the ingenious reader has guessed
who was the stout gentleman who called upon Georgy at his school
in company with our old friend Major Dobbin. It was another old
acquaintance returned to England, and at a time when his presence
was likely to be of great comfort to his relatives there.

Major Dobbin having easily succeeded in getting leave from his good-
natured commandant to proceed to Madras, and thence probably to
Europe, on urgent private affairs, never ceased travelling night and
day until he reached his journey's end, and had directed his march
with such celerity that he arrived at Madras in a high fever.

He recovered, rallied, relapsed again, having undergone such a
process of blood-letting and calomel as showed the strength of his
original constitution. He was almost a skeleton when they put him on
board the *Ramchunder* East Indiaman, Captain Bragg, from Calcutta,
touching at Madras; and so weak and prostrate, that his friend who
had tended him through his illness prophesied that the honest Major
would never survive the voyage, and that he would pass some morning,
shrouded in flag and hammock, over the ship's side, and carrying
down to the sea with him the relic that he wore at his heart. But
whether it was the sea air, or the hope which sprung up in him afresh,
from the day that the ship spread her canvas and stood out of the
roads towards *home* our friend began to amend, and he was quite
well (though as gaunt as a greyhound) before they reached the Cape.
"Kirk will be disappointed of his majority this time," he said, with
a smile; "he will expect to find himself gazetted by the time the regiment reaches home." For it must be premised that while the Major
was lying ill at Madras, having made such prodigious haste to go
thither, the gallant —th, which had passed many years abroad, which
after its return from the West Indies had been balked of its stay at
home by the Waterloo campaign, and had been ordered from Flanders
to India, had received orders home; and the Major might have accompanied his comrades, had he chosen to wait for their arrival at Madras.

Perhaps he was not inclined to put himself in his exhausted state
again under the guardianship of Glorvina. "I think Miss O'Dowd

would have done for me," he said laughingly to a fellow-passenger,
"if we had had her on bcard; and when she had sunk me, she would
have fallen upon you, depend upon it, and carried you in as a prize
to Southampton, Jos, my boy.

For indeed it was no other than our stout friend who was also a
passenger on board the *Ramchunder*. He had passed ten years in
Bengal. Constant dinners, tiffins, pale ale and claret, the prodigious
labour of cutcherry, and the refreshment of brandy-pawnee which he
was forced to take there, had their effect upon Waterloo Sedley. A
voyage to Europe was pronounced necessary for him; and having
served his full time in India, and had fine appointments, which had
enabled him to lay by a considerable sum of money, he was free to
come home and stay with a good pension, or to return and resume
that rank in the service to which his seniority and his vast talents
entitled him.

He was rather thinner than when we last saw him, but had gained
in majesty and solemnity of demeanour. He had resumed the mustachios to which his services at Waterloo entitled him, and swaggered
about on deck in a magnificent velvet cap with a gold band, and a
profuse ornamentation of pins and jewellery about his person. He
took breakfast in his cabin, and dressed as solemnly to appear on the
quarter-deck, as if he were going to turn out for Bond Street, or the
Course at Calcutta.

Many and many a night, as the ship was cutting through the roaring
dark sea, the moon and stars shining overhead, and the bell singing
out the watch, Mr. Sedley and the Major would sit on the quarter-deck
of the vessel talking about home, as the Major smoked his cheroot,
and the civilian puffed at the hookah which his servant prepared for
him.

In these conversations it was wonderful what perseverance and
ingenuity Major Dobbin would manage to bring the talk round to the
subject of Amelia and her little boy. He coaxed, wheedled, cajoled,
and complimented Jos Sedley with a perseverance and cordiality of
which he was not aware himself, very likely; but some men who have
unmarried sisters or daughters even, may remember how uncommonly
agreeable gentlemen are to the male relations when they are courting
the females, and perhaps this rogue of a Dobbin was urged by a
similar hypocrisy.

The truth is, when Major Dobbin came on board the *Ramchunder*,
very sick, and for the three days she lay in the Madras Roads, he did
not begin to rally, nor did even the appearance and recognition of his
old acquaintance, Mr. Sedley, on board much cheer him, until after
a conversation which they had one day, as the Major was laid languidly
on the deck. He said then he thought he was doomed; he had left a
little something to his godson in his will; and he trusted Mrs. Osborne
would remember him kindly, and be happy in the marriage she was
about to make. "Married? not the least," Jos answered. "He had

heard from her; she made no mention of the marriage: and by the way, it was curious, she wrote to say that Major Dobbin was going to be married, and hoped that *he* would be happy." What were the dates of Sedley's letters from Europe? The civilian fetched them. They were two months later than the Major's; and the ship's surgeon congratulated himself upon the treatment adopted by him towards his new patient, who had been consigned to shipboard by the Madras practitioner with very small hopes indeed, for from that day, the very day that he changed the draught, Major Dobbin began to mend. And thus it was that deserving officer, Captain Kirk, was disappointed of his majority.

CHAPTER LVIII

OUR FRIEND THE MAJOR

OUR Major had rendered himself so popular on board the *Ramchunder*, that when he and Mr. Sedley descended into the welcome shoreboat which was to take them from the ship, the whole crew, men and officers, the great Captain Bragg himself leading off, gave three cheers for Major Dobbin, who blushed very much, and ducked his head in token of thanks.

Major Dobbin made his appearance the next morning very neatly shaved and dressed, according to his wont. Indeed, it was so early in the morning, that nobody was up in the house except that wonderful Boots of an inn who never seems to want sleep. Then Jos's native servant arose and began to get ready his master's ponderous dressing apparatus, and prepare his hookah; then the maid-servants got up, and meeting the dark man in the passages, shrieked, and mistook him for the devil. He and Dobbin stumbled over their pails in the passages as they were scouring the decks of the Royal George. When the first unshorn waiter appeared and unbarred the door of the inn, the Major thought that the time for departure was arrived, and ordered a postchaise to be fetched instantly, that they might set off.

He then directed his steps to Mr. Sedley's room, and opened the curtains of the great large family bed wherein Mr. Jos was snoring. "Come up! Sedley," the Major said, "it's time to be off; the chaise will be at the door in half an hour."

Jos growled from under the counterpane to know what the time was; but when he at last extorted from the blushing Major (who never told fibs, however they might be to his advantage) what was the real hour of the morning, he broke out into a volley of bad language, which we will not repeat here, but by which he gave Dobbin to understand that he would jeopardize his soul if he got up at that moment—that the Major might go and be hanged—that he would not travel with Dobbin, and that it was most unkind and ungentlemanlike to disturb a man out of his sleep in that way; on which the discomfited Major was obliged to retreat, leaving Jos to resume his interrupted slumbers.

The chaise came up presently, and the Major would wait no longer. Every minute incident of his last meeting with Amelia was present to the constant man's mind as he walked towards her house. The arch and the Achilles statue were up since he had last been in Piccadilly; a hundred changes had occurred which his eye and mind vaguely noted. He began to tremble as he walked up the lane from Brompton, that well-remembered lane leading to the street where she lived. Was she going to be married or not? When he came up to the row of houses, at last, where she lived, and to the gate, he caught hold of it and paused.

The window of the parlour which she used to occupy was open, and there were no inmates in the room. The Major thought he recognized the piano, though, with the picture over it, as it used to be in former days, and his perturbations were renewed. Mr. Clapp's brass plate was still on the door, at the knocker of which Dobbin performed a summons.

A buxom-looking lass of sixteen, with bright eyes and purple cheeks, came to answer the knock. She looked him hard in the face for a moment—and then turning white too, said, "Lord bless me—it's Major Dobbin." She held out both her hands shaking. "Don't you remember me?" she said. "I used to call you Major Sugarplums." On which, and I believe it was for the first time that he ever so conducted himself in his life, the Major took the girl in his arms and kissed her. She began to laugh and cry hysterically, and calling out, "Ma, Pa!" with all her voice, brought up those worthy people, who had already been surveying the Major from the casement of the ornamental kitchen, and were astonished to find their daughter in the little passage in the embrace of a great tall man in a blue frock-coat and white duck trousers.

"I'm an old friend," he said—not without blushing though. "Don't you remember me, Mrs. Clapp, and those good cakes you used to make for tea?—Don't you recollect me, Clapp? I'm George's godfather, and just come back from India." A great shaking of hands ensued. Mrs. Clapp was greatly affected and delighted; she called upon Heaven to interpose a vast many times in that passage.

The landlord and landlady of the house led the worthy Major into the Sedleys' room (whereof he remembered every single article of furniture, from the old brass ornamented piano, once a natty little instrument, Stothard maker, to the screens and the alabaster miniature tombstone, in the midst of which ticked Mr. Sedley's gold watch); and there, as he sat down in the lodger's vacant arm-chair, the father, the mother, and the daughter, with a thousand ejaculatory breaks in the narrative, informed Major Dobbin of what we know already, but of particulars in Amelia's history of which he was not aware—namely, of Mrs. Sedley's death, of George's reconcilement with his grandfather Osborne, of the way in which the widow took on at leaving him, and of other particulars of her life. Finally, he was informed that Mrs. O.

was gone to walk with her pa in Kensington Gardens, whither she always went with the old gentleman (who was very weak and peevish now, and led her a sad life, though she behaved to him like an angel, to be sure), of a fine afternoon, after dinner.

"I'm very much pressed for time," the Major said, "and have business to-night of importance. I should like to see Mrs. Osborne though. Suppose Miss Polly would come with me and show me the way."

Miss Polly was charmed and astonished at this proposal. She knew the way. She would show Major Dobbin.

That officer, then, in his blue frock-coat and buckskin gloves, gave the young lady his arm, and they walked away very gaily.

They were too soon (for he was in a great tremor at the idea of a meeting for which he had been longing any time these ten years) through the Brompton lanes, and entering at the little old portal in Kensington Garden wall.

"There they are," said Miss Polly, and she felt him again start back on her arm.

"Suppose you were to run on and tell her," the Major said. Polly ran forward, her yellow shawl streaming in the breeze.

Old Sedley was seated on a bench, his handkerchief placed over his knees, prattling away according to his wont, with some old story about old times, to which Amelia had listened and awarded a patient smile many a time before. As Mary came bouncing along, and Amelia caught sight of her, she started up from her bench. Her first thought was, that something had happened to Georgy; but the sight of the messenger's eager and happy face dissipated that fear in the timorous mother's bosom.

"News! news!" cried the emissary of Major Dobbin. "He's come! he's come!"

"Who is come?" said Emmy, still thinking of her son.

"Look there," answered Miss Clapp, turning round and pointing; in which direction Amelia looking, saw Dobbin's lean figure and long shadow stalking across the grass. Amelia started in her turn, blushed up, and, of course, began to cry. At all this simple little creature's *fêtes* the *grandes eaux* were accustomed to play.

He looked at her—oh, how fondly—as she came running towards him, her hands before her, ready to give them to him. He took the two little hands between his two, and held them there. He was speechless for a moment. Why did he not take her in his arms, and swear that he would never leave her? She must have yielded; she could not but have obeyed him.

"I—I've another arrival to announce," he said, after a pause.

"Mrs. Dobbin?" Amelia said, making a movement back—Why didn't he speak?

"No," he said, letting her hands go. "Who has told you those lies? —I mean, your brother Jos came in the same ship with me, and is come home to make you all happy."

"Papa, papa!" Emmy cried out, "here are news! My brother is in England. He is come to take care of you.—Here is Major Dobbin."

Mr. Sedley started up, shaking a great deal, and gathering up his thoughts. Then he stepped forward and made an old-fashioned bow to the Major, whom he called Mr. Dobbin, and hoped his worthy father, Sir William, was quite well.

"He is very much shaken," Emmy whispered, as Dobbin went up and cordially shook hands with the old man.

Although he had such particular business in London that evening, the Major consented to forego it upon Mr. Sedley's invitation to him to come home and partake of tea.

Amelia was very happy, smiling, and active all that evening, performing her duties as hostess of the little entertainment with the utmost grace and propriety, as Dobbin thought. His eyes followed her about as they sate in the twilight.

At his accustomed hour Mr. Sedley began to doze in his chair, and then it was Amelia's opportunity to commence her conversation, which she did with great eagerness: it related exclusively to Georgy. She did not talk at all about her own sufferings at breaking from him—for indeed this worthy woman, though she was half-killed by the separation from the child, yet thought it was very wicked in her to repine at losing him—but everything concerning him, his virtues, talents, and prospects, she poured out. She described his angelic beauty; narrated a hundred instances of his generosity and greatness of mind whilst living with her; how a Royal Duchess had stopped and admired him in Kensington Gardens; how splendidly he was cared for now, and how he had a groom and a pony; what quickness and cleverness he had; and what a prodigiously well-read and delightful person the Reverend Lawrence Veal was, George's master. "He knows *everything*," Amelia said. "He has the most delightful parties. You who are so learned yourself, and have read so much, and are so clever and accomplished —don't shake your head and say no; *He* always used to say you were —you will be charmed with Mr. Veal's parties. The last Tuesday in every month. He says there is no place in the bar or the senate that Georgy may not aspire to.

"O William," she added, holding out her hand to the Major, "what a treasure Heaven has given me in that boy! He is the comfort of my life; and he is the image of—of him that's gone!"

"Ought I to be angry with her for being faithful to him?" William thought. "Ought I to be jealous of my friend in the grave, or hurt that such a heart as Amelia's can love only once and for ever? O George, George, how little you knew the prize you had, though." This sentiment passed rapidly through William's mind, as he was holding Amelia's hand, whilst the handkerchief was veiling her eyes.

"Dear friend," she said, pressing the hand which held hers, "how good, how kind you always have been to me! See, papa is stirring. You will go and see Georgy to-morrow, won't you?"

"Not to-morrow," said poor old Dobbin. "I have business." He did not like to own that he had not as yet been to his parents' and his dear sister Ann—a remissness for which I am sure every well-regulated person will blame the Major. And presently he took his leave, leaving his address behind him for Jos, against the latter's arrival. And so the first day was over, and he had seen her.

When he got back to the Slaughters', the roast fowl was of course cold, in which condition he ate it for supper. And knowing what early hours his family kept, and that it would be needless to disturb their slumbers at so late an hour, it is on record that Major Dobbin treated himself to half-price at the Haymarket Theatre that evening, where, let us hope, he enjoyed himself.

CHAPTER LIX

THE OLD PIANO

WE have adroitly shut the door upon the meeting between Jos and the old father and the poor little gentle sister inside. The old man was very much affected; so, of course, was his daughter; nor was Jos without feeling.

The result of the interview must have been very satisfactory; for when Jos had reascended his post-chaise, and had driven away to his hotel, Emmy embraced her father tenderly, appealing to him with an air of triumph, and asking the old man whether she did not always say that her brother had a good heart.

Indeed, Joseph Sedley, affected by the humble position in which he found his relations, and in the expansiveness and overflowing of heart occasioned by the first meeting, declared that they should never suffer want or discomfort any more; that he was at home for some time at any rate, during which his house and everything he had should be theirs; and that Amelia would look very pretty at the head of his table —until she would accept one of her own.

It was a matter of great delight and occupation to Jos to superintend the building of a small chariot, which he and the Major ordered in the neighbouring Long Acre; and a pair of handsome horses were jobbed with which Jos drove about in state in the Park, or to call upon his Indian friends. Amelia was not seldom by his side on these excursions, when also Major Dobbin would be seen in the back seat of the carriage. At other times old Sedley and his daughter took advantage of it; and Miss Clapp, who frequently accompanied her friend, had great pleasure in being recognized as she sate in the carriage, dressed in the famous yellow shawl, by the young gentleman at the surgery, whose face might commonly be seen over the window-blinds as she passed.

Shortly after Jos's first appearance at Brompton, a dismal scene, indeed, took place at that humble cottage at which the Sedleys had passed the last ten years of their life. Jos's carriage (the temporary one, not the chariot under construction) arrived one day and carried off old Sedley and his daughter—to return no more.

Major Dobbin was exceedingly pleased when, as he was superintending the arrangements of Jos's new house, which the Major insisted should be very handsome and comfortable, the cart arrived from Brompton bringing the trunks and bandboxes of the emigrants from that village, and with them the old piano. Amelia would have it up in her sitting-room, a neat little apartment on the second floor, adjoining her father's chamber, and where the old gentleman sate commonly of evenings.

When the men appeared then bearing this old music box, and Amelia gave orders that it should be placed in the chamber aforesaid, Dobbin was quite elated. "I'm glad you've kept it," he said, in a very sentimental manner. "I was afraid you didn't care about it."

"I value it more than anything I have in the world," said Amelia.

"*Do* you, Amelia?" cried the Major. The fact was, as he had bought it himself, though he never said anything about it, it never entered into his head to suppose that Emmy should think anybody else was the purchaser, and as a matter of course he fancied that she knew the gift came from him. "Do you, Amelia?" he said; and the question, the great question of all, was trembling on his lips, when Emmy replied:

"Can I do otherwise? did not *he* give it me?"

"I did not know," said poor old Dob, and his countenance fell.

Emmy did not note the circumstance at the time, nor take immediate heed of the very dismal expression which honest Dobbin's countenance assumed, but she thought of it afterwards. And then it struck her, with inexpressible pain and mortification too, that it was William who was the giver of the piano, and not George, as she had fancied.

Then, according to her custom, she rebuked herself for her pettishness and ingratitude, and determined to make a reparation to honest William for the slight she had not expressed to him, but had felt for his piano. A few days afterwards, as they were seated in the drawing-room, where Jos had fallen asleep with great comfort after dinner, Amelia said, with rather a faltering voice, to Major Dobbin, "I have to beg your pardon for something."

"About what?" said he.

"About—about that little square piano. I never thanked you for it when you gave it me, many, many years ago, before I was married. I thought somebody else had given it. Thank you, William." She held out her hand. But the poor little woman's heart was bleeding; and as for her eyes, of course they were at their work.

But William could hold no more. "Amelia, Amelia," he said, "I did buy it for you. I loved you then as I do now. I must tell you. I think I loved you from the first minute that I saw you, when George brought me to your house, to show me the Amelia whom he was engaged to. You were but a girl, in white, with large ringlets; you came down singing—do you remember?—and we went to Vauxhall. Since then I have thought of but one woman in the world, and that was you. I think there is no hour in the day has passed for twelve years that I haven't thought of you. I came to tell you this before I went to India, but you did not care, and I hadn't the heart to speak. You did not care whether I stayed or went."

"I was very ungrateful," Amelia said.

"No, only indifferent," Dobbin continued desperately. "I have nothing to make a woman to be otherwise. I know what you are feeling now. You are hurt in your heart at the discovery about the piano, and that it came from me and not from George. I forgot, or I should never have spoken of it so. It is for me to ask your pardon for being a fool for a moment, and thinking that years of constancy and devotion might have pleaded with you."

"It is you who are cruel now," Amelia said with some spirit. "George is my husband, here and in heaven. How could I love any other but him? I am his now as when you first saw me, dear William. It was he who told me how good and generous you were, and who taught me to love you as a brother. Have you not been everything to me and my boy—our dearest, truest, kindest friend and protector? Had you come a few months sooner, perhaps you might have spared me that—that dreadful parting. Oh, it nearly killed me, William. But you didn't come, though I wished and prayed for you to come; and they took him too away from me. Isn't he a noble boy, William? Be his friend still and mine"—and here her voice broke, and she hid her face on his shoulder.

The Major folded his arms round her, holding her to him as if she was a child, and kissed her head. "I will not change, dear Amelia," he said. "I ask for no more than your love. I think I would not have it otherwise. Only let me stay near you and see you often."

"Yes, often," Amelia said. And so William was at liberty to look and long, as the poor boy at school who has no money may sigh after the contents of the tart-woman's tray.

CHAPTER LX

RETURNS TO THE GENTEEL WORLD

GOOD fortune now begins to smile upon Amelia. We are glad to get her out of that low sphere in which she has been creeping hitherto, and introduce her into a polite circle; not so grand and refined as that in which our other female friend, Mrs. Becky, has appeared, but still having no small pretensions to gentility and fashion. Jos's friends were all from the three presidencies, and his new house was in the comfortable Anglo-Indian district of which Moira Place is the centre. Minto Square, Great Clive Street, Warren Street, Hastings

H

Street, Ochterlony Place, Plassy Square, Assaye Terrace. Jos's position
in life was not grand enough to entitle him to a house in Moira Place,
where none can live but retired Members of Council, and partners of
Indian firms (who break after having settled a hundred thousand
pounds on their wives, and retire into comparative penury to a country
place and four thousand a year). He engaged a comfortable house of
a second or third rate order in Gillespie Street, purchasing the carpets,
costly mirrors, and handsome and appropriate planned furniture.

It was a modest establishment. The butler was Jos's valet also, and
never was more drunk than a butler in a small family should be who
has a proper regard for his master's wine. Emmy was supplied with a
maid grown on Sir William Dobbin's suburban estate—a good girl,
whose kindness and humility disarmed Mrs. Osborne, who was at first
terrified at the idea of having a servant to wait upon herself, who did
not in the least know how to use one, and who always spoke to
domestics with the most reverential politeness. But this maid was very
useful in the family, in dexterously tending old Mr. Sedley, who kept
almost entirely to his own quarter of the house, and never mixed in
any of the gay doings which took place there.

Numbers of people came to see Mrs. Osborne. Lady Dobbin and
daughters were delighted at her change of fortune, and waited upon
her. Miss Osborne from Russell Square came in her grand chariot with
the flaming hammercloth emblazoned with the Leeds arms. Jos was
reported to be immensely rich. Old Osborne had no objection that
Georgy should inherit his uncle's property as well as his own. "Damn
it, we will make a man of the feller," he said; "and I'll see him in
Parliament before I die. *You* may go and see his mother, Miss O.,
though I'll never set eyes on her;" and Miss Osborne came. Emmy,
you may be sure, was very glad to see her, and so be brought nearer
to George. That young fellow was allowed to come much more frequently than before to visit his mother. He dined once or twice a week
in Gillespie Street, and bullied the servants and his relations there, just
as he did in Russell Square.

He was always respectful to Major Dobbin, however, and more
modest in his demeanour when that gentleman was present. He was a
clever lad, and afraid of the Major. George could not help admiring
his friend's simplicity, his good-humour, his various learning quietly
imparted, his general love of truth and justice. He had met no such
man as yet in the course of his experience, and he had an instinctive
liking for a gentleman. He hung fondly by his godfather's side, and it
was his delight to walk in the Parks and hear Dobbin talk. William
told George about his father, about India and Waterloo, about everything but himself. When George was more than usually pert and con-
ceited, the Major made jokes at him, which Mrs. Osborne thought very
cruel.

Georgy never tired of his praises of the Major to his mother. "I like
him, mamma, because he knows such a lot of things; and he ain't like

old Veal, who is always bragging and using such long words, don't you know? The chaps call him 'Longtail' at school. I gave him the name; ain't it capital? But Dob reads Latin like English, and French and that; and when we go out together he tells me stories about my papa, and never about himself; though I heard Colonel Buckler at Grandpapa's say that he was one of the bravest officers in the army, and had distinguished himself ever so much. Grandpapa was quite surprised, and said, '*That* feller! why, I didn't think he could say Bo to a goose.' But *I* know he could; couldn't he, mamma?"

Emmy laughed; she thought it was very likely the Major could do thus much.

If there was a sincere liking between George and the Major, it must be confessed that between the boy and his uncle no great love existed. George had got a way of blowing out his cheeks, and putting his hands in his waistcoat pockets, and saying, "God bless my soul, you don't say so," so exactly after the fashion of old Jos that it was impossible to refrain from laughter. The servants would explode at dinner if the lad, asking for something which wasn't at table, put on that countenance and used that favourite phrase. Even Dobbin would shoot out a sudden peal at the boy's mimicry. If George did not mimic his uncle to his face, it was only by Dobbin's rebukes and Amelia's terrified entreaties that the little scapegoat was induced to desist. And the worthy civilian being haunted by a dim consciousness that the lad thought him an ass, and was inclined to turn him into ridicule, used to be extremely timorous, and of course doubly pompous and dignified, in the presence of Master Georgy.

Before long Emmy had a visiting-book, and was driving about regularly in a carriage, calling upon Lady Bludyer (wife of Major-General Sir Rodger Bludyer, K.C.B., Bengal Army); Lady Huff, wife of Sir G. Huff, Bombay ditto; Mrs. Pice, the Lady of Pice the Director, etc. We are not long in using ourselves to changes in life. That carriage came round to Gillespie Street every day; that buttony boy sprang up and down from the box with Emmy's and Jos's visiting-cards; at stated hours Emmy and the carriage went for Jos to the Club, and took him an airing; or, putting old Sedley into the vehicle, she drove the old man round the Regent's Park. The lady's-maid and the chariot, the visiting-book and the buttony page, became soon as familiar to Amelia as the humble routine of Brompton. She accommodated herself to one as to the other. If Fate had ordained that she should be a duchess, she would even have done that duty too. She was voted, in Jos's female society, rather a pleasing young person—not much in her, but pleasing, and that sort of thing.

The men, as usual, liked her artless kindness and simple, refined demeanour. The gallant young Indian dandies at home on furlough— immense dandies these, chained and moustached, driving in tearing cabs, the pillars of the theatres, living at West End hotels—nevertheless admired Mrs. Osborne, liked to bow to her carriage in the Park, and to be admitted to have the honour of paying her a morning visit. Swankey of the Body Guard himself, that dangerous youth, and the greatest buck of all the Indian army now on leave, was one day discovered by Major Dobbin *tête-à-tête* with Amelia, and describing the sport of pig-sticking to her with great humour and eloquence; and he spoke afterwards of a d—— King's officer that's always hanging about the house—a long, thin, queer-looking, oldish fellow, a dry fellow though, that took the shine out of a man in the talking line.

Had the Major possessed a little more personal vanity, he would have been jealous of so dangerous a young buck as that fascinating Bengal Captain. But Dobbin was of too simple and generous a nature to have any doubts about Amelia. He was glad that the young men should pay her respect, and that others should admire her. Ever since her womanhood almost, had she not been persecuted and undervalued? It pleased him to see how kindness brought out her good qualities, and how her spirits gently rose with her prosperity. Any person who appreciated her paid a compliment to the Major's good judgment—that is, if a man may be said to have good judgment who is under the influence of Love's delusion.

After Jos went to Court, which we may be sure he did as a loyal subject of his Sovereign (showing himself in his full Court suit at the Club, whither Dobbin came to fetch him in a very shabby old uniform), he who had always been a staunch Loyalist and admirer of George IV. became such a tremendous Tory and pillar of the State that he was for having Amelia to go to a Drawing-room too. He somehow had worked himself up to believe that he was implicated in the maintenance of the public welfare, and that the Sovereign would not be happy unless Jos Sedley and his family appeared to rally round him at St. James's.

Emmy laughed. "Shall I wear the family diamonds, Jos?" she said.

"I wish you would let me buy you some," thought the Major. "I should like to see any that were too good for you."

CHAPTER LXI

IN WHICH TWO LIGHTS ARE PUT OUT

There came a day when the round of decorous pleasures and solemn gaieties in which Mr. Jos Sedley's family indulged was interrupted by an event which happens in most houses.

The period of mourning for Mrs. Sedley's death was only just concluded, and Jos scarcely had had time to cast off his black and appear in the splendid waistcoats which he loved, when it became evident to those about Mr. Sedley that another event was at hand, and that the old man was about to go seek for his wife in the dark land whither she had preceded him.

So there came one morning and sunrise when all the world got up and set about its various works and pleasures, with the exception of old John Sedley, who was not to fight with Fortune or to hope or scheme any more, but to go and take up a quiet and utterly unknown residence in a churchyard at Brompton by the side of his old wife.

"You see," said old Osborne to George, "what comes of merit and industry, and judicious speculations, and that. Look at me and my banker's account. Look at your poor grandfather Sedley and his failure. And yet he was a better man than I was this day twenty years —a better man, I should say, by ten thousand pound."

Beyond these people and Mr. Clapp's family, who came over from Brompton to pay a visit of condolence, not a single soul alive ever cared a penny piece about old John Sedley, or remembered the existence of such a person.

When old Osborne first heard from his friend Colonel Buckler (as little Georgy has already informed us) how distinguished an officer Major Dobbin was, he exhibited a great deal of scornful incredulity, and expressed his surprise how ever such a feller as that should possess either brains or reputation. But he heard of the Major's fame from various members of his society. Sir William Dobbin had a great opinion of his son, and narrated many stories illustrative of the Major's learning, valour, and estimation in the world's opinion. Finally, his name appeared in the lists of one or two great parties of the nobility, and this circumstance had a prodigious effect upon the old aristocrat of Russell Square.

The Major's position as guardian to Georgy, whose possession had been ceded to his grandfather, rendered some meetings between the two gentlemen inevitable; and it was in one of these that old Osborne, a keen man of business, looking into the Major's accounts with his ward and the boy's mother, got a hint which staggered him very much, and at once pained and pleased him, that it was out of William Dobbin's own pocket that a part of the fund had been supplied upon which the poor widow and the child had subsisted.

On one or two evenings the Major came to dine with Mr. Osborne (it was during the time of the sickness of Mr. Sedley), and as the two sate together in the evening after dinner all the talk was about the departed hero. On the second evening old Osborne called Dobbin William, just as he used to do at the time when Dobbin and George were boys together; and the honest gentleman was pleased by that mark of reconciliation.

On the next day at breakfast, when Miss Osborne, with the asperity of her age and character, ventured to make some remark reflecting slightingly upon the Major's appearance or behaviour, the master of the house interrupted her. "You'd have been glad enough to git him for yourself, Miss O. But them grapes are sour. Ha! ha! Major William is a fine feller."

That old Osborne's mind was changing was pretty clear. He asked
George about his uncle sometimes, and laughed at the boy's imitation
of the way in which Jos said, "God-bless-my-soul," and gobbled his
soup. Then he said, "It's not respectful, sir, of you younkers to be
imitating of your relations.—Miss O., when you go out a-driving to-
day, leave my card upon Mr. Sedley, do you hear? There's no quarrel
betwigst me and him anyhow."

The card was returned, and Jos and the Major were asked to dinner
—to a dinner the most splendid and stupid that perhaps ever Mr.
Osborne gave: every inch of the family plate was exhibited, and the
best company was asked.

More than once Mr. Osborne asked the Major about—about Mrs. George
Osborne—a theme on which the Major could be very eloquent when he
chose. He told Mr. Osborne of her sufferings; of her passionate attachment to her husband, whose memory she worshipped still; of the tender
and dutiful manner in which she had supported her parents, and given
up her boy when it seemed to her her duty to do so. "You don't know
what she endured, sir," said honest Dobbin, with a tremor in his voice;
"and I hope and trust you will be reconciled to her. If she took your
son away from you, she gave hers to you; and however much you
loved your George, depend on it she loved hers ten times more."

"By God, you are a good feller, sir," was all Mr. Osborne said. It
had never struck him that the widow would feel any pain at parting
from the boy, or that his having a fine fortune could grieve her. A
reconciliation was announced as speedy and inevitable, and Amelia's
heart already began to beat at the notion of the awful meeting with
George's father.

It was never, however, destined to take place. Old Sedley's lingering
illness and death supervened, after which a meeting was for some time
impossible. That catastrophe and other events may have worked upon
Mr. Osborne. He was much shaken of late, and aged, and his mind
was working inwardly. He had sent for his lawyers, and probably
changed something in his will. The medical man who looked in pronounced him shaky, agitated, and talked of a little blood and the seaside; but he took neither of these remedies.

One day when he should have come down to breakfast, his servant
missing him went into his dressing-room, and found him lying at the
foot of the dressing-table in a fit. Miss Osborne was apprised; the
doctors were sent for; Georgy stopped away from school; the bleeders
and cuppers came. Osborne partially regained cognizance, but never
could speak again, though he tried dreadfully once or twice, and in
four days he died.

When the will was opened, it was found that half the property was
left to George, and the remainder between the two sisters; Mr. Bullock
to continue, for their joint benefit, the affairs of the commercial house,
or to go out, as he thought fit. An annuity of five hundred pounds,
chargeable on George's property, was left to his mother, "the widow

of my beloved son, George Osborne," who was to resume the guardian-ship of the boy.

"Major William Dobbin, my beloved son's friend," was appointed executor; "and as out of his kindness and bounty, and with his own private funds, he maintained my grandson and my son's widow, when they were otherwise without means of support" (the testator went on to say), "I hereby thank him heartily for his love and regard for them, and beseech him to accept such a sum as may be sufficient to purchase his commission as Lieutenant-Colonel, or to be disposed of in any way he may think fit."

When Amelia heard that her father-in-law was reconciled to her, her heart melted, and she was grateful for the fortune left to her. But when she heard how Georgy was restored to her, and knew how and by whom, and how it was William's bounty that supported her in poverty, how it was William who gave her her husband and her son —oh, then she sank on her knees, and prayed for blessings on that constant and kind heart; she bowed down and humbled herself, and kissed the feet, as it were, of that beautiful and generous affection.

And gratitude was all that she had to pay back for such admirable devotion and benefits—only gratitude! If she thought of any other return, the image of George stood up out of the grave, and said, "You are mine, and mine only, now and for ever."

William knew her feelings; had he not passed his whole life in divining them?

In her capacity of guardian to Georgy, Mrs. Osborne, with the consent of the Major, her fellow-trustee, begged Miss Osborne to live in the Russell Square house as long as ever she chose to dwell there; but that lady, with thanks, declared that she never could think of remaining alone in that melancholy mansion, and departed in deep mourning to Cheltenham, with a couple of her old domestics. The rest were liberally paid and dismissed—the faithful old butler, whom Mrs. Osborne proposed to retain, resigning, and preferring to invest his savings in a public-house, where, let us hope, he was not unprosperous. Miss Osborne not choosing to live in Russell Square, Mrs. Osborne also, after consultation, declined to occupy the gloomy old mansion there. The house was dismantled; the rich furniture and effects, the awful chandeliers and dreary blank mirrors packed away and hidden, the rich rosewood drawing-room suite was muffled in straw, the carpets were rolled up and corded, the small select library of well-bound books was stowed into two wine-chests, and the whole paraphernalia rolled away in several enormous vans to the Pantechnicon, where they were to lie until George's majority. And the great heavy dark plate-chests went off to Messrs. Stumpy & Rowdy, to lie in the cellars of those eminent bankers until the same period should arrive.

The female Bullock, aunt of Georgy, although despoiled by that little monster of one-half of the sum which she expected from her

father, nevertheless showed her charitableness of spirit by being reconciled to the mother and the boy. Roehampton is not far from Richmond, and one day the chariot, with the golden bullocks emblazoned
on the panels, and the flaccid children within, drove to Amelia's house
at Richmond; and the Bullock family made an irruption into the
garden, where Amelia was reading a book, Jos was in an arbour
placidly dipping strawberries into wine, and the Major in one of his
Indian jackets was giving a back to Georgy, who chose to jump over
him. He went over his head, and bounded into the little advance of
Bullocks, with immense black bows in their hats, and huge black
sashes, accompanying their mourning mamma. "He is just of the age
for Rosa," the fond parent thought, and glanced towards that dear
child, an unwholesome little Miss of seven years of age.

"Rosa, go and kiss your dear cousin," Mrs. Frederick said—"Don't
you know me, George? I am your aunt."

"*I* know you well enough," George said; "but I don't like kissing,
please," and he retreated from the obedient caresses of his cousin.

"Take me to your dear mamma, you droll child," Mrs. Frederick
said; and those ladies accordingly met, after an absence of more than
fifteen years. During Emmy's cares and poverty the other had never
once thought about coming to see her; but now that she was decently
prosperous in the world, her sister-in-law came to her as a matter of
course.

So did numbers more. Our old friend Miss Swartz and her husband
came thundering over from Hampton Court, with flaming yellow
liveries, and was as impetuously fond of Amelia as ever. Miss Swartz
would have liked her always if she could have seen her; one must do
her that justice. But, *que voulez-vous?*—in this vast town one has not
the time to go and seek one's friends; if they drop out of the rank
they disappear, and we march on without them. Who is ever missed
in Vanity Fair?

But so, in a word, and before the period of grief for Mr. Osborne's
death had subsided, Emmy found herself in the centre of a very genteel
circle indeed, the members of which could not conceive that anybody
belonging to it was not very lucky.

CHAPTER LXII

AM RHEIN

THE above everyday events had occurred, and a few weeks had
passed, when on one fine morning, Parliament being over, the
summer advanced, and all the good company in London about to quit
that city for their annual tour in search of pleasure or health, the
Batavier steamboat left the Tower stairs laden with a goodly company
of English fugitives.

Jos was seated at that moment on deck under the awning, and pretty

nearly opposite to the Earl of Bareacres and his family, whose proceedings absorbed the Bengalee almost entirely. Both the noble couple
looked rather younger than in the eventful year '15, when Jos remembered to have seen them at Brussels (indeed, he always gave out in
India that he was intimately acquainted with them). Lady Bareacres'
hair, which was then dark, was now a beautiful golden auburn; whereas
Lord Bareacres' whiskers, formerly red, were at present of a rich black,
with purple and green reflections in the light. But changed as they were,
the movements of the noble pair occupied Jos's mind entirely. The
presence of a lord fascinated him, and he could look at nothing else.

"Those people seem to interest you a great deal," said Dobbin,
laughing and watching him. Amelia too laughed. She was in a straw
bonnet with black ribbons, and otherwise dressed in mourning; but
the little bustle and holiday of the journey pleased and excited her,
and she looked particularly happy.

"What a heavenly day!" Emmy said; and added, with great
originality, "I hope we shall have a calm passage."

In due time this happy party landed at the quays of Rotterdam,
whence they were transported by another steamer to the city of
Cologne. Here the carriage and the family took to the shore, and Jos
was not a little gratified to see his arrival announced in the Cologne
newspapers as "Herr Graf Lord von Sedley nebst Begleitung aus
London."

It was at the little comfortable Ducal town of Pumpernickel (that
very place where Sir Pitt Crawley had been so distinguished as an
attaché; but that was in early, early days, and before the news of the
battle of Austerlitz sent all the English diplomatists in Germany to the
right about) that I first saw Colonel Dobbin and his party. They had
arrived with the carriage and courier at the Erbprinz Hotel, the best
of the town, and the whole party dined at the *table d'hôte*. Everybody
remarked the majesty of Jos, and the knowing way in which he sipped
or rather sucked the Johannisberger, which he ordered for dinner.

It was what they call a *gastrolle* night at the Royal Grand Ducal
Pumpernickelisch Hof, or Court theatre, and Madame Schroeder
Devrient, then in the bloom of her beauty and genius, performed the
part of the heroine in the wonderful opera of *Fidelio*. From our places
in the stalls we could see our four friends of the *table d'hôte*, in the
loge which Schwendler of the Erbprinz kept for his best guests; and
I could not help remarking the effect which the magnificent actress and
music produced upon Mrs. Osborne—for so we heard the stout gentleman in the mustachios call her.

The performance over, the young fellows lounged about the lobbies,
and we saw the society take its departure. The Duchess Dowager went
off in her jingling old coach, attended by two faithful and withered old
maids of honour, and a little snuffy spindleshanked gentleman in waiting, in a brown jasey and a green coat covered with orders, of which

the star and the grand yellow cordon of the Order of St. Michael of Pumpernickel were most conspicuous. The drums rolled, the guards saluted, and the old carriage drove away.

Then came His Transparency the Duke and Transparent family, with his great officers of state and household. He bowed serenely to everybody. And amid the saluting of the guards and the flaring of the torches of the running footmen, clad in scarlet, the Transparent carriages drove away to the old Ducal Schloss, with its towers and pinnacles standing on the Schlossberg. Everybody in Pumpernickel knew everybody. No sooner was a foreigner seen there than the Minister of Foreign Affairs, or some other great or small officer of state, went round to the Erbprinz, and found out the name of the new arrival.

CHAPTER LXIII

IN WHICH WE MEET AN OLD ACQUAINTANCE

MR. Sedley, the very next morning, at breakfast, pronounced his opinion that Pumpernickel was the pleasantest little place of any which he had visited on their tour.

Doctor von Glauber, Body Physician to H.S.H. the Duke, speedily convinced Jos that the Pumpernickel mineral springs and the Doctor's particular treatment would infallibly restore the Bengalee to youth and slimness.

Jos's mind was made up; the springs, the Doctor, the Court, and the Chargé d'Affairs convinced him, and he proposed to spend the autumn in these delightful quarters. And on the next day the Chargé d'Affairs presented Jos and the Major to Victor Aurelius XVII., being conducted to their audience with that sovereign by the Count de Schlüsselback, Marshal of the Court.

They were straightway invited to dinner at Court, and their intention of staying in the town being announced, the politest ladies of the whole town instantly called upon Mrs. Osborne; and as not one of these, however poor they might be, was under the rank of a Baroness, Jos's delight was beyond expression.

Everybody—everybody that was noble, of course; for as for the bourgeois, we could not quite be expected to take notice of *them*—visited his neighbour. H.E. Madame de Burst received once a week, H.E. Madame de Schnurrbart had her night, the theatre was open twice a week, the Court graciously received once; so that a man's life might, in fact, be a perfect round of pleasure in the unpretending Pumpernickel way.

Before the winter was far advanced it is actually on record that Emmy took a night and received company with great propriety and modesty. She drove about with one of her dear German friends, and Jos asleep on the back seat of the barouche.

He was becoming very sweet upon the Gräfinn Fanny de Butterbrod, a very gentle, tender-hearted, and unassuming young creature, a Canoness and Countess in her own right, but with scarcely ten pounds per year to her fortune; when—when events occurred, and those grand *fêtes* given upon the marriage of the Hereditary Prince of Pumpernickel with the lovely Princess Amelia of Humbourg-Schlippenschloppen took place.

Everybody was asked to the *fêtes* of the marriage. Garlands and triumphal arches were hung across the road to welcome the young bride. The great St. Michael's fountain ran with uncommonly sour wine, while that in the Artillery Place frothed with beer.

Jos, having only peeped, came eagerly to part of the entertainment, and hankered round the tables where the croupiers and the punters were at work. Women were playing; they were masked, some of them; this licence was allowed in these wild times of carnival.

A woman with light hair, in a low dress, by no means so fresh as it had been, and with a black mask on, through the eyelets of which her eyes twinkled strangely, was seated at one of the roulette tables with a card and a pin, and a couple of florins before her. As the croupier called out the colour and number, she pricked on the card with great care and regularity, and only ventured her money on the colours after the red or black had come up a certain number of times. It was strange to look at her.

But in spite of her care and assiduity she guessed wrong, and the last two florins followed each other under the croupier's rake as he cried out with his inexorable voice the winning colour and number.

Jos was no gambler, but not averse to the little excitement of the sport now and then, and he had some napoleons chinking in the embroidered pockets of his Court waistcoat. He put down one over the fair shoulder of the little gambler before him, and they won. She made a little movement to make room for him by her side, and just took the skirt of her gown from the chair there.

"Come and give me good luck," she said, in a foreign accent. The portly gentleman, looking round to see that nobody of rank observed him, sat down; he muttered, "Ah, really, well now, God bless my soul. I'm very fortunate; I'm sure to give you good fortune," and other words of compliment and confusion.

"Do you play much?" the foreign mask said.

"I put a nap or two down," said Jos, with a superb air, flinging down a gold piece.

"Yes; ay, nap after dinner," said the mask archly. But Jos looking frightened, she continued, in her pretty French accent. "You do not play to win. No more do I. I play to forget, but I cannot. I cannot forget old times, Monsieur. You—you are not changed—but yes, you are. Everybody changes, everybody forgets; nobody has any heart."

"Good God, who is it?" asked Jos, in a flutter.

"Can't you guess, Joseph Sedley?" said the little woman, in a sad voice; and undoing her mask, she looked at him. "You have forgotten me."

"Good heavens! Mrs. Crawley!" gasped out Jos.

"Rebecca," said the other, putting her hand on his; but she followed the game still, all the time she was looking at him.

"I am stopping at the Elephant," she continued. "Ask for Madame de Raudon. I saw my dear Amelia to-day; how pretty she looked, and how happy! So do you! Everybody but me, who am wretched, Joseph Sedley." And she put her money over from the red to the black, as if by a chance movement of her hand, and while she was wiping her eyes with a pocket-handkerchief fringed with torn lace. The red came up again, and she lost the whole of that stake. "Come away," she said—"come with me a little; we are old friends, are we not, dear Mr. Sedley?"

CHAPTER LXIV

A VAGABOND CHAPTER

WE must pass over a part of Mrs. Rebecca Crawley's biography with that lightness and delicacy which the world demands—the moral world, that has, perhaps, no particular objection to vice, but an insuperable repugnance to hearing vice called by its proper name.

If we were to give a full account of her proceedings during a couple of years that followed after the Curzon Street catastrophe, there might be some reason for people to say this book was improper. The actions of very vain, heartless, pleasure-seeking people are very often improper (as are many of yours, my friend with the grave face and spotless reputation; but that is merely by the way); and what are those of a woman without faith, or love, or character?

She lingered about London whilst her husband was making preparations for his departure to his seat of government. The revenues of the Governor of Coventry Island are not large. A part of them were set aside by His Excellency for the payment of certain outstanding debts and liabilities; the charges incident on his high situation required considerable expense. Finally, it was found that he could not spare to his wife more than three hundred pounds a year, which he proposed to pay to her on an undertaking that she would never trouble him. Otherwise—scandal, separation, Doctor's Commons would ensue. But it was Mr. Wenham's business, Lord Steyne's business, Rawdon's, everybody's, to get her out of the country, and hush up a most disagreeable affair.

She was probably so much occupied in arranging these affairs of business with her husband's lawyers, that she forgot to take any step whatever about her son, the little Rawdon, and did not even once propose to go and see him. That young gentleman was consigned to the entire guardianship of his aunt and uncle, the former of whom had always possessed a great share of the child's affection. His mamma wrote him a neat letter from Boulogne when she quitted England, in which she requested him to mind his book, and said she was going to take a Continental tour, during which she would have the pleasure of writing to him again. But she never did for a year afterwards, and not, indeed, until Sir Pitt's only boy, always sickly, died of whooping-cough and measles; then Rawdon's mamma wrote the most affectionate composition to her darling son, who was made heir of Queen's Crawley by this accident, and drawn more closely than ever to the kind lady whose tender heart had already adopted him. Rawdon Crawley, then grown a tall, fine lad, blushed when he got the letter. "O Aunt Jane, you are my mother!" he said; "and not—and not that one." But he wrote back a kind and respectful letter to Mrs. Rebecca, then living at a boarding-house at Florence.

Becky's history was after all a mystery. Parties were divided about her. Some people, who took the trouble to busy themselves in the matter, said that she was a criminal; whilst others vowed that she was as innocent as a lamb, and that her odious husband was in fault. She won over a good many by bursting into tears about her boy, and exhibiting the most frantic grief when his name was mentioned or she saw anybody like him. She gained good Mrs. Alderney's heart in that way, who was rather the Queen of British Boulogne, and gave the most dinners and balls of all the residents there, by weeping when Master Alderney came from Dr. Swishtail's academy to pass his holidays with his mother. "He and her Rawdon were of the same age, and *so* like," Becky said, in a voice choking with agony; whereas there was five years' difference between the boys' ages, and no more likeness between them than between my respected reader and his humble servant. Wenham, when he was going abroad, on his way to Kissingen to join Lord Steyne, enlightened Mrs. Alderney on this point, and told her how he was much more able to describe little Rawdon than his mamma, who notoriously hated him, and never saw him; how he was thirteen years old, while little Alderney was but nine; fair, while the other darling was dark—in a word, caused the lady in question to repent of her good humour.

Whenever Becky made a little circle for herself with incredible toils and labour, somebody came and swept it down rudely, and she had all her work to begin over again. It was very hard—very hard—lonely and disheartening.

From one colony to another Becky fled uneasily—from Boulogne to Dieppe, from Dieppe to Caen, from Caen to Tours—trying with all her might to be respectable, and alas! always found out some day or other, and pecked out of the cage by the real daws.

Then she tried keeping house with a female friend; then the double *ménage* began to quarrel and get into debt. Then she determined upon a boarding-house existence, and lived for some time at that famous mansion kept by Madame de Saint Amour in the Rue Royale, at Paris, where she began exercising her graces and fascinations upon the shabby dandies and fly-blown beauties who frequented her landlady's *salons*.

But it is probably that her old creditors of 1815 found her out, and

caused her to leave Paris; for the poor little woman was forced to fly
from the city rather suddenly; and went thence to Brussels.

Here, as at Paris, Becky was a boarding-house queen, and ruled in
select *pensions*. She never refused the champagne, or the bouquets, or
the drives into the country, or the private boxes; but what she preferred was the *écarté* at night, and she played audaciously.

So our little wanderer went about, setting up her tent in various cities
of Europe, as restless as Ulysses or Bampfylde Moore Carew. Her
taste for disrespectability grew more and more remarkable. She became a perfect Bohemian ere long, herding with people whom it would
make your hair stand on end to meet.

There is no town of any mark in Europe but it has its little colony
of English raffs—men whose names Mr. Hemp the officer reads out
periodically at the Sheriff's Court—young gentlemen of very good
family often, only that the latter disowns them; frequenters of billiard-
rooms and *estaminets*, patrons of foreign races and gaming-tables.
They people the debtors' prisons; they drink and swagger; they fight
and brawl; they run away without paying; they have duels with
French and German officers; they cheat Mr. Spooney at *écarté*; they
get the money, and drive off to Baden in magnificent brizkas; they try
their infallible martingale, and lurk about the tables with empty
pockets, shabby bullies, penniless bucks, until they can swindle a Jew
banker with a sham bill of exchange, or find another Mr. Spooney to
rob. The alternations of splendour and misery which these people
undergo are very queer to view. Their life must be one of great excitement. Becky—must it be owned?—took to this life, and took to it not
unkindly. She went about from town to town among these Bohemians.
The lucky Mrs. Rawdon was known at every play-table in Germany.
She and Madame de Cruchescassée kept house at Florence together. It
is said she was ordered out of Munich; and my friend Mr. Frederick
Pigeon avers that it was at her house at Lausanne that he was hocussed
at supper and lost eight hundred pounds to Major Loder and the
Honourable Mr. Deuceace. We are bound, you see, to give some
account of Becky's biography; but of this part the less, perhaps, that
is said the better.

CHAPTER LXV

FULL OF BUSINESS AND PLEASURE

THE day after the meeting at the play-table, Jos had himself arrayed
with unusual care and splendour; and without thinking it necessary
to say a word to any member of his family regarding the occurrences
of the previous night, or asking for their company in his walk, he
sallied forth at an early hour, and was presently seen making inquiries
at the door of the Elephant Hotel. In consequence of the *fêtes* the
house was full of company, the tables in the street were already surrounded by persons smoking and drinking the national small-beer, the

public rooms were in a cloud of smoke, and Mr. Jos having, in his pompous way and with his clumsy German, made inquiries for the person of whom he was in search, was directed to the very top of the house, above the first-floor rooms, where some travelling pedlars had lived, and were exhibiting their jewellery and brocades; above the second-floor apartments, occupied by the *état-major* of the gambling firm; above the third-floor rooms, tenanted by the band of renowned Bohemian vaulters and tumblers; and so on to the little cabin of the roof, where, among students, bagmen, small tradesmen, and country-folk, come in for the festival, Becky had found a little nest—as dirty a little refuge as ever beauty lay hid in.

As Jos came creaking and puffing up the final stairs, and was speech-less when he got to the landing, and began to wipe his face and then. to look for No. 92, the room where he was directed to seek for the person he wanted, the door of the opposite chamber, No. 90, was open, and a student, in jack-boots and a dirty *schlafrock*, was lying on the bed smoking a long pipe, whilst another student, in long yellow hair and a braided coat, exceedingly smart and dirty too, was actually on his knees at No. 92, bawling through the keyhole supplications to the person within.

"Go away," said a well-known voice, which made Jos thrill; "I expect somebody—I expect my grandpapa. He mustn't see you there."

"Angel Engländerinn!" bellowed the kneeling student with the whity-brown ringlets and the large finger-ring, "do take compassion upon us. Make an appointment. Dine with me and Fritz at the inn in the park. We will have roast pheasants and porter, plum-pudding and French wine. We shall die if you don't."

"That we will," said the young nobleman on the bed. And this colloquy Jos overheard, though he did not comprehend it, for the reason that he had never studied the language in which it was carried on.

"*Newmero kattervang dooze, si vous plair*," Jos said in his grandest manner, when he was able to speak.

"*Quater fang tooce!*" said the student, starting up, and he bounced into his own room, where he locked the door, and where Jos heard him laughing with his comrade on the bed.

The gentleman from Bengal was standing disconcerted by this incident, when the door of the 92 opened of itself, and Becky's little head peeped out full of archness and mischief. She lighted on Jos. "It's you," she said, coming out. "How I have been waiting for you! Stop! not yet; in one minute you shall come in." In that instant she put a rouge-pot, a brandy-bottle, and a plate of broken meat into the bed, gave one smooth to her hair, and finally let in her visitor.

She had, by way of morning robe, a pink domino, a trifle faded and soiled, and marked here and there with pomatum; but her arms shone out from the loose sleeves of the dress very white and fair and it was tied round her little waist so as not ill to set off the trim little figure of the wearer. She led Jos by the hand into her garret. "Come in," she said—"come, and talk to me; sit yonder on the chair," and she gave the Civilian's hand a little squeeze, and laughingly placed him upon it. As for herself, she placed herself on the bed—not on the bottle and plate you may be sure—on which Jos might have reposed, had he chosen that seat; and so there she sate and talked with her old admirer.

"How little years have changed you!" she said, with a look of tender interest. "I should have known you anywhere. What a comfort it is amongst strangers to see once more the frank, honest face of an old friend!"

The frank, honest face, to tell the truth, at this moment bore any expression but one of openness and honesty; it was, on the contrary, much perturbed and puzzled in look. "I should have known you anywhere," she continued; "a woman never forgets some things. And you were the first man I ever—I ever saw."

"Was I, really?" said Jos. "God bless my soul, you—you don't say so."

"When I came with your sister from Chiswick, I was scarcely more than a child," Becky said. "How is that dear love? Oh, her husband was a sad, wicked man, and of course it was of me that the poor dear was jealous. As if I cared about him, heigh-ho! when there was somebody—but no—don't let us talk of old times;" and she passed her handkerchief with the tattered lace across her eyelids.

"Is not this a strange place," she continued, "for a woman, who has lived in a very different world too, to be found in?" And she began forthwith to tell her story—a tale so neat, simple, and artless, that it was quite evident from hearing her that if ever there was a white-robed angel escaped from heaven to be subject to the infernal machinations and villainy of fiends here below, that spotless being, that miserable unsullied martyr, was present on the bed before Jos—on the bed, sitting on the brandy-bottle.

Jos went away, convinced that she was the most virtuous as she was one of the most fascinating of women, and revolving in his mind all sorts of benevolent schemes for her welfare. Her persecutions ought to be ended; she ought to return to the society of which she was an ornament. He would see what ought to be done. She must quit that place, and take a quiet lodging. Amelia must come and see her, and befriend her. He would go and settle about it, and consult with the Major. She wept tears of heartfelt gratitude as she parted from him, and pressed his hand as the gallant stout gentleman stooped down to kiss hers.

Jos walked over to Dobbin's lodgings with great solemnity, and there imparted to him the affecting history with which he had just been made acquainted, without, however, mentioning the play business of the night before. And the two gentlemen were laying their heads together, and consulting as to the best means of being useful to Mrs. Becky, while she was finishing her interrupted *déjeuner à la fourchette*.

As for Mrs. Amelia, she was a woman of such a soft and foolish disposition, that when she heard of anybody unhappy her heart straightway melted towards the sufferer; and as she had never thought or done anything mortally guilty herself, she had not that abhorrence for wickedness which distinguishes moralists much more knowing.

When the Major heard from Jos of the sentimental adventure which had just befallen the latter, he was not, it must be owned, nearly as much interested as the gentleman from Bengal. On the contrary, his excitement was quite the reverse from a pleasurable one; he made use of a brief but improper expression regarding a poor woman in distress, saying, in fact, "The little minx, has she come to light again?" He never had had the slightest liking for her, but had heartily mistrusted her from the very first moment when her green eyes had looked at and turned away from his own.

"Well, well, let's ask Mrs. George," said that arch-diplomatist of a Major. "Only let us go and consult *her*. I suppose you will allow that *she* is a good judge, at any rate, and knows what is right in such matters."

Jos opened the business with his usual pomp of words. "Amelia, my dear," said he, "I have just had the most extraordinary—yes, God bless my soul! the most extraordinary adventure. An old friend—yes, a most interesting old friend of yours, and I may say in old times— has just arrived here, and I should like you to see her."

"Her!" said Amelia. "Who is it?—Major Dobbin, if you please not to break my scissors." The Major was twirling them round by the little chain from which they sometimes hung to their lady's waist, and was thereby endangering his own eye.

"It is a woman whom I dislike very much," said the Major doggedly, "and whom you have no cause to love."

"It is Rebecca, I'm sure it is Rebecca," Amelia said, blushing, and being very much agitated.

"You are right—you always are," Dobbin answered. Brussels, Waterloo, old, old times, griefs, pangs, remembrances, rushed back into Amelia's gentle heart, and caused a cruel agitation there.

"Don't let me see her," Emmy continued; "I couldn't see her."

"I told you so," Dobbin said to Jos.

"She is very unhappy, and—and that sort of thing," Jos urged. "She is very poor and unprotected, and has been ill—exceedingly ill— and that scoundrel of a husband has deserted her."

"Ah!" said Amelia.

"She hasn't a friend in the world," Jos went on, not undexterously, "and she said she thought she might trust in you. She's so miserable, Emmy. She has been almost mad with grief. Her story quite affected me—'pon my word and honour it did; never was such a cruel persecution borne so angelically, I may say. Her family has been most cruel to her."

"Poor creature!" Amelia said.

"And if she can get no friend, she says she thinks she'll die," Jos proceeded, in a low, tremulous voice. "God bless my soul! do you know that she tried to kill herself? She carries laudanum with her —I saw the bottle in her room—such a miserable little room—at a third-rate house, the Elephant, up in the roof at the top of all. I went there."

This did not seem to affect Emmy. She even smiled a little. Perhaps she figured Jos to herself panting up the stair.

"She's beside herself with grief," he resumed. "The agonies that woman has endured are quite frightful to hear of. She had a little boy, of the same age as Georgy."

"Yes, yes, I think I remember," Emmy remarked. "Well?"

"The most beautiful child ever seen," Jos said, who was very fat, and easily moved, and had been touched by the story Becky told—"a perfect angel, who adored his mother. The ruffians tore him shrieking out of her arms, and have never allowed him to see her."

"Dear Joseph," Emmy cried out, starting up at once, "let us go and see her this minute." And she ran into her adjoining bedchamber, tied on her bonnet in a flutter, came out with her shawl on her arm, and ordered Dobbin to follow.

He went and put her shawl—it was a white Cashmere, consigned to her by the Major himself from India—over her shoulders. He saw there was nothing for it but to obey; and she put her hand into his arm, and they went away.

"It is No. 92, up four pair of stairs," Jos said, perhaps not very willing to ascend the steps again; but he placed himself in the window of his drawing-room, which commands the place on which the Elephant stands, and saw the pair marching through the market.

It was as well that Becky saw them too from her garret; for she and the two students were chattering and laughing there. They had been joking about the appearance of Becky's grandpapa, whose arrival and departure they had witnessed; but she had time to dismiss them, and have her little room clear before the landlord of the Elephant, who knew that Mrs. Osborne was a great favourite at the Serene Court, and respected her accordingly, led the way up the stairs to the roof-story, encouraging Miladi and the Herr Major as they achieved the ascent.

CHAPTER LXVI

AMANTIUM IRÆ

FRANKNESS and kindness like Amelia's were likely to touch even such a hardened little reprobate as Becky. She returned Emmy's caresses and kind speeches with something very like gratitude, and an emotion which, if it was not lasting, for a moment was almost genuine. That was a lucky stroke of hers about the child "torn from her arms shriek-ing." It was by that harrowing misfortune that Becky had won her friend back, and it was one of the very first points, we may be certain, upon which our poor simple little Emmy began to talk to her new-found acquaintance.

And so the two women continued talking for an hour or more, during which Becky had the opportunity of giving her new friend a full and complete version of her private history. She showed how her marriage with Rawdon Crawley had always been viewed by the family with feelings of the utmost hostility; how her sister-in-law (an artful woman) had poisoned her husband's mind against her; how he had formed odious connections, which had estranged his affections from her; how she had borne everything—poverty, neglect, coldness—from the being whom she most loved, and all for the sake of her child; how, finally, and by the most flagrant outrage, she had been driven into demanding a separation from her husband, when the wretch did not scruple to ask that she should sacrifice her own fair fame so that he might procure advancement through the means of a very great and powerful but unprincipled man—the Marquis of Steyne, indeed. The atrocious monster!

This part of her eventful history Becky gave with the utmost feminine delicacy and the most indignant virtue. Forced to fly her husband's roof by this insult, the coward had pursued his revenge by taking her child from her. And thus Becky said she was a wanderer, poor, unprotected, friendless, and wretched.

Whilst the ladies were carrying on their conversation, Amelia's constant escort, the Major (who, of course, did not wish to interrupt their conference, and found himself rather tired of creaking about the narrow stair passage of which the roof brushed the nap from his hat) descended to the ground-floor of the house and into the great room common to all the frequenters of the Elephant, out of which the stair led.

"And so this devil is still going on with her intrigues," thought William. "I wish she were a hundred miles from here. She brings mischief wherever she goes." And he was pursuing these forebodings and this uncomfortable train of thought, with his head between his hands and the *Pumpernickel Gazette* of last week unread under his nose, when somebody tapped his shoulder with a parasol, and he looked up and saw Mrs. Amelia. She wanted to see Jos that instant. The Major laughed at the impetuous affection Mrs. Amelia exhibited; for, in truth, it was not very often that she wanted her brother "that instant."

They found the Civilian in his saloon on the first floor. He had been pacing the room, and biting his nails, and looking over the market-place towards the Elephant a hundred times at least during the past hour, whilst Emmy was closeted with her friend in the garret, and the Major was beating the tattoo on the sloppy tables of the public room below; and he was, on his side too, very anxious to see Mrs. Osborne. "Well?" said he.

"The poor dear creature, how she has suffered!" Emmy said.

"God bless my soul, yes," Jos said, wagging his head, so that his cheeks quivered like jellies.

"She may have Payne's room; who can go upstairs," Emmy continued. Payne was a staid English maid and personal attendant upon Mrs. Osborne, to whom the courier, as in duty bound, paid court, and whom Georgy used to "lark" dreadfully with accounts of German robbers and ghosts.

William, in a state of great indignation, though still unaware of all the treason that was in store for him, walked about the town wildly until he fell upon the Secretary of Legation, Tapeworm, who invited him to dinner. As they were discussing that meal, he took occasion to ask the Secretary whether he knew anything about a certain Mrs. Rawdon Crawley, who had, he believed, made some noise in London; and then Tapeworm, who of course knew all the London gossip, and was besides a relative of Lady Gaunt, poured out into the astonished Major's ears such a history about Becky and her husband as astonished the querist, and supplied all the points of this narrative—for it was at that very table ten years ago that the present writer had the pleasure of hearing the tale. Tufto, Steyne, the Crawleys, and their history—everything connected with Becky and her previous life—passed under the record of the bitter diplomatist. He knew everything, and a great deal besides, about all the world—in a word, he made the most astounding revelations to the simple-hearted Major. When Dobbin said that Mrs. Osborne and Mr. Sedley had taken her into their house, Tapeworm burst into a peal of laughter which shocked the Major, and asked if they had not better send into the prison, and take in one or two of the gentlemen in shaved heads and yellow jackets who swept the streets of Pumpernickel, chained in pairs, to board and lodge, and act as tutor to that little scapegrace Georgy.

When at length, in the afternoon, the Major gained admission to Amelia, instead of the cordial and affectionate greeting to which he had been accustomed now for many a long day, he received the salutation of a curtsy, and of a little gloved hand, retracted the moment after it was accorded to him.

Rebecca, too, was in the room, and advanced to meet him with a smile and an extended hand. Dobbin drew back rather confusedly. "I—I beg your pardon, ma'am," he said, "but I am bound to tell you that it is not as your friend that I am come here now."

"Pooh! damn! don't let us have this sort of thing!" Jos cried out, alarmed, and anxious to get rid of a scene.

"I wonder what Major Dobbin has to say against Rebecca?" Amelia said, in a low, clear voice, with a slight quiver in it, and a very determined look about the eyes.

"I will *not* have this sort of thing in my house," Jos again interposed—"I say I will not have it; and, Dobbin, I beg, sir, you'll stop it." And he looked round trembling and turning very red, and gave a great puff, and made for his door.

"Dear friend!" Rebecca said, with angelic sweetness, "do hear what Major Dobbin has to say against me."

"I will *not* hear it, I say," squeaked out Jos, at the top of his voice, and gathering up his dressing-gown he was gone.

"We are only two women," Amelia said. "You can speak now, sir."

"This manner towards me is one which scarcely becomes you, Amelia," the Major answered haughtily; "nor, I believe, am I guilty of habitual harshness to women. It is not a pleasure to me to do the duty which I am come to do."

"Pray, proceed with it quickly, if you please, Major Dobbin," said Amelia, who was more and more in a pet. The expression of Dobbin's face, as she spoke in this imperious manner, was not pleasant.

"I came to say—and as you stay, Mrs. Crawley, I must say it in your presence—that I think you—you ought not to form a member of the family of my friends."

"Yours is a very modest and convenient sort of calumny, Major Dobbin," Rebecca said. "You leave me under the weight of an accusation which, after all, is unsaid. Let me go, Emmy. It is only to suppose that I have not met you, and I am no worse to-day than I was yesterday. It is only to suppose that the night is over and the poor wanderer is on her way. Don't you remember the song we used to sing in old, dear old days? I have been wandering ever since then—a poor castaway, scorned for being miserable, and insulted because I am alone. Let me go; my stay here interferes with the plans of this gentleman."

"Indeed it does, madam," said the Major. "If I have any authority in this house——"

"Authority, none!" broke out Amelia.—"Rebecca, you stay with me. *I* won't desert you because you have been persecuted, or insult you because—because Major Dobbin chooses to do so. Come away, dear." And the two women made towards the door.

William opened it. As they were going out, however, he took Amelia's hand, and said, "Will you stay a moment and speak to me?"

"He wishes to speak to you away from me," said Becky, looking like a martyr. Amelia gripped her hand in reply.

"Upon my honour, it is not about you that I am going to speak," Dobbin said.—"Come back, Amelia," and she came. Dobbin bowed to Mrs. Crawley as he shut the door upon her. Amelia looked at him, leaning against the glass; her face and her lips were quite white.

"I was confused when I spoke just now," the Major said, after a pause, "and I misused the word 'authority.'"

"You did," said Amelia, with her teeth chattering.

"At least I have claims to be heard," Dobbin continued.

"It is generous to remind me of our obligations to you," the woman answered.

"The claims I mean are those left me by George's father," William said.

"Yes, and you insulted his memory. You did yesterday. You know you did. And I will never forgive you—never!" said Amelia. She shot out each little sentence in a tremor of anger and emotion.

"You don't mean that, Amelia?" William said sadly. "You don't mean that these words, uttered in a hurried moment, are to weigh against a whole life's devotion? I think that George's memory has not been injured by the way in which I have dealt with it; and if we are come to bandying reproaches, I at least merit none from his widow and the mother of his son. Reflect afterwards, when—when you are at leisure, and your conscience will withdraw this accusation. It does even now." Amelia held down her head.

"It is not that speech of yesterday," he continued, "which moves you. That is but the pretext, Amelia, or I have loved you and watched you for fifteen years in vain. Have I not learned in that time to read all your feelings and look into your thoughts? I know that your heart is capable of: it can cling faithfully to a recollection, and cherish a fancy; but it can't feel such an attachment as mine deserves to mate with, and such as I would have won from a woman more generous than you. No, you are not worthy of the love which I have devoted to you. I knew all along that the prize I had set my life on was not worth the winning; that I was a fool, with fond fancies, too, bartering away my all of truth and ardour against your little feeble remnant of love. I will bargain no more; I withdraw. I find no fault with you. You are very good-natured, and have done your best; but you couldn't —you couldn't reach up to the height of the attachment which I bore you, and which a loftier soul than yours might have been proud to share. Good-bye, Amelia! I have watched your struggle. Let it end; we are both weary of it."

Amelia stood scared and silent as William thus suddenly broke the chain by which she held him, and declared his independence and superiority. He had placed himself at her feet so long that the poor little woman had been accustomed to trample upon him. She didn't wish to marry him, but she wished to keep him. She wished to give him nothing, but that he should give her all. It is a bargain not unfrequently levied in love.

William's sally had quite broken and cast her down. *Her* assault was long since over and beaten back.

"Am I to understand then—that you are going—away—William?" she said.

He gave a sad laugh. "I went once before," he said, "and came back after twelve years. We were young them, Amelia. Good-bye. I have spent enough of my life at this play."

Whilst they had been talking, the door into Mrs. Osborne's room had opened ever so little; indeed, Becky had kept a hold of the handle, and had turned it on the instant when Dobbin quitted it, and she heard every word of the conversation that had passed between these two. "What a noble heart that man has," she thought, "and how shamefully that woman plays with it!" She admired Dobbin; she bore him no rancour for the part he had taken against her. It was an open move in the game, and played fairly. "Ah!" she thought, "if I could have had such a husband as that—a man with a heart and brains too! I would not have minded his large feet;" and running into her room, she absolutely bethought herself of something, and wrote him a note beseeching him to stop for a few days—not to think of going—and that she could serve him with A.

The parting was over. Once more poor William walked to the door, and was gone; and the little widow, the author of all this work, had her will, and had won her victory, and was left to enjoy it as she best might. Let the ladies envy her triumph.

At the romantic hour of dinner Mr. Georgy made his appearance, and again remarked the absence of "Old Dob." The meal was eaten in silence by the party—Jos's appetite not being diminished, but Emmy taking nothing at all.

After the meal Georgy was lolling in the cushions of the old window, a large window, with three sides of glass, abutting from the gable, and commanding on one side Market Place, where the Elephant is, his mother being busy hard by, when he remarked symptoms of movement at the Major's house on the other side of the street.

"Hallo!" said he, "there's Dob's trap; they are bringing it out of the courtyard." The "trap" in question was a carriage which the Major had bought for six pounds sterling, and about which they used to rally him a good deal.

Emmy gave a little start, but said nothing.

"Hello!" Georgy continued, "there's Francis coming out with the portmanteaus, and Kunz, the one-eyed postilion, coming down the market with three *schimmels*. Look at his boots and yellow jacket! ain't he a rum one? Why, they're putting the horses to Dob's carriage. Is he going anywhere?"

"Yes," said Emmy, "he is going on a journey."

"Going on a journey! and when is he coming back?"

"He is—not coming back?" answered Emmy.

"Not coming back!" cried Georgy, jumping up. "Stay here, sir!" roared out Jos. "Stay, Georgy," said his mother, with a very sad face.

"By Jove, I *will* go!" screamed out Georgy. "Give him this," said Becky, quite interested, and put a paper into the boy's hand. He had rushed down the stairs and flung across the street in a minute; the yellow postilion was cracking his whip gently. William had got into the carriage, released from the embraces of his landlord. Georgy bounded in afterwards and flung his arms round the Major's neck (as they saw from the window), and began asking him multiplied questions. Then he felt in his waistcoat pocket and gave him a note. William

seized at it rather eagerly, he opened it trembling, but instantly his
countenance changed, and he tore the paper in two, and dropped it out
of the carriage. He kissed Georgy on the head, and the boy got out,
doubling his fists into his eyes, and with the aid of Francis. He
lingered with his hand on the panel. *Fort, Schwager!* The yellow
postillion cracked his whip prodigiously, up sprang Francis to the box,
away went the *schimmels*, and Dobbin with his head on his breast.
He never looked up as they passed under Amelia's window; and
Georgy, left alone in the street, burst out crying in the face of all the
crowd.

CHAPTER LXVII

WHICH CONTAINS BIRTHS, MARRIAGES, AND DEATHS

EMMY was not very happy after her heroic sacrifice. She was very
distraite, nervous, silent, and ill to please. The family had never
known her so peevish. She grew pale and ill. She used to try to sing
certain songs ("Einsam bin ich nicht alleine," was one of them; that
tender love-song of Weber's, which, in old-fashioned days, young
ladies, and when you were scarcely born, showed that those who lived
before you knew too how to love and to sing)—certain songs, I say, to
which the Major was partial; and as she warbled them in the twilight
in the drawing-room, she would break off in the midst of the song, and
walk into her neighbouring apartment, and there, no doubt, take refuge
in the miniature of her husband.

Some books still subsisted, after Dobbin's departure, with his name
written in them: a German Dictionary, for instance, with "William
Dobbin,—th Reg.," in the fly-leaf; a guide-book with his initials, and
one or two other volumes which belonged to the Major. Emmy cleared
these away, and put them on the drawers, where she placed her work-
box, her desk, her Bible, and Prayer-book, under the pictures of the
two Georges. And the Major, on going away, having left his gloves
behind him, it is a fact that Georgy, rummaging his mother's desk
some time afterwards, found the gloves neatly folded up, and put
away in what they call the secret drawers of the desk.

It was June, and, by consequence, high season in London. Jos, who
read the incomparable *Galignani* (the exile's best friend) through every
day, used to favour the ladies with extracts from his paper during their
breakfast.

Jos read a brief announcement: Major Dobbin had joined the —th
regiment at Chatham; and subsequently he promulgated accounts of
the presentations at the Drawing-room, of Colonel Sir Michael O'Dowd,
K.C.B., Lady O'Dowd (by Mrs. Molloy Malony of Ballymalony), and
Miss Glorvina O'Dowd (by Lady O'Dowd). Almost directly after this,
Dobbin's name appeared among the Lieutenant-Colonels; for old
Marshal Tiptoff had died during the passage of the —th from Madras,

and the Sovereign was pleased to advance Colonel Sir Michael O'Dowd to the rank of Major-General on his return to England, with an intimation that he should be Colonel of the distinguished regiment which he had so long commanded.

After June all the little Court society of Pumpernickel used to separate, according to the German plan, and make for a hundred watering-places, where they drank at the wells, rode upon donkeys, gambled at the *redoutes* if they had money and a mind, rushed with hundreds of their kind to gourmandize at the *tables d'hôte*, and idled away the summer. The English diplomatists went off to Toplitz and Kissingen; their French rivals shut up their *chancellerie* and whisked away to their darling Boulevard de Gand. The Transparent reigning family took too to the waters, or retired to their hunting-lodges. Everybody went away having any pretensions to politeness, and of course, with them, Doctor von Glauber, the Court Doctor, and his Baroness. The seasons for the baths were the most productive periods of the Doctor's practice—he united business with pleasure; and his chief place of resort was Ostend, which is much frequented by Germans, and where the Doctor treated himself and his spouse to what he called a "dib" in the sea. His interesting patient, Jos, was a regular milch cow to the Doctor, and he easily persuaded the Civilian, both for his own health's sake and that of his charming sister, which was really very much shattered, to pass the summer at that hideous seaport town. Emmy did not care where she went much.

At last she took a great resolution—made the great plunge. She wrote off a letter to a friend whom she had on the other side of the water; a letter about which she did not speak a word to anybody, which she carried herself to the post under her shawl, nor was any remark made about it, only that she looked very much flushed and agitated when Georgy met her, and she kissed him, and hung over him a great deal that night. She did not come out of her room after her return from her walk.

Two mornings after, although the day was rainy and gusty, and Amelia had had an exceedingly wakeful night, listening to the wind roaring, and pitying all travellers by land and by water, yet she got up early, and insisted upon taking a walk on the Dyke with Georgy; and there she paced as the rain beat into her face, and she looked out westward across the dark sea line, and over the swollen billows which came tumbling and frothing to the shore. Neither spoke much, except now and then, when the boy said a few words to his timid companion indicative of sympathy and protection.

"I hope he won't cross in such weather," Emmy said.

"I bet ten to one he does," the boy answered. "Look, mother, there's the smoke of the steamer." It was that signal, sure enough.

But though the steamer was under weigh, he might not be on board—he might not have got the letter—he might not choose to come.

A hundred fears poured one over the other into the little heart, as fast as the waves on to the Dyke.

The ship came swiftly nearer and nearer. As they went in to meet her at the landing-place at the Quay, Emmy's knees trembled so that she scarcely could run. She would have liked to kneel down and say her prayers of thanks there. Oh, she thought, she would be all her life saying them! It was such a bad day that as the vessel came alongside of the Quay there were no idlers abroad; scarcely even a commissioner on the look-out for the few passengers in the steamer. That young scapegrace Georgy had fled too; and as the gentleman in the old cloak lined with red stuff stepped on to the shore, there was scarcely any one present to see what took place, which was briefly this—

A lady in a dripping white bonnet and shawl, with her two little hands out before her, went up to him, and in the next minute she had altogether disappeared under the folds of the old cloak, and was kissing one of his hands with all her might; whilst the other, I suppose, was engaged in holding her to his heart (which her head just about reached), and in preventing her from tumbling down. She was murmuring something about—forgive—dear William—dear, dear, dearest friend—kiss, kiss, kiss, and so forth—and in fact went on under the cloak in an absurd manner.

When Emmy emerged from it, she still kept tight hold of one of William's hands, and looked up in his face. It was full of sadness and tender love and pity. She understood its reproach, and hung down her head.

"It was time you sent for me, dear Amelia," he said.

"You will never go again, William?"

"No, never," he answered; and pressed the dear little soul once more to his heart.

As they issued out of the Custom-house precincts, Georgy broke out on them, with his telescope up to his eye, and a loud laugh of welcome. He danced round the couple, and performed many facetious antics as he led them up to the house. Jos wasn't up yet; Becky not visible (though she looked at them through the blinds). Georgy ran off to see about breakfast. Emmy, whose shawl and bonnet were off in the passage in the hands of Miss Payne, now went to undo the clasp of William's cloak, and—we will, if you please, go with Georgy, and look after breakfast for the Colonel. The vessel is in port. He has got the prize he has been trying for all his life. The bird has come in at last. There it is with its head on his shoulder, billing and cooing close up to his heart, with soft outstretched fluttering wings. This is what he has asked for every day and hour for eighteen years. This is what he pined after. Here it is—the summit, the end—the last page of the third volume. Good-bye, Colonel. God bless you, honest William!—Farewell, dear Amelia. Grow green again, tender little parasite, round the rugged old oak to which you cling!

Perhaps it was compunction towards the kind and simple creature who had been the first in life to defend her, perhaps it was a dislike to all such sentimental scenes, but Rebecca, satisfied with her part in the transaction, never presented herself before Colonel Dobbin, and the lady whom he married. "Particular business," she said, took her to Bruges, whither she went; and only Georgy and his uncle were present at the marriage ceremony. When it was over, and Georgy had rejoined his parents, Mrs. Becky returned (just for a few days), to comfort the solitary bachelor, Joseph Sedley. He preferred a Continental life, he said, and declined to join in housekeeping with his sister and her husband.

When Colonel Dobbin quitted the service, which he did immediately after his marriage, he rented a pretty little country place in Hampshire, not far from Queen's Crawley, where, after the passing of the Reform Bill, Sir Pitt and his family constantly resided now. All idea of a Peerage was out of the question, the Baronet's two seats in Parliament being lost. He was both out of pocket and out of spirits by that catastrophe, failed in his health, and prophesied the speedy ruin of the Empire.

Lady Jane and Mrs. Dobbin became great friends; there was a perpetual crossing of pony-chaises between the Hall and the Evergreens, the Colonel's place (rented of his friend Major Ponto, who was abroad with his family). Her Ladyship was godmother to Mrs. Dobbin's child, which bore her name, and was christened by the Rev. James Crawley, who succeeded his father in the living; and a pretty close friendship subsisted between the two lads George and Rawdon, who hunted and shot together in the vacations, were both entered of the same college at Cambridge, and quarrelled with each other about Lady Jane's daughter, with whom they were both, of course, in love. A match between George and that young lady was long a favourite scheme of both the matrons, though I have heard that Miss Crawley herself inclined towards her cousin.

Mrs. Rawdon Crawley's name was never mentioned by either family. There were reasons why all should be silent regarding her. For wherever Mr. Joseph Sedley went, she travelled likewise, and that infatuated man seemed to be entirely her slave. The Colonel's lawyers informed him that his brother-in-law had effected a heavy insurance upon his life, whence it was probable that he had been raising money to discharge debts. He procured prolonged leave of absence from the East India House, and indeed his infirmities were daily increasing.

Three months afterwards Joseph Sedley died at Aix-la-Chapelle. It was found that all his property had been muddled away in speculations, and was represented by valueless shares in different bubble companies. All his available assets were the two thousand pounds for which his life was insured, and which were left equally between his beloved "sister Amelia, wife of, etc., and his friend and invaluable attendant during sickness, Rebecca, wife of Lieutenant-Colonel Rawdon Crawley, C.B.," who was appointed administratix.

The solicitor of the Insurance Company swore it was the blackest case that ever had come before him; talked of sending a commission to Aix to examine into the death; and the Company refused payment of the policy. But Mrs., or Lady Crawley, as she styles herself, came to town at once (attended with her solicitors, Messrs. Burke, Thurtell, & Hayes, of Thavies Inn), and dared the Company to refuse the payment. They invited examination; they declared that she was the object of an infamous conspiracy, which had been pursuing her all through life; and triumphed finally. The money was paid, and her character established; but Colonel Dobbin sent back his share of the legacy to the Insurance Office, and rigidly declined to hold any communication with Rebecca.

She never was Lady Crawley, though she continued so to call herself. His Excellency, Colonel Rawdon Crawley died of yellow fever at Coventry Island, most deeply beloved and deplored, and six weeks before the demise of his brother, Sir Pitt. The estate consequently devolved upon the present Sir Rawdon Crawley, Bart.

He, too, has declined to see his mother, to whom he makes a liberal allowance, and who, besides, appears to be very wealthy. The Baronet lives entirely at Queen's Crawley, with Lady Jane and her daughter; whilst Rebecca, Lady Crawley, chiefly hangs about Bath and Cheltenhan, where a very strong party of excellent people consider her to be a most injured woman. She has her enemies. Who has not? Her life is her answer to them. She busies herself in works of piety. She goes to church, and never without a footman. Her name is in all the Charity Lists. The Destitute Orange-girl, the Neglected Washerwoman, the Distressed Muffinman, find in her a fast and generous friend. She is always having stalls at Fancy Fairs for the benefit of these hapless beings. Emmy, her children, and the Colonel, coming to London some time back, found themselves suddenly before her at one of these fairs. She cast down her eyes demurely and smiled as they started away from her; Emmy skurrying off on the arm of George (now grown a dashing young gentleman), and the Colonel seizing up his little Janey, of whom he is fonder than of anything in the world—fonder even than of his "History of the Punjaub."

"Fonder than he is of me," Emmy thinks, with a sigh. But he never said a word to Amelia what was not kind and gentle, or thought of a want of hers that he did not try to gratify.

Ah! *Vanitas Vanitatum!* which of us is happy in this world? Which of us has his desire? or, having it, is satisfied?—Come, children, let us shut up the box and the puppets, for our play is played out.